BLUE
FALL

THE TOURNAMENT: VOLUME ONE

—————

B. B. GRIFFITH

GRIFFITH PUBLISHING

DENVER

Griffith Publishing
Denver

Publication Information
Blue Fall
ISBN: 978-0-9824817-4-5
Copyright: Griffith Publishing LLC ©2011
First published 2011
Written by B. B. Griffith
Designed by B. B. Griffith

All rights reserved. No part of the publication may be reproduced, stored in
a retrieval system or transmitted in any form by any means without the prior
written permission and consent of the copyright owner.
Enquiries should be made to the publisher:
info@griffithpublishing.com

Publisher Information
Griffith Publishing LLC is a registered trademark.
www.griffithpublishing.com

This is a work of fiction. Names, characters, places, and incidents
either are the product of the author's imagination or are used
fictitiously, and any resemblance to actual persons, living or dead,
business establishments, events, or locales is entirely coincidental.

For more information about the Tournament
visit us online at www.griffithpublishing.com

If you've been known to open up
a book simply to escape, then *Blue
Fall* is dedicated to you.

"Frankly, I'd like to see the government
get out of war altogether and leave the
whole field to private industry."
~Milo Minderbender
Catch-22
by Joseph Heller

BLUE
FALL

PROLOGUE

WILLIAM LEE BEAUCHAMP WHISKED his desk chair into the center of the cordoned test zone of his team's lab, hundreds of feet below the rocky ground of Cheyenne Mountain State Park in Colorado Springs. He wheeled a monitoring device behind him to which he was attached via five sticker tipped cords. He checked his surroundings before plopping down upon the chair and positioning the machine next to him. It beeped softly in time with his heart.

He slapped his hands on his thighs. "Let's do this."

One of his colleagues, a cardiologist named Baxter Walcott, pleaded with him. He held up one ink stained hand as if to ward off evil and rubbed his eyes under wire framed glasses as he spoke.

"Bill, please. We have no idea what will happen here. It's late. We're tired."

"Nonsense! How many times do we have to run around in circles here? I'm in my prime, Baxter. I'll be fine. Shoot."

"Absolutely not," Baxter said, turning away.

"Fine. Wuss. Sarah, you do it."

Sarah Foss was rolling what looked to be a standard bullet up and down her forefinger with her thumb. She popped it into the middle of her palm and held it up to her eye, as if checking its lines.

"I don't know, Bill. Just because the mice recovered doesn't mean…"

"And the rabbits. And the chimps. What else can we test? You want us to shoot cats and dogs? Why don't you round us up a giraffe? Will that put you at ease?" Bill leaned back heavily in his chair, hands resting behind his head. "You said it yourself. The ratios are exact. The mice recovered, so will I."

Baxter Walcott shook his head and gazed at his cluttered lab table, his back to Bill.

Until we test it on one of us, on *me*, we're at the end of our research," Bill said. "We can believe that we've eliminated the side-effects all we want, but we need real time feedback. You know this."

"It's extremely painful. You've seen it. The animals scream. We're talking pain on every level. If we're wrong it means severe vascular bruising."

"If the mice can bounce back, so can I," Bill insisted, popping his neck back and forth like a boxer and settling in his chair once again. When his neck cracked, he winced and tried to cover it by smoothing his hair back into place.

Sarah snorted.

"Just shoot me, Sarah."

Sarah looked at Baxter, still turned away like a petulant child. She picked up a dull gray handgun from the workstation in front of her.

"Attagirl Sarah."

"Bill—"

"Bill nothing. Just do it."

Baxter allowed a look back at them, eyes widening, but he said nothing. Sarah swallowed and slowly sighted the gun at the trim, graying man in the lab coat twenty feet in front of her. The gun trembled so she grasped it with both hands. Bill straightened himself and gripped his armrests. His breathing quickened but he nodded.

Sarah fired.

Bill lurched in his seat and his chair rolled backward as he took the shot, pulling the monitoring cords taught. The snap-bang retort echoed loudly and acrid sulfur tinged the air. Bill heaved a breath.

He let loose a garbled, primal scream of pain, and then he went limp, slumping over himself in his chair.

Baxter ran to him and shook him violently.

"Bill!" he screamed, one hand to his pulse as he moved his ear by Bill's mouth. He glanced at Sarah, where she stood immobile, horrified.

For ten seconds of eternity, their small, secluded laboratory was as silent as a tomb. Then Baxter nodded.

"He's breathing! The adrenal! Get me the adrenal!"

Sarah was rooted and useless…terrified. Baxter swore at her and scrambled back to his desk where he withdrew an inoculation with a wicked needle from a cache of similar shots encased in bright red plastic. He primed it as he moved back to Bill, then popped it into his thigh and depressed it as steadily as he was able.

"C'mon Bill, c'mon. Please," he whispered, placing his ear next to Bill's slack mouth once more and feeling for a pulse. "It's so light. It's barely there."

For another ten seconds, all was silent.

Then Bill Beauchamp sighed softly and took in a deep breath.

Dr. Baxter Walcott dropped his forehead to Bill's chest in exhaustion. "Thank God. You stupid, stupid man," he muttered as Sarah found herself and rushed to Bill's side.

"You sonofabitch! I thought I'd killed you, you sonofabitch!" she screamed.

Bill smiled weakly, eyes still closed.

"See? Piece of cake." Then he rolled slightly to his side and vomited on the linoleum flooring.

Just over one month later, as Bill Beauchamp was dancing with his wife Jeanie at the wedding of their eldest niece, Bill suddenly stood back and away. He rubbed his left arm and looked at his wife as if she had asked him a particularly perplexing question.

"Bill?" she asked.

Bill dropped dead on the dance floor.

CHAPTER ONE

FRANK YOUNGSMITH WAS UP in the middle of the night visiting the toilet. Last night he felt the beginning of a cold coming on, and in a preemptive strike had swallowed three multivitamins and three full glasses of water. At four in the morning he was up and in the bathroom when his phone rang.

He heard it, but didn't move. His face had an oily sleep sheen to it. There were pillow lines down one baggy cheek and a patterned dimpling across his upper forehead that resembled his blanket. His hair, usually a springy bed of tight little curls where he still had it, was flung awry around the back of his domed head. Dried spittle flaked the beginnings of stubble on his rounded jaw. The phone still rang. Answering wasn't an option. He could barely open his eyes in the harsh fluorescent light, much less hold a conversation. Probably a wrong number. He finished up, climbed back into the bowed spot at the middle of his twin bed, and was drifting off when the phone rang again. He jostled violently awake. His bed creaked for a moment even after he settled himself.

"Yes?" he answered hoarsely.

"We need you to go to investigate an incident first thing in the morning. One of our major policy owners just had a heart attack."

"What time is it?"

Winston Pickett, Frank's boss, ignored Frank's question and rattled off a residential address.

"The life insurance payout is outrageous in this one, Frank. The numbers don't add up. I want a full report on my desk tomorrow afternoon before we pay out dime one."

Pickett hung up. Frank sighed and clattered his phone back onto its cradle. Groggy though he was, Frank was still unable to sleep for the final two hours of his night. He shook his head and cursed his job as he stared at the water-stained ceiling above his bed.

Frank's neighbor, a thin, wiry fellow named Andy Billings, called out hello just as Frank locked his door behind him on his way out. Dressed in a small, pin-striped shirt tucked into thin, charcoal gray pants, Andy's appearance suggested a vaudeville performer, but he was in fact employed as a security guard at a telecom company just south of the city. His bushy gray hair was combed back in tufts and frozen in place with hairspray, and the walrus moustache he had grown to offset his meager stature was waxed into a handlebar with two severe upswings. Just as he did every morning, Andy tried to strike up a conversation with Frank as Frank was running late.

"I heard your phone ringing last night neighbor! Is everything all right?"

"Everything's fine, Andy. It's just work."

"I'm up playing solitaire and I can hear it through the wall. Right through the wall! I figure a late night phone call is never a good thing, am I right?"

"It's just work Andy, always work."

"Just making sure no one you know's dead."

"Nope, everyone's alive. Thanks though. I really do have to go."

"No prob Frank, I'll be seeing you."

Andy waved goodbye as Frank drove up his narrow street to the wider end where he could flip his two-seater around, backtrack, and head to the highway. When Frank passed Andy again, Andy waved again. Frank didn't want to wave, but did anyway.

The streets were practically empty as Frank turned his cramped coupe east into the sun glare. He drank his coffee and followed the badly written directions he had scrawled on a Chinese takeout menu while half awake. He missed his exit twice, peering at the number seconds too late both times. His assigned interview, Mrs. Jeanie Beauchamp, wife of the deceased, lived in the affluent Monhannon suburbs by Colorado College. Pickett hadn't told him the actual numbers involved on the life insurance policy; he insisted his adjusters proceed objectively, but perhaps a high payout wasn't so inconceivable after all. Frank steeled himself, as he did every time, by shutting off the radio and listening to the rhythmic clanks emanating from his car. He dreaded the job ahead, as he did every time.

There was simply no way *not* to come across as a coldhearted bastard when grilling the newly widowed about the cash they are about to receive. He had lost the drive for it. It made him feel slimy. Worse, he wasn't even good at it. Frank had played the part of investigative adjuster countless times, endured numerous blowouts, and was even hit in the face once, but in all his years, his work had never led to a conviction. He sometimes hoped for an assignment to an outrageous case of blatant fraud—anything to get his name recorded somewhere in perpetuity, even if only in the vast records of a courthouse. The only thing worse than doing something you hate is doing something you hate without a damn thing to show for it.

Frank found the address and parked behind a long row of much larger and cleaner vehicles. Naturally Jeanie would have company in her grief, family and friends to help her through these worst first days in which she would be vulnerable, reeling right along with her freshly unhinged world. Unfortunately, this was also the best time to unearth evidence of fraud. Traumatized people slip up. Sometimes there are inaccuracies in the telling of chains of events, or questionable grieving behavior: Too sad was a tipoff. Not sad enough was a tipoff. Frank was trained to read emotions like these.

Frank straightened his tie, cleared his throat, and knocked three times on her open door. He was called inside. He was often mistaken for a friend come to pay his respects at first. They would soon learn otherwise.

Once inside the foyer, Frank joined an encircling group of perhaps fifteen soberly dressed men and women murmuring and sipping on drinks. In the middle, on a wide leather chair, sat the ample form of Mrs. Jeanie Beauchamp. She wore a wide black satin dress and a black gem the size of a goose egg hung from a bright gold chain around her neck. A glittering black butterfly broach perched on her heaving bosom as she silently wept into the shoulder of a large woman sitting next to her, no doubt her mother. As the circle opened, Jeanie looked up to see this newest arrival, leaving an outrageous caking of makeup on her mother's shoulder.

Frank wiped the sweat from his palms on his slacks and began the speech he'd memorized years before.

"Mrs. Beauchamp, I'm terribly sorry for your loss. My name is Frank Youngsmith, I'm with Barringer Insurance."

"We'll deal with the money in good time, man. All she needs at the moment is to grieve." This from an older fellow weaving to Jeanie's left, probably the father. His face was ruddy and an amber liquid sluiced from the edges of an overfilled plastic cocktail cup in his hands. Frank let out a short breath.

"Mrs. Beauchamp, may I speak to you alone for a moment?" Frank asked, already knowing the answer.

"Who the hell do you think you are, sir? My Jeanie is going nowhere!"

"Ma'am, I'd really rather speak—"

"You'd better goddamn well say what you're going to say right here, or by God I'll throw you right out on your ass," the man blustered, his white walrus mustache twitching. Several others stepped towards Frank with squared shoulders.

"Ma'am, your husband's life insurance policy has caught the eye of Barringer's wrongful claims division. I'm an adjuster that Barringer sent to determine if a case needs to be opened. Trust me when I say it is in your best interest to speak to me," Frank said, warding the group off with his pudgy hands.

The moustached man tossed a full glass of scotch into Frank's face and moved to follow it with his fist when Jeanie warbled aloud.

"Stop! Stop it! Dad, you're off your face! Someone get a hold of him!"

A younger man intervened and pulled Jeanie's snorting father back into the recesses of the house while Frank sputtered and blinked away the sting in his eyes. His every breath now reeked of hand-warmed scotch. He smacked his mouth like a dog and blew out of his nostrils. He hated scotch.

"Good Lord. Someone grab the man a towel. Wipe yourself off."

At her weak gesture, a dish towel appeared. Frank swiped at his hair and face and dabbed at his collar. It could have been worse. It *had* been worse before.

"Forgive my father," she said hoarsely. "He's had a bit much. What's this all about?"

Frank rubbed his eyes as he spoke. "Your husband's policy was modified close to his death. Are you aware of that?"

"I've no idea about the details of my husband's life insurance policy. His work handled all of that," Jeanie said, wiping her own eyes and slumping in her chair. Her mother absently rubbed circles around her large back while glaring at Frank.

"Are you aware of how much you stand to gain from this?"

Jeanie sniffled loudly and swallowed. She continued to look down at her hands in her lap as she said, "I've no idea. Nor do I much care."

"A significant amount of money."

Jeanie drooped in silence. Those around her studied Frank, interest replacing animosity.

"Several million dollars, Mrs. Beauchamp."

Some in the mourning party gasped outright and set to muttering. Jeanie fluttered her eyelids and clenched her jaw. There was grief in her face, Frank knew, but it now conflicted with some other emotion. Surprise? Fake surprise? Disbelief? Frank stopped himself short of stooping to get a better look at her.

"Now perhaps you'd feel more comfortable discussing this with me in private? It was never my intention to make your personal matters so…public," Frank said, digging at some residual stinging in his tear duct.

"No," Jeanie said softly. "Right here is fine."

Frank shook his head. If she wanted to play it this way, fine. He took out his dampened reporter's pad and patted at himself until he located a chewed ball point in his breast pocket.

"Did you adjust the insurance policy, ma'am?"

"No."

Feeling as though he should use the pad under the watchful eyes of those around him, Frank wrote *no* and then scribbled about in an official manner.

"Did your husband adjust the plan?"

"I don't know."

"Your husband never mentioned that he increased his payout by several million dollars?"

"No."

"He never spoke of the substantial monthly payment increases that would entail?"

"No."

"It would have been in the thousands per month, Mrs.

Beauchamp," Frank said, lowering his voice. "Had he lived to make a payment, that is."

The muttering around him increased in volume and animosity. Frank cleared his throat and stood up out of the slouch he'd found himself incrementally falling into of late.

"You understand why this looks questionable, don't you ma'am?"

"I do," Jeanie said, ever quieter.

"You'll have to forgive me if I say you're not very forthcoming."

Jeanie started a sort of silent, breathless weeping that reminded Frank of dainty dry heaving. Her mother continued to rub her back, but stared at Frank with abject hate, as if Frank had killed Bill Beauchamp himself.

"I'm afraid I'm going to have to recommend an inquiry," Frank said, suddenly very tired. He let the pen and pad flop to his waist.

"I think you probably should," Jeanie said, so softly Frank could barely hear.

"What? Ma'am, do you know what an insurance inquiry entails? It's like an IRS audit, but without the charm."

"Do what you must, but leave me in peace right now," she said, dabbing at her eyes with a marred and wadded tissue.

So Frank did.

The Colorado Springs branch of the Barringer Insurance conglomerate occupied an old converted medical building snatched up on the foreclosure market. Frank's office was a modified patient room, windowless, with hooks still on the doors from which clipboards once hung, and roughly patched screw-holes in the walls where disposal containers had once been. Everything in the office felt exposed and unfinished, like a temp building. It was a M.A.S.H. Unit of insurance salesmen.

Frank sat in a decade old chair behind his cluttered desk and formally requested an inquiry of the Beauchamp claim. Before he could even submit, his gray block of a phone buzzed and he was summoned to see his boss. He sat back and narrowed his eyes at the off-white wall across from him before getting up. On his way he passed the water cooler, stopped, went back to the water cooler, poured a cone full of water and sipped for a minute. That finished, and with nothing else to detain him between where he stood and the big converted doctor's office at the end of the hall, Frank walked in to see Winston Pickett.

Winston Pickett was a small, round, and dismissive man in his mid-forties, proud as hell of his large office and convinced of his singular right to occupy it. He insisted that his management and his management alone kept the Colorado Springs satellite division of Barringer Inc. afloat. He had a window but he sat with his back to it, choosing instead to plop his desk in the middle of the room facing his door. The door was always closed because Pickett reasoned that in the three seconds it took for a visitor to open the door he might prepare himself for their arrival, which meant sitting back in his chair, steepling his fingers, and staring at the door as if he expected a visit all along.

"Fraaaank," he said, smiling.

His squatty, rotund appearance had inspired nicknames. Frank's favorite was Winnie the Pickett. Frank fought the urge to turn right around much as he fought the urge to peer up in to

Jeanie's weeping face back at her husband's wake

"I was just in the process of submitting a request for inquiry," said Frank.

"So you think we have something then!" Pickett chirped.

"She was genuinely distraught," Frank said, ignoring his boss' grating enthusiasm. "But something doesn't smell right."

"Doesn't smell right!" Pickett barked. "Atta boy! Look at you! We got a regular Dick Tracy over here!"

Frank said nothing.

"And that's good! Because you're heading up the inquiry!"

"Sir, I really don't think—"

"Don't think *what*? You're a pretty bright guy. You're familiar with the case."

"They aren't very happy with me over there," Frank said lamely.

"They'd hate anyone else I sent over there just as much. Nature of the beast, Frank."

"Sir, I—"

"Ah!" Pickett chirped again, holding up a single finger as if warning a dog. "You can do it, Frank. Just do it. Status report on my desk at the end of the week."

Pickett warded off any further protest with a dismissive wave.

For the rest of the day, Frank halfheartedly researched the claim through the Barringer database. He succeeded in finding nothing other than the fact that Bill Beauchamp had signed the coverage increase form himself, and that he had been employed by a company named BlueHorse Holdings. Their co-sign on every pertinent document had been a rubber stamp, a generic swoosh and scribble.

Though he'd accomplished little, at the end of the day, Frank felt twice as exhausted as normal. When he left his darkened office he fought another urge: this one to keep walking and never return. He won out. Barely.

When he could catch Frank at home, Frank's neighbor Andy Billings often talked to Frank through the thin walls of their respective housing units. In an especially shameful display of unit-to-space maximization their duplex had been designed to share a bathroom wall. When Andy spoke to his mirror, he was in effect speaking to Frank on the other side. The acoustics of the conversations reminded Frank of the tin can telephones he had made as a kid, but Frank could hear every word. He could even hear whenever Andy turned on a faucet, or flushed his toilet, or dropped his shaver onto his linoleum floor, a floor identical to Frank's in every way. It all made Frank slightly ill, but Andy enjoyed it.

"You in there good buddy?" Andy shouted, and Frank shook his head.

Andy began to whistle, and when Frank didn't respond, he spoke again, "Frank! You over there?"

"I'm really tired. It was a very long day. I think I'm just going to sleep for as long as I am able."

"Goodnight Frank!"

"Goodnight Andy," Frank said, already on the way to his bedroom.

Settled into the well worn groove in the center of his twin, Frank listened to the clatter and roll of various sundry items as Andy completed his clumsy nighttime routine.

In the morning, he would do it all over again.

And in the morning, he would find that Jeanie Beauchamp jumped ship on him.

He'd called on her again to follow up and found that she'd promptly cremated her husband's body and then conveniently "taken some time off" to "get herself together" in Boca Raton... which meant he had hit a brick wall in his investigation. And pressing him up against that wall with the slow, relentless pressure of a garbage compactor was his horse's ass of a boss. The mere thought of Pickett's status report made Frank claustrophobic.

BlueHorse Holdings. Glendale, California.

Frank wasn't going to get anything else done in the Beauchamp case unless he got to Beauchamp's employer, but they'd stonewalled him on the phone the day before during his meandering research. Database documents told Frank that Blue-Horse Holdings had employed Bill, contracted through Barringer for his insurance, and approved the payout increase in case of untimely death. They were Barringer's actual client. They were the key.

Perhaps someone at BlueHorse would be a bit more forthcoming in person. A business trip might not be so bad; it would at least get him away from Winston Pickett and his sad-sack office. He needed a change of scenery. What he really needed was a change of life, to jump track and veer wildly away from his current path. The very air was drying him out, turning him into an empty husk of a man, day by day.

But in lieu of quitting his job, defaulting on his car lease and condo loan, draining his several credit cards to their limit and taking it all to some remote location in Switzerland, a little business trip to Glendale, California would have to do.

Frank's desk phone lit up. Winston Pickett.

Frank sighed.

If you hate what you do, you might as well be in California when you do it.

CHAPTER TWO

GREER NICHOLS HAD A large office of dark wood. His desk was a sweeping mahogany arc gone near black with lacquering. On it sat a large, flat computer monitor, its screen a dull black. On the far wall in front of him an array of winking camera lenses mimicked the curve of his desk and looked down upon him like stage lights; they too were off. Things were quiet now. Greer could hear the whisper of the fan units cooling all of his hibernating hardware. Sitting in a large brown leather desk chair, he took a moment to consciously enjoy this quiet. He knew it wouldn't last much longer.

Greer was a large, naturally angular man. He wore well-tailored jackets and sharp-collared shirts. His head was shaved to a gleaming black even darker than the color of his desk, and he often whisked his right hand over it when contemplating. At the moment he contemplated the note that had been placed in front of him upon his arrival that morning.

Bill Beauchamp is dead.

Greer pressed a small red button to the side of his keyboard. Within one minute there was a tap on his door. A trim, young man, dressed in pressed track pants and a reflective athletic shirt, took two impatient steps inside of Greer's office.

"Problem?"

"Is this your delivery, Allen?"

"It is."

"Who is Bill Beauchamp, and why do I care that he is dead?"

Allen Lockton pulled an electronic pad from a single strapped messenger's bag behind his back and tapped through several pages until he found what he needed.

"Bill Beauchamp is…was…on the Tournament lead weapons development team."

"The diode?"

"His team was charged with continually developing the diode insertion system, yes."

"And now he's dead."

"That's right."

"And how does this concern me?"

The courier fidgeted with the corner of his pad. Greer Nichols waited.

"It would appear that his death may be work related."

"Ah," Greer said, followed by a heavy, "Oh."

"Yes. It looks as though he tested the newest version of the diode on himself. It went poorly."

Greer rubbed his face. "Bill Beauchamp," Greer said, thoughtfully. "An old guy?"

"Sixty-two, I believe."

"Jesus. I thought we made it clear to all of the lab staff that they were only to test the diodes on animals."

"Bill Beauchamp's team had been perfecting that diode delivery system for years. He knew what he was doing. My guess is he finally wanted to see what it felt like."

"At sixty-two? Unbelievable. For a scientist he was a goddamn idiot. May he rest in peace," Greer added, and his gaze wandered to rest upon the arc of cameras peering down upon him like the eyes of a massive insect. The courier shied away from their dead gaze.

"Are you going to tell them?" he asked, gesturing at the cameras with the back of his head. "I mean, a Tournament employee has died, after all, as a result of Tournament work, in all likelihood."

Greer ran his thumb down the sharp line of his jaw as he pondered the cameras.

"I don't contact them. They contact me. When they're ready. And I doubt they would be interested in the goings on of one such as Bill. His team was one of many. They don't care about the *how*. We're all just players in the game to them. As long as the next cycle of the Tournament starts when they want it to, as long as they can still bet on the world's biggest game of chance, everything else is irrelevant."

"And you think it's coming again?"

"They give me reason to believe the Tournament is coming again, yes. Any moment now, actually."

"Who are they?"

"That is the wrong question to ask." Greer turned to

look him evenly in the eye. "I want you to listen to me now. You are a runner. You get information where it needs to go. That is all. Don't ever ask me that question again."

Hours later, the courier long gone, Greer Nichols was still watching the centermost lens with a silent intensity, pondering, when a small light below blinked an angry red. It could only mean one thing. He pressed another button, one on the underside of his desk. The angry red blinking became muted green. He could see the eyes focus on him, each in time, like a spider awakening.

"This is Greer Nichols," he said clearly.

The voice on the other end was singular, but Greer knew it spoke for many. An unknown number of faceless bettors, an elite group of patrons he would never know. The voice was distorted, low and guttural, like rolling rocks.

"The task of Master of Ceremonies for this, the fifth round of the Tournament, has come to rest upon your shoulders. Has it not?"

"It has," Greer said, as formal acknowledgement of the job that had fallen upon him by rightful rotation of participating country administrations.

"And do you pledge to fulfill the position of Master of Ceremonies with total objectivity?"

"I do," Greer said without hesitation.

"Then, Greer Nichols, for the duration of this cycle, you will cease to be Administrator for Team Blue, and will become Master of Ceremonies, beholden to no team."

"I understand," Greer said solemnly.

"Master of Ceremonies. It is time. Disperse the Couriers. Notify the teams. Start the countdown."

Greer nodded at the cameras, and they lingered upon him for several moments before shutting off once more. Their lenses unfocused as the green light first turned red and then went black.

CHAPTER THREE

M OST OF THE TWENTY-FOUR people who would receive the page indicating that the Tournament would begin again were caught unawares, but Alex Auldborne was not. Auldborne never questioned how he ended up with his remarkable lot in life. Auldborne took his station for granted. His entire life he'd been wholly unaware of limitations. The lack of money, the lack of a myriad of convenient familial connections, lack of respect, lack of sex appeal—no such limitations applied to Alex Auldborne. Becoming the leader of England's team, coded Team Grey, seemed the natural progression of things to him.

Before Grey recruited him, Auldborne was dealing cocaine to fellow students in his last year at Eton College in Windsor. Up until then he had been nothing more than a name on a list, another potential amongst hundreds watched for years by the Tournament's unseen eyes.

Auldborne didn't deal drugs for money; he had never wanted for money. He dealt because of the reputation it provided him. He didn't even like the drug itself. He considered narcotics beneath him, but he savored the power to provide it and deny it on a whim to those he'd made addicts. He was successful in the way that the reckless are: wildly and briefly. Then he was caught.

Having successfully distributed to all who wanted it on campus, often blatantly within the administration buildings, and sometimes during class, Auldborne grew bored. The next time he spoke to his supplier over the phone, he decided to change things for the sake of changing things.

"Tell you what. I'm not paying you what we agreed upon any more. I'm halving it," he said, his crisp accent enunciating each word. He then went silent and awaited the reaction, as if he were merely adding a new ingredient into a soup.

"Oh, is that what you goin' ta do, Alex?" came the reply, a growling mix of dirty British and Jamaican English, fast and slow at intervals, dangerously upbeat.

"Yes, Draden," Auldborne replied, emphasizing the name on purpose. Very few people called him Alex and it sounded odd and disrespectful to him. "It is what I'm doing."

"Then you a stoopid basta'd. You an Aie? We fuckin' done."

Draden hung up with a single click.

Auldborne was intrigued. No one had ever spoken to him like that before. He filed the experience away, unperturbed.

The next morning he was pulled out of class and arrested on charges of supplying a class A narcotic, which carried a maximum penalty of life in prison and an unlimited fine. It wasn't hard to find the evidence. Auldborne hadn't bothered to hide it very well. Doing so never occurred to him.

But this was Eton, the Crown Jewel of preparatory schools. Princes were educated here. Boys worth millions were placed on the waiting list well before they were even conceived. What was the faculty to do? Let this, the oldest and most respected of boarding schools in all of England, become synonymous with drugs? Let it be known that one of their own had run over a thousand grams of cocaine through their hallowed halls, and that all of it was eagerly snatched up? No. It simply would not do. They would quietly usher Alex Auldborne out, let the law deal with him, but nowhere near Eton. Auldborne took in his situation mechanically, scientifically, for future reference: *so this is what happens when rich people panic*. He filed it away.

They quietly passed him through, handed him his A levels, and told him never to return under any circumstances. He left Eton under subtle police escort.

He was not surprised to learn that the law held no power over him—not because he was above it, but because for Auldborne the law hadn't the presence it held for others. For most, the law of the land was the nameless stitching in the fabric of society, a gigantic, untouchable thing synonymous with modern living. To Alex Auldborne the law was a person, frail but regal, and ultimately fallible like all humans are.

Madeleine Auldborne presided over some of the highest profile cases brought before the courts of England and Wales, but she was also Alex Auldborne's mother, and so for him the line between High Court Judge and mother blurred. As a justice she rarely faltered—she was as pithy and decisive as she perceived the law itself to be—but as a mother she would always be marked by what Auldborne perceived as her one great failure: his father.

Peter Auldborne, a portly, ruddy man, was too fond of wine and did nothing but live off the wealth and status that Madeleine had earned. This made him absolutely worthless in the eyes of his only son. If the law was his mother, and his mother could make a mistake like Peter, then the law, by extension, had to be fallible as well.

Madeleine was well aware that certain rulings accrued certain favors from certain unsavory elements in her profession, but she also knew better than exploit them, because that path, once trodden, is often impossible to backtrack out of again. For over thirty years she never once pandered to the darker side of jurisprudence, until the day that the very law she served threatened to jail her only child for the rest of his life. Aside from the fact that she genuinely loved her troubled son, she would not allow it to be said that she had failed as a mother, even if she had. She decided that she would break herself to wipe his slate clean, if that's what it came to.

Marcus Pinkton, the prosecuting barrister for her son's case, was a man who Madeline had dealt with in the past and would no doubt preside over in the future. In the end it was a remarkably easy operation. She simply approached him one afternoon after proceedings in which he was involved. A deceptively clean looking fellow, long and neat in his three piece suit under full barrister regalia, he seemed to know what was coming and yet smiled politely, fully aware of what a woman in Madeleine's position could offer. He was young, only in his early thirties, his face smooth and square with not a speck of stubble. He had a deep, unnatural tan and smelled of heavy aftershave that masked another subtly cloying scent that Madeleine couldn't pinpoint.

"Justice Auldborne," he said, looking expectantly at her through peering, dark brown eyes. Madeleine suddenly abhorred him but she shoved the revulsion down inside of her. The only sign of her distaste was a subtle thinning of the lips, but it was not lost on Marcus.

"You are prosecuting my son," she said, and then stopped. He cocked his head in mock misunderstanding. Madeleine realized that he was going to force her to say it. She clasped her elegant hands in front of her and softly sighed.

"I need you to make his offense probationary."

"Done," he said quickly, flashing a straight but slightly tea-stained set of teeth. Madeleine cocked one eyebrow, wary.

"We can't very well have a High Court Judge's son go up for narcotics charges, can we?" he asked. Madeleine remained silent; it was with effort that she endured his gaze.

"All sorts of questions would arise, including those into your own person, My Lady. As a mother. As a public figure."

Madeleine looked into him much as she would look into a defendant, trying to separate the truth from the lies, but Marcus was too shrewd. His smile was of the vacant sort that wraps just as easily around both truth and lies, and his tone was disconcertingly congratulatory.

"Naturally," he continued, dipping his countenance a bit, as if almost embarrassed to continue, "Naturally I'll have to do some…maneuvering. I'll have to put up with a few unwelcome questions."

He leaned in a bit closer to Madeleine and she instinctively leaned away. He appeared to take no notice.

"But I'm more than happy to take the brunt of them, your ladyship. People will eventually tire of questions. They always have in the past." His mouth was balanced between a leer and a smile. His expression seemed to change as he moved.

"Thank you," she said haltingly, unsure of how to further proceed, only sure of wanting to be elsewhere.

"Of course," he said, and then, seemingly as an afterthought, "Please keep this in mind, if you would, in the future."

Then he whisked off without a word, leaving behind only

his musk. Madeleine was left looking at the floor and suddenly she felt as if her very footing was in danger of shifting out from under her at a whim.

Auldborne's offence was forgotten, shuffled off into a twelve month probationary sentence that was then shuffled off into nothing, lost amidst piles of paperwork never to be seen again. Madeleine didn't know how and she didn't ask. Auldborne himself had his diploma from Eton and from there went on to attend the London School of Economics, where in mere months he had endeared himself to those he wished with his fluid charm, and yet already he was probing his surroundings, looking for his next opportunity to experiment, to add an ingredient and step away. It was both a fortunate and an unfortunate return to normalcy for Auldborne. On the one hand, he was in no legal trouble. On the other, he was once again mired in the very status quo that made him increasingly bored.

Once beyond the confines of Eton, Alex Auldborne had taken to women extremely well. His mechanic reasoning had always been glossed with a charming exterior, but in the slick streets of London this charm was allowed to flourish, and the result was a cool approachability that endeared him to a certain type of woman. The kind that preferred to hold to their own wild speculations about him. The kind that preferred not to know anything more about the man they were with other than what they saw. What they saw was a slim, well dressed, wealthy young man. He often sat at a reserved table in the choicest of clubs with his own bottle of liquor, surrounded by people who leaned in to listen to him. His light skin and small, barely colored lips spoke of a type of aristocratic refinement of old, while his storm gray, unblinking eyes and close cropped hair, sharply widow peaked and already peppered with the same gray as his eyes, hinted at something darker, something to inspire a second glance. It wasn't just women who often watched him in these settings. Those that recruited for England's team in the Tournament did as well, and they increasingly liked what they saw.

Then, midway into Auldborne's first year at the LSE, Marcus Pinkton called in his favor.

One of Pinkton's associates was defending a man accused of supplying amphetamines, a class B narcotic, in a case over which Madeleine would never preside. Pinkton asked that the court appointed solicitor be replaced for reasons "best left unspoken." He told her who was to be replaced by whom, and that was that. Madeleine Auldborne had sway in slating solicitors, and could, should she wish, change the council. It was rarely done and would arouse suspicion, especially considering her rank and the relative unimportance of this case, but the man had taken care of her son, after all.

Madeleine rearranged some dates, effectively suspending the hearing until there was a scheduling conflict with the slated solicitor. Then she dismissed the man in lieu of the prior engagement. Later that week Madeleine heard that, for one or another reason she dared not delve into, the defendant had been found innocent. Regardless of whether the defendant was actually innocent or not, Madeleine felt soiled. But if shuffling around some lawyers was all it took, then she figured her son's freedom cheaply bought.

Then Pinkton called in his favor again. This time he asked that she mitigate the sentencing of a man in a case over which she *was* presiding, a high profile trial in the Crown Court, and in which Pinkton had no visible part.

"You needn't let the man walk free. Simply reduce his sentencing to the minimum."

"I won't do that," she hissed. "It's too much Marcus. It'll

cause an outrage. We're even."

"I suppose I'll have to let a few things slip then? Perhaps let others take a bit of a closer look at Alex's file?" His voice slid into a rougher intonation as he spoke, unpolished, but clearly more natural. Madeleine stepped back, mouth agape.

"Are you threatening me?"

Marcus said nothing.

"Marcus, you've nothing to do with this case."

"With all due respect, My Lady," he said, all polish returned, as if he had briefly stepped off stage and was now back. "You cannot possibly know what I am and am not involved in."

Alone in her study at home, Madeleine wracked her brain for any way to do as Pinkton had asked, but she couldn't think of anything that wouldn't raise outright objection, much less creeping suspicion. The evidence in question was perfectly in order. The man was guilty. There was simply no way to reject any of it to mitigate.

And it wouldn't end there. She'd been a fool. Marcus Pinkton had her under his thumb and they both knew it.

Once a week Alex Auldborne hopped on the Temple Tube stop and exited Westminster to meet his mother for lunch. Usually Madeleine Auldborne was forthcoming about her work, proud of her job and her position of influence, so when she began to steer the topic elsewhere during their conversations, Alex knew something was wrong. He could read concealed despair in her face, in the deepening lines about her small eyes, and in the way that her cheekbones became more pronounced. Her mouth was slack when once it was prim and compressed, as if she longed to speak but could not. His mother was beaten down. It didn't take him long, either, to realize that her dismay was the result of unusual circumstances surrounding the dismissal of his drug dealing case. The fact that he had paid nothing for his crime was not lost on him, and he figured she had sacrificed dearly for him. Still, he never spoke of it to her, and she, too proud, never spoke of it to him.

Auldborne felt no remorse for his crime. Nor did he feel guilt for his mother's current position. He had made a decision and had gotten caught just as she had made a decision and chosen to absolve him. He saw only the immediate circumstances: Someone, somewhere, was taking advantage of his mother. Someone was using her power to raise themselves above their station, possessing it as if it was their own, getting something undeserved.

A cold, hard fury stirred inside him at this thought, a fury that threatened to explode if he couldn't control it, so control it he did. He compressed it and pushed it in on itself, snapping his emotions shut like an overstuffed suitcase. But every time his gray eyes saw his weary mother, something inside very nearly snapped.

The most Madeleine could do for Marcus Pinkton was delay the trial to better assess the submitted evidence, and even this raised concern. The evidence had been submitted earlier to no interest; why was a deeper probe suddenly needed? It seemed unlike Madeleine to quibble over details like this. She was generally decisive, forgoing bureaucracy in favor of letting the law work its course.

This was not enough for Pinkton, and Madeleine could tell he was losing patience. Several times they ran across each other in Parliament Square and he eyed her coolly, allowing his gaze to linger as she passed. She didn't acknowledge him. She had nothing to say; nothing she *could* say.

In fact, Pinkton was livid. It was all he could do to control himself when he saw her in all of her judicial livery. He had more tied up in this case than she knew. He had made promises to people. He had been paid in advance. He had spent in advance. For a High Court Judge she was terribly daft, he thought. Did she not comprehend the situation? He could have both her and her son disgraced and jailed. It was the scandal of the decade, and he was the one working the strings. What about this did she not understand? He said what to do and she did it, or she suffered the consequences.

He had seen this Alex Auldborne out at night. He often went to the same clubs as the boy. He had seen him at his table upstairs, looking down upon everyone. Pinkton could see in the boy's face that he didn't care about what he'd done. He would, in all probability, do it all again. He was a criminal. He *deserved* jail. They were all the same, these rich, young punks, surrounded by their things, crying out for attention. It made him sick. Perhaps he should take a different approach? Perhaps he should have a few words with Alex the next time he saw him. He would probably quiver behind his imported bottle of vodka at the first mention of his little issue. He probably thought everything was over and done with, but he was about to find out otherwise. Yes, that's what he would do—go straight to the problem himself. That just might shake things up enough to get his old bird of a mother moving.

That very weekend Marcus saw Auldborne at The Meridian, a popular night spot just off of Covent Garden. It played deep beats with Middle Eastern flair and specialized in infused vodka concoctions. The bar itself was darkly lit with warm colors and made of brick and wood. The overall impression was that of drinking and dancing in a large wine cellar or a hollowed tree.

Pinkton had seen Auldborne here twice before, and had correctly guessed he would eventually return. When he saw him, he finished his drink at the bar, straightened his coat, and excused himself from a woman to whom he wasn't listening. He moved directly over to Auldborne's table upstairs, figuring that this approach would be even more likely to intimidate him.

Auldborne was sitting back in his chair, sipping his drink and talking quietly to the woman on his left. His head moved every now and then, nodding or shifting, always engaged. He was leaning slightly in her direction and she seemed enthralled. Around him several other men and women chatted amongst themselves, occasionally glancing at him, looking for an opening to speak. He held a measure of control over everything about him, like a man playing several games of chess at once.

Pinkton crested the stairs, moved over to the edge of the nearest table and blatantly glared at Auldborne until eventually one and then another of the conversations surrounding him dropped off. Last of all to acknowledge Pinkton was Auldborne himself.

With a small smile, Auldborne politely excused himself from his conversation. Auldborne leveled his gaze at Pinkton with eyes the light gray of sleeping coals, flecked here and there with a darker ash.

"I think you and I need to talk," Pinkton said.

"What about?" Auldborne replied, still sitting.

"Your mother."

And in that moment Auldborne knew who this man was and what he was doing here. The anger he had packed away stirred dangerously, expanding and creaking, but his face betrayed nothing. In one fluid motion he rose and casually walked around the table to Pinkton, where he stood level with him. His companions at the table looked awkwardly at them both and, sensing their need for some privacy, started up insignificant conversations of their own.

"I was wondering if you might ask her...*what the bloody hold up is!*"

Auldborne just looked at him.

"She'll understand my meaning."

Auldborne ran his right hand smoothly down the left side of his jaw, but still said nothing. Pinkton was growing annoyed at Auldborne's lack of emotion; he looked like he was studying a particularly intriguing piece of art, not confronting a man who held his wellbeing in the palm of his hand.

"You might also tell her, 'My welfare hinges upon it,'" Pinkton suggested.

"Yours?"

"No you fucking ponce, not mine. Yours," he spat back, leaning in close to Auldborne's face.

"And hers," Pinkton added.

He then straightened himself and brushed absently at his front, as if to dust himself of the whole encounter. Auldborne continued to watch.

"Is that all?" Auldborne asked congenially. Pinkton simply shook his head in disbelief, in pure exasperation at the inherent idiocy of today's youth. Turning away, he walked back towards the bar down in front.

For a moment Auldborne stood where he was, watching him go. Then he moved back to his seat and sat down. The women and men around him looked at him questioningly and he reassured them each with a glance and a small smile and a few words, but as he reached for his drink and took a sip he seemed preoccupied, his jaw set itself and he worked it loose with a subtle grinding motion. His eyes, slate gray now, were elsewhere: watching Pinkton as he paid his tab, watching Pinkton as he said goodbye to his companions, watching Pinkton as he made his way to the door and stepped out.

Auldborne took a small, wistful breath, and set his drink back down. "Pardon me a moment, will you. I'll be right back."

His company thought nothing of it, but peppered about the bar several sets of eyes discreetly followed him, slowly peering over their shoulders or over the rims of their glasses. As Auldborne stepped out through the door these eyes looked at one another, and then one of their number, a nondescript male, perhaps thirty, stood up and walked out half of a minute later, following.

Outside, Auldborne looked about for a moment before spotting Pinkton walking over to a black BMW. It looked to be illegally parked in a back-alley about a block away from the dark-bricked rear wall of The Meridian. He was fishing about in his pockets for his keys as he walked, in no particular hurry.

"It's just you then, isn't it, holding this over my mother. I thought and I thought about who it could possibly be, but I must admit I had quite given it up," Auldborne said in his detached way of thinking aloud. Pinkton stopped, looked over his shoulder for a moment, and then spun around. He squinted his eyes in the dark. Auldborne kept walking until they were within arm's reach of each other.

"You really are an idiot," Pinkton said, leaning in to jab his point home on Auldborne's chest, but he never got the chance. Auldborne shot out both of his hands, dug them into the fleshy hollows on either side of Pinkton's neck just behind his collarbone, and with one forward tug snapped them both. It was a single, fluid motion, like a bird plunging its beak into the soft earth after spying movement. The cracking sounded wet and hollow. Pinkton collapsed and let out a scream that was quickly cut off as Auldborne slammed his hand over Pinkton's mouth.

"If you make another sound I'll break your neck," Auldborne said, as if murmuring to a friend over dinner at a quiet restaurant. There was no anger in his voice and his face was a sculpted calm, but Pinkton looked up into Auldborne's eyes and saw within their flecked depths a terrible malice. They were now the gray of milling sharks glimpsed briefly through the light-filtered waters of a rolling wave.

"Thank you for your part in this messy business. It saved me a good deal of trouble. Now. You are done with my mother. If you ever talk to her again I will kill you. Accounts are settled. Do you understand me? I will kill you."

Auldborne's hand still clamped over the lower half of his pale green face, and streaming silent tears, Pinkton nodded. Auldborne slowly took his hand away. Pinkton didn't scream, he only muttered softly to himself and twitched weakly about on the ground.

Auldborne stood and wiped his palm off on his leg. When he turned around he saw a man watching him, just one, in a dark shirt and dark slacks, perhaps thirty years old, hands in his pockets. Tucked nonchalantly under his right arm was a file folder.

For a moment the two looked at each other. Auldborne watched the man as if wholly unaware of the danger of his current circumstance, having just assaulted a man in a dark alley. Neither did this stranger show any emotion. Both seemed detached from the dark world about them.

After a moment the man slowly approached Auldborne,

his patent leather shoes clicking on the sidewalk, one foot after the other. He stopped in front of Auldborne and looked distastefully down at Pinkton whimpering in the fetal position, his hands hovering over his disfigured, purpled collar bone as if afraid of what they might touch.

The man removed one hand from his pocket and grabbed the folder with it, glanced at it perfunctorily, and handed it out to Auldborne who took it without speaking. The folder was gunmetal gray in color; its sheen reflected the harsh orange of the utility lights about the alley. The cover was adorned with a single, stylized letter T.

"Read what you find in there," the man said, in a slightly nasal Birmingham drawl. "If you're interested, let us know. We'll contact you in two days."

Auldborne looked silently from the folder to the man, down to Pinkton, and back to the folder.

"You had better get back inside. Your alibi will only hold for so long. We'll take care of…this," he said, gesturing dismissively towards Pinkton, who had finally slipped into unconsciousness.

Auldborne looked at the man for a moment more, lightly rubbed his chin, and set off towards the club again. He didn't look back, but clutched the folder tightly in one hand. He was already having difficulty recalling the man's face. Perhaps his mind, surging with adrenaline, had chosen not to remember it, or perhaps he had never even really seen it in the first place. The folder was very heavy and, without really knowing why, he decided to hide the symbol on its cover. But as he strolled through the doorway once again, he was sure that somehow he had shattered the status quo that was threatening on the horizon, perhaps forever.

Later, alone in his loft, Alex read through the folder, and

would have perhaps thought its contents to be a joke were it not for the way the faceless stranger had handled the situation in the alley, and for the fact that in subsequent days his mother's problem vanished. Not only did Pinkton drop the issue, but he left the court system of England and Wales altogether.

Madeleine never spoke to her son about this sudden turn in events, nor did he tell her what had happened. She kept waiting for the other shoe to drop, but it never did, and if she thought he had anything to do with the way things had turned out, she never let on. After a time she started to breathe easier, but she wasn't exactly sure she liked what she occasionally saw in her son's eyes as they sat across from each other on their once-a-week lunch dates, casually conversing. They were dancing, almost shimmering with what she could only describe as happiness.

Madeleine could not possibly know the path that the faceless stranger and his folder had set her son upon. She could not possibly know that two days after that night at The Meridian Auldborne was visited by a woman he had never seen before. Madeleine couldn't fathom the ramifications of the promise Auldborne would make to this woman.

He was walking from the Temple stop back to his loft when she appeared beside him, matching his pace. She was small, smartly dressed in a dark linen pantsuit that flowed about her as she moved. She was, at most, five years older than Auldborne. As they talked, she looked over at him congenially, like they were old friends. She seemed excited, but was trying to conceal it and only partially succeeding.

"Alex Auldborne?"

He looked over at her and then forward again, still walking.

"What's your verdict?"

He stopped and then she stopped a step after. She slid back in next to him.

"I'm only going to ask this once, and then never again," he said. "I want you to look at me."

She looked up at him.

"Is this real?"

"Absolutely." She seemed to know that how she answered the question was just as important as what the answer was. "Far more real that you can even guess. Soon, if you agree to lead us, you'll come to see what I mean."

Auldborne looked down at her for a moment, and then across the way, at all the bustling activity of Leicester square, the shops, the cars, the bars, the buskers working the crowds, the London that he knew.

"Yes."

The woman seemed prepared for this, and smiled only slightly. She reached in the pocket of her three-quarter length coat and pulled out a small pager with a pink screen.

"Then you'll be needing this," she said, as she handed it to Auldborne, "Keep it on you always."

She straightened herself and exhaled a clipped breath.

"Now then," she said, "let's take you to meet your team."

Around a small circular table, at the very restaurant where he met his mother on a weekly basis, sat two others. They eyed him warily as he approached. Neither stood.

To Auldborne's immediate left sat a young woman with cold, black eyes and a small, perfectly proportioned face, smooth and doll-like, but not a child's doll. She reminded Auldborne of the kind of doll that, beautifully poised, watches from a shelf on high, gaining in value while everything around it ages and goes to sod. This was Christina Stoke. She had the position of sweeper on what would become Auldborne's team.

And to his right sat the very same young man that had been the first person on earth to speak frankly to Auldborne, over the phone, all those years ago:

"You and Aie? We fuckin' done," he had said.

Except that they weren't.

This man, who was positioned as Auldborne's striker, was a second generation Jamaican citizen of Great Britain. His hair was set in an explosive motley of ponytailed dreadlocks that geysered off of the back of his head. His name was Draden Tate and he was built like a brick wall.

Auldborne immediately recognized Draden when the woman introduced them. Auldborne walked right over to him and shook his hand.

"It's wonderful to be back in business with you, I have only myself to blame for our earlier...falling out," he said, smiling. Draden eyed him for a moment, and then let out a deep, roaring laugh that bared all of his pearl white teeth.

—

Alex Auldborne was contemplating the London that he'd left

behind, even as he still lived within it, when the pager he'd been given on that day five years ago flashed and buzzed for only the fifth time since he'd owned it. Auldborne felt its movement upon his chest inside the breast pocket of his jacket and let it be for a moment. Then he withdrew it. On its normally blank screen a countdown appeared, already ticking down.

Auldborne allowed himself a slight smile. The time had come once again, as he knew it would. Things had ended badly for him in the last cycle. That they'd lost in the second round didn't bother him nearly as much as to whom they had lost, and how.

When he saw the Americans of Team Blue this time around, as he knew he would sooner or later, he'd make very sure that they paid dearly. Their captain he would personally break. He made a vow to himself that Grey would shatter Blue once and for all, no matter what.

CHAPTER FOUR

AT LAX FRANK RENTED a white two-seater and drove north on I-5, windows down. He had been to California only once before, when one of the Youngsmith Family Reunions happened to be in Anaheim. He was young at the time, and had forgotten most of it. This was his first real voyage to the west coast as a man, and he was determined to enjoy it, despite the circumstances.

As the blacktop flew under him, Frank went over what he was to say. Pickett had made it clear that he wasn't to appear confrontational, but he was to look like he had the power to bring BlueHorse Holdings to task if he had to. Insurance fraud was prosecuted by the Attorney General of individual states. Barringer could only make a case for their interests, but one of the finer points of Frank's occupation was looking as if he had the power of authority behind him when in fact he didn't. In reality, all he had behind him was his fat little boss.

He reached Glendale in the early afternoon. From there he got horribly lost twice, even with the help of a laminated map he'd purchased at a gas station. His mind wandered and he forgot himself entirely when stuck in traffic for extended periods of time, and he wasn't quite confident enough to make the required quick merges and exits. By the time he actually found BlueHorse it was just past four, and naturally he was unprepared for what he saw.

It was massive. The lot itself encompassed several acres in the far north of the city. It had numerous corporate looking roundabouts with decorative cactus displays in their centers, out of which sprouted neatly printed directional signs. Frank saw brass statues of corporate art peppered about, including one of the California state bear looking bored and radiating heat. He saw a bird alight upon it and then take off again just as fast.

Frank looped absurdly about as he followed the arrowed signs marked *Visitor's Entrance*. The brass statues began to look the same, and he was increasingly worried that everything would be closed if he ever made it inside. Thankfully, there were still a few cars parked in the visitor's lot as Frank pulled up. He got out, stretched, and made his way inside.

The front lobby was a dry, air-conditioned cool. Several chairs were aligned along one wall, a few occupied by tired individuals who flipped idly through out-of-date magazines. Opposite the entrance a prim young woman sat behind a standalone mahogany desk in front of closed double doors. She was talking softly on the phone and writing something on a pad in front of her. She looked up at Frank as he entered and smiled absently. When he made no move towards her, she went back to her writing.

The room was quiet to begin with, but just as the secretary hung up the phone the air conditioner also shut off and the silence became a heavy, palpable thing. One young man waiting against the wall even looked up, as if the disturbance had been the result of added activity and not retracted. Suddenly, Frank wanted very badly to move off to one corner of the room. He reminded himself that he knew none of these people, and that he would likely never see any of them again, and so he forced his way up to the front desk.

To Frank's immediate left a lean, slightly constipated

looking fellow dressed in immaculate and shiny tracksuit pants was pulling letters from a single strap tote bag slung around his back and placing them in a series of locked mailboxes set in the wall. As Frank approached, he was dimly aware of the mailman watching him with undue interest.

"Can I help you?" the secretary asked.

Perhaps it was a combination of her small stature and the massive mahogany desk, but suddenly the woman seemed very far away and the doors even farther. For a moment the scene reminded him of talking to Pickett back at Barringer, but he quickly forced that disconcerting thought out of his mind. He had to look legitimate here, confident.

"I hope so," he said, clearing his throat. "I'm with the criminal investigations unit of Barringer Insurance," Frank said, standing straight. The woman politely wrinkled her forehead.

"I'm here to undertake a formal inquiry into a claim filed by an employee of yours, recently deceased. A man named William Lee Beauchamp."

At this Frank thought that the mailman might have frozen briefly in his deliveries, but when he looked over the man had continued about his business, although his unlocking and dropping movements seemed far too deliberate. After each delivery he would re-lock the box and check that it was thoroughly sealed, as if he was waiting, drawing it out. Frank frowned.

The woman finished her searching and looked at the screen for a prolonged moment before turning back to Frank.

"We don't have any record of a William Beauchamp in our system, sir," she said, but she seemed to focus on the top button of Frank's shirt. Frank watched her for a moment. She itched under her nose and seemed, unbelievably, to glance at the mail-man of all people for reassurance.

"Ma'am, with all due respect, I have a copy of his policy, signed by this company. So let's not make a big deal out of this, shall we? It's very hot and we're all tired."

"What are you, a policeman?"

This from the mailman. Frank spun around. The man seemed to be standing slightly on his toes, his legs pressed tightly together and his fists in little balls at his hips. Frank almost laughed until he realized that his own fists were also in little balls at his own hips. He sighed instead.

"No. I'm an insurance agent, actually."

"Well then we're under no obligation to tell you any-thing."

With visible effort, Frank eased the tension in his body. His characteristic slump returned. He rubbed the back of his damp neck as he shuffled towards a seat against the wall. He sat heavily. The entire room was still watching him.

"You're right. I'm just an insurance guy. But I'm kind of at the end of my rope here, and I've got a boss who's…" Frank shook his head. "Look. I've been doing this for way too long, long enough to know a red flag when I see one. Something is not right here, and I'm about to throw the whole file at the Attorney General and say to hell with it and let them sort it out. Then it turns into a mess. Especially if the case crosses state lines and the FBI throws their hat into the ring. A mess for everyone involved. If you've got nothing to hide here, then you need to work with me, or we're all screwed."

Frank deflated in his chair as if his very words were all

the substance he had within him. The secretary still looked to be deferring to the mailman. The air conditioning kicked on with an exaggerated click and whoosh. Allen Lockton looked down at the rumpled and scruffy figure Frank cut with both pity and disgust. His use of the collective "*we*" concerned the courier. Allen Lockton never wanted to stand any chance of being thrown in with the same lot as the wilted individual slumped in front of him. The man looked desperate. The Tournament would do well to steer clear of desperate men.

"Deborah," he said, addressing the secretary behind the desk. "Did you cross reference the name Bill? I don't think he ever went by William Beauchamp. Just Bill."

The assistant took the hint. She tapped on her keyboard a few moments more. Frank glanced up.

"Ah," she said as the courier moved behind her to check the screen himself. "Yes. Bill Beauchamp. Here he is."

"But Hank…" the courier began.

"Frank."

"Yes, Frank, our records do nothing but coincide with yours. It shows he is recently deceased and claiming full benefits. I'm not sure what more we can do for you," the courier said with a pronounced clearing of his throat. He looked blatantly from Frank to the door behind Frank.

"Well, there is one way to clear this all up once and for all," Frank said, heaving himself to his feet once more. "Answer me this. Was Bill Beauchamp's policy an abnormality?"

"How's that?"

"Did Bill work in a team?"

"I'm not sure I'm at liberty to…"

Frank closed his eyes. All of this was giving him a head-ache, and it certainly wasn't helping BlueHorse Holding's case. Why couldn't these people see that they were all the same? Frank was a pencil-pusher and paper-shifter just as surely as they were. This anal-retentive mailman was a *mailman* for crying out loud. His loyalty to his job unnerved Frank, as if any one company could possibly be fundamentally different from another.

"Listen, all I'm getting at here is that if Bill worked with anyone else and they were insured in an equally ridiculous man-ner, it would certainly go a long way towards dropping this case."

"And then everyone would know the precise manner in which we ensure our high-risk employees," the courier snipped.

"Oh for God's sake. Fine. In that case, can you tell me where the Glendale Attorney General offices? You'll almost cer-tainly be implicated for signing off on this."

"All right. Just hold on," the courier said, motioning the entire room down with his hands. "Yes. Bill did work as a member of a team. And yes. They were all insured the exact same. To the dollar. Is that enough for you, Mr. Youngsmith?"

"A copy of those records should suffice."

"Can't do that."

"Then a statement from a member of that team saying as much should suffice to end the inquiry," Frank said, his voice monotone. The air had shut off again. He was sweating through his collar.

The courier looked torn. He glanced at the screen in front of him, and then behind him, as if seeking approval from behind the double doors. He sucked at his teeth for a moment before coming to a decision. He grabbed a small pad, took a name from the screen in front of him and scribbled it violently down, then tore it off and thrust it out to Frank.

"His name is Dr. Baxter Walcott. Down in San Diego. Not convenient, but the closest there is."

Frank took the sheet and backed away from the courier.

"Now listen to me, Mr. Youngsmith. Once you get that statement, that's it. There will be nothing else. Right?"

"That should do it," Frank said haltingly.

"Good. That's good," the courier said. "Then you can go on back to whatever it is you do wherever it is you do it."

CHAPTER FIVE

WHEN NIKKIE HIX'S PAGER went off she was visiting her favorite cousin in Tempe, Arizona. They were watching a movie and eating Chinese takeout on the couch when her cousin felt a vibration in the small of her back. She jumped up and let out a little yelp and after looking around for a moment noticed that she had been sitting on Nikkie's hooded sweatshirt.

"I think you're vibrating," she said.

Nikkie, absorbed in the movie, looked at her blankly.

"Hmm?"

"Your sweater."

Nikkie was so used to carrying the silent pager around with her that at first she had no idea what her cousin might mean.

"Vibrating?"

She picked up the sweater, a thin, wash worn Tennessee hoodie, and reached into the front pouch.

She was still for a moment.

"You're gonna miss the call," her cousin said, eyes back on the screen.

Nikkie pulled out the pager, muting its angry buzzing in her hands. Its pink screen bathed her face in a fluorescent glow. She read the display.

Ten days until the draw. The Tournament was back.

"Well how 'bout that," she said softly.

"Is that a *pager?* I didn't think they even *made* those anymore."

Nikkie didn't answer her cousin.

"…Nikkie? What is it? Is everything okay?"

"It's nothing," she said, her eyes still fixed on the pink screen. "Just work. They want me to come in early."

Nikkie had told her cousin that she worked as a traveling rep for a sports apparel company, giving out free merchandise at various sporting events, trade shows, and concerts. She had even gone so far as to purchase a pair of shoes, a watch, and a sports bag and given them over to her, nonchalantly claiming that they were left over from her most recent promotion. All lies.

"How early?" her cousin asked.

"Soon. Next couple of days."

"Aw. Man. Work sucks."

"Sometimes, for sure," Nikkie said, slipping the pager back in her pocket. She hunkered back down into the couch and, drawing her knees up to her chest and popping another bit of orange-flavored chicken in her mouth, she thought of her captain, Johnnie Northern.

—

Ten doctors in five separate hospitals across the U.S. were trained to complete the pre-draw medical exam Nikkie Hix and every other player required, and the closest Tournament doctor to Tempe, Arizona was Dr. Baxter Walcott in San Diego. So it was that two days after getting the page, Nikkie Hix walked in to San Diego's University Medical Hospital. Dr. Walcott was behind the main reception desk dropping off a file and absently recording observations of his last patient into a Dictaphone when he saw her walk in. At first he thought it was his daughter Sarah, and he waved briefly even as he recorded. Seconds later, however, he clicked it off mid-sentence.

As Nikkie approached, her smile was perfectly disarming. Dr. Walcott was struck by how she even smiled like his daughter; it started as a near-smirk and seemed to roll fully across her face. She had a harmless, welcoming look to her muted green eyes, but over the years Walcott had learned better. It was as if their real hue was loosely draped by a thin, white lace, and when she narrowed them, as she did when she smiled, the lace was tightened, and for a moment Walcott saw something in the green behind that spoke of a type of passion he couldn't understand, of a fierce pride frightening in one such as her, and that he had only ever seen in two others, and they were of her ilk.

Dr. Walcott had grown fond of Nikkie in a fatherly way, but he hated to see her. Seeing her meant the Tournament was around the corner. She was one of three members of Team Blue, and as the chief cardiologist at UCSD Medical, and indeed one of only a handful nationwide who could, it fell to him to sign off on sending her out into the madness. Of the three on the team, it was always hardest with her.

"It must be that time again," he said darkly.

"I got the page. 'Suppose I'm first?'"

Walcott looked at her at length. She stood comfortably, hands in the front pouch of her sweatshirt, heels together, toes out, like a cross between a soldier and a ballerina. After several moments, Walcott turned to the receptionist.

"Push all of my appointments back an hour, will you? I have to see this patient."

Walcott went over to a far cabinet and pulled a string of perhaps twenty keys from the side pocket of his white lab coat. He flipped through them, chose one, and unlocked the drawer lowest to the floor. He flipped through several manila folders until he came upon three blue folders in succession in the far back. The very last of the three read **Hix.** Walcott pulled it and, with a loud popping of the knees, stood once again.

"This way," he said, managing to keep the defeat out of his voice. To the receptionist it was almost humorous; this girl couldn't be older than twenty-five and yet here the head of Cardiac was catering to her. She hadn't spoken but five words and yet he was already motioning for her to follow him back into the depths of the hospital. But something in Dr. Walcott's heavy mannerism gave her pause and kept her mouth closed.

They passed many patient rooms as they walked, some open, some closed. Here and there gurneys rolled by and now and then a passing doctor or resident would say hello to Dr. Walcott. The hospital had a distinctive smell, inhumanly clean and slightly animal at the same time, like the laundry room in which the dog spends the majority of its time. They turned several corners and went into one surgical room only to pass through a small door in its rear into another, larger room in which several sets of glistening chrome machines sat inert. Dr. Walcott directed Hix to a patient bed where she sat; the butcher-paper covering the bed crinkled as she settled herself. Walcott gently closed the door behind them and turned to face her. She looked about the room, her feet dangling off the edge of the bed.

"So you're back," he said.

"I'm back."

"I assume I'll be seeing Northern and Haulden shortly, then?"

"Northern, yeah. Max is up east somewhere. He'll probably get checked up there," she said, her slight southern twang rising every now and then. Although she seemed at ease Walcott couldn't help feeling that she was very far from home.

He went to the closest of the machines, a black computer monitor situated on an ornate subterfuge, and flipped it on. He then opened up her file, removed a sheet of paper, and began writing remarks as the machine whirred intermittently.

"Blood sample first. To let it process."

Nikkie hopped down from the bed and sat at the desk near the monitor. She pushed one sleeve up and rested her elbow on the desk, as if preparing to arm wrestle. At first Walcott was worried he might not find the vein, but her forearm, if small, was strong and defined and had a prominent blue vein that he tapped easily. She never winced. She watched the blood shoot through the piping and spatter into the first of two vials with interest.

After he had both samples he secured each in its own centrifuge, closed the lids, and set them spinning. On the attached monitor a spreadsheet opened and numbers appeared in the columns.

"If you could take off your shirt, please."

She moved back to the bed and took off her sweatshirt and the t-shirt under it, leaving only her light pink bra on. She looked as strong and healthy as she ever had, her small form more athlete than actress. Her smooth, unblemished skin belied the unique medical turmoil of her inner system. Her only noticeable scar was just at her bellybutton where there once was a piercing, a remnant of her collegiate years before the Tournament. It had since been torn out. She couldn't precisely remember when. By the time she noticed it was gone the wound had already scabbed over, leaving only a swath of red blood on her shirt.

What always got Dr. Walcott was her tattoo.

How a girl like Nikkie Hix could sport any tattoo at all, and wear it well, was still beyond Walcott, even five years after he had first seen it.

On her, as on all three of them, the inking seemed less like a man-made design and more like a natural patterning of the skin. Like veins of mineral in a rock, or a striking whorl of graining in a piece of lumber. It covered her right shoulder and extended halfway down her upper arm. Because the ink flowed with the curves of her shoulder and arm muscles, the design seemed of two pieces, like plate armoring, but symmetrical. It took the shape of two reverse-teardrops, one falling from her shoulder and the other climbing from the top of her bicep. From a distance the drops seemed filled in. A closer look revealed the design fractured here and there by slopes and dips, always reflected symmetrically on both sides.

Walcott had asked Nikkie Hix, upon first seeing her, what it was. "*What do you think it looks like?*" she'd replied. Walcott said that while the shapes looked like water from a distance, it reminded him of a flame close up, something that would come from a single candle in a dark window.

"A light in the dark," she said.

Dr. Walcott put on his stethoscope and began to softly probe Nikkie's stomach, listening here and there for abnormal acidic activity. He moved up to her chest and told her to take several deep breaths. Nikkie watched his face the entire time.

"You can quit, you know. You don't have to do this. There are other doctors."

Walcott looked at her for a moment before popping the earpieces out and turning around to another of the machines.

"You'd think that, wouldn't you, from your end," he said, as he flicked another of the chrome displays on, his back to her, "but it's a good deal more difficult when you three keep coming in on gurneys. Or those around you do."

Nikkie was silent as Walcott took a bottle of rubbing alcohol and several cotton balls from the top shelf of a cabinet. He then proceeded to gently clean five separate spots on Nikkie's upper body, one on either shoulder, one just below her sternum, and two just below her waist. To each of these spots he attached suction cups of the type normally used in EKG testing. He checked the monitor on the centrifuge once more and then moved to a locked cabinet just below. He took out his set of keys, located the correct one, and unlocked it. From it he pulled an apparatus that looked like a center-punch. Nikkie's gaze moved from Walcott's face to this new instrument.

"We're very good about not endangering others when we can help it" she said, softly.

"You are very good. But not perfect."

Walcott moved over to her and took her hand in his, palm up. "You know what this is. It replicates a diode hit, on a much smaller scale, of course. You should immediately go numb within the localized area."

Walcott pressed the device to his own palm and fired it. He felt a small static shock but nothing more; as it should be. He then positioned the punch on her palm, looked up at her, and pressed a red button on its top. It gathered tension and then snapped into the center of her palm. Nikkie grit her teeth and instinctively tried to pull her hand away, but Walcott held her fast.

To Nikkie it felt like she had slammed her funny-bone on a sharp corner, only the feeling was in her palm and not on her elbow; a moment of intense numbness followed by needle pricks that slowly spread themselves out over the surface of her palm to her fingertips. It was as if someone had squeezed her fingers shut over a fistful of thistles. Her hand contracted of its own accord.

This pain lasted for perhaps ten seconds and then slowly dissipated. The only evidence of the punch was a small wet mark, merely a few drops of liquid.

Walcott was grim as he repeated this test four more times in the four other areas on Nikkie's body. The results were similar, although the pain varied slightly. Each left a small wet mark that Walcott wiped off with a cotton ball. The punch just below the waist was the most painful; it momentarily took her breath away, and the numbness was replaced by ten or so seconds of what felt like extreme menstrual cramps that spread from her uterus throughout her lower intestines. Thankfully, they also shortly abated.

"It says in your file that you were hit in the left shoulder last time, also below the left breast, and on the left hip," he said.

"That's right."

"Your NRS readings confirm that."

"What's that mean?"

"It means that even a year later your body is still showing effects."

"You're always sayin' this."

"I'm still not convinced that a body can fully heal from what they've done to you, Nikkie."

"You say that every year too."

"You know, I just lost a colleague to this ridiculous organization."

Nikkie narrowed her eyes.

"A doctor?"

"He was the head of our research team. Older fellow. He took a full hit and died not even three weeks later of cardiac arrest. I'm positive it was the damn diode."

The centrifuges slowed to a stop, beeped twice, and suddenly the corresponding monitor displayed a long data sequence. Walcott moved over to the monitor and sat down on a small swivel stool. He slowly scrolled down through the numbers, checking them against past readouts in Nikkie's file.

"I'm sorry to hear that," Nikkie said quietly.

Walcott printed the results, all three pages of them, and took them back to Nikkie. He set them on her lap. Nikkie picked them up and cocked her head as she scanned them.

"But it doesn't change your opinion, naturally," Walcott said.

Nikkie shrugged. "This is what I do. I'm young. I can recover," she said, offhand. "This looks like a mess of numbers to me. Just tell me: will I work?"

"You're still prone to it, if that's what you mean. The diode will hurt you."

"C'mon Doc, don't look so sad," she said, smiling slightly.

"This spits in the face of the oath I swore," he muttered.

"Then stop! If you feel so bad about it, stop."

"It's far too late for anything like that," he said, looking down at her as he shook his head kindly. "My leaving won't stop that courier with his tracksuit from coming into this hospital and handing me that blue folder, and it won't stop *you* from coming in this hospital, conscious or not." He gently took the papers from her and clipped them onto his board.

"It's you that has to stop," he said, looking into her face. "I can only go if you go. And you're not planning on quitting any time soon, are you?"

"Never."

Nodding slowly, Dr. Baxter Walcott signed the bottom of the report and handed it back to Nikkie.

"In that case, you're cleared." Convincing any of these players of the harm they were doing to themselves was like trying to reason with a fanatic. He wasn't going to die on that hill. There were other ways.

Nikkie hopped up and put her shirt and sweatshirt back

on. She folded up the report and stuffed it into her front pouch. "I'll see you around, Doc."

"Don't get shot, Nikkie. We still don't know how deeply the diode affects you."

"I never plan on it." She winked at him and strode from the room.

Dr. Walcott sat down heavily on the swivel stool.

His daughter winked just like that.

CHAPTER SIX

ALLEN LOCKTON FELT CLEAR-HEADED only when he was exercising.

This isn't to say that he zoned out when working out… quite the opposite. He made decisions, he formulated plans, and he did his work on the run quite literally.

With the fifth cycle of the Tournament imminent, Lockton was feeling overwhelmed. They had him running all over the USA and soon he would be running all over other countries. He would have job after job, one after another. On top of all that there was now, apparently, a frumpy balding guy asking too many questions.

How in the world did that *happen?* And yet he'd seen it himself, with his very eyes. Problems were meshing together, layering on top of each other, like so many loose sheets of paper strewn about on a desk. Where did one issue end and the next begin? This was especially hard for a man like Allen Lockton, who needed things compartmentalized. He could tackle everything in the world if it was presented to him in a single file line, but now it seemed like it was coming from all sides.

I need to work out, he thought as he looped about the roundabouts in his car exiting the BlueHorse grounds.

As a Tournament courier, driving was his least favorite mode of transportation. Trapped in a car, the pressures of the day amplified, rebounding against the roof and windows like caged animals, only intensifying. He was easily annoyed sitting worthlessly at stoplight after stoplight and moving in and out of traffic, waiting to shoot ahead and gain a little time. It seemed like a big pointless pinball game.

He preferred running. He loved the speed and the sweat. It felt clean. He loved plowing bodily into the air in front of him, and he shaved his legs so he could feel it more intensely. He started shaving for high school track meets years ago and continued when he ran long distance for the Fighting Illini at the University of Illinois. He liked to think that his lack of leg-hair had increased his overall lifetime streamlining.

In high school, a rail thin, prepubescent Allen "Stocky Locky" Lockton, recently arrived on the track team, was often heckled for his running style. He ran with his head held high, his back stick straight, forearm and bicep at ninety degrees, knees popping high, back leg extended for maximum thrust. All of this, naturally, was the correct way to run, but his teammates, and all of the football players practicing on the same field, had none of it.

"You run like a faggot, Stocky. It looks fucked up," one said eventually, after several days of snickering.

That night, running in place before his mirror, his stick thin legs and bony shoulders jutting and shifting all about and looking more like a crude, angular rendering of a boy than an actual boy, Allen acknowledged that he did look a bit funny. But it felt right; it felt like the logical way to run.

When, two months later, he ran that very same "fucked up" style all the way to second place at State as a fifteen year old freshman, he wasn't heckled anymore. Soon he saw a few teammates running the same way. He told his mother so and she clasped her hands proudly and ran to tell his father.

"Oh honey," she said to James, "Allen says people are copying the way he runs now!"

"They should," he heard his father say from his chair in the living room. "The boy's no idiot."

At U of I he always ran early in the morning, to the amazement of his roommates. He tried to put in five miles before the sun broke on the Illini Union, and he always stayed up late to run in the cool dead of night as well, under the buzzing lights. He left very little room for anything else in his life, least of all school-work, and as a result he nearly failed out. His physical endurance was remarkable, but his aptitude for academia was another matter. He was still convinced that the only reason he did graduate was because of a few choice words spoken to a few choice people on his behalf by the track and field coaching staff.

But while he certainly wasn't an intellectual, he was no idiot either, a fact his father constantly impressed upon him. Whenever his son got discouraged about school, James Lockton would say, "The last thing the world needs in another literati," pronouncing it *lituratee*, and, "You got it where it counts, son."

While books infuriated him, Allen Lockton had always shown a lightening quick propensity for logic. Most often this would manifest itself in his remarkable ability to find things.

When the Lockton's terrier ran off, as it was prone to do, and his sister sat blubbering, as she was prone to do, Allen went out after it, reasoning that since the dog always barked furiously at their neighbor's pink Mary Kay Cadillac, the neighbor's garage might be a good place to start. He found the dog either there or at a myriad of other locations he quickly deduced over the years, and he always brought it back home.

Seeing the dog safely squirming about in his arms, his mother would clasp her hands in pride and run off to tell his father, who would look up from his paper, shrug, and proclaim, "The boy's no idiot."

After all his schooling was done and he had no more years of NCAA eligibility left, he felt lost. Struggling through the gap year between college graduation and whatever lay beyond, unemployed and dispirited, Allen was meandering around Chicago looking for a job when he came across a flyer stapled to a pocked wooden post in Grant Park:

Bike Couriers Wanted

Pay Variable

Trinity Bank Building

21 South Dearborn

The bottom of the paper was cut like a row of teeth, each sporting the number to call. Allen tore one off and two days later he walked into the Trinity Bank Building for an interview.

"Now you know we can't be held responsible for whatever happens to you out there,"

The head of courier services for the Trinity Bank Building, a middle-aged, military looking fellow dressed in a short-sleeve shirt and tie, looked at him over thick glasses. He gestured outside at the honking, chugging traffic snaking around the building like water through a series of sluices. Allen looked out of the glass doors of the lobby along with him. He saw the vendors, the sun glaring off the cars, he saw the billowing effects of the hot wind surging down the crosshatched streets of South Dearborn and West Madison, peeling around the corners and kicking up debris. It looked like Chicago to him, the Chicago he knew.

"But that said," the man continued, "we pay you by the job. So, ah, you know, the more you deliver, the more money you make."

"Makes sense."

"You got a bike?"

"I do."

"And you know Chicago?"

"I've lived here all my life, aside from college."

"Good. Then you're hired. But be careful flyin' around out there. You know, there's a lot of morons. There's a reason we're always hiring couriers, if you catch my drift."

The Trinity Bank Building shot up sixty stories into a tapered edge that cut a prominent spot on the Chicago skyline. It was made of granite and reflective black glass, and when the sun set it often took on the look of massive and bloodied obsidian arrowhead. Although named for the Trinity Bank, it housed an array of institutions, mostly financial firms, but also a variety of legal firms, a food court, and an organic supermarket. Allen Lockton would be delivering all manner of correspondence for any and all of them that wished it, all over downtown Chicago.

Despite having what he thought was a working knowledge of the city, the other couriers beat him hands down at first, sometimes delivering two or three items to his one. He quickly found out that riding down the streets, even in and out of cars, was not always the quickest way. The best ways often meant he had to cut across corporate lawns, in and out of courtyards, up the sidewalls of stairs, and in and around loading docks and back alleys that he had never before noticed. Split second decisions often meant the difference between a twenty-five minute delivery and a fifteen minute delivery. By the end of his first week he was averaging twenty minutes a job.

At home he would study overhead maps of the city, noting each place he delivered to and marking the clusters of buildings he trafficked most. He mapped out routes and marked out potential shortcuts. By the end of the first month he knew exactly how much passing room certain models of certain cars allowed and where their corresponding blind spots were. In that first month he fell twice: Once he took a rough tumble off the retaining wall of a concrete island near the Carbide and Carbon building and scraped a thin layer of skin off the back of his arm. The other was an incident in which a car door opened as he passed and he clipped his left handle on its side-view mirror, flipping himself head over end. The woman driving the car thought she'd killed him and shrieked, but the fall looked a lot worse than it was. He was able to ride away.

After the first month he never fell, and although he did buzz a few pedestrians and garnered his share of loud curses, he never hit anything else.

Soon he was averaging fifteen minutes a delivery and companies were requesting him by name for their most pressing documents. By the middle of his second month at work he was beating every other courier and was one of only three that had remained on from the time of his hiring. As with every task to which he applied himself, Allen had become a well-oiled machine. He formed blisters that split and reformed as calluses on his palms and his legs grew strong and corded. He got a deep biker's tan that made the rest of his covered body look onion white. By the end of his third month he could quote just about any delivery time to within one minute: City Hall or Daley City Center? Seven minutes. Prudential Plaza? Ten. Citicorp Center? That's across the river, so it'll take eleven minutes there, seven minutes back.

One day, after he had been working as a courier for almost half of a year, Allen was asked to deliver to a place that he didn't recognize. A company called BlueFox Financial, occupying half of the very top of the Trinity Bank Building, hired him for the delivery. He'd run for them a handful of times before, always tightly sealed packages and letters addressed to strange, nondescript locations; once he delivered a sealed letter from them to one of a series of warehouses on the east-side that he had always thought were abandoned. Another time they asked him to deliver a small package to someone's car in the Cooper Residential area. He was given the keys, told to place the letter on the driver's seat, and then lock the keys in the car. These were among the oddest of his deliveries, so when he reported to the top floor that day he was expecting another strange ride. He got something else entirely.

The secretary for the office was an endearing elderly woman who had always given him his mail and directions in the past, but this time she told him to pass through the thick wooden doors himself. There, a tall, gaunt fellow in a dark suit gravely shook his hand and led him into a sparsely lit conference room.

Unsure if he should remove his helmet, Allen sat awkwardly in a large leather chair that faced a table cluttered with maps of every sort. There were maps on the walls and maps on the floor. Some were rolled up and shoved halfway in various cubbyholes along the walls while others lay limply strewn about in the corners. One large map of the world, prominently placed on the wall to his left, was studded with hundreds of tacks of every color. He was surprised to see that of all the maps visible, only one was of Chicago, partly covered by others and hanging half off of the table.

The man introduced himself as Henry as he sat heavily opposite Allen. Henry rested his head back and sighed audibly. Then he closed his eyes for a moment and didn't move at all, as if struck by a sudden fit of narcolepsy. Henry's hair was unkempt and stuck out a bit over either ear the way a child's bowl-cut might. Under his eyes were deep, purplish bags so prominent that they looked painted. Allen glanced at one of the five clocks in the room, the one that read **CHICAGO**, and was about to say something about keeping to his schedule when Henry suddenly spoke, his eyes still closed.

"Allen, I need help here. This has all gotten to be…more than I can handle."

"What do you need?"

"If I ask you to deliver to a place for me, without knowing anything beyond the few details that I give you, could you find it? Find him?"

"Yes," said Allen, and then, "Him? A person?"

Henry seemed not to have heard him and continued talking, eyes still closed.

"It's rather out of the way, and God knows you won't get any help from the locals."

"Where is this? Up north? On Chicago Ave? If I just take

Dearborn up I can usually get that far north in twenty minutes."

Henry opened his eyes and looked directly at Allen, who was already putting his helmet back on.

"St. Petersburg."

Allen stopped, mid-strap.

"St. Petersburg? Is that that suburb out by South Pond?"

"It's that city. In Russia."

"Is this a joke?"

Henry's tired eyes peered at him with such scrutiny that Allen wished he would close them again. Henry shook his head.

"This is no joke, Allen. We would want you working full time for us. Something like a…a worldwide courier."

"Can't you just use FedEx?"

"The things we need delivered are special things. Things we can trust to very few people. Almost nobody."

"I don't deliver drugs."

Henry laughed weakly and the stubble on his face lifted into something of a smile.

"No, nothing like that. Mostly just letters. And we'll also need you to find people…people we need to get signatures from, people we need to keep tabs on."

Allen looked at him, and then glanced about the room at the maps.

"We would pay you very well. If, that is, you can find

these people for us. Starting with one man in particular. In St. Petersburg." Henry shook his head apologetically. "This one is a trial by fire if there ever was one."

"What's his name?"

"His name is Eddie Mazaryk, and he lives in St. Petersburg sometimes, and that's all you get because that's all we know. That, and this credit card, which will cover every expense you need, regardless of what it might be."

Henry slowly slid a black charge card across the desk.

"No one else has ever contacted Eddie Mazaryk with any regularity whatsoever. We thought that perhaps you might be the right…type."

Allen took the card and looked at it. It was a black American Express card with **Allen Murrow Lockton** inscribed on it in raised black lettering.

"Is this what I—"

"If you can find him and deliver to him, we'll take you on full time to deliver to all of our players worldwide. Then we'll tell you everything you want to know. Or, you could walk out and forget I ever asked. Up to you."

Allen paused for a long moment in which only the ticking of the clocks could be heard.

Finally, Allen stood up and took the card off the desk. Henry nodded, and Allen left the room. The elderly receptionist out front smiled kindly at him as he went out.

In the ensuing months and years, Allen flew, ran, swam, climbed, slid, dropped, biked, and drove all across the world finding people and delivering things for the Tournament. He came to realize that this new job was simply an extension of his old job, really of the jobs he had been doing all of his life. Only now instead of looking under Mrs. Massey's Pink Cadillac in her garage, he might have to jet across the Sahara to some casino in Sun City, or run down the Amalfi Coast to a fish shack off Via Quasimodo.

Hardly anyone called him Allen anymore. He wasn't even sure he would turn around if someone yelled his first name in a crowded room. Now people called him Lock, because he was a sure thing. He got the job done, no matter what.

But he still hated driving. Without the open air around him he felt restricted and muddled, even while doing what likely was the freest job in the world.

Lock eyed himself in his rearview mirror, as he often did, and ran his thumb down the rail-straight part in his brown hair, smoothing any errant flyaways. He would have to take each task as it came, as he always did. One at a time. But this whole issue with Bill Beauchamp and Frank Youngsmith was bothering him more than he allowed himself to show. It seemed a bad omen to open the fifth cycle on the tail-feathers of the death of one of their own. And the insurance agent, he was a rare kind of desperate. He was searching for something, even if he didn't know it yet.

Lock's gut told him the Tournament hadn't seen the last of Frank Youngsmith. And Lock's gut was never wrong.

CHAPTER SEVEN

IN THE TWO AND a half hours it took Frank Youngsmith to drive from Glendale down south to San Diego and the UCSD Medical center, Lock notified Greer Nichols about the unfortunate inquiry Frank had brought to their doorstep, and about what Lock had done to get rid of him.

"You sent him to Baxter?" Greer cried. "You *know* how that *man* feels about *this organization!*"

"There was nothing else I could do!" Lock snipped back. "He was threatening to go to the Attorney General!"

In his office, Greer rubbed at his head and glanced up at the dead cameras above him. He let out a big breath.

"I don't know, Lock. Baxter Walcott can be a pain in the ass. Might have been better off letting him toss the file to the Attorney General and leave the rest up to our legal people."

"All this Frank guy is going to do is get Dr. Walcott to sign a simple statement regarding his benefits. Then this whole issue gets shuffled off," Lock said, but his high pitch betrayed his lack of confidence. He knew he'd overstepped himself. Greer shook his head.

"If he really gets to talking with Baxter, there is no way this issue is gonna disappear."

At that very moment, many miles away, Frank Youngsmith walked into the crowded triage ward of UCSD Medical Center in San Diego and began to wait. Frank waited for almost twenty minutes just to get to the front desk, where he was immediately told by an exasperated secretary that there was simply no way he was going to see Dr. Walcott today. Walcott was the chief of the cardiac wing. He didn't take walk-ins, and even if he did, he wouldn't today. He was outrageously busy.

"Ma'am," Frank said, sweating a bit upon the counter, "I flew from Colorado to see Dr. Walcott. I need less than five minutes with the man."

The secretary eyed him skeptically. His face was ruddy from the heat and his sparse mop of springy hair was smeared to his forehead. He looked half ready to keel over.

"Dr. Walcott is in surgery," she said pityingly.

"I'll wait."

The secretary shrugged and pointed towards one of the few empty chairs in the waiting room. Frank shuffled over, sat down, closed his eyes, and fell asleep. He awoke some time later to a large orderly with flappy arms tapping him on the shoulder.

"I wasn't really sleeping, just…kind of closing my eyes, you know?"

The woman grunted and gestured at the front desk. Frank glanced behind her and saw that the secretary was twitching strangely, shifting one shoulder back and to her left where stood a thin and graying man, hunched slightly in his white lab coat. He was speaking into a Dictaphone with one hand and rubbing his eyes with the other. The secretary looked at Frank emphatically and Frank realized that Dr. Walcott had emerged for what was likely to be only a few moments.

Frank jumped up, startling the orderly and causing several people in the waiting area to wince.

"Dr. Walcott! A moment!"

Baxter Walcott paused in recording and eyed Frank with discomfort. He stepped back towards the patient rooms in preparation to bolt.

"Please, wait! I just need a moment," Frank said, stopping himself so as not to startle the doctor further.

Walcott quietly spoke something to the secretary, who shrugged in feigned ignorance and suddenly busied herself with her computer.

"I'm sorry, but unless you're suffering acutely, you'll have to book an appointment," Walcott said, tucking a fresh pen into a sagging pocket and turning to leave.

"Wait! No! It's about Bill Beauchamp!"

Baxter Walcott froze.

"Yes! Yes, it's about Bill!" Frank fumbled a few steps closer.

"What about Bill?" Walcott asked, his voice deadly quiet.

"We insured Bill Beauchamp. I'm investigating his claim," Frank said, sensing the need to be both brief and to the point.

Walcott peered at Frank.

"It shouldn't be an inconvenience, really, I just need to clear up a few things. A brief statement should do it."

"Who are you with?"

"Barringer Insurance."

"You mean you're not…with *them*…" Walcott began, before tapering off and glancing about. His eyes alighted for half of a moment upon one of the many cameras screening the waiting room of the ward.

Frank blinked. "Like I said, I'm with Barringer Insurance."

Baxter Walcott stared at Frank and looked to be thinking very hard.

"Dr. Walcott? Maybe I'm not sure what you're talking about."

Dr. Walcott suddenly said: "Take a walk with me."

He grabbed Frank at the shoulder and ushered him around the desk and the secretary, all but pulling him behind as he walked from the waiting room into the depths of the ward. They passed room after room, some open and some closed.

"Where are we going?" Frank clopped along behind Dr. Walcott.

"Sh."

"Maybe you misunderstood me, Doctor. I just need this basic statement signed—"

Walcott crowded him inside a darkened exam room and closed the door. He then rushed to the back of the room and began fishing around in a drawer near a gleaming piece of expensive looking machinery. Frank itched his arm and looked warily about.

"I think I caught you at a bad time."

"You wanna know what killed Bill Beauchamp?" Walcott asked, his voice a harsh whisper over the rattling of the drawer's contents.

"Not particularly, but it's my job to know if he's defrauding Barringer."

Walcott let out a derisive snort in the darkness.

"Money, money, money! That's the least of their worries. They throw money around like autumn leaves. This is much bigger than money."

"You were on his research team. Are you insured for the same amount as Bill Beauchamp? That's all I want to know, then I'll be gone. Totally gone."

"Of course I was. I still am. None of that matters."

Frank exhaled. Just like that, another potential criminal was proven harmless. No fraud here after all. Despite his exhaustion, Frank felt a bit disappointed. Again. He fished in his thin jacket for the statement he'd drawn up and notarized himself in the car on the drive over.

"If you could just sign this then—"

"No."

Frank paused and closed his eyes. He nodded to himself. It somehow seemed fitting that he would finally get to the bottom of it all and falter at the very last step.

"With all due respect to your friend, how he died doesn't really concern me right now," Frank said, his voice hollow in the darkened exam room.

"Bill didn't *die*," Walcott said, grabbing something from

the drawer and spinning back around to face Frank. "He was *murdered*."

Frank stepped back. He couldn't see what was in Dr. Walcott's hands, but he didn't like it, whatever it was. He fished around behind him for the doorknob with one hand while warding Walcott away with the other.

"Whoa, whoa. Don't tell me that. *Do not tell me that!* My work is done here! I'm kind of out of my depth!"

Frank managed to pop the door open just as Walcott reached him with what he held. A white sliver of light from the hallway fell upon the doctor's open hand. In it rested a strange bullet: dull ceramic in color with a tiny red capping.

"Bill was trying to solve the glass and water issues..." Walcott said, staring at the diode as if seeing it for the first time.

"The *what* issues? What the hell is that thing?"

"The diode has a minor charge to it that zaps the solution inside of it when it hits its target, but it's always reacted poorly on contact with glass and water. I'm not sure of the mechanics of it. That was Bill's job. He was the engineer. He thought he had it fixed...but he didn't."

"And what am I supposed to do with it?" Frank asked, shying away from the doctor's open palm as if it held some poisonous insect.

Walcott snatched Frank's wrist before he could react and pressed the diode into his hand. Frank squeezed his eyes shut, bracing for impact.

"Don't be an idiot. It's not going to blow up on you. It needs to be shot out of a gun. And even then it won't work. Not on you anyway. Although it'll hurt like hell." Abruptly, Walcott started like a spooked rabbit. "They'll have noticed my absence already. I've been gone far too long."

He sidestepped around Frank and out to the hall, pressing Frank further into the room.

"Wait here," he whispered. "Leave in another five or so minutes."

"I still don't know what you expect me—"

"Tell everyone. I wish I could be of more help, but I've said too much already and I can't afford a *reassignment* like Sarah got. She was our third team member. Now she's God knows where."

"This is not my area. I'm an *insurance agent!*"

"That doesn't matter anymore," Walcott hissed. "You're the best shot those kids have got. Get the word out, Frank, or Bill's death will just be the first in a long, long line."

With that Baxter Walcott swept out of view and back down the hallway, leaving Frank alone with the diode in the antiseptic silence and the dark.

CHAPTER EIGHT

MAX HAULDEN WALKED ALONE under the September-tinged leaves of the chestnut trees of Annapolis, Maryland. Their canopies spread above him like yellow sheets of linen and even the sunlight that filtered through them felt weighty with age. Annapolis was an old, solemn town, beautifully quiet in the fall.

Max could see the copper dome of the Naval Academy chapel, oxidized to a sharp turquoise, from the front porch of his parent's house. Every time it tolled the hour with its muted ringing he caught a faint whiff of his childhood, and he frowned. The Naval Academy was the reason he was no longer welcome in the house of his father. Every time he returned to this place he saw his father, and his grandfather before him, everywhere he looked—whether he wanted to or not.

All that physically remained of his grandfather were his pictures, his medals, and his house. Such was not the case with his father: his father could still sting him, or at least try to, although his son's employ with the Tournament had sapped Frederick Haulden of any real ability to hurt Max. But whatever problems the Tournament took away it also replaced. Max had long since learned that problems never go away: they just change faces.

Max was eighteen and still a student at NAPS, the Naval Academy Preparatory School, when he and his father parted ways. Max's classmates had finally accepted him for what he was after

two years of trying to befriend him to no avail, and then another
two years of trying to bully him–again, to no avail. He was a cold
and distant boy, and they eventually gave up bothering with him.
Still, his demeanor fascinated them. Whereas other unpopular
students were actively rejected from social circles, Max Haulden's
seclusion was self-inflicted. Moreover, he didn't bother trying to
move beyond it. His nonchalance confused his peers. Nonchalance
was the hallmark of popular people, not loners.

The girls also liked his hair. It was light-brown and a
bit longer than most. Tired of it falling in his face while he read,
Max pushed it all back with cheap gel, for functionality only. This,
combined with his slightly pinked cheeks, gave the impression
that he was romantically windblown most of the time, and even
rather attractive. No girl would ever admit it, though. They knew
where he stood in the pecking order. Max knew nothing about
any of this, and if he did he would have thought it ridiculous.

All Max ever seemed to want to do was read and observe,
but he was a senior, so he was also entangled in the long, involved
process of applying to the Naval Academy—or rather, Fredrick
Haulden was entangled in the long, involved process of applying
for his son. Frederick took it upon himself to ensure that Max
was to become the third generation of Hauldens to grace the halls
of "The Academy."

Fredrick was an imposing figure. He was taller than his
son even at fifty-five, but frumpier, and with the barely perceptible beginnings of a stoop. He was still fairly muscular, but what
was once bulk was beginning to settle downward. He had the
distinct look of an aging military man, like a wet camping tent,
where the basic outlines remain true to form, but the filler is a
bit saggy. He still had a commanding voice, however, the voice of
a captain. That had never left him. Frederick was frequently away
while Max grew up, so when Max thought of his father, his mind

brought forth the voice first and foremost.

His mother, however, he could describe without error, down to the gold and pearl broach she always wore on the lapel of her jacket, and the jade-butterfly clip that kept her peppered hair pulled tightly back from her forehead. Nancy Haulden was a predictable woman. She had known his father since childhood, almost twenty-five years before Max was born. She and his father grew up next to each other, not half of a mile from where their house now sat just southwest of Church Circle. It was the house that his grandfather had given them as a marriage present.

Max knew his father's father, the only grandfather anyone in his family ever talked about, through pictures and stories only, but he figured he had about enough of them to write a tome. They shared the same nickname although his grandfather's full name was Maximilian, whereas his was Maxwell. His mother often said that this was because he was "so like his grandfather, and yet his own man." How they had known this at the time of his birth, Max had no idea.

Max did look remarkably like the young cadet he saw in framed, black and white photos on high shelves and coffee tables about his father's house. They had similarly thin, small noses, and the same light complexion. Mostly, though, it was the expressions that the two wore that likened one to the other: it was a worried look, almost sad, in which their eyebrows sloped gently down and away from a softly ridged forehead, their eyes always a shade shy of fully open.

Perhaps it was partly because of this resemblance that his father took it so hard when, upon receiving his inevitable acceptance, Max told him he would not be attending the Naval Academy.

"Excuse me?" Fredrick said.

"I said I'm not going."

"Of course you are, son. The commendation is in, the acceptance is back. It is what is happening."

"Georgetown also accepted me."

"Is that so?"

"Yes."

"Then get out of my house," he said in his captain's voice: not a yell, not a statement. A command.

So Max left. He left his father's house and moved into his grandfather's, where his mother had often stayed when Fredrick was away during his tours of duty back before he had retired. It was still family property, but nowadays his mother mostly used it to entertain guests. She felt it had a friendlier atmosphere than her and Fredrick's own.

His mother came to see him that first night. She found him in his grandfather's old study reading in his old desk-chair, and for a moment she silently stood and watched. Absorbed as he was in his book, he seemed not to notice her. He looked so much like Maximilian that it seemed to her that the house had been transported back in time sixty years. Despite the blowout earlier, Max looked calm, if a little sad. Or perhaps it was just the same look he always wore made more profound by the day's events.

"I'm not going to that school, mom," he said softly without looking up from his book.

"You broke your father's heart."

"It was handed to him, just like it was handed to me. The only man that earned a spot there was granddad."

Nancy approached and embraced him and pulled him
in close to her, and Max knew then that she would support him
regardless.

Twice a week throughout the summer following Max's
graduation from NAPS, Nancy would visit him at her late father-
in-law's house where he took up residence, always on the pretense
of bringing food, but in reality just to talk to him. He never saw
his father, and if the two of them ever spoke about Fredrick it was
always within the context of Maximilian. When Nancy would
visit she would often find her son reading in the study. "You
know, your grandfather loved that book," she would say, or "In
high school I would often come up to this study just to talk with
your grandfather. He used to keep a jar of caramels right there."
Back at his own home he had found these stories repetitive, even
a bit burdensome, as if he was in constant comparison, but in
his grandfather's house he found them empowering. It was only
when he was surrounded by the ghost of his grandfather that he
began to understand the man he was.

The longer Max lived in that house, the more he came to
realize that Maximilian would have supported his choice to aban-
don the Naval Academy. His grandfather's spirit wasn't a military
one; it was entrepreneurial. He came from a family of doctors, but
struck out on a different path and succeeded in the military. Max
would do the same, even if it meant leaving his father behind.

Max went away to Georgetown that fall, as good as his
word, but he always returned to his grandfather's house during the
summers. His mother would find him in the study or on the back
porch. More often than not he was reading, but sometimes he
would be writing or just watching the movement around him. He
made several friends at Georgetown, and was even dating a girl for
a few months during his sophomore year, but he put everything
on hiatus during the summers when he came back to Maryland.

He was transient, unable to commit fully to either residence as home.

One day during the summer of his junior year, as he sat reading in the study, he thought he heard his mother come in the house and start up the stairs. He quickly finished the paragraph he was on and marked his space as the door to the study opened.

"Mom, I was thinking that we could fix up the—" he began, but then he looked up and saw that the person standing in the door frame wasn't his mother at all: it was a tall black man wearing a cream-colored suit, his head shaved to a gleam. Max froze. Only his bobbing Adam's apple betrayed the alarm coursing through his body.

The man moved to a leather seat in front of the desk and sat down in it. He leaned forward, rested his elbows on his knees, and steepled his fingers. He looked directly into Max's eyes.

"Can you take an order, Max?"

Max quietly closed his book and set it on the desk in front of him, but kept his hand upon it.

"Who are you? Did my father send you?" he asked, his voice level.

"Your father? No. My name is Greer Nichols. We'll get to me and what I do in time. What I need to know right now is if you can take an order. From someone other than your mother."

"My father did send you. Get out of this house."

Max looked at his grandfather's old rotary phone, sitting on its own stand just to the right of the desk. It looked to weigh at least twenty pounds. Perhaps he could throw it…

"I wouldn't do that Max, not yet. At least not until you've heard me out."

Something in the tone of the man's voice made Max stop. Despite its low rumbling, it contained no threat. The man ran a well-manicured hand over his head and sat back in his seat. The leather creaked.

"Who are you?" Max repeated, again, more worried this time. The man's lack of hostility bothered him, and the calm way that he sat in his chair was unsettling, like this was his own study, like nothing at all was out of the ordinary.

"Can you take an order? We've been watching you, and are divided on this."

"Who's we?"

"Just answer the question. Please."

The man was looking around the office as he spoke and seemed to be paying only peripheral attention to the conversation. Suddenly Max had the feeling that somehow the man in front of him, a man he had never seen before, knew precisely how Max would answer the question even before he asked it. He felt like he was already caught in something—that he'd been caught as soon as this man walked in the room. Max looked at Greer for a moment, waiting until his focus fell back upon him before answering.

"If it's from the right person, yes," Max said.

Greer nodded immediately: obviously this was in line with whatever he was thinking himself. Max was faintly annoyed as well as alarmed. Perhaps he should have lied.

The man then took a dark blue folder with a metallic sheen from the left breast of his jacket and set it on the desk before Max.

"Take a look at this. If you like what you see, call the number written inside and we'll take you to meet the rest of your team. If you don't like what you see, or you think this is some sort of joke, do us all a favor and throw it away and never speak of our conversation again. The choice, as always, is entirely up to you"

Greer got up, flattened his lapels, and moved towards the door. Max noticed that Greer removed another folder, identical to the one in front of him, from beneath the right breast of his jacket.

"Whose is that?" Max blurted out. Greer paused.

"Not yours," he said simply, before nodding a brief farewell and stepping out.

Max heard him go down the stairs, and he heard the clanging of the screen door as it shut behind him. In the ensuing quiet, Max could faintly hear the chittering of birds by the feeder on the back porch. Somewhere out front a car door slammed and an engine whirred softly off into the distance. Max looked at the file for a moment as it lay on the desk, then he turned it towards him and read the lettering in the seal on the front:

The Tournament

Team Blue

(USA)

Maxwell Haulden

Striker

—

Max was unique among his colleagues: He never once doubted what he was told or what he read about the Tournament, even that first time in his grandfather's study. In five years, under the leadership of Johnnie Northern, and side by side with Nikkie Hix, he had become a ruthless striker. In all that time he never told his mother what he was doing or where he went on his extended trips. He only ever said that work called him away. They were alike in more ways than he knew, Max and Nancy, because every time he said that he was off, as he did when his pager buzzed this fifth and most recent time, she never asked questions. She hugged him and told him to be safe, and every time she said it, Max was again reminded why he could never tell her what it was that he really did.

There was nothing remotely safe about it.

CHAPTER NINE

<hr>

IT WAS SUNDAY AFTERNOON in Belfast when Ian Finn's pager went off. He didn't have it on him. He never carried it on him when he was working out back, and at the time he was smoking a cigarette and sitting on a dark brown tarp, leaning against the sun warmed side of his father's work shed taking a break. He'd been up since Mass at six in the morning. A long time.

The muggy fall weather made him sweat and the flashes of wind had then dried it alternately throughout the late morning and past noon so that his pale brow was gritty and his shirt was wet in some places and tracked with white salt lines in others. Work dust and flecks of dried paint peppered his hair as if sifted there. He was stripping the shed's ceiling; it hadn't been touched in a long time. Where he pushed his damp hair out of his eyes it dried wildly in big curls that looped about and behind his ears and halfway down his neck. As he smoked he watched the sun wane across the town, illuminating one side of each of the weatherworn single-story houses and rain-stained brick buildings seemingly at random, as if highlighting particular pieces of some industrial art show. He crossed his thin arms around himself and inhaled deeply in one side of his mouth before exhaling around the cigarette. His dark green eyes, muted always by the soft black bags that hung below them, reflected nothing. Not even the setting sun seemed able to pass through to them.

The shed behind him had stood derelict for five years

until Ian decided to do something about it. In the last two years it had taken to slouching slightly to one side as if drunk. The lead-based paint his father coated it with a decade ago bled into the ground and was slowly killing the grass in an ever expanding circle. By now the building itself looked contagious.

As he smoked he was thinking of what Father Darby said to him that morning, in passing, as he and his mother were leaving the gray stone church with the rest of the congregation, filing slowly out under the carved eaves, their once sharp masonry now blunted by rain and time. They all thanked the old priest, as was the custom for as long as Ian could remember. As Ian received his blessing, Father Darby briefly touched him on his shoulder. "Keep your eyes open," he had said, quietly. "I think it's almost time."

Only Ian heard him, and Ian simply nodded, crossed himself, and walked out into the growing light to catch up with his mother.

Everyone knew that Ian was close to Father Darby. He'd known him for almost a decade now, but none could guess at the true relationship that Ian had with the slightly stooped, white haired priest. Although Ian had been involved in St. Mary's church from a very young age, for a long while he only ever garnered a gracious nod or a blessing from Father Darby. In all those years he hadn't the slightest idea that the man was watching him very closely.

As a child, Ian was often teased about his father. Ian and his classmates were all far too young to understand why Peter Finn was in jail, but they still ridiculed Ian. No doubt most of the children had been told by their parents to avoid Ian, and so they did, but they weren't told why. Some thought Ian's dad was sick, and Ian by proxy. His hitched left arm, a minor birth defect, contributed to these fancies. Some feared to touch Ian in case they contracted his 'wonky arm'.

He could move his left arm in exactly the same way as his right if he concentrated fully upon it, but when he left it to its own devices it tensed up and cocked itself awkwardly as if he were wearing an invisible sling. Over the years he'd tried to hide it, and in turn had developed a slightly hunched walk. When in school, Ian frequently caught the tail end of exaggerated shows the other kids put on to mock it.

Youth was hard on Ian, but he did befriend one child, a younger boy named Toby. Ian was walking home from school one day when Toby caught up with him. Ian, unused to company, stopped dead in his tracks and looked down at the small, mousey boy.

"Hello," the boy said.

Ian looked from Toby back down the street the way he had come, and then back at Toby again.

"Hullo," Ian said.

"You're Ian Finn."

"I am."

"My name is Toby."

Ian said nothing.

"My mother told me about you."

"And what's that she said?" Ian asked, halfheartedly stepping forward a bit, having long ago tired of the action needed to back up his words.

"Said your father's a patriot," Toby said, backing up a bit

and hunkering down in front of Ian as if he'd heard a loud noise and didn't know where from. Ian stopped and stepped back. He looked down at the ground, confused and slightly ashamed for the cowering boy. Both were silent.

"D'you live over there?" Toby asked, pointing down the road, still hunched.

"Yes."

"So do I."

And so they became friends.

But Toby was too small to help Ian in the schoolyard. When the other boys tried to bait Ian into fighting, Toby slinked back into the wall and wouldn't meet anyone's eye. Ian expected this, however, and never held it against him, but Ian wouldn't allow himself to do nothing, even if it was only to vehemently repeat *You don't know my father* again and again. He was often galled by a particularly spiteful and vicious boy named Matthew, who worked himself into a splotchy faced redness as he berated Ian, smiling ever broader as he went.

"I know he's in The Maze," Matthew said.

"You know nothing about him."

"That's all I need ta know"

"You know nothing about him," Ian repeated wearily. He would often be sitting during these interchanges, his back against the brick wall of his classroom, and the boys would look down on him. He sat simply, his knees propped up near his chest where he could rest his gimped hand upon them and it would look normal. It was a vulnerable position, but Ian's apparent lack of concern confused Matthew. Matthew could strike out at Ian if he wanted, he could spit on him or kick him easily, but the ease with which he could do it was the very thing that kept him from it.

Ian rarely looked at Matthew and his posse when they taunted him, but he always looked at whomever he addressed. He would squint into the light and peer up, always seeking direct eye contact. His eyes betrayed nothing: no fear and no hate. This also disconcerted his aggressors. After Matthew had the last laugh, he and the rest of the boys would generally leave him alone, and Toby would come wandering back to sit down next to Ian again in silent companionship.

During the early spring of his final year in middle school there was a particularly long stretch of gray and rainy days. Ian awoke to rain, trudged through it to school, listened to its patter on the windows during class, and walked back home in it. For three straight weeks every jacket was damp, every corridor thinly tracked with mud and water, every window fogged and dripping, and it gnawed at everyone, students and teachers alike. Despite the weather the teachers made the kids all go outside for recess, more for their own sanity than that of the students.

During these recesses all of the students huddled under the overhanging eaves of the buildings and doorways. It wasn't long until Matthew and his friends, bored and uncomfortable, sought out Ian and Toby where they stood quietly talking and gazing out into the mist. Toby was biting his nails and spitting them out over the rail. The playground stood empty and muddy, its metallic structures dripping. The students all hung about its edges as if it was a cordoned-off police zone.

Matthew came up behind Toby and pushed him out under the roof runoff and held him there. Toby, too startled to say anything, sputtered and paled instantly.

"Hey, you all right there Tobe?" Matthew said, laughing

and rubbing hard on Toby's head. Toby scrunched down.

"Didn't see ye there, mate," Matthew said. "Here, come back a bit, outta the rain." He moved Toby behind him and patted his head in mock affection. Then he stepped up next to Ian.

"Hello Ian."

"Didn' have ta do that Matthew."

"Hard ta find room around here."

Ian shook his head and looked out into the rain.

"It's terrible they make us sit out here, right Ian?"

"It's not so bad."

"I bet they don't even make yer dad run around the yard on days like this, eh?"

Ian was silent. Around him conversations tapered off. Toby moved under the doorway behind everyone, wiping his coat and eyes and smoothing his hair. Ian couldn't tell if he was crying or just wet.

"It must be hard, being a criminal. Days like this."

"Shut yer mouth, Matthew."

"You only ever get that one jumpsuit, can't get it wet."

"I said shut your mouth."

"One day you'll probably end up in there with him."

And Ian hit him.

Ian stepped out into the rain and drove his shoulder back

under the eave and into Matthew's chest. Matthew staggered back into the wall and his head snapped back into a window, feathering it around the break. In a flash Ian's bad hand was at Matthew's throat and his other was pushing hard on his face, as if he was trying to force his head back through the glass. The window creaked and moaned. Matthew didn't have time to react initially, but now he tried to fight back. His hands flailed around Ian's grip and his feet slid about on the gravel below, fighting for purchase. He tried to raise a knee, but Ian pressed himself into him, almost as if he was about to kiss him. He placed his thumb over the slight pit in Matthew's throat and suddenly his bad hand quickly seized up, closing off Matthew's airway. Ian never blinked, but Matthew's eyes rolled wildly, resting again and again on Ian's bum left hand.

"Why the surprise Matthew? It's gimp, not dead," Ian said, looking at his own hand as if it was something foreign and beyond his control. Ian's voice wavered when he spoke because he was close to tears and his mouth was set in a strained frown in fighting to keep them back. He looked more sad than angry.

Behind Matthew's head the pane of glass popped and cracked, but then several teachers descended upon them and Ian was pulled away from Matthew. Matthew was coughing violently and hugging himself and everyone else in the yard started yelling and pointing, describing the fight to everyone and no one. As Ian was pulled inside he never took his eyes off of Matthew. Suddenly Ian started to cry, and then Toby cried.

Ian was suspended for a week, but his mother wasn't angry. She only told him that he needed to guard his feelings and that what people said meant nothing. She said his father would have been proud, but this only made Ian feel worse because he wasn't sure if he wanted his father to be proud of him. Ian wasn't sure of his father, and he hated people like Matthew all the more for making him aware of it. In truth, Ian knew little about his father. His mother rarely spoke of James' incarceration, having deemed Ian too young to understand the politics. The few times he'd broached the subject directly, most often after schoolyard altercations, Mary Finn had replied truthfully and simply that some people thought James was a hero, but some also thought he was a criminal, and one day Ian would have to decide for himself. This only confused Ian further, so he dropped the subject. Instead he stole his first cigarette from Mary's purse and went out to his father's old shed and smoked it and looked up at the cobwebs in the ceilings and absently shuffled around the gardening tools with his feet. The cigarette burned his throat, but he finished it and buried the butt outside under the dead grass so his mother wouldn't know.

Four months later Father Darby first came to see Ian. He never recalled speaking directly with the priest for more than a few minutes, so Ian was surprised to see the man, already old, walking towards where he sat with Toby. The two were throwing pebbles at a hitch in the splintering wooden fencing that surrounded the school's parking lot. Classes had finished, but Ian lingered to kill time between when he got out of school and when his mother finally got home from working at the stationary store in Castle Court where she was the cashiers' manager.

"Good afternoon boys," Darby said, looking at both in turn before glancing about at the mostly empty car lot. Although people still moved about here and there inside the school buildings, most of the rooms were dark. Ian could hear the faint hum of a vacuum cleaner somewhere inside.

"Afternoon Father," Ian offered awkwardly. Toby nodded his small head by way of greeting.

"Getting late," Darby said.

"We were just about to take off."

"Need a ride?"

"It's only a few blocks. Thank you though."

"I heard you're still having some trouble at school."

Ian looked down briefly and then focused on the hitch in the post that had been their target.

"Sometimes," he said.

"What about?"

Ian was silent.

"Ian, your father—"

"My father is a good man," Ian said suddenly.

"…He's more than that. James is a good friend as well. And a patriot."

Ian looked at Father Darby for a moment. Beside him Toby coughed briefly.

"You know my father," Ian said, more a statement than a question.

"I do. You're right handed?" Father Darby asked, as if it was the natural progression of the conversation. Ian wrinkled his brow.

"What?"

"You write with your right hand?"

"Course I do."

"But you choked that Matthew boy with your left hand. 'S what yer mother says."

Darby started towards Ian and Ian involuntarily stepped back. Both froze and Toby got up and scampered a short distance away. A hot August breeze gusted low across the blacktop parking lot, scattering small bits of sand and fluffing Father Darby's sparse white hair. Ian heard small bits of windblown debris clack against Darby's thick eyeglasses. Ian blinked rapidly.

"It's all right son, I just wantae see yer hand."

"Why."

"I think I can fix it."

"I'm allrigh' with it."

"Are you sure?"

Ian looked at Toby. Toby already had his backpack on.

"Fix it how? It's already 'bin looked at."

"I would pay for it. All of it."

Ian narrowed his eyes.

"I've spoken ta yer mother. And yer father."

"You spoke to my dad."

"I did."

"Are you lyin' to me."

"I don't lie. Ever."

"That so."

"It is."

"Well."

"I just would like tae see it. If I may. Nothin' more son. I promise."

Ian said nothing.

"May I?"

"My mother? You talked to my mom?"

"Yes."

"All right," Ian said finally.

Darby moved over to Ian and reached out with both hands to touch his left arm. Ian slowly held it out to him with considerable effort. It still hitched up slightly. Darby cradled it in both hands like a small animal, moving it slightly about to the left and right and extending it. All the while Ian never took his eyes off of Darby's face.

Darby turned Ian's hand palm up and took his index finger and traced a particularly defined muscle that ran from the crux of Ian's arm towards his pale, veined wrist. At the halfway point Ian snapped his hand back very quickly: One moment Darby held it, the next it was back across Ian's chest like he was preparing to ward off a strike.

"Sorry," Ian said. "That wasn't me. It was, I mean, but it wasn't. I didn't mean to do it."

"That's all right," Darby said, smiling broadly. "That's perfect, Ian. Perfect."

—

"Your pager, Ian!"

Ian peeked from around the shed. His mother stood in the doorway, a faded blue smock strung around her hips, hung low and folded over itself so that its ties brushed the linoleum floor just inside. She was splashed with something white, either paint or flour, and she wore jeans and bright red clogs of the type used often in gardening work. Ian smiled despite himself.

"Shut that damn pager up!" she yelled.

"What?"

"Are you smoking?"

"Yes."

She put her hands on her hips and cocked her head at him.

"You could at least lie about it."

"I don't lie. I believe you taught me that one," Ian reminded as he gently crushed the ember out on the tarnished broadside of his old silver Zippo lighter. The rest of the cigarette he stuck behind his ear for future use.

"Well at least do something about this pager. It's like an alarm or something."

Ian quickly righted himself from the shed.

"My pager? Wait, *my* pager?" he asked, pointing at himself.

"Who else owns a pager these days? Stop it or I toss it!"

Ian dashed across the lawn, squeezed inside around his mother, and stopped dead staring at the metal folding table next to their back window. Sure enough, a small black pager was slowly rattling its way to the far edge. Ian could only watch it for a moment, but just before it was about to drop to the floor he snatched it. He turned it around. Its screen pulsed pink. The clock was already ticking down.

Chapter Ten

D R. Baxter Walcott was setting out the lasagna he spent two hours preparing, a long time to spend on a dish that was essentially cheese, noodles, and meat, but Baxter didn't care. His daughter Sarah loved his lasagna, and he loved that Sarah loved it, so he was more than happy to make it when she visited.

He placed the ceramic dish on a hotpad in the center of their large wooden dining table, covered it with a glass lid, and sat a towel over that. Three place settings were clustered to one side of the table, Sarah's at the head, his wife Sheila's to one side of her, and his own to the other. He set out plates and silverware and then an oversized wine glass at the head of each place setting. He still liked to think that wine was a special treat for Sarah, although he guessed it had lost its luster now that she was in college and could get whatever booze she wanted. Not for the first time did Baxter shove thoughts from his head, thoughts of liquored up Cali-boys thrusting cup after cup of high-proof poison into Sarah's hand in the drippy basement of some dodgy house party. No sir. Not his daughter.

The monthly dinners had been Baxter's idea, and one that he had proposed to the family upon Sarah's departure to UCSD almost two years ago. Although the dinners were ostensibly a chance for Sarah to come home for a night and catch up with her parents, they were also for Sheila, whom he felt he was seeing less of because of his work. With the draw in three days, there was a real possibility of longer and stranger hours at the hospital, and he wanted to enjoy the calm before the storm.

He was uncorking the wine when his wife's car drove past the front windows. He heard the garage door opening a moment later. It amazed him how he could look up at almost the exact time his wife was driving by, as if he sensed it. Perhaps he did. When Sarah was in high school, he'd often wake up moments before he heard her come in late. Now, of course, with her gone, he never knew her comings and goings. Her freshman year she had sometimes pleasantly surprised him at work for lunch, and other times she would stop off at home occasionally, but this year she visited less. Perhaps it was a natural progression, but Baxter would insist upon these monthly dinners as long as all three of them were able. They were about much more than food.

At almost the time Sheila opened the door from the garage, Sarah rang the doorbell. Walcott still thought it odd that his daughter rang the doorbell at her own house, but Sarah always did it now. He shouted for her to come in just as Sheila turned the corner to the kitchen and kissed him on the cheek. She looked surprisingly fresh, and he knew that she had put on makeup in the car on the way home. Her blond hair hung flatteringly around her shoulders. She colored it recently, refusing to allow any gray to show despite Baxter's insistence that she looked just as beautiful with it as she did without.

Sheila was carrying garlic bread, balancing precariously atop a fresh load of junk brought from her ailing parents' small ranch house twenty minutes away: a bedside lamp, several books, and a shadowboxed display of military medals, no doubt her grandfather's. Every time she came from them she acquired more of their possessions. Baxter wasn't sure why they felt the need to unload all of their things on her. It was as if they were having one last massive yard sale, except that it had lasted for three years now.

He never had to deal with his own parents in this manner. They died when he was in medical school in St. Louis, first his father and then his mother shortly thereafter, and so he always stepped lightly around the subject of his wife's parent's care. Was their longevity a blessing or a curse? He silently chastised himself. It was a blessing, wasn't it? She smiled at him and looked at the table spread.

"She's going to love it," she said.

"Of course I love it," he heard Sarah call as she wiped her feet at the door. "I smelled the lasagna from the porch, dad."

Sheila ran to her daughter with exaggerated, mother-hen attentiveness. Sarah submitted to all her kisses and rolled her eyes, but her smile was genuine.

They took their traditional spots at the table, said a quick blessing in which Baxter kept his eyes open and looked back and forth from his wife to his daughter, and they dug in to the food.

"Room looks different," Sarah observed, eating a hunk of garlic bread with one hand and pushing a strand of hair behind her ear with the other. She wore a pair of delicate glasses that nicely set off her eyes. Her face looked like a picture. Every glance seemed an unintentional pose, like she moved in a series of snap-shots. She was getting dangerously beautiful.

"You know your mother, she's always moving things," Walcott said. And suddenly he was reminded of Nikkie Hix. What if Sarah was in Nikkie's place? The sweet nausea of catastrophe avoided tapped at Walcott. Thank God his daughter could simply be a normal college girl.

"Do you hate it?" Sheila asked, looking around at the room. Sarah laughed.

"No mom, it looks good. And yes, it still feels like home."
Sheila was constantly worried that Sarah would come home and
not recognize the house. "I love this place. It's so much better than
our apartment," Sarah said.

"Well this is a *house*, honey. It took us eight years to get it
like this," Sheila said.

"How are Alice and, ah," Baxter said, he always forgot that
other one.

"It's Annie. Annie and Jessica, dad. What's this, two years
now I've lived with them?"

"You have a lot of friends," Baxter began, and trailed off.
Sarah had already forgiven him. She knew about her dad and
names.

"Jess found a cockroach two days ago in our bathroom.
A baby one," Sarah said, shivering. "Gross. Just gross. Boys are supposed to have that stuff. We're girls."

"What did you do?" Baxter asked, smiling.

"We used a can of bug spray on it and put a bucket over
it until Jess's boyfriend could come and get rid of it. I had to leave
the apartment."

"A whole can?"

"Yeah. David said they come up through the drains, so we
put cups over all the drains when we aren't using them. I want to
move."

"Just the one?"

"Yeah."

"Well, honey, maybe it came in through the window. Are you sure it was a cockroach?"

"It was a bug. Or something."

"Well, see how it goes the next couple of weeks before you start packing."

"Dad."

"What?"

"This is serious."

"Oh I know. Terribly."

"No bug talk at the table. How is Nick?" Sheila asked. Sarah had accidentally let the name drop in one of her phone conversations. Sheila had picked up on it instantly.

"Oh, fine. I haven't seen him for a few weeks." Sarah said, suddenly concentrating on cutting her lasagna into smaller portions.

"I see. Not working out?"

"I dunno. He's a nice guy."

"Uh huh."

That was all they would get out of her.

"Your grandparents gave me a bunch of notepads to give you," Sheila said, shaking her head. "That and a desk lamp. It's in the kitchen."

"I'm all right."

"I know."

"Is the lamp nice?"

"No. It's a sort of stained porcelain tulip lamp. If you could take it to the trash on your way out, that would help us out a lot," Sheila said, smiling sadly.

"How are they doing?" Sarah asked, half looking up at her mother.

"They're hanging in there."

"How are you?"

"I'm fine, sweetheart."

"Growing old. It's hard," Sarah said.

"It can be."

Baxter refilled the wine glasses.

"It was nice when you stopped by work last week," Baxter said. "Let me know next time and we can get lunch. Like we used to."

"No problem. Is there still that place nearby?"

"The deli? It's a coffee shop now, but there are others."

Sarah nodded and took her wineglass up, she twirled it around and watched the legs drip down the inner rim.

"Who was that guy you were with? Does he work at the hospital?"

"What guy?"

"Really short blonde hair. Cute. I saw him talking with you."

Baxter stopped his fork midway from plate to mouth, but Sarah seemed not to notice. She was absently watching the wine in her glass, unconcerned. Baxter took a sip of wine and let it rest on his tongue. Sheila looked up at him. He swallowed.

"Probably just a patient. Doesn't sound like an employee."

"I think he goes to UCSD. What's his name?"

"You know I can't give out patient information. It's private."

"Oh come on dad. A name. I'm just curious. I think I've seen him around."

Baxter itched at his nose and was suddenly aware of his hands. To make them seem more natural he reached for the lasagna plate and took up the spatula. He looked intently at the food and then at his daughter.

"You *do* know who I'm talking about," Sarah said, smiling.

"It's nobody Sarah. Just a patient. And trust me, he doesn't go to UCSD."

"What's wrong with you dad?"

"Johnnie—John. It's John."

" Johnnie John?"

"No. Yes. John. He's a patient of mine."

"Well, put in a good word for me, eh? He's got great forearms."

Baxter said nothing.

"Dad. I'm just joking. C'mon. I'm twenty. You do know I like boys, right? Mom, tell him I'm joking."

Shelia started laughing. Baxter managed a poorly mustered smile.

"All right, I'll talk to him myself, if I ever see him," Sarah said, after a moment more of her father fiddling with the lasagna.

"No, I'll tell him. Don't—just leave that one alone. For me. Okay?"

Shelia's smile changed into a something more questioning, one eyebrow half-cocked. Sarah leaned back in her chair and looked at him for a moment through narrowed eyes. He had been too hasty in replying. He already knew that this would rebound against him tenfold. He had just propelled what might have been a passing interest into full-blown curiosity.

"Why?" she asked simply.

Baxter's mind raced; he was in damage-control mode.

"It's just medical issues. I can't talk about it. He isn't the most…stable of men," he said, choosing his words carefully, acutely aware of Sarah's awareness of his doing it. "I really cannot discuss confidential patient matters. You know this."

Sarah shrugged and went back to eating.

"Really, it's no big deal," he lied, trying to backtrack. "He's just not…he's not a good man."

"Wow, dad. All I did was see him through the glass doors."

"I know."

Sarah let out a big breath. Sheila puffed out her lower lip.

They all went back to eating.

"How's the car holding up?" Baxter asked, a few moments later. "That service light still beeping?"

"I was going to ask you how to make it stop. It drives me crazy. Every time I start the damn thing."

"I can't turn it off. Dealer has to do it."

"Well that's convenient, isn't it?"

And so they moved on. But Sarah never forgot her father's reaction, and Baxter knew it. His daughter wanted to meet Johnnie Northern. Captain of Blue. As he kissed her goodbye and told her to start the new school year strong, he prayed that Frank Youngsmith was well on his way to dismantling the organization before Sarah had any chance to get involved with the likes of Northern. What a pathetic outside shot that was. Daughters were like pendulums: if you pushed them away from a thing, they came swinging right back. Or perhaps she might forget about it. Perhaps it was nothing but passing conversation. He pondered this as he fell asleep later that night, trying to will his mind into peace, but his dreams unsettled him and he awoke tired.

Sarah saw him on her way back from her *Age of Lincoln* pro-seminar not even one week later. The class was a once weekly, four-hour beast that she, as an American Culture Studies major, was required to take some time in her undergraduate tenure. She put it off for the first two years, and she didn't want the notoriously difficult class hanging over her senior year, so she bit the bullet. Now, almost a month in to the first semester, she was quite sure the class was going to kill her.

Because of the shortening fall days it was nearly dusk

when Sarah got out of the class and began the long walk back
to her car. The San Diego weather was characteristically beautiful and best enjoyed just then, when the dark was cooling but
the breeze was warm. She turned on to Gilman Drive, the main
campus thoroughfare, and walked while idly watching people flit
about the student center to her right. Exhausted and distracted,
she allowed her mind and eyes to wander, but then she saw him
watching her.

He was sitting on one of the many cut-concrete slabs
strewn across the campus that functioned as benches. He was
dressed simply, in a dark and smooth t-shirt and jeans. Sarah immediately looked at his shoes, as she was prone to do, and saw that
he wore faded boat shoes and no socks. In the waning half-light
he looked very dark. Only the blond sheen of his close-shaved
hair and a hint of blue in his eyes stood out at a distance to dif-
ferentiate any of his facial features, and yet Sarah knew it was the
man she'd caught her father speaking to before stopping in to
visit. He was lightly running his right thumb over his lower lip, as
if lost in thought about her without even knowing her. It seemed
insane that her old, lovable fud of a father could be associated
with this young wolf. Closely associated, if the way she'd seen
them speaking was any indication.

If she had ever talked to him before, or indeed if she
thought he had ever actually seen her before, she might have
thought he was waiting for her. But he was a total stranger, so the
effect of seeing him watch her was disquieting—and flattering.
At first she looked behind her, thinking that perhaps his gaze was
focused elsewhere, but then she turned back around and saw that
his thumb had stopped moving.

"You're Baxter Walcott's daughter," he offered after a
moment of her standing in place. She could hear the smile in her
voice and see the white flash of his teeth as he spoke. "I recognize
you from pictures, in his office. I believe I was told to stay away

from you."

"I was told the same about you," she said, suddenly aware of how she was standing and of the odd sound of her voice. He laughed briefly, a sound that bubbled up and then went down just as quickly, like the settling of boiling water when the pot is removed from the stove. Dangerously disarming. She stepped forward.

"What…are you doing here?" she asked, immediately disliking how it came out.

"I'm waiting for a friend."

Sarah perfectly masked the touch of disappointment she felt that he should not be there solely for her. She dared not ask whether the friend was male or female.

"I think I've maybe seen you around campus before," she said, moving closer still. He watched her for a moment in silence before sliding slightly over on the bench, leaving the decision to her. In several delicate moves she sat down and positioned herself an acceptable distance from him. She smelled a hard, clean scent like cold water coming from him.

"I grew up here," he said, gesturing vaguely with the back of his head at the gathering dark behind him, his eyes still on her. "But I'm not around much anymore, unfortunately."

"Why not?" she asked, lowering her voice to match his.

"Work. I have to move about a lot."

"What do you do?"

"All sorts of things. Different things for different times."

"What about right now?"

"I guess I'm in between jobs."

"Don't know why he would have said to watch out for you," Sarah said, shaking her head. "My dad, he's not very comfortable with any man that might be near my age, no matter who he is."

He cocked his head a bit and looked right into her. She could see the tips of his teeth just a touch below his upper lip.

"What did your father say about me?"

"Nothing. Just to stay away. So naturally I came up to meet you."

Northern nodded.

"You ever think maybe you should listen to him?" he asked, smiling in the dark.

"I'd like to think I'm a pretty good judge of character on my own."

As she spoke his eyes drifted briefly behind her to where a taxi cab had pulled up to the curb. His expression never changed. She looked behind her.

"Is that them?"

"That's him. Sorry Sarah, I have to go," he said, slowly rising. "I'll see you again."

From the bench, she watched him meet the man who emerged from the taxi. She faintly heard their greetings; they met like business associates might, but then she heard Northern call the man Max, and then watched them embrace like brothers. She saw Max nod several times in a conversation she could no longer hear, and suddenly knew that he, like most people, probably deferred to Johnnie Northern.

Although she thought often of their meeting, and although she always looked for him again whenever she was out, especially coming home from her seminars, it would be nearly a month before she saw him again.

CHAPTER ELEVEN

IAN SAT AT THE small metal dining table of his mother's house, his back to the open window and the old woodshed beyond. With his right hand he idly flipped a pack of cigarettes end over end. His left hand he absently squeezed, doing the physical therapy exercises that were once a part of his daily routine after the surgery, out of habit. He watched the pager as it sat quiet, but now alive, its pink screen silently ticking down.

In the kitchen his mother talked to him as she taped the corners of the cabinets in preparation for painting. With the changing season, she aimed to make the kitchen a warmer color than stark white. Stark white was for summer, and summer was gone.

"So who paged you?" She looked over her shoulder at Ian.

"McGee Trucking again. They want me to do a few runs, say they'll pay me time and a half," Ian lied.

"You're never around when you work for them," she said. "In and out, here and there. I can hardly get a hold of you."

"Only for a short while," Ian said eyeing the pager, squeezing his hand, flipping the pack.

Whenever the Tournament buzzed him, he told his

mother that his boss at McGee Trucking Company had paged and wondered if he could run cargo across Britain for a few weeks. He told her that they paid him well and under the table. Ian actually had worked for McGee Trucking just out of sixth form, years ago. They ran out of nearby Lisburn. Three weeks into the job he quit because they wouldn't let him smoke in the cab. But the excuse still worked well because truckers had odd hours and were always running off here and there at a whim.

"Ian?" His mother stood in the kitchen doorway, looking at him.

"Yes? Sorry. I was—I guess I kind of spaced out there."

"Are you going to take the job?"

"I think so. The money's too good."

She nodded slowly.

"Is your hand bothering you?"

Ian realized he was still squeezing and releasing his left hand. He snapped it open.

"Force of habit, 'suppose. It never bothers me anymore. Not for years since it was fixed."

In July of Ian's seventeenth summer Father Darby took the young man to see Dr. Marcus Shay, a muscular surgeon who had once worked for Belfast Mercy Hospital, but who had elected to open a private practice at the age of sixty. He was a wiry man, thin and spry for his age. He insisted upon dying what hair he had left on his head a dark brown and made absolutely no attempt to hide the fact. He prided himself on the mustache that he could still grow, which he also dyed the same color. He examined the tendons in Ian's damaged left forearm with a light and sure touch. His hands never wavered or trembled, and his nails were immaculate. When he spoke it was quick and abrupt, but kind.

"I can tell you right now that you have a truncated flexor tendon. It seems to have fused unnaturally with the muscle grouping about halfway up your forearm. You can feel it. Here."

He took Ian's right hand and placed his index finger on the pale underside of his left forearm. Ian knew exactly what Dr. Shay was talking about. Where he pressed there was a minor bump, barely noticeable to the naked eye. Ian could push it around a bit under his skin.

"My guess is that whenever your hand quickly seizes up it's because you've tensed a muscle somewhere in your upper arm, connected in some way to the fusion point. It, in turn, snaps your hand shut. Like dominos."

"To find out just how each muscle is connected, we'll need to do some further testing, perhaps a muscle dye injection," Shay said. All the while Father Darby stood to the side, his hands crossed over his black cassock, listening and nodding.

"Will he be able to control it?" Darby asked softly.

"Before I can comment any further on that, I'll need to see the results of testing."

"Whatever you have to do, you do it," Darby said. "Money is not a factor here."

Dr. Shay looked at Father Darby for a moment. Then he nodded.

"Fine then. We'll start now. Today. With an X-ray for

muscle motion. It'll give us a thorough base to work with."

The two men seemed to have temporarily forgotten about Ian, who sat on the examination table, legs dangling. Adolescence had not been kind to him. Recently seventeen, he was in the thick of puberty, and his pale coloring made the spots on his face that much more apparent. He was already acquiring the slightly sunken, haunted look he would never quite grow into. Already there were hints of the pale shadowing that would settle in varying degrees under his soft green eyes and make him look perpetually exhausted. All in all he was a sickly looking boy.

"Wait here for a moment while I prepare," the doctor said before ambling out of the room. Father Darby stood leaning against a sink nearby. Ian looked at his left arm, and then up at Darby.

"Why're you doing this? Why now?"

"I thought you said you wanted it."

"No, I do, I suppose. I mean, I suppose I don't care one way or the other. Neither does my ma. It's my father that said to take advantage of this." There was skepticism in his voice. Darby simply nodded.

"Your father tells me you don't visit him much."

Ian watched him for a moment, trying to read him. Darby leveled his gaze back at Ian.

"Probably not as much as I should."

Darby nodded again.

"Why does my father want me to do this?"

"That's between you and him."

"Why are you doing it?"

"I owe your father."

"Why?"

"That's between me and him."

Ian exhaled sharply and shook his head in exasperation.

"The decision to go through with this surgery is entirely yours, Ian. You know this. If you want to walk out right now, you walk out right now, son."

Ian remained seated. Perhaps if his mother had said outright that he didn't need anything done then he would have walked out. His mother's ambivalence coupled with his father's strange endorsement made him stay. Part of the reason he would go through with the surgery was the residual guilt he felt for not visiting his father, as if it was somehow penance. Before the visit a week ago, it had been almost six months since he'd seen Peter Finn. Something about his father, his incarceration and his attitude towards it, his complete indignation, as if it was an affront to him and a shame upon those who held him, did not sit well with Ian. It never had. But he had to know his dad's role in this strange turn of events. Naturally, he'd gotten nothing more out of his father than his confirmation of approval and a few wry smiles. The trip had been short.

Twice a week over the next two months Dr. Shay tested Ian's left arm and hand, from the end of summer into the beginning of Ian's final year of sixth form. Often Father Darby was with him, but not always. By the end of the testing period, Shay had constructed several multi-layered models of the entirety of Ian's left arm, from his shoulder joint down to the tip of his middle finger. It resembled a plastic print flipbook of the creation of an arm, from bone to vein to tendon to muscle and skin. Shay marked certain spots on all of the films, most often around the area in the middle of Ian's left forearm where the slight bump was. On several of the films Shay drew a fan of straight lines leading from this area up to his deltoid muscle and down to the muscles in his pointer and index fingers. When compared to a sample film of a normally developed left arm, Ian's appeared similar save in the area of the bump, which contained an abnormally high concentration of muscle tissue and veins. Although Ian couldn't see it very well, Shay showed him with a laser pointer how this fused muscle development affected his entire arm: it pulled on his muscle slightly, which was why his hand curled inward. Certain shoulder muscles were also affected and pulled tighter than normal, which was why his arm unnaturally hitched itself upward and in towards his body.

"When you quickly seize your hand, it's because you've unknowingly tensed this muscle grouping," Shay said, pointing out the bump.

"And you can fix it?" Ian asked.

Shay looked at Father Darby, who had come for this, the last testing session, and was sitting quietly, legs crossed, in a chair at the back of the room. He stood up, put his hands in the pockets of his black slacks, and walked slowly to the front of the room.

"We can."

Darby studied the prints, hung from their tops all along the wall, lit with a cold white light. He turned around and looked at Ian.

"Are we going to do this?" he asked.

"I'm willing."

Darby then looked at Shay for what seemed to Ian like an

uncommonly long time.

"And you?" Darby asked. "Are you willing?"

"I am," Shay said, after a moment. "Whenever Ian is ready for the surgery, I'll schedule a team. It's not going to be a particularly difficult procedure, but it's no appendectomy either. I estimate three hours for surgery, one day of in-hospital recovery, and then physical therapy—probably a month. All said, about a month and a half before he'll be totally recovered."

Darby looked at Ian. Ian nodded.

"Sooner the better," Ian said quietly. "Just get this over with."

They scheduled the surgery for the following Thursday. He arrived early in the morning on an empty stomach per the request of the anesthesiologist. Father Darby sat in the waiting room reading a book. He greeted Ian and Mary with a smile and a handshake and didn't reference the surgery at all. He simply gestured into the operating room.

All told, the operation took just shy of three and a half hours. Minor incisions were made at pertinent muscle groupings on Ian's forward left deltoid and just to the left of his elbow, but the extensive work was done on his forearm. Throughout the surgery, Ian's left arm was palm-up, forearm exposed. Dr. Shay made a six inch long cut and extended it three-quarters of the way up his forearm. At either end of the primary cut, Shay made a smaller, perpendicular cut. Together, the three incisions looked like an angry, seeping letter "I".

The cuts were just deep enough to expose the abnormal muscle grouping beneath. Ian's skin was flayed out to either side of his arm. Underneath the skin was a series of grainy red lines, here and there peppered by knobby bits of what looked like gristle. On these Dr. Shay went to work for three long hours, assisted by his small team.

When Ian awoke four hours later, his arm was spray-on-tan orange and an "I" had been stitched midway up his forearm like a personal monogram. There were also smaller groups of sutures near his elbow and on his shoulder. His left arm was totally numb and he had a lingering headache. He felt very groggy and stiff, as if he had slept long without once moving.

"Everything went very well," Shay said, studying Ian's arm like an artist stepping back from a finished painting. "Exactly as planned." Father Darby was in the room as well. Ian wondered when he had come in.

"Now we just wait for it to heal."

Something about the way he referred to his arm as a separate entity unnerved Ian, but his mind was still sloshy and things didn't stick. Ian nodded and closed his eyes, shutting out the bright operating lights.

For three weeks Ian wore a sling around his left arm, but for the first time in his life his arm felt held there by the sling only. It was a strange sensation, having an arm that felt inclined to the ground. Although he didn't move it much for fear of splitting the stitches, he could already feel a difference. Everything felt loose.

It didn't hurt much, but it itched terribly. Ian babied it, cleaning it gingerly, touching it lightly, barely a tickle, and reveling in the self control it took to not tear into it. At three weeks his shoulder stitches had healed and were removed by Dr. Shay, after which he no longer needed the sling. He stood in front of the thin, rectangular mirror in his room for a long time that first night after he no longer had a sling, admiring how symmetrical his body now looked all of its own accord.

In physical therapy Ian worked with a very small and very kind lady, Mrs. McKinney, who constantly talked to him while she prodded and maneuvered his arm, warning him, in her calming, motherly voice, of certain pains he might feel, and oo-ing and aww-ing when Ian flinched or sucked in a breath, as if she also felt his pain even though she was relentless. Father Darby often joined him for these sessions. It was he who found Mrs. McKinney and set up the appointments, twice a week for two hours.

Ian's left arm was naturally weaker from its lack of use over the years of his life, so the surgery just made what was already bad even worse. Once the sling and primary sutures were removed and all that remained was the welted "I", Mrs. McKinney started Ian on light weight training. Wrist curls were the worst. Ian was already skinny: He had never lifted weights in his life. One set of ten curls with a ten pound weight was excruciating, especially since he had to go through the motions so slowly. The day after his first weight training session, his left forearm was so sore he could have sworn he ruptured something.

Four weeks into the therapy, Mrs. McKinney started gently back-stretching Ian's left hand, and for the first hour it felt like someone was kneading a big bruise on his body. The second session was less painful, but Ian's left hand could still be bent back to only roughly half of the angle of his right. He asked Mrs. McKinney why this was even after a month of therapy.

"All in good time, Ian," she said, tutting. "Therapy is about patience."

"But it doesn't feel like a simple tight muscle. It's…I dunno, *harder.* It feels like it *can't* move past that point. Like I'm pressing back on a wall."

"All in good time."

At the end of that session she gave Ian a grip-squeeze device. She told him he must use it twice a day for half an hour a time. Ian did so without fail, yet he gained no more backward rotation on his left hand.

Ian was dozing in class when he first snapped his hand forward.

It was an unseasonably hot September day, one week before physical therapy ended. There was no wind, and the air in the classroom was muggy with the collective breathing of thirty teenagers. It happened during Literature class, Ian's least favorite subject. The students had been asked to re-read five pages of a particular chapter in James Joyce's *A Portrait of the Artist as a Young Man*, a novel that Ian found particularly ridiculous. While reading, Ian's eyes drooped and he dropped the book off of the corner of his desk. In a hazy daze he bent over to pick it up, resting the tip of the mechanical pencil he had been holding in his left hand on to his thigh as he did so. It happened faster than he could have imagined, faster than he could make himself aware, so that at first he noticed nothing more than his pencil clattering across the wood floor.

Then Ian looked down at his thigh and saw a clean, deep gash, about a foot long, starting just shy of the hemline of his shorts and ending above his knee. At first it was simply a white line, even his body was caught unaware, but soon an angry red rose up and out of the split skin until it overflowed and spilled down either end of his leg, dripping to the chair and pooling, then dripping to the floor. Still Ian didn't understand what had happened, but a girl who sat next to him was roused by the clattering pencil. She screamed right as the pain hit Ian like hot water on sunburned skin. He started to sweat.

"I think I've cut myself," he said, gone past pale.

His teacher ran to get some paper towels from the dispenser and shoved them at him.

"Press it! Press it!"

Ian pressed it, and the red soaked upward upon the papers, creeping like an exotic spider walking up a wall. He was handed more towels and he pressed them over the old ones. One particularly quick student jumped up and moved his desk over to where Ian sat.

"Put yer leg up! Elevate it! Jeysus Christ. Look at all that."

By now Ian was surrounded and he was breathing heavily and swallowing profusely.

"It's all right, Ian," Toby said. "It's all right mate. Step back! Give him some air!"

The students all looked at Toby for a moment, surprised at the vehemence behind the voice of the normally silent boy. Then they stepped back. The teacher handed Ian more towels until the nurse arrived, and by then Ian had stopped the flow, if only by the sheer force of pressing down. Having done that, he was terrified at the prospect of having to remove the towels to allow the school nurse a look. Thankfully, when she arrived she took one look at the spattered floor around him and told everyone that it would be best if he got to a hospital.

Later that evening, with twenty new stitches to echo those he had only recently freed himself of, Ian sat out on his front porch and leaned against the banister, his left leg stretched out sideways along the length of the top step. He was squeezing the grip-builder Mrs. McKinney had given him and staring off into the darkness beyond the glow of his houselights. His leg throbbed and itched and generally felt like it was going to burst.

Outside, the remaining bugs had been fooled into think-ing it was still the thick of summer and were chirping again. They could be heard all around him. It was here that Father Darby found him. As he approached the house, Ian looked up at him but said nothing.

"Don't be disappointed, Ian," Darby said.

"It didn't work. Something is still wrong with my hand."

"No. Your hand is exactly as it should be."

Ian furrowed his brow and shook his head.

"I don't even know what happened. I didn't see it. I couldn't even feel it at first."

Darby nodded, and then with much popping and groan-ing he sat himself down on one of the lower steps, his back towards Ian.

"I know what happened," Darby said, talking out into the night. He almost sounded cheerful. Behind him Ian shifted about as much as his leg would allow, trying to peer around to see Darby's face.

"What are you talking about?"

"You triggered your hand."

"But I thought that was one of the things the surgery was supposed to fix, that…twitching."

"It wasn't like the twitching though, was it? Like the twitching before?"

"No. It was way more…fast. Stronger."

Darby nodded. Ian watched the bobbing of his wispy head.

"Wait a fu—wait a minute. Are you telling me this was supposed to happen?"

Darby slowly stood and turned. He scratched the faint gray stubble that was growing under his nose. He fixed Ian with a gaze that held him; even if Ian wasn't nursing a cut-bruised leg, he wouldn't have been able to move. Ian recognized it from his most impassioned sermons, those in which it seemed he was speaking directly to you alone.

"What were you doing when you cut yourself, Ian?" he asked, his voice calm and oddly mismatched with the rest of him.

"Sleeping. I was dozing off."

"No. Right when it happened."

Ian thought for a moment. He looked out beyond Father Darby. Then it came to him.

"I dropped my book. We were reading and I dropped my book."

Father Darby smiled and nodded slowly, encouraging him.

"I leaned over my desk. I switched hands with my pencil and leaned off to the right, to get it."

"And what was your left hand doing? When you did this?"

Ian thought for a moment, shook his head, and then

moved his body slightly in a lesser mimicking of how he leaned over to get the book in class that day. As he moved himself out and over the stairs, his left hand moved up a few inches. That was all. Nothing more. Ian looked at Father Darby and shrugged.

"I don't think my hand was doing anything."

"It was," Darby said calmly. "You positioned it for those muscles to click."

"Click?"

"You drew."

"I what? Drew?"

"I'd like for you to learn to fire a handgun, Ian."

Ian leaned back, away from Father Darby.

"A handgun?" His voice cracked.

"Left handed," Darby said quietly.

It was a moment before Ian spoke.

"Hold on. You think I can…pull a gun, like a—like a quick draw or something? What is this? Is this what this is all about? Some sideshow?"

Father Darby stood watching as Ian shuffled forward to the edge of the stairs. Their talking had hushed the insects nearby and a strange calm settled over the front of the house. Darby seemed to be weighing options. He worked his jaw slightly and looked from Ian off into space and then back to Ian again. He seemed agitated. When he spoke, he spoke slowly and Ian felt that his words had a particular weight, and that they had been mulled over for a long while, well before Darby had appeared at his front porch that night:

"There is an organization. They are interested in you. And have been for some time."

"What organization? Does this have something to do with my father?"

"It's not what you think. I can't tell you anything more. They have forbidden it. They think you are too young at the moment. I disagree, but in matters such as this…I answer to them."

At these words Ian felt a strange twinge deep in his stomach, near his guts. It reminded him of the sensation he once got after his mother had pulled him back from an intersection just before a bus barreled through; like all the blood that was surging through his veins switched directions on a dime. It wasn't just the words themselves—it was Father Darby. In all his years of knowing the old priest, he had never heard him speak like this. Ian was speechless. A man of God had just asked him to learn to fire a weapon. A man he had thought answered to nobody but God apparently answered to someone, or something else, and he had already brought Ian into it, without him even knowing.

"I trust you not to insult me by asking if I'm serious," Darby said.

"Insult *you*? You had plans for me all along! You *used* me! You're *still* using me! And I don't even know what for! I went through surgery for *you*! This was never about me, was it?"

"You have every right to be angry. All I can say is that I know you very well. Far better than you think. I made some assumptions. I made decisions on your behalf. I trust that if you knew the full story, you would be behind these decisions as well."

"Well *tell* me the full goddam story!"

"Ian I *cannot!*" Darby yelled, raising his voice for the first time.

For a moment he stood to his full height, as if a surge of power had rocked through him, but it was fleeting. Then he seemed to deflate, and shortly was his hunched self again. Ian was suddenly very aware of how old Darby was. He had been yelling, cussing even, at a man nearly eighty—at a priest nearly eighty.

"I'm sorry, Father."

Darby looked up at him and smiled sadly. Both the yellow porch lighting and the shades of night dappled his face at once, accentuating the wrinkles and lines.

"Ian, this is as frustrating for me as it is for you. It's true I've betrayed your trust. If it was up to me, you would know everything, but it isn't. And I know I've no right to ask you to trust me once again, but it's all I can do."

"How much does my father know?"

"I'm not sure."

"A gun? You want me to learn to shoot a gun? I don't know if I want to be part of a group like that. No guns in the UK, Father, in case you didn't know. Not for priests and not for students."

Darby stepped towards him and leaned a bit down, grasping with his gaze for Ian's eyes. He found them and brought them up to his own.

"Never mind that. You'll want to be part of this, Ian. I'd bet my life on it."

CHAPTER TWELVE

FROM CERTAIN VANTAGE POINTS, mostly high ones, the city of St. Petersburg, Russia, seems an endless myriad of towers. At dawn or at sunset in particular all that can be seen of these many spires are their outlines, black against the sky. Some are bulbous, others needle tipped, and still others are a mixture of both, as if in creating the city God had tossed handfuls of sharp objects across the land like dice, and all of them had landed tip up.

The spires soar into the sky on behalf of several gods. Cathedrals and temples mingle with a small handful of mosques, all blackened by the same dust and soot, all stained by the same passing of the same years. Some are older than others, but almost all are very old, some ancient. St. Petersburg is a city of two parts, much of it destroyed in the Second World War during one of the most destructive sieges of any modern city in history. It was known as Leningrad then, and afterwards it was built anew around the scattered surviving portions. One might, without knowing it, be walking down dark and twisted streets of cobblestones many centuries old, or be leaning upon a wall that has stood for half of a millennium.

The collective lives of generation upon generation of St. Petersburg citizens, their comings and goings, their births and deaths, their passions and secrets, has imbued the city with a heavy and quiet air. Its beauty is unique, tinged with pain, but nonetheless deep and vintage.

It was through this history that Allen "Lock" Lockton walked, down the curved and twisted streets, among the towering spires and dark rock. He walked quickly, as was his way, but quicker than normal for all that. He carried with him a glossy, jet black folder emblazoned with the Tournament seal, and therefore he felt that all of St. Petersburg was somehow watching him. Though his arrival was unannounced, he felt that Eddie Mazaryk and Team Black were expecting him. The very air was expectant. It chilled him and made him see things in the darkened windows and doors that couldn't be there. He imagined that people watched him specifically, random people at odd intervals on the street corners and under the umbrellas of sidewalk cafes who looked at him as if they knew him. The whole city, he nearly believed, worked for Mazaryk.

Lock himself was only aware of a few individuals who had direct contact with Black, and he was on the lookout for them. They would lead him to the captain. Lock could only go to where he had last met these strange individuals and look from there, and the last time he had seen any of them had been here in St. Petersburg.

He knew all three of them by sight: a tall woman, middle aged, who wore her white hair long and down; an elderly man stooped and with a cane, its handle in the shape of an ivory eagle; and a dark-skinned Turkish child, no more than ten, who wore a gold pendant and never spoke. After five years with the Tournament he had deduced only these three to be in direct contact with Black, but there were no doubt others. How many more, he couldn't guess. How many of those casting errant glances his way were in league with Black? And yet even the three he knew were three more than any other Tournament courier had found. That was why it was always Lock who had to deliver to Black, even though the region was well out of his zone. Eddie Mazaryk was notoriously difficult to reach, and Lock was the best the Tournament had at finding people.

Lock listened to the sounds around him, the sibilant Russian of which he knew some, and here and there bits of other languages of which he knew none. He smelled the air, damp from recent rain, and with it the mingled scents of wet wool and the meaty smell of food from a nearby stall. He caught a whiff of coffee here and of vodka there. He wiped his brow of mist and looked about a small, dark courtyard. At its center bubbled a stone fountain so grooved and blunted by the passing of water that whatever shape it once possessed was now just a lump of glittering rock. It was here that he had last been approached. He moved inside of the square, under a rod-iron gate that was chained open, and sat down on one of the flaking wooden benches that ringed it. He sat for twenty minutes, until he could no longer stand the waiting, and he got up once more. He would not find help there this time. But he knew they were watching.

Outside the courtyard he assessed the situation, weighing his options. He glanced down a nearby market street and saw nothing intriguing; he combed the cafes and terraces with his most suspicious eye, marking anything potentially out of place. People moved about the windows doing their own business. Oddly, no one even glanced his way now. Two teenage girls in full school uniforms came around a nearby corner and were walking up the street in his direction, chatting away in rapid Russian. They looked up at him briefly as they passed around him, but took no real notice. He walked to the corner around which they had come and looked down the alleyway there. It was thin, and down its center ran a shallow, trickling storm gutter.

A clothesline was strung above him in the alley and it drooped with saturated sheets that had been caught out in the rain. They dripped heavy drops in a dark line stretching out in front of him, beckoning.

Lock turned around and looked back out onto the main street and saw a few people moving about in the gathering dusk. No one took any notice of him. He turned back towards the alleyway. It was empty. He wiped his brow again and started walking forward. He skirted the dripping sheets, only to walk under more dripping laundry. The rain had come without warning. The alley was silent save for the random splattering of water from the lines above, and the soft murmur of that water as it gathered in the shallow center gutter to flow back out onto the main street. Lock walked slowly, moving from one side of the alley to the other, stepping over the water as he went. He followed it around a soft bend, choosing not to walk down any of the side streets that opened up at intervals to his right and left, and not quite knowing why not.

Ten minutes later he saw the Turk boy.

The alley progressed in a wide, left-leaning circle and Lock was never able to see that far down it at any one time, so he came upon the boy suddenly, and when he did, the boy was staring at him. He was dressed in a small raincoat that reached his knees and he wore black galoshes. A shiny gold chain glinted off his dark skin. His hair was very wet and plastered down about his head and it made his ears stick out. Lock stopped dead and watched him, afraid that if he moved or said anything too quickly he would scare the boy, who might dash off like a rabbit.

But the boy didn't look scared. In fact, the boy smiled at him, albeit briefly. Then he pointed down a side street just to his left and stood still, like a small statue dripping in the quiet drizzle. Lock moved slowly up to him and looked down the way he pointed. The boy simply watched him, his arm held out.

This side street looked identical to the countless number he had already passed, save for a single ornate lantern burning brightly under a tattered overhang. The lantern illuminated an old wooden sign written in faded Russian, and a dark red, solid-wood door that stood open. Lock looked back at the boy, who looked only at him. Then Lock moved over to the door and inside.

It was an old tavern. The walls were papered in a raised pattern of red felt, and the tables and chairs were the same dark red wood as the door. Two men in the corner played chess on a board that had been carved into the surface of their table. A man smoked a cigarette behind the bar, and another stood reading a paper in front of a thin, spiral staircase. All four looked up at Lock when he entered, lingered briefly upon him, and then resumed their business.

In the silence Lock could hear the clicking of the chess pieces very clearly and the soft hiss of the bartender drawing on his cigarette. He walked up to the bar and the barman looked at him expectantly but said nothing. Behind him, the newspaper rustled as the man by the staircase turned the page. Lock turned to look at him, and after a moment stepped back from the bar and moved over to the staircase. He expected the man to challenge him, or to at least say something, but he never even looked up. Lock set one foot on the staircase, and when the man didn't respond, Lock slowly climbed the stairs.

Waiting just at the top was Goran Brander, the striker for Black. A towering man, he wasn't far from the second-story ceiling even leaning casually against the wall as he was. Although he was tall, over six and a half feet, he wore his height well, so that you were only really aware of the full extent of it when standing right next to him. Only then did one sense the power that can be housed in a body with a near-seven foot wingspan. His face was long and aquiline, his nose sharp and extended, not outward but downward. His sharp jaw line begat a sharper, triangular chin. In his trim black suit and thin black tie he looked the type of figure to avoid, and yet despite this, upon seeing him, Lock let out a breath of relief.

"Brander," he said, regaining something of his steadfast, ramrod composure, "*Finally.*"

The striker laughed deeply and softly. "You are welcome. As always." His voice was slightly accented in the eastern-European way, yet inexplicably gentle. Even now, five years after first speaking with him, it still threw Lock every time he heard that voice come out of that man. It was as if his body and voice were separate entities.

"We're over here," he said, lazily pointing through the doorway at his side. After gesturing, he stepped through. Lock followed after.

The room inside was silent. Lock heard the creak of his shoes on the dusty carpeting, and the occasional rattle of wind jostling the windows and slipping through cracks in the foundation below. The room was dark, lit only by the faltering light through two thin, rectangular windows, and by the glow of a small fire in the fireplace in the back. In the shadow of its mantle stood a second man, the firelight reflecting erratically off his small, round eyeglasses. By his short height Lock knew him to be Ales Radomir, the sweeper for Black, lurking silently, as always.

Offset of the fire, another man sat in a massive and faded wingback chair. His hand rested around an amber drink sat upon a thin stand to his right. Brander walked forward towards the chair, nodded once, and then took his place standing next to Ales by the fire. Neither man acknowledged the other. Both scrutinized Lock. Brander's gaze was calm, but Lock couldn't see past the fire that flitted over Ales spectacles and this bothered him.

The man himself, Eddie Mazaryk, sat deep in the wingback. His face and skin were smooth and light and his lips small and carved like a doll's. His hair was fine and dark and long enough to cover the back of his neck. Most of it was held together with a band behind his head, but a few wisps hung down the sides of his face. In the gathering darkness, his eyes picked up the firelight. They were of so pure a shade of brown that they reminded Lock of soil brought up from deep below the earth, or of the rich mud of a lake bed. Eddie Mazaryk held his right hand up in greeting.

"Hello Allen."

"Eddie."

"I'm glad you found the place."

"Yes. Well. They sent me after our first courier wasn't so lucky," Lock snipped.

"I'd heard," Mazaryk said calmly.

"Natasha Saslow is a perfectly capable courier. She's *your* courier, Eddie. Let her do her job."

"She's new," Mazaryk said, amused, unused to being spoken to in such a manner.

"She'd find you if you let her," Lock continued, glancing back at the two by the fire. "I've worked with her personally, she trained in my hemisphere—"

"I know you. And she's new," Mazaryk said, a bit harder this time.

"I don't have time," Lock said, exasperated. "They stretch me too thin just running correspondence for the Americas—"

"You have time. You just don't *like* it. It makes you uncomfortable here."

Lock paused and righted himself. In the dark glow of the firelight he saw Ales Radomir smile strangely.

"You love a challenge. This little jaunt is not what bothers you."

"You bother me, Eddie. All I know of you is what I hear. What I've heard I don't like. To be frank."

"What a terrible thing to say, my friend," Brander chimed in from behind. He sounded genuinely hurt, yet Lock knew this was absurd. As if he, Allen Lockton, could possibly hurt a man like Brander. Allen carried letters. Brander fired a .50 caliber handgun like it was a supermarket cap gun. He glanced up at Brander, who smiled benevolently down at him. Suddenly Lock felt that he needed to get out of the building. He suppressed a wild urge to run by reminding himself that these three, no matter what their agenda, surely had no issue with a courier. Whoever shot the messenger?

"Let's get this over with," Lock said.

He flipped his messenger's bag around to his front and unzipped it. From a padded pocket within he removed a small handheld device.

"I assume your physician has cleared you to participate," Lock said.

Still seated, Mazaryk reached over to the stand at his right and grabbed a flat black cellphone. He tapped it. The soft blue glow of the phone's screen seemed out of place in the old room.

Lock waited for the beep from his handheld. He scrolled through documents until he found the electronic signature of a Dr. Vigo Valclav, a Tournament doctor stationed in Kalingrad, Russia. Dr. Valclav had marked all three members of Black as fit for participation.

"Everything is in order," Lock said.

He called for the sweeper first and Ales Radomir stepped silently forward. Lock held the screen towards him, thumb-pad first. Ales pressed lightly upon it, waited for the beep, and then removed his thumb and stepped back in the shadows.

"Striker," Lock then said, and Brander stepped forward, pressing his thumb down in turn.

"And how are things out west?" Brander asked kindly.

"Fine. They're just fine."

"Good. That's good. We're quite excited for things to begin again."

Lock looked up at him for a moment and nodded briefly, unsure, as always, how to take him. The screen beeped, and Brander stepped back next to Ales.

"Captain," Lock said, moving over to where Mazaryk sat. He took the handheld from Lock and pressed his thumb down on its pad until the beep, then he handed it back.

"On behalf of Tournament Administration, and in lieu of your *assigned courier*," Lock said, the emphasis clear, "I hereby pronounce all members of Team Black present and accountable." He pressed his own thumb down and then typed in a code.

"You're cleared for the draw," he said quickly, eager to be gone. He packed the handheld away again.

"Leaving so soon?"

"Look at your pager. The countdown is under seventy

hours and I have other teams to check in."

"I had noticed. It's at sixty-eight."

"So if you'll *excuse* me, I—"

"I noticed Johnnie Northern checked in just fine."

"What's that supposed to mean?"

"You're his courier."

"I'm neutral. I run for many teams. What's your point?"

"I hope to run into him again this time around," Mazaryk said quietly, narrowing his gaze.

Lock recalled the last time the two teams had met. They racked up an accumulated six million in fines and hospitalized no fewer than 14 citizens of Anchorage in their battle. The vast majority of the damage was done by the hands of the very man sitting before him.

"Yes. Well." Lock said, swallowing. "I've got to go, Eddie."

Lock moved out of the door without another word, nor did any of Team Black call after him.

CHAPTER THIRTEEN

NATASHA SASLOW REMINDED KAYLA of a stock of wheat. She was tall, thin, and blond, and she moved with the grace of a swaying field. She was also very quiet, almost silent. Unlike her counterpart Allen Lockton, she would often wait for another to speak before doing so herself. But it was getting late, and couriers were always on the clock. To her credit, though, the only way Kayla could tell that she was annoyed at the delay in checking in Team Green was her occasional questioning look. *Lock would have blown a gasket by now*, Kayla thought.

"They'll be here. Probably Ian's fault. The fucker's never on time," Kayla said, in her clipped Irish way.

"I'm sure," Natasha replied, looking into the distance.

They fell quiet once more while all around them the sounds of Dublin whirled. Cars sped up and slowed down; laughter and shouts echoed out of the concrete banks of the nearby River Liffey. They sat at a table outside of a small pub. Dusk approached and the Temple Bar district was waking up. Kayla started tapping a booted foot on the table stand and bit the nail on her right forefinger.

"Who checked in Grey? Lock?" Kayla asked.

"I did," Natasha replied. "Lock was needed elsewhere."

"How were they?"

"Fine. Alex Auldborne was as cordial as ever."

"I'll bet," Kayla said acidly. Natasha swayed to look at Kayla briefly, and then returned her gaze outward. No love was lost between the teams of England and Ireland, but as a courier she was ever impartial. Kayla sniffed and played around with her pager on the table for a moment.

"There they are," Natasha said, checking her watch and pointing out to a couple walking around the corner. Kayla snapped up, smiling. She shoved her seat out and ran around the table while Natasha slowly rose in her wake, picked up her messenger's bag, and began deftly opening its various pockets, gathering her tools.

The two walked her way like brother and sister, and Kayla couldn't help but smile. Seeing them there, walking and talking, it was proof. The Tournament had come alive again. This was her family once more. She found herself trembling with excitement. She tried to replicate this sensation in the seemingly interminable off-season, but she always failed. No man, no drug, no sport—nothing else could compete. *This*, she thought, *is a pure thing. A holy thing to me.*

Pyper Hurley saw her first. Pyper, just a tad taller than Ian, was dressed conservatively in fitted corduroy slacks and a small khaki jacket, its high collar accentuating her slender neck and prim jaw line. Her long brown hair was pulled back and fell down her shoulders. She struck an aloof, regal figure and Kayla thought her beautiful. Kayla herself was short and decidedly child-like in ways that Pyper was not. Her complexion was darker and freckled where Pyper's was a creamy white. Her hair was dirty blonde, and she hated the feeling of it on her shoulders so she cut it short and pinned it back and down in random places. It was tousled and wild, which was all right, she supposed, but she often wondered how people would take her if she held herself like Pyper. By *people* she really only meant one person: Ian Finn.

Her gaze lingered longest on Ian. On the cigarette that hung from his lips, suspended. He was lighting up when he saw her. He paused and took it out and smiled at her with open arms. For a moment his dull green eyes flashed.

He was in a plain white t-shirt, so she could see the entirety of their team mark on him. It wound around his left forearm and licked the base of that deadly left hand of his. It was alternately sharp and smooth in shape, and of a dark green ink so pure it almost glistened. It had no definitive design, but from a distance suggested a snake. Unconsciously she touched her own left forearm where she had one exactly like it. The tip of Pyper's mark, same as theirs, could just barely be seen where it poked out beyond her cuff.

Kayla reached Pyper first. They hugged and stood back and appraised each other, Pyper's hands on her shoulders. Then Ian was finally close enough and she hugged him too, wondering how long she could linger. She felt Pyper looking at her, and was reminded of her words of caution: "*Tread carefully, Kayla.*" And Kayla did tread carefully. She saw in Ian's eyes at least a brother's love, but also something of a cornered animal, teeth half-bared, growling low. When he fought, the line between bravery and terror was blurred, desperation and courage were slammed together in each pull of that gun. Right now, though, he was smiling. And he was close. That was enough.

"They still payin' you Ian? Don't they know you aren't even really Irish?" Kayla said, smiling wickedly.

"Check the passport, love. And anyway, we north-Irish are more Irish than you," he responded, softly tracing with his finger the lines of freckles under her eyes. It was a small show of affection he sometimes made, and one that Kayla had spent long hours at night trying to interpret. He stepped back to look at her fully, and she did a mock curtsy.

"Dublin," he said, shaking his head slightly and gesturing about. "I saw five hen parties on the way in, and ten tour groups. I'm surprised they don't have you dressed up like a leprechaun, selling Guinness."

"I like Guinness," she said, hitting him on the arm.

"So do I." He smiled.

"And we are three once again," Pyper said quietly. "Are you ready Kayla?"

Kayla stepped back and straightened herself. Pyper always asked this of them upon their reunion.

"I am."

"And Ian?"

"Always."

"Good, then I am as well. Hello, Natasha. Sorry to keep you waiting."

With something of a start Kayla turned back to Natasha, slightly embarrassed that she had so lost herself. If she was annoyed, Natasha didn't show it. She brought out her handheld.

"We've received and confirmed your physical exams in which all three of you were pronounced fit for the draw," she said, looking up pointedly from her screen. "Now for each of you. Sweeper first. Kayla MacQuillan."

She passed the handheld over to Kayla, who pressed her thumb on the pad until it beeped. Natasha took it back and clicked in a confirmation.

"Striker. Ian Finn," she said.

Ian transferred his cigarette from his right hand and set it lightly in his mouth again. Leaning forward, he pressed his right thumb onto the pad until the beep. Then he leaned back again and lit up.

"Captain. Pyper Hurley."

Pyper took the handheld and contemplated it for a moment before pressing her own thumb on the red square. She watched it closely, as if the machine gave the final say. A strange thought, she knew, and an incorrect one. She and she alone would ultimately be culpable for the ensuing success or defeat of her team. Such was the captain's burden.

The handheld beeped and she handed it back to Natasha. "On behalf of Tournament Administration, I pronounce Team Green present and accountable," Natasha said. She pressed her own thumb down on the pad and pocketed the handheld.

"And Grey?" Ian asked suddenly, exhaling smoke as he spoke. "Are they clear?"

Natasha looked at him and then at Kayla. Kayla shrugged.

"As I've told Kayla, Grey are ready and accounted for, if you must know," she said, her voice decidedly monotone. "You're the last. You make eight. That's all I need," Natasha said, shouldering her bag and placing her hands on her hips. They would get no more information.

"Thank you, Natasha," Pyper said.

"Good luck at the draw. You have just over 25 hours."

After one last nod, she set off in long strides down the river's sidewall. All three members of Green watched her depart, already falling back into the type of comfortable silence that comes with years of practice.

CHAPTER FOURTEEN

M URDER.

It was far too heavy a word for Frank Youngsmith. The doctor's foreboding charge hung upon him on the flight back to Colorado Springs, the strange bullet tucked amongst his socks in his checked bag, buried like pornography.

"Get the word out, or Bill's death will be just the first in a long, long line."

Was that a threat? A warning? Frank took his scotch-stained paper pad from his fraying breast pocket and decided to make a list of what he knew.

First, there was no fraud. The doctor, in his strange haste, had said as much when he affirmed that all members of the research team on which Bill worked were insured equally by the company BlueHorse Holdings. For whatever reason, the company had actually insured Beauchamp's research team for the ludicrous amount that they did days before he died.

Second, he had no way of proving this. The one thing his waddling boss wanted him to get, he had failed to get. The anal retentive man in the tracksuit at BlueHorse had ushered him out without ceremony, and the good doctor had flat refused to sign the statement. Unless, that is, Frank *got the word out.* Whatever that meant. Then he'd slapped the strange bullet in his hand and dashed away.

When he finally reached home, dried out and hoarse from the stale cabin air, he set the unwanted spoils of his trip upon the tiny nightstand by his unmade bed and pondered it in the dark. It wouldn't satisfy Winston Pickett. His boss wouldn't give a damn about the bullet. The bullet wasn't the signed statement. And since his boss didn't give a damn about Frank, he wouldn't be happy taking his word and dropping the case because Bill Beauchamp's death was going to cost the company big time. In leaving for California, Frank had patched up a wound only to return and find it festering. That a job he hated could make him feel so terribly only worsened things. In a slow and pathetic act of defiance, Frank pushed the bullet and file off and to the floor, and eased his head onto his single pillow. He heard the sound of his over-exuberant neighbor, Andy Billings, dropping something into his sink through their shared wall.

"Hey Andy," Frank said, not knowing quite why.

"I thought you might be back, Frank! How was the trip?" Andy yelled. Andy still didn't seem to understand that one need only murmur to be heard through their walls.

"Not too good. Work. It sucks, Andy—"

"I hear you, buddy."

"You don't happen to know anything about bullets, do you?"

"Are you kidding me?"

"Yeah, I know. Just checking, anyway—

"—I *make* the goddamn things, Frank!"

Frank looked up at his bathroom wall, right where he guessed his neighbor would be standing.

"You there, Frank?"

"What do you mean you make them?" Frank asked, very evenly.

"I mean it goes hand in hand with my huntin'! I got a machine, a new one just this August for my birthday even. See we call it *swaging* though. Bullet *swaging.* Just a fancy word. Debbie got it for me. It's a Corbin! Best on the market."

"Can you take apart a bullet with your machine?"

"Take apart, put together, pick your jacket, pick your core, fashion your point—"

"Yeah, Andy—"

"They've even got this new thing now where you can put your name on your bullets all tiny. Your *name!*"

"I need you to—"

"This Corbin, they call it a *Mighty Mite Precision Press.* It's got needles and scopes and magnification—"

"Listen, Andy, *Andy!* I need to come over. For a second. "

It was Andy's turn to be silent. He'd lived next to Frank for almost a year now, and never once had Frank shown the slightest neighborly interest.

"Are you telling me you want to swage with me?" Andy asked slowly, the anticipation audible.

"Something like that."

"Well hell! Of course! The neighbors united!"

Frank was already scrabbling about on his knees, scooping fistfuls of dust bunnies out from under his bed until he felt the tiny solidness of the bullet. He blew the dust off of it.

"I've got something I want you to look at," Frank said.

"What the hell kind of thing is this, Frank? 'Cause it sure ain't a bullet. Not any bullet I ever seen." Andy squeezed his left eye shut in concentration as his right peered through the magnification scope of his Corbin. With surprising delicacy he held the diode between the needle thin clamps of miniature pliers and rotated it in the light of a high-beam halogen. Frank watched over his shoulder.

"Well I was hoping you could tell me. It *looks* like a bullet."

"See this tip though? It's not metal. Come to think of it, this ain't lead in here neither. It's not shinin' right.

"Looks metal to me," Frank said, moving his head in next to Andy. He smelled stale tobacco in what was left of Andy's hair.

"Well sure, the jacket's metal, but the jacket stays with you. It's what's inside that counts," Andy said, winking.

"Can you take the jacket off? Can you make sure?"

"I could…" Andy said, rising from his scope and eyeing the bullet warily.

"But…" Frank prompted

"But I'm not guaranteeing Imna be able to get 'er back

together again. This here, it's a strange thing," Andy said, shaking his head.

"That's fine. Whatever you can tell me has to be better than what I'd get from the thing sitting on my nightstand, even if you do ruin it."

"All right, all right then. Let's see what we can do." Andy sat down once again and moved to pick up the bullet with his tools.

"See now, in swagin' the rule is *keep your hands off the ass*," he looked from the bullet up to Frank and grinned. "But that's just swagin', know what I mean Frank?"

"Not particularly."

"What that means is this. Don't mess with the rear of the bullet. The hammer point. Otherwise it's liable to pop off in your face."

Frank took a small step back.

"Oh don't worry Frank," Andy said, his eyes on his work. "I do this all the time. I've screwed up a helluva lot of bullets in my day, and you can't just toss the damn things and risk Joe Blo's little boy eating 'em out of the trash and blowing his gut up. You gotta dismantle 'em, right?"

"Makes sense," Frank said, leaning in a tad. As Andy spoke he set one tool down, something akin to a tiny monkey wrench, and picked up an instrument with a needle thin tip. It was like redneck surgery.

"My buddy Manx, he used to just toss his bum bullets until one day his wife dropped the garbage bag on the pavement outside their house and shot their neighbor's cat. Hand to God.

Theeere we go…" Andy said, easing the brass jacket up and over the tip of the bullet.

"Oh shit," Andy said, freezing mid-motion.

"Shit? What's shit?"

"It's caught on something. I don't wanna lean over it to see neither."

"Put it back!"

Andy slowly slid the jacket back down the bullet, but froze again.

"Nope, it's not going back. I had to warp the edges a bit to slip it up in the first place."

"Well great. That's just great."

"It's not supposed to catch on the upward motion!"

"So what do we do?"

"Well, might as well just pull."

"Pull it? Just yank it?"

"Up. If I yank it up the powder can't ignite. At least, it's not supposed to."

"Jesus…"

"I gotta do something Frank, I can't just hold it all my life."

"All right, fine, just yank it up. I'll be over here."

"Okay. Here goes."

Andy swallowed and then sat for a second in silence. Frank could hear the soft buzzing of the naked overhead bulb above him. The hour was late and the traffic was intermittent, more distant than usual.

With one swift pull, not quite a jerk, but small and controlled, Andy popped the jacket off of the bullet. At the same time, in the relative silence of the garage, both men clearly heard a tiny fizz, like a damp firework.

"That sounded electric," Frank said, moving quickly in near Andy once again.

"What the hell…" Andy set the brass jacket down on his worktable and held up what he had found inside.

Where the lead should have been was a tiny, thin and partially cracked cylinder made of what looked like ceramic. A liquid with the consistency of spit slowly dripped down from within. There was a sudden and powerful acrid smell in the garage, like burning plastic, then an abrupt popping sound. Andy dropped the entire thing and began to flick his left hand about and suck in air through his teeth.

"What? Did you burn yourself?"

"That tip cracked it open. It did something. It flashed blue inside the jacket. I saw it," said Andy, leaning back.

"It *was* electric. That tip was a circuit of some sort," Frank said, bewildered.

"That watery shit and electricity. Not safe, man. I got some of it on me. It feels weird," Andy held his hand out to Frank and pointing just above his thumb. Whatever liquid might have been there was gone now. It had absorbed right in, or evaporated away like rubbing alcohol.

"It *shocked* you," Frank said.

"It did *somethin'*," Andy said, looking spitefully at where the bullet lay on the worktable. The liquid that was inside of the ceramic cylinder had completely disappeared.

"Say that electric bit and the liquid hit you hard, right on your heart…"

"Well that would suck."

"And you were old. Say you were old and that thing slammed into your chest. You only got a part of it, but say the whole thing hit you full on in the chest."

"That wouldn't be good at all."

"It might even kill you."

"Might," said Andy, nodding.

"Excuse me Andy, I have to make a phone call," Frank said as he dashed out of the garage.

Frank picked up his phone and dialed the UCSD Hospital triage ward. He tapped his hand repeatedly upon his sticky counter as the phone rang.

"This is triage. How can I direct your call?"

"I need Dr. Walcott, please."

"One moment."

Frank tapped and paced.

"May I ask who is calling, please?"

"This is Frank. He'll know."

"One moment."

Frank thought about Andy Billings in his garage, waiting by his bullet machine with his goggles on. What a strange man. Perhaps he was thinking the same thing about his loner neighbor Frank.

"He's not available at the moment."

"The hell he's not, ma'am. If you wouldn't mind telling him that I'm dropping everything unless he gets on the phone right now."

"Pardon?"

"Say just that. Say Frank is dropping everything unless you get on the phone. Please. Thank you."

There was a pause in which Frank heard a muffled scratching on the other end, and then a longer pause in which Frank thought he might have been hung up on, before someone spoke. His voice was a harsh whisper.

"What the hell do you think you're doing, you maniac?"

"Dr. Walcott. I know what happened. The bullet diffuses something into whomever it hits. It shuts them down."

"Have you lost your mind, calling me like this?" hissed Walcott.

"And now I'm telling you that I'm done. I don't know who you think I am, but you should know that I'm a nobody. A *nobody*. Understand? I'm on the verge of getting fired from a desk job at an insurance agency. A job that I hate, but am terrified to lose. I can't do anything for you about any new weapon technology. Bottom line. I'm out."

"You are a fool," said Walcott with a genuine sadness that disturbed Frank.

"This organization that's after you, that you say killed Bill Beauchamp, I want nothing of it."

"They aren't hunting me, Frank. They need me. You are the one that's expendable. And they've already found you."

"What?"

"No doubt they're listening. Say hello."

Frank was silent.

"Why did you call me? I thought I made it clear, but it's too late now. It's over for you, friend," he said, heartbreak in his tone. Then Dr. Walcott hung up.

CHAPTER FIFTEEN

THERE WAS LESS THAN an hour left on the pagers. Every team had cleared the physicals, and every team had been personally checked in by the global couriers. All that remained was to watch and wait as each minute ticked down.

Blue was holed up in a hotel off of Pacific Highway in San Diego. Johnnie Northern reasoned that should anything happen immediately following the draw, they were on the coast, not far from San Diego International Airport, and they could move. With fifteen minutes to go Northern was kicking back on a sofa bed, idly flipping through channels on the TV embedded in the dresser. He was conversing lightly with the sallow Max Haulden, who was having a good deal more difficulty hiding his nerves. Max lay ramrod straight on one of the two twin beds, his eyes wide.

On the sofa to Northern's right sat Nikkie Hix. She pulled her pajamas tight around her legs and closed her eyes. Her stomach always hurt during the hours before the draw, although she would never admit it to her teammates. She didn't know that both of them already knew.

Across the pond, Alex Auldborne was at a dinner party hosted by a recent appointee to the Chancery Division of the High Court of Justice who had clerked for his mother. Auldborne pondered, briefly, awaiting Grey's draw at a more secluded and intimate venue, but then thought better of it. Here was much more interesting. There were simply too many wealthy and powerful people to talk to; too many rich interactions to watch and take part in.

Many in the room noted that Auldborne spoke most often to a small, porcelain beauty in one corner. This woman sipped upon a gin and tonic, never once acknowledged advances from anyone other than Auldborne, and never smiled.

While it looked to everyone else like Christina Stoke was having a miserable time, Auldborne knew better. He knew that Stoke loved rejecting men far more than she enjoyed being with them. His theory was that she derived more pleasure from embarrassing a man than she could derive from sleeping with him. To her, pleasure was power, and power was dominance.

Both Auldborne and Stoke kept their pagers in the breast pocket of their jackets—as did Draden Tate, their hulking striker, who had taken one look at the guests, decided against the party, and was pacing the perimeter of the gardens in the dark. All three awaited the buzz that would notify them of their first-round matchup.

The Irish of Team Green sat around a table, eating with Pyper Hurley's father, Daniel. Bailey, Pyper's little sister, ran around the dining table and darted this way and that, too excited at the sight of Kayla and Ian back once again to sit still. She gave both of them crayon drawings as welcome gifts. Kayla's depicted her and Bailey and Daniel in a forest of Christmas trees. Kayla was distinguished by short and spiky brown hair and a huge smile, Daniel Hurley by his distinctive squat, boxy frame, and Bailey, as always, had a large green bow on top of her head. Her real green ribbon clip, one of her mother's final gifts and without which she couldn't live, sat securely upon the crown of her small head.

Ian's picture was in the same vein as almost every one he had ever received from Bailey. It was of him and Bailey holding hands inside of a heart, surrounded by other hearts of various colors. Bailey really liked Ian.

As the four adults ate they talked about everything except the Tournament. Pyper's father and sister knew nothing of it and Pyper had made it clear that they were to stay in the dark. Instead they spoke comfortably of the weather and the work week. As the pagers ticked down, Ian became antsy and excused himself for his third cigarette of the meal.

Team Black sat in the dark. For them, the draw would come at three in the morning. They situated themselves in a small bungalow in northern Russia in the middle of which sat a freestanding fireplace with a tarnished brass chimney. The fire in it burned to white coal, and from there slowly receded so only its pinkish core remained.

Ales Radomir, the silent and bespectacled sweeper, was sleeping on top of many cushions spread about the corner nearest the door. His small, round glasses sat in the exact center of a chair that he brought over to where he lay. Without them on, and in the low light, his face looked smooth and round and devoid of all emotion, like a clay model awaiting an artist. He made no sound at all as he slept.

Goran Brander, the towering striker, had fallen asleep in an old scratched leather lounger near the window on the right wall of the room. His long legs sprawled outward and his head sank into his broad shoulders. His arms hung to either side of the chair, his fingertips brushing the ground.

Eddie Mazaryk watched the heat waves radiate outward from the copper chimney-tube before him. The metal was so hot that in places it had been discolored to a dark rainbow of purples, like iridescent drops of oil. It was a beautiful color and it seemed to shift and expand as if alive. Ales had touched the copper the last time they were all here, almost a year and a half ago, even though he knew how hot it was. It had seared the fingerprint off his right pointer finger after only a few seconds. He hadn't made a sound.

Mazaryk's gaze was fixed but his mind was elsewhere. He debated which team would move first once the draw was in and the matchups set. After the draw the Tournament would be open and any team could move as they wished. Some teams preferred to wait for the fight to come to them while others brought the fight to their opponents. Those that moved and those that waited had remained more or less consistent over the years. Whether a captain chose to await the fight or to go to it depended upon a number of factors, both personal and professional, but it was not a decision to be taken lightly. A brash move could get an entire team killed very quickly.

Patient observation had won his team the past two Tournaments in a row. Since their debut, they had never lost. Black was well on the way to achieving a legacy. Mazaryk and his teammates had crafted a plan of attack for every team based largely upon psychological profiles. Black had a thick file on every captain, striker and sweeper for all eight teams across the world. These profiles were begun years ago and continuously updated, but they were far from complete. Players changed, sometimes in ways that Mazaryk doubted they noticed themselves. Remaining abreast required strict vigilance. Of particular interest to Mazaryk was Team Blue.

The Tournament was changing. Insidious vendettas between teams were beginning to warp the system. Johnnie Northern and Blue were becoming flashpoints. Sometimes they fought with an almost archaic genteel like infantry in the wars of centuries past. Other times they lashed out with disturbing cruelty. The English of Grey had learned this fact painfully last time.

Blue coined an entirely new phrase in Tournament vernacular as a result: *The Bludgeon Blackout.* The English had been humiliated. Auldborne was not quick to forget an affront, to say the least. He was one of the most proud.

Furthermore, Northern was increasingly unconcerned with maintaining the secrecy that they had all been sworn to upon their commissioning, nor was he unique in this. Admittedly, keeping the Tournament secret was difficult, but the United States was the worst of all places for its existence to become known. Americans in general had no tact; it seemed every one of them felt entitled to know everything and to tell everything, and took even the slightest suggestion to the contrary as a violation of their "rights". It never occurred to any American Mazaryk had ever known that certain knowledge might hurt them, or that they might be happier kept in the dark about certain things. The entire nation gossiped like adolescent children. If the story broke in the United States, rumors and half-truths would spread like a virus. It would only make all of their jobs more difficult.

Mazaryk looked from where Ales slept as if dead over to where Brander slept in a bundle, like a massive child. If a stranger were to walk in that dark room he would have no idea who they were, or of what each could do. And yet combined they were even more: They were his arms and he was their head. In the dark and in the waning heat he was, for a moment, moved by their loyalty. He took it for granted. But then again, in order to survive in this game their loyalty and their ability to function as one unit had to be such that he was able to take it for granted.

Thousands of miles away, a deceptively calm Greer Nichols prepared before his arc of hollow eyed cameras. The curved wooden desk in his enormous office had been removed, and in its place stood a slightly elevated platform. It was on this that he stood, dressed in a fitted, crème colored suit that seemed molded to his broad shoulders and long arms. His rounded, bald head gleamed black, and his brown eyes glittered from within like pennies dunked in syrup. His nostrils flared slightly with each controlled breath. He brushed one hand over his gleaming head and nodded once at his long-time assistant, a quiet young man named Bernard.

At the press of a button the soft green light under the cameras turned red.

"Welcome, ladies and gentlemen, to the fifth draw of our Tournament. My name is Greer Nichols. Many of you know me. More of you do not. I am a recruiter for Team Blue. According to custom, and in adherence to the rotation, the honor of Master of Ceremonies has fallen upon my shoulders this time around—an honor that I gladly accept."

The lenses glinted and shifted to focus as his signal was securely broadcast to a select mass of individuals scattered across the globe. It was unsettling to be the only living thing in his office save his Bernard and yet to be seen by countless unknown eyes. Aside from Greer himself, the only other noticeable object in the shot's frame was a large digital countdown display suspended at the top of a black data board behind him.

"Every one of you joining me tonight is either part of the recruitment wing of a team, or is prepared to make a wager on the Tournament to come. As you know, as soon as the draw is finished our systems stand ready to receive wagers of any type: personal, professional, monetary or otherwise. Anything and everything can be settled here. Once entered, all wagers are documented and final. There are absolutely no exceptions. As always, no member of any team will ever become aware of any wager made on their performance in this or any subsequent Tournament round. If any of the three members of a team should discover the wagers placed upon them, that team will be dismissed not only from this round, but from the entire Tournament and all subsequent Tournaments. Ours is to anonymously enjoy, theirs is to act unbeknownst to all. This is the way it has always been."

With a practiced poise, Greer stepped to the side of his dais and turned his gaze up and behind him to the clock, now in its final minute. In absolute silence, Greer along with untold others watched the seconds blink away.

Three seconds…two…one…

And in the impossibly long pause between the darkening of the clock and the brightening of the draw board, everything was decided. With rapid-fire quickness, the matches were displayed above Greer's head, each black space lighting up and rolling to its proper letter like train times at Union Station, one after the other.

For those moments Greer ceased to be M.C. and was once again a Team Blue recruiter. He and his colleagues had mapped out their response, from an administrative and financial level, to every possible match-up. He held his breath as Blue was matched.

The completed board read as follows:

GREY *(England)* vs. **WHITE** *(Mexico)*

BLACK *(Russia)* vs. **SILVER** *(France)*

GOLD *(Italy)* vs. **GREEN** *(Ireland)*

BLUE *(USA)* vs. **RED** *(Japan)*

The final letter clicked in place and the draw was over. In that same instant, all across the globe an unthinkable amount of money, blue-blood and newly minted fortunes alike, was pooled as odds were calculated and wagers were placed. Other, stranger wagers came in, odd and cryptic and written in contract form. Greer learned long ago that it was best not to delve into the dark minds of those who gambled with things more precious than money, sometimes their limbs or organs—or, worst of all, their entire selves, all to settle a score. The odds moved and shifted with the momentum of the wagers and the excitement that came with knowing that at any time they could be called to term, for the Tournament was now open and the teams could attack at any second.

Greer Nichols stepped up and on to the raised platform once again. He cleared his throat and brought his hands together in front of him as he slowly shifted his gaze across each of the lenses that watched him. After a moment he spoke. His deep voice once more took on an uncharacteristically proper air, more subdued.

"It has been our practice in this, the highest circle of the Tournament, to be as forthcoming with each other as is possible, and it is with this pledge in mind that I speak to you once again."

Greer paused for several moments to allow for his words to be translated across multiple languages and dialects.

"Until now, the Tournament has been used as a forum for wagers of every type, provided they were of a certain scale. We have seen some of the most extraordinary sums exchanged and deeds passed, objects of every sort won and lost. Many debts have been settled in this forum that would not otherwise have been settled without issue. Today things are changing, and I felt the collective administrations should know of it. Time will tell if I am wrong."

Greer paused again and shifted his gaze up behind him at the board. His look was slow and deliberate.

"As you can see, we at Blue have drawn Team Red for the first round. We are both pleased and excited by this, because it allows us to put into place a plan we have been formulating for quite some time."

Greer turned back to look directly at his audience of lenses once more. His face, unreadable until that point, now held the faintest hint of a grin.

"We've decided to take our first round opponents up on a wager of a different type. Both of our teams have within the ranks of their patrons certain government officials who wish to settle a long-standing foreign policy point of contention between our two countries. As you may know, the matter of the Futenma Air Station in Okinawa has become newsworthy. Without going into too much detail, the Japanese government wishes all of the Marines stationed there withdrawn and the land requisitioned. The United States government does not. Negotiations on behalf of our two governments have not yielded satisfactory results. We are at a political standstill. Obviously, neither country has faith in the other's politics. Certain agents in both governments do, however, have complete faith in their respective teams. It seems only natural, then, that the matter should be decided in that manner."

"The point is this. For the first time, the Tournament is being used to quickly and decisively settle a matter of foreign policy between nations. Both the United States and Japan have agreed to adhere to this contract and to the result of this round between our two teams."

Greer paused momentarily and imagined the various scenes on the receiving ends of the cameras. Were they shocked? Angry? Greer doubted it. It would be very hard to overestimate the collective power of those unseen eyes. No, these men and women were never shocked, and if they were angry it was because they lacked Greer's foresight to use the Tournament in this way. Very soon they would all come to agree that the Tournament was born to be used in this way.

"This is the future of this organization, ladies and gentlemen, the natural progression! No one team would dare renege on a contract made public to ones such as us. No team would risk expulsion. It is one team against another, true, but as always, the weight of every team in this body lies behind each contract. The contract is final. Such accountability can be found nowhere else on earth. It's time we took advantage. This, friends, is our future."

Greer cleared his throat. "Let the games begin."

CHAPTER SIXTEEN

ROUND ONE

A T THE DAWNING OF the second straight day in which Andy
Billings had yet to see or hear anything of his neighbor
Frank, Andy began to worry.

For as long as Frank had lived next door, Andy had seen
him almost every morning. It was rare, in these times, for neighbors to look out for each other. It wasn't like the old days, Andy
thought, when a man's neighbor was practically family. Now it
seemed that everybody suspected everybody else. That's why it
was important to Andy that he kept up with Frank. The man lived
alone, never had any callers that Andy had ever seen, worked all
day and slept all night. He could use a good friend. And what
with their proximity, Andy could hear the guy pee every morning
for crying out loud. It would be downright indecent of them not
to be regular acquaintances at least.

And what's more, it was plain odd, him running out of
the garage without even a word, especially given the nature of
that wacko bullet he'd asked Andy to look at. The thing was still
sitting on the Corbin where Andy had accidentally broken it and
then dropped it when it shocked him. His thumb still smarted a
bit from that damn thing.

Around nine in the morning Andy decided to go knocking and see just what was going on. Andy strode up to Frank's
door, taking the concrete steps two at a time. The house was

dark. He saw four days' worth of the *Denver Post* piled up against Frank's front door. Andy paused for a moment, picked them up, and rang the doorbell. He then stepped back a stride and waited, both hands clasped on the newspapers in front of him.

There was no answer, so he rang again, and knocked on the door this time as well.

"Frank? Buddy you there? Frank, it's Andy!"

No answer.

Now it fell upon Andy to make a difficult decision. Should he walk away, or should he try the doorknob? He stopped to think for a moment. First thing's first. Just try the damn door and see if the sucker's locked.

Andy slowly turned the knob and gently pushed on the door. It swung open a half an inch. Andy froze. It might be a little forward to just barge on in. Or would it? He had a responsibility for Frank—a neighbor's responsibility. What if Frank had hurt himself? Tripped on the phone cord and gone down hard right onto the edge of the Formica island he had in his kitchen? Debbie did that once. Gashed her forehead up bad too. Andy knew Frank had that exact same damn island.

Andy pushed open the door and moved in, moustache first.

"Frank? Hey man, haven't seen you in a while. Everythin' okay?"

No answer. No turning back now. Andy gingerly stepped into the tiny foyer, leaving the door open behind him. He looked about. He wasn't encouraged by what he saw.

Somebody had been in the house, all over it. Random

sheets of paper were strewn about the foyer. In the living room too, on the stairs, and in the hallway leading to the kitchen off to Andy's left. It looked as if someone had been going through a manuscript as they walked the house, tossing page after page as they read. Frank's carpet was scuffed through the living room in front of where Andy stood. Andy peered into the kitchen: every cabinet was open and every drawer extended.

He bent to examine the footprints. They were big, larger than Frank's foot for sure. Andy slowly walked forward into the living room, following the paper trail and calling out to Frank. Nobody. Now edgy, Andy trotted upstairs. Somebody, or some people, had been through everything. Frank's bedroom in particular, where his meager study was, looked a mess. All of the books and binders Frank had, most of them with the Barringer logo on them, were splayed open on his bed. Certain sheets were torn out. Some lay strewn across the bed and floor. His mattress was off-kilter and his dresser drawers had been completely removed and stacked in the corner, their contents rifled through. No sign of Frank anywhere.

Back at his own home, Andy called the police to report a robbery. Nothing of any real value had been taken, as far as Andy could see, but what else could it be? Frank was a plain fellow with no enemies that Andy knew of. It had to be a robbery.

"911 emergency response."

"Yes, I'd like to report a break-in at 15B South Plaza Circle, Colorado Springs."

"All right, sir. Is the break-in in progress?"

"No. It's maybe a few days old."

Andy waited while the woman on the other end typed

and he watched Frank's house out of his window, dark and foreboding. It was the scene of a crime now, something cold and impersonal, no longer a home. Almost half of a minute passed without the dispatcher speaking.

"Ma'am?" Andy asked.

"South Plaza Circle?"

"That's right."

"15B?"

"Yes."

"The police have already been there."

"What's that?"

"We have a first responder's report on file already, sir."

Andy narrowed his eyes at the house. Could the police have really already come? He hadn't seen anything. No lights, no sirens, no police tape, nothing.

"Maybe there's some sort of mistake…" Andy began.

"No mistake, sir."

"Who called the police?"

"I can't give that information out, sir."

"Well then I'd like to file a missing person report."

"What is the name?"

"Frank Youngsmith. He's my neighbor."

"There is already a department bulletin out for any information regarding his whereabouts."

Andy shook his head. "What's that supposed to mean? That sounds bad. Like he's wanted or something."

"No, it just means that the police are already looking for him, sir. If you have any information, I can patch you through to the Colorado Springs Police Department."

"I don't have any information."

"All right then sir. Will that be all?"

"I suppose so."

"Thank you for calling."

Andy hung up and put his hands on his hips. He called upstairs to where his wife was reading in bed. She would worry if he told her everything. She was terrified of intruders; they were her number one fear. She would be hysterical. Andy was the gun connoisseur of the family, but it was Debbie who insisted upon keeping two loaded revolvers under the bed, one for each of them.

"Hey Deb?"

"What honey?" she yelled back.

"Anybody come to the door today? Or yesterday?"

"Not that I can remember," she said, her tone already wary. "Why?"

"Nothing, I was just expecting Frank to drop by, that's all."

"Well, not when I was here anyway."

Andy walked outside into the cooling night, across his driveway and the thin, knee high hedge that separated his property from Frank's. He stopped on Frank's identical driveway and stared at the house. In its emptiness and violation it had taken on a haunted air. Nothing about it looked as though the police had been there.

Andy feared the worst kind of worst.

CHAPTER SEVENTEEN

FIVE YEARS AGO, WHEN a consortium of powerful Mexicans decided that they needed a Tournament team, they sent recruiters far and wide looking for a worthy captain. They would have to go north before they finally found him. Far north. Across the border and all of the way to Bay City, Texas, in Matagorda County. They tracked him to the sprawling vacation homes of a wealthy, gated community called Foxwood Estates. He was mowing lawns there, working for his family company.

It was mid-summer and already steaming hot at eight in the morning. Diego, his first cousin Adrian, and two of his distant cousins, Luis and young Gabriel, made up the June to August crew of Vega Lawn Service, and they were already on their second job of the morning. The Vega family lived in Mexico City almost exclusively from the profits the two rotating lawn crews made throughout the growing season. Every year each man in the family filed for and received a temporary work visa from the United States, and for three months, each man made the trek up to Bay City. While they lived in Texas they did nothing but work. To cut costs they ate communally, usually cabbage rich stews, rice, and beans. All four of them lived in a small flat off of I-35. Their only vehicles were two old Chevy trucks they used to haul their four stand-and-ride mowers, two industrial trimmers, and one hedger. The mowers alone cost the equivalent of a small fortune in Mexico. Diego purchased them with money his sister gave him, the lion's share of her wedding dowry. Diego refused the money for two weeks but was convinced when his sister announced her pregnancy. The family was growing. They would need to turn money into more money, and Diego was their best hope.

Diego and his brother Miguel agreed at the outset that one or the other needed to be with each crew to lead them and keep them in line. When Diego was gone Miguel stayed with the family in Mexico, and vice versa.

On the morning that they found him, Diego was mowing his least favorite house in Foxwood Estates. He dreaded the house not because of the size of its lawns—the standing mowers could mow nearly any size of lawn in short order—but because this house neighbored a home owned by a woman every Vega man had been warned about.

If anyone mowed anywhere near her house before noon, this woman—none of them knew her name even after two years of mowing her neighborhood—unfailingly stormed out of her door, waddled as fast as she could down her winding walkway in a silk robe and house slippers, and screamed for ten straight minutes. Either Diego or Miguel, whoever happened to be the lead man, always volunteered to mow the area nearest her house and take the brunt of the yelling, mostly because they weren't confident that the other men in the crew would keep their cool.

As he rounded the sprawling Red Oak adjacent to her walkway she popped open her front door and huffed down the sidewalk as if on cue, her face reddening with righteous indignation. Diego sighed, choked the mower engine, and stepped off of the platform on to the grass. He took off his weather beaten, wide brimmed cowboy hat, wiped his brow, and awaited her arrival.

He wasn't tall; even with his grass-stained cowboy boots he barely matched her height, but of the two of them he looked by far the more respectable even after an hour's worth of mowing in the gathering heat. He was dressed as always in an impeccably clean, white t-shirt, and faded blue jeans. He was trim and stood straight, his lean, dark arms resting harmlessly at his sides. His face was kind, shaved clean save for a thin, down-turned moustache he'd had since he had been able to grow it. His face was deeply tanned, even beyond his normally dark complexion, and lined outward around his dark eyes where he squinted off the sun every day. He looked older than his twenty-six years and was often mistaken for being in his mid-thirties. Years of outdoor work will go a long ways towards blotting out anyone's youth, but his wide smile shaved a good ten years off of his face, and he smiled often, exposing a bright gold cap on his left incisor.

He even retained the smallest trace of his smile when confronted with this hysterical, fat peacock of a woman. Not a full smile—that would insult her, but Diego had found that when dealing with such people the barest upturning of the mouth, a small dimpling of his cheeks, gave the impression that he was a harmless simpleton. Just a Mexican farmer in the big city. Diego spoke very little English, so with the exception of the occasional *que?* or *lo siento*, he remained silent throughout her diatribe.

"Listen to me. Do you speak English?" Her voice was nasally and her jowly face turned upward to gain that extra inch. Diego shook his head slowly but she barreled ahead anyway.

"I speak to one or another of you Mexicans every time. Every time! You *must* wait until the afternoon to mow here. Do you understand me? I *cannot* have this noise! DO YOU UNDER-STAND?" She spoke slowly and heavily, as if to a small child or a dog. Diego shook his head.

Luis, fluent in English and mowing nearby, stopped work-ing when he saw her frump out of the door. He called out to his cousin in very polite Spanish, disguised as a harmless question.

"Diego, you need me to come help with this bitch?"

Diego calmly waved him away.

"I'll tell her it's almost nine o'clock and she has to get her fat ass up sometime."

Diego never broke his bovine gaze just below the woman's wide nose as he slowly shook his head. He knew you couldn't reason with these types of people; it was much better to let them run their course.

"What is he saying? Does he speak English? Hey! YOU! DO. YOU. UNDERSTAND. ME? THIS. IS. A. COVENANT. CONTROLLED. COMMUNITY. WE. HAVE. NOISE. RE-STRICTIONS. DO YOU UNDERSTAND WHAT A NOISE RESTRICTION IS?"

Luis looked at Diego and Diego warned him with a sudden flash of his eyes. Luis looked at the woman and back at Diego and gritted his teeth into a stupid smile. He gave an exaggerated shrug and spoke in Spanish.

"Sorry pig, but I'm not supposed to understand you. Seventy-two lawns we mow and you are the only one that ever complains. You make me sick. Can you understand that? You understand me? I want to vomit whenever I see you."

She looked blankly from Luis back to Diego, who smiled and shook his head slowly once more.

"If you Mexicans want to come and live here, you learn to speak English. Can you do that for me?"

"Unbelievable. She really has nothing better to do," Luis said, as the two men watched her grumble all of the way back to her door and inside her house. They sat in silence until they saw her

round face glare at them one last time through the window and then disappear behind the flick of a curtain. Diego turned to his cousin and cocked one eyebrow at him accusingly.

"*One day someone is going to understand your Spanish. Then we're both in deep shit,*" said Diego, his voice rolling easily over each word.

"*These people? Understand me? Please. Half of them can't even speak their own language correctly. If that cow spoke even one full sentence of Spanish I'd eat my mower,*" said Luis, laughing as he stepped back on his machine and pressed the starter. Despite his best efforts at maintaining a reproachful, fatherly air, Diego couldn't help but laugh himself.

Fifteen minutes later, having mown the entire lawn down to a final patch in the corner, Diego prepared for his last pass when he noticed another potential complaint walking towards him: a man, dressed in a starched and pressed white button up shirt, jet black slacks, and shimmering black cowboy boots. Diego sighed, stepped off of his mower onto the bleeding grass, and took off his cowboy hat once again. Then he noticed that another man, dressed similarly to the first but shorter and wearing fat, reflective aviator glasses, was leaning gently on an old Cadillac parked nearby, quietly watching.

Luis choked his mower once more. Diego glanced at him and saw him eye both men nervously. All of his snap seemed to have deserted him.

"*Police,*" he said in a whisper. "*What do they want?*"

The police terrified Luis, mostly because men like Luis and Diego, honest, hard-working Mexicans, had the most to lose in a causal encounter with any one of them. Men like Diego, who worked tirelessly to distance themselves from those few migrant workers who took a different, more violent path, could lose all that they had built up over years of saving and toil in one careless swipe of a the long, overworked arm of the South Texas law. All too often the police went looking for the type of men who gave Luis and Diego a bad name, but instead found Luis and Diego. It had happened to almost all of the Vega men; their nationality sometimes inspired instant mistrust. They all worked constantly to rise above it, but the battle was so sharply uphill that every one of them had at one point pondered another way. Perhaps the single greatest measure of the true character of the Vega family was the fact that despite their extensive knowledge of the English language, the border routes, the visa procedures, and even the crime circuit of the Texas borderlands, not a single member of their large, extended family had even once succumbed to that temptation.

Diego thought that the woman had finally called the police on them and was already preparing a rational argument for them so that, through Luis, he could explain that the woman was unhinged. The man in the white collared shirt reached where Diego stood and for a very long moment simply looked Diego over, scanning him up and down. Then, most unnervingly, the man smiled and stood in silence.

Diego rubbed the sweat off of his face and brushed his hands off over the grass. He waved Luis over and was about to start talking to the man when the man spoke first.

"Diego Vega. It's about time, no?"

It took Diego a full ten seconds before he realized that the man had spoken in fluent Spanish. Not textbook Spanish either, his was a practiced Spanish, southern in dialect. Far from reassuring Diego, this knotted his stomach. He was sure the men were worse than the normal police. They had to be some sort of special police—perhaps even ICE or the FBI. A million terrible possibilities flashed through Diego's mind: There was an immigration problem, a customs issue, maybe something had happened to Gabriel or Adrian as they mowed several blocks away, or worst of all, maybe something had happened back home, to his family.

"*Sir, what is this about?*" he asked, his voice softer than he intended, but twice as strong as he felt.

The man ignored him and continued talking. "*Do you have any idea what we've gone through to find you? You've got a good brother in Miguel. Mistrustful, but loyal as an old junkyard dog.*"

Diego froze. This man knew Miguel. Something had happened at home.

"*Please. Just tell me what happened. What is the problem?*"

"*We didn't get anything out of him. It could have saved us a lot of time,*" the man said, shaking his head. "*But what can you do? There is no way he could have known…*"

"*Known what?*" Diego shifted to get a better look at the man in the glasses near the car. They both looked Mexican but there was nothing particularly notable about either of them. No badges or guns. Their sunglasses covered much of their faces.

The man put his hands in the pockets of his loose slacks.

"*We've been watching you for a long time, Diego.*"

"*Who are you?*"

"*My name doesn't matter. Should you take us up on our offer you'll find out more. Either way, you will most likely never see me again.*"

"*What offer?*" asked Diego, looking to Luis who, having caught a few words of the Spanish, blanched noticeably. He seemed glued to his spot behind his mower, torn between pretending he couldn't hear and eavesdropping.

> *"We want you to work for us."*

> *"I have a job."*

> *"You'll like ours more."*

> *"Who do you work for, the police?"*

> *"No."*

> *"Drugs? I don't do drugs. I won't deal with them."*

> *"Neither do we."*

> *"Then who do you work for?"*

> *"Mexico."*

> *"Mexico what?"* asked Diego, nervously running his thumb and middle-finger down the sides of his moustache.

> *"Just Mexico."*

> *"Like the government?"*

> *"No. Just Mexico."* The man gestured backwards at his partner, and in response his partner reached in through the passenger window of the old Cadillac and took out a shiny folder of metallic white. He walked a few paces, delivered it to the man in front of Diego, and returned to his post leaning on the driver's side door. The man held it out with two hands as if presenting an award.

> *"It's a significant opportunity."*

Diego took it and slowly turned it around to face him.

He flipped open the cover, read a few lines of the first page he saw, and looked back up, his brow furrowed.

"La Tournamenta?" he asked, reading slowly over each syllable, as if testing its feel.

"Tell only who you must. Believe me when I say that in that line of work," he pointed briefly at the embossed "T" on the cover, *"the fewer people who recognize you, the better off you are."*

He smiled at Diego, a strange smile coming from a stranger, one in which Diego sensed admiration. He looked at the folder in his hands. The light reflected brightly off the cover and Diego blinked several times. When he looked up again the man was already walking back to the car and his partner was already inside.

Diego stammered after him. *"What do I—"*

"It's all in the folder, Diego. Good luck my friend," the man called over his shoulder as he popped open the driver's side door and closed it gently behind him. Diego and Luis watched in silence as he rolled the engine over for a few seconds, kicked the car to life, and slowly pulled out into the street. His partner flicked a type of farewell salute to them both as they passed, skittering stray pebbles in their wake.

—

It was now five years later. Diego read the folder countless times since that day, and still sometimes did even now, despite being firmly entrenched in the organization as the captain of Team White. He still thought often of that first day. They were right, of course. The job was an unbelievable opportunity, and once he was sure that the Tournament was real, that the men had been serious, he agreed to take part. Of the men themselves he knew next to nothing, only that they had helped find him and assign him his role on Mexico's team. He hadn't heard from them since, nor had he seen them again.

His world changed so dramatically that he often caught himself thinking about his old life much like a man would recall a movie viewed long ago. Since then he had been there to lead his team through four consecutive tournaments, and when he needed it they were there for him as well. The second time he was called to fight for Mexico he managed, tooth and nail, to bring his team all the way through to the glorious finish, but the Tournament had a short memory and in the past years his team hadn't fared well. In contrast that mirrored their colors, it seemed as though Black had fallen into an almost supernatural groove since they had arrived, stopping every opponent before they could really start. Still, Diego Vega had never been so confident in his team, and the slates were all clean once more.

The world had shifted under Diego's feet in the past five years, but the man himself changed remarkably little. He still wore his moustache as he always had: thin, trimmed, and brushed downward. He still preferred t-shirts and jeans, buying new versions of the same whenever either wore out. His hat remained the same, faded to a ghostly off-white by the sun and the sweat around the band. His only upgrade was the pair of cowboy boots he allowed himself to purchase after winning it all three years prior. He loved them dearly and would never part with them, but he often wondered if their purchase had brought bad luck down upon them. For all his stolid leadership Diego was a superstitious man, fond of routine, who never bucked what won. If his tried and true methods of leadership failed him, he often blamed some small deviation from procedure as the missing bolt that caused the machine to seize up.

The only noticeable physical difference between the man that was Diego Vega of Vega Lawn Services and the man that was now Captain Vega of White was the tattoo on his right outer forearm. His skin was dark and tough, weathered by the sun already, so the tattoo had to be dark and bold in order to stand out. He instantly knew what the design would be: the eagle of Mexico, noble and reserved even as it battled a snake. He much preferred the Mexican eagle to its counterpart in the United States, a depiction of the great bird that Diego had always found violent and panicked, in perpetual motion. But how to portray the symbol of his country in a manner that would be White's alone? Countless of his countrymen had inked the bird on themselves as a show of pride. Most often the eagle was depicted as menacing: a show of machismo surrounded by garish colors, or clutching a bloody something in its talons, its curved beak gleaming like a scythe. The bird he knew was pure and simple in its beauty; a fluid animal, not jagged. His eagle would never draw attention to itself, it would be a presence more felt than seen or heard.

In depicting this on his forearm, Diego took the traditional picture of the Mexican eagle and broke it into thirty-one pieces, one for each of Mexico's states. These thirty-one pieces were small and clear; rolling shapes, gently curved and sloped, each about the size of a dime. He fashioned these shapes into an outline of the bird as if lit from behind. The result was a simple, elegant illustration that was part hard lines and part negative space.

Only two others shared his vision of the eagle, and both wore it in exactly the same way on their own right outer forearms. A woman, Lilia Alvarez, had been chosen as his striker, plucked right out of jail and armed again with the make and model of gun that had put her there in the first place. His sweeper was Felix Ortiz. A gentleman, observant and professional, the recruiters had found him when he was pumping his entire life and soul into a doomed little hotel on the coast of Mazatlan. Their journey together hadn't been easy, and more than once one or the other had almost walked away, but ultimately Diego so endeared himself to them that neither could walk away from the man.

And now all three of them were faced with the first round of the Tournament come again. They had drawn Grey. The English were coming for them—of that Diego Vega was certain. He knew Alex Auldborne as well as anybody. Better than most. Auldborne was the type of captain to move first.

"It's a funny thought, the English wandering around Mexico," said Lilia, her nose touching the stained wooden floor of a small, single room ranch that the team owned off of the Huapango Lake in Mado, fifty miles northwest of Mexico City. She stretched her small body in anticipation of what lay ahead, making sure that every part of her legs and butt remained flattened to the ground as she leaned first over her right thigh and then her left. She draped herself easily and completely over her legs, so that her long black hair rested in flowing waves down and around her body, dark as India ink.

"There is absolutely nothing funny about those three criminals running around my country," said Felix.

He sat across from Diego at a thick, squat work table, pocked and crossed with deep gouges. Felix was tall for a Mexican, and possessed of a somber, patient intelligence unique to men forced to grow up too soon. He wore a dark, solid colored button-down shirt and khaki slacks with old and faded penny loafers. He spoke strongly but betrayed very little emotion. His small eyes were set back behind dark, full eyebrows and stray wisps of dark brown hair. Whatever expression they provided was hidden.

"You call them criminals as if it is a bad thing. I was a criminal once," Lilia said, looking up from her folded position. Her teardrop face seemed to be resting of its own accord on the wooden floor. She winked up at him and grinned.

"Not like them," said Felix, looking down at her. *"You did what you had to do to survive. Those three are lunatics."*

"*They're coming. Nothing we can do about that,*" said Diego, tracing the length of a deep gouge in the table with his forefinger.

"*Auldborne is hot-headed. Like a cowboy with something to prove, angry all of the time. His power comes from the head of steam he builds up like a locomotive to run over everyone in front of him.*"

"*Then let's not get in front of him,*" said Felix.

Lilia slowly unwound herself and rocked into a ball on her back. Felix watched his captain as he swept his hand across the scars of the table.

"*But he is still just a man. All of them are only human,*" said Diego. "*He will tire. And when he does, we will be there. This is our land.*"

Diego looked first at his striker as she rocked slowly back and forth on the floor, and then at his sweeper who waited calmly across from him, both hands palm down on the table.

"*Let him chase us around a strange land until he falters. Let him lose himself in Mexico. Then let us put an end to him, and be done with them all.*"

CHAPTER EIGHTEEN

THE FRENCH TRIPLETS OF Team Silver were told of their draw, that Eddie Mazaryk and Black were coming for them, so they started drinking heavily. They only managed to rouse themselves when they learned that Black had filed a flight plan and were flying towards them presently.

They learned this because Eddie Mazaryk himself called them as they lay prone in various positions throughout the pub they owned.

Tristan Noel, the sweeper, was the only one to awaken for the call. A persistent ringing worked its way into his dream for a while until he sat up with a nauseating jolt. He was behind his bar again and he hadn't dreamed the noise: The slop sink was definitely ringing. The only other sound in the downstairs bar came from his brother and captain Yves Noel, who snored under a table out front. As his head cleared he realized that the slop sink itself wasn't ringing, but something inside of it was. He blinked for a moment until the pieces came together and he picked the phone out of the sticky mess at the bottom of the sink, cursing to himself.

"Allo?" answered Tristan, his voice thick and dry.

"*We're boarding an airplane, Tristan,*" said Mazaryk in pitch perfect French.

"Who is this?" asked Tristan. He saw Yves stir and then moan.

"You know who this is. We're boarding an airplane. Tell your worthless brothers we're coming for the three of you," said Mazaryk. He hung up.

Tristan looked at his brother pawing his way to a sitting position against the trunk of the table.

"Merde," said Tristan. *Shit.*

"Everyone is far too loud. Phones ringing. People swearing. This place smells like stale sweat," complained Yves, squinting up at his younger brother. *"It must have been a good night."*

The two looked alike in almost every fashion: both were square jawed, with prominent, boxy cheekbones and small, beaked noses. Both had long, thick, brown hair, down to the base of their neck; remarkably well behaved hair that stayed wherever they brushed it, in part because it was a tad greasy. Yves called it *natural product.*

The only noticeable difference between their two appearances was that the captain, Yves Noel, wore his hair loose and brushed back in waves, and the striker, his younger brother Tristan Noel, had a perky pony tail. A closer look revealed a long, thin scar that ran the length of Tristan's right temple, a Tournament souvenir from an errant blade of shattered glass. It tightened the skin to the right of his right eye just enough to give the impression that he was carefully examining everything at which he looked.

"So what was all of that about?" asked Yves, resting his head back on the trunk of the table and watching the ceiling fan slowly rotate.

"They're on their way," said Tristan, his voice flat. He grabbed the cleanest tumbler glass he could find, washed it out, and began to rummage around the bottles for the vodka.

Yves closed his eyes. He didn't have to ask who was coming. *"Fucking Russians. Call Dominique. He's upstairs."*

"You call Dominique."

"Just call him. I think I might throw up."

"That nervous?"

"No. I'm never drinking port again so late," Yves said, rubbing his face.

"Dominique, you shit! Wake up! We have a problem!"

Tristan found the vodka, poured three fingers of it into his glass, and topped it off with warm tomato juice. Dominique appeared at the top of the stairs, naked and grinning stupidly. He was the best looking of the triplets, the only one of any of them that spent any time at all lifting weights or exercising. As the youngest he loved to flaunt whatever advantages he had. As a result, and because of his taste for any type of woman at all, he was often naked. The only thing he never seemed to take off were his aviator glasses; lenses the size of fists, either on his face or holding back his hair. He had them on now as he stood proudly at the top of the stairs, his hands balled into fists at his hips.

Dominique had several tattoos scrawled on both arms and one on his left shoulder, but the most impressive was inked across his upper chest, centered over his sternum. It stretched across the interior of his pecs, and was perhaps three centimeters from top to bottom. It featured three separate and distinct lines. In the center of the design each of the lines braided itself once with every other, forming a simple knot at its heart. This was the only tattoo that all three brothers shared: the mark of Silver.

"*Tristan, dear brother,*" he said, cloyingly sweet. "*You're waking my lady friend.*"

Tristan narrowed his eyes at Dominique, took a sucking sip from his drink, and nodded towards Yves. Dominique turned to his captain, who had righted himself and moved over to the bar. Yves motioned for his brother's drink.

"*Remember that terrible draw we had two days ago?*" he said, sipping gingerly at the cloudy red.

"*Oh no…*" Dominique said, closing his eyes.

"*Yes. It seems they will be landing in mere hours.*"

"*Those fucking Russians!*"

"*That's what I said.*"

"*So what do we do?*"

"*Start by putting on some clothes,*" said Yves, finishing off the drink and handing the cup back to his brother, who filled it again.

"*And after that?*" asked Dominique. "*We didn't do so hot against them last time.*"

"*Nobody did,*" Tristan said.

Yves willed himself to stand and popped his neck first one way and then the other. He was starting to feel better. It was a strong drink.

"*Yes. Eddie Mazaryk is good. They are all very good. The man is some sort of mind reader.*"

The two brothers waited for their captain to continue.

"*So…*" Yves said.

"*So…*" Tristan repeated.

"*So.*" snipped Dominique.

"*So what if we aren't in our right minds?*" asked Yves.

"*Well then it would be hard for him to predict anything at all, would it not?*" quipped Tristan, grinning as he brought two more tumblers to the bar top.

Dominique sauntered naked down the stairs and up to the bar. Both brothers looked sharply away but Tristan poured him a drink nonetheless.

"*Cheers, brothers. To the Russians. Let's see them try to forecast our moves when we don't even know them ourselves. Predict this, you Cossack bastards,*" Yves pronounced, holding up his glass. All three brothers clinked and drank.

—

Team Black disembarked at Charles De Gaulle International. They packed nothing and carried only guns. They dressed in trim black suits and immaculate white shirts that looked no worse for the four hour flight from Moscow. Goran Brander wore a thin black tie and smoothed out any errant wrinkles he found as he walked alongside Ales, his long, loping gait equaling two full strides of his shorter teammate. Ales calmly cleaned his round spectacles with the silk of his tie as he walked. He replaced them a tad below the bridge of his nose, where they were most comfortable, and surveyed the immediate scene over them. Out of long habit, he computed distances and approaches, mapped out routes and firing lines.

Eddie Mazaryk wore no tie, just a three-button black jacket over a white collared shirt. The dark brown wisps of his bangs were held back by a black band, the rest of his hair hung freely down to just above his shoulders. There was no trace of sleep on him. His eyes were dark and hard. All three walked silently.

As soon as they reached immigration they were waved to the side of the room where one entry kiosk stood dormant. A jowly customs official asked Mazaryk for his identification in rapid French. Mazaryk removed a thin wallet from his breast pocket and took from it a card. The official swiped it and asked for a thumb print, which he gave. Mazaryk then unbuttoned his jacket as another officer, a bullish young man bulky with a protective vest and equipment, approached haltingly. Mazaryk calmly watched him, his eyes following the man's every move.

The official cleared his throat. *"Where is your gun?"*

"In a shoulder holster above my left hip," replied Mazaryk in quiet, fluent French.

The officer pushed open Mazaryk's jacket with one gloved hand and reached inside. He popped open the shoulder holster there and withdrew an angry looking .34 caliber black Beretta. Mazaryk watched his gun as the man carefully passed it to his jowly superior, who scanned a metal barcode at the butt of its hilt with what looked like a supermarket check-out gun. The device beeped twice. The officer watched Mazaryk through heavily lidded eyes.

"What is the purpose of your visit?" he asked.

"Give me my gun," Mazaryk said in quiet French.

The young man tensed, his hand straying to his hip, but

the elder simply returned Mazaryk's gun and stepped aside to allow him to pass through.

Eddie Mazaryk patiently waited while his teammates went through the same procedure, watching every move everybody made. Once past customs the three were waved though immigration without event. Several officers watched them pass, as did a throng of travelers who had been in the front of nearby lines and seen the men remove their weapons only to have them returned to them.

Thirty minutes later the three arrived at the Noel Bar in Belleville on the right bank of Paris. They drove two blocks beyond it, paid their driver, and exited to the street. They approached on foot.

Mazaryk looked at the dingy building as it rose up before him. It was old and soot stained, the windows streaked and gummy. There was no sign to speak of, but the address was correct. He spat. He pulled out his gun and his other two did the same. He pushed open the door easily and snapped about in every direction as Brander and Ales fanned out to flank him. No one was there. Ales immediately moved over to the stairs and leveled his gun up them. Nothing moved.

Mazaryk heard a shuffling behind the bar and snapped it to sight. He nodded at Brander, who padded to the bar and reached over it as if replacing the salt shaker on the far side of a dinner table. The shuffling behind the bar stopped and they heard a small squeak.

In very polite French, Brander spoke. *"Get up young one."*

A small boy rose slowly from behind the bar holding a mop. From where he stood Mazaryk could see only his head.

"Come here," Mazaryk said, his gun pointing at the child, his voice level. The boy stood frozen, mouth agape.

"You had better go," Brander said after a moment.

The boy dropped his mop and its handle snapped on the floor. Ales swung his gun around to sight and the boy wailed in fright.

"Come here!" Mazaryk barked.

The boy stumbled out from behind the bar and stood in front of Mazaryk with his head bowed. His breathing was shallow and he was losing his color.

"Where did they go?" Mazaryk asked. The boy started to cry.

"He's going to faint," Brander said.

"Where did they go!" Mazaryk snapped.

The boy cringed into a squatting position before buckling into a heap at Mazaryk's feet.

"Ales, upstairs."

Ales took the stairs one at a time, sweeping his gun to account for every nook on the way.

Mazaryk stooped to the boy's level and grabbed his face, bringing the boy's eyes up to his own. The boy stirred. *"Listen to me child. Tell me what happened to the men who own this bar, and we will leave you forever."*

Tears streaming down his face, the boy pointed a shuddering arm towards the door. Mazaryk followed: an envelope was nailed just under the inside handle. They had missed it on their way in. Mazaryk stood.

"Watch the boy. Don't let him move."

Brander leveled his massive gun down at the child, who buried his face into the filthy floor and moaned.

Mazaryk ripped the envelope from the nail and tore open one end. Inside he found a damp letter. It read:

Dear Black

Welcome to France.

Why not come dancing?

Frieze: Rue De Montpellier.

P.S.

You Russian Bastards.

-Silver

Ales Radomir came down the stairs and shook his head. Mazaryk looked back at Brander who was watching the sobbing boy intently.

"Time to go," he said.

———

Club Frieze occupied a massive converted warehouse on *Rue De La Forge Royale* in the east warehouse district of Paris. It was an old storage building that had fallen into disrepair, indistinguishable from those surrounding it, so neglected that half of the roof was caved in. Where most people saw a haven for derelicts and drug abusers, one enterprising and wealthy young Parisian saw possibilities. He purchased the entire lot, kicked every bum out of it, and went to work. He removed the entirety of the warehouse roof, even the part still standing, and erected a peaked and sloped canvas roofing in its place. At the rear of the building he raised a DJ booth ten feet high on a single, thick steel pole and surrounded it with curved glass. Fully stocked bars spanned both sides of the rectangular building, and round, port hole like windows were embedded every ten feet behind them. To top it off, he literally blew a hole in the front wall for the front door. Three months later he had one of the hottest nightclubs in Paris.

The night was deeply black when Mazaryk and his team approached Frieze and the club stood out like a jewel. Deep, throbbing music and a misty red light escaped from breaks in the tented roofing and out through the jagged front door. All around the club loomed the shadows of darker, derelict buildings, illuminated occasionally by a stray beam. A line of beautiful young men and women waited to get in, all smartly dressed and shivering in the late October night. Many talked on their phones and most of them smoked. Their cigarettes burned brighter here and there like sporadic fireflies as one and then another took a drag. Mazaryk looked upon them for a moment, his breath puffing small, even clouds into the air.

"A nightclub. They think this is some sort of game," said Mazaryk, his Russian soft and clipped. Brander looked at him and popped a large eyebrow. If Mazaryk's voice betrayed even a slight annoyance, he was furious. Eddie Mazaryk disliked games not of his own contrivance.

"Let's move," said Mazaryk, placing his gun hand inside his jacket as he stepped off the sidewalk.

They bypassed the line and walked directly to the door. As they approached the bouncers there, Mazaryk spoke to Brander. *"Take care of them, I'm walking in."*

Brander withdrew his massive handgun from his jacket and leveled it at the nearest bouncer.

"If you move, I'll kill you," he said, his voice a base growl loud enough to be heard over the waves of music. All three men manning the door froze and Eddie Mazaryk stepped deftly inside. Brander knew he had at most ten seconds within which he must act before someone screamed. Ales moved in, his teeth clenched, and leveled his own gun at another bouncer. Ales nodded at Brander who swept inside just as the screaming began. It was immediately clipped by the roaring music.

Yves Noel waited inside for Mazaryk. He stood against the bar to the left of the room, about twenty feet towards the back. He leaned over his handgun to shield it from whoever might look his way, but snapped it up as he saw Mazaryk appear and then disappear into the crowd just as quickly. He only just managed to duck out of view himself before he saw the towering frame of Goran Brander enter the club. For almost five seconds he had a clear shot at the man but reasoned that if he took it, he would reveal his position to Mazaryk, who couldn't be more than ten feet away. Mazaryk was the head of the snake. He wouldn't risk the striker with that prize in reach. Yves ducked again and lost sight of Brander.

Seconds later Yves saw a slim man in a black suit weaving about just in front of him. He turned the man about and jammed the silencer of his gun into his gut, but it wasn't Mazaryk. The man was drunk and tried to grab Yves in return, but Yves shoved him behind and ducked further, nosing about like a hound.

Mazaryk was nowhere. Yves cursed. All three men of Black would be in by now. He was too late, and they could be anywhere. He only hoped his brothers stalking the perimeter had a better vantage than he did. He should have shot that behemoth when he had the chance. He had Brander in his sights for five full seconds. He swore at himself again as he ducked and weaved, scanning the room.

Tristan Noel *did* see Brander when he came in and he shot at him twice with his silenced automatic, but the distance was too far and he missed. Yves had ordered them to make their shot clusters quick and precise and then to holster their guns so as not to cause a panic. His diodes slammed against the front wall while the crowd danced on to the blaring music none the wiser. By the time Tristan was able to see the length of the club again, Brander was gone. He shook his head. For a giant, the man was frighteningly mobile.

Dominique Noel had backed into the shadows at the edge of the large room and leveled his gun at the entrance, hoping to drop one or all of them as they walked in, but something was wrong outside. No one was moving in or out and both bouncers had disappeared from view. Had Mazaryk come in? Had Ales Radomir? The club was so loud and the visibility so low and erratic that nothing was certain. Yves had designed it this way so that all communication between Team Black would be cut off, but as the strobe lights kicked on and the entire club plunged into an eerie stop-motion animation, Dominique wondered if it was any advantage at all.

Twice Eddie Mazaryk thought he had one or more of the triplets cornered, and twice it was nobody, and his anger was mounting. Team Black practiced methods of movement, formations that they followed in a fight, and normally they never lost each other. Ever. Still, at times like this, when communication with his team was impossible, Mazaryk was thankful for his striker's height. They found each other almost at once. Mazaryk grabbed Brander and pulled him down to his eye level and spoke directly into his ear.

"Ales will only be able to hold the door for at most another minute. If the police come here or they turn on the lights, you, at least, will be shot very quickly. I think they are in the corners. That is where I would be."

Brander started off towards the back corners but was stopped by Mazaryk, who flipped him about again.

"No!" he hissed. *"They'll see you coming. They'll see any of us coming."*

He looked around himself at the jostling crowd, squeezing into each other and around each other and bobbing up and down in unison like a bucket of worms. He shook his head and snuffed a derisive breath.

"Cowardly French," he said. *"They risk everyone in this building, but we're running out of time."*

He hung his head momentarily, and for a moment he looked very sad—so sad that Brander was about to speak to him, but then Eddie Mazaryk brought his head up and the look Brander saw in his eyes stilled him. The man had totally separated himself. Mazaryk perceived the flowing masses with a new distance, objectively, as if they were no longer people but mere *things*, moveable and usable. When Brander saw this he began to unscrew the silencer on his gun.

"They use this chaos against us. It is time we turned the tables," said Mazaryk as he unscrewed his own silencer. *"Go to the door and follow my lead."*

Mazaryk shifted his way to the center of the dance floor, surrounded on all sides by the pressing horde. The music was rising, gaining in pitch, the beat intervals closing. The bass drop was coming and the clubbers sensed it, tensing in anticipation and raising their heads to the elevated booth that was its source as if preparing to receive a blessing. Mazaryk calmly raised his gun at the glass enclosed DJ and fired four times just as the low notes of the drop tapped the sternum of the crowd. The cracks were muffled by the music but not covered completely, like the settling of wood under carpeting, and four of them in a row got the immediate attention of everyone nearby. The mob froze in terror, unable to react for a stretch of moments.

When the DJ booth exploded into a million tiny glass fragments, people fell to the floor and screamed and whoever was still standing in the rear corners of the building, Eddie Mazaryk shot.

If Mazaryk's gun was a loud pop under the music, Brander's .50 sounded like a cannon in the music's abrupt absence. Those still standing under the shower of glass began to run en masse for the door but were immediately turned away by Brander, who sighted the corners opposite him and fired at anything that resembled the triplets. He fired in measured time: *blam, blam, blam, blam,* a devastating metronome. Three people hit the ground in succession, one lay still, but two writhed about in a grotesque parody of the dancing moments before.

Ales appeared through the doorway already firing in the same direction as his captain, as if the bespectacled sweeper was simply awaiting his cue. He shot a bartender in the face. The impact snapped her head back owlishly and she dropped a drink as she collapsed.

Surrounded on all sides by madmen with guns, most of the clubbers simply dropped to the ground and screamed. Several buried their heads in their shirts and dresses. A handful stood dead still. One girl near Mazaryk screamed herself to her knees. One very drunk man tried to settle the matter by lunging at Mazaryk, who sidestepped him easily and shot him in the face twice. He dropped like a sack of coins.

In the dead space both teams now saw each other clearly for the first time. Ales stood at the door, Brander to his far left. Mazaryk still stood at the dead center of the dance floor. Dominique and Tristan were at either corner opposite the door, Yves near the left bar, twenty paces from his brothers. Everything from the time Team Black walked in until that moment spanned barely five minutes. For a split-second, both teams simply looked at each other. Then, at once, everything happened.

The Russians fired first and the French were forced to move because they took half of a beat longer to sight in an effort to spare as many of their countrymen as possible. Black had no such qualms and fired at everyone standing between them and their targets. Dominique ducked low, his back against the wall under the bar. He was hit by a tooth as he sought a vantage point from which to fire between the jumbles of legs. He watched it in horrified fascination as it bounced off of his arm and skittered on the smeared linoleum floor. Tristan, drunk on vodka and high on adrenaline, walked himself into the middle of the dance floor with a fresh clip in his gun. He shoved men and women to the floor as he shot at Brander and Brander only. It was unbelievable to Tristan that a man of Goran Brander's size was not yet incapacitated. It was unnatural. He was five shots into his ten shot clip before Mazaryk got a bead on him.

Brander found himself inundated with Tristan Noel's fire. He managed to flinch out of the direct line of one diode just as a second slammed into a bottle of whisky behind him, exploding it into an auburn colored fine debris inches from his head. With whisky burning his eyes and fresh cuts on his face, Brander leaned heavily on the bar. Above him, another shot struck one of the porthole windows and blew its glass inward and onto the cowering bartenders.

Then Tristan was shot in the shoulder, just above his heart, and his firing stopped.

It had taken Eddie Mazaryk almost six bullets to finally hit the French sweeper. Three people lay screaming on the ground in their wake, brought low as Mazaryk cleaved a clean sight through those that still stood between them. Tristan hitched back with the force of the shot. Yves saw his brother get hit and screamed in anger as he propelled himself off of the bar at Mazaryk. Mazaryk turned to aim at him, but Ales got to him first with a single shot to the neck. Yves gargled as he fell to the ground in front of Mazaryk, who hissed at him, his face furious.

"You think this is a game? The blood tonight is on your hands!"

Yves coughed and jerked as Ales stepped forward to finish him off with four shots clustered in the small of his back. The captain of Silver lay still.

Through force of will Tristan still stood, but he was gasping with the pain of his wound. Every breath hitched up high in his chest and would go no further. He could not exhale. His body was failing him, growing numb. His eyes were wild, but his gun was still sighted on Goran Brander. Mazaryk, momentarily distracted by Yves' charge, was about to finish Tristan when Dominique popped up from the floor to his right. Mazaryk coolly readjusted his aim at this newest threat and fired into Dominique's stomach. He absorbed it as if he was catching a ball and fell to his knees, but not before unloading two wild shots towards the front of the room. Neither of them hit anyone, but in the second that Mazaryk was forced to duck, Tristan fired once. The diode whizzed past Mazaryk's cheek and slammed into Goran Brander's right temple. Brander slumped over the bar, unmoving.

Mazaryk looked at his striker for a moment as he lay draped on the bar.

Dominique Noel still laughed from his knees at his brother's kill. He spat and moved to speak, but Mazaryk shot him once in the head and he went silent. Mazaryk turned to Tristan, the only Silver man still standing, albeit in a leering manner. He popped out his spent clip and reloaded in one swift movement while Tristan sucked in air and fumbled with his gun. Mazaryk walked around Tristan and shot him three times in the back of the head. He slammed to the ground as if a weight had dropped upon him. Mazrayk turned once again to look at his felled striker, contemplating. Then he turned back to Tristan and fired once more into the back of his head.

Ales Radomir dashed over to his teammate. He shoved people away and felt for a pulse in his long neck. He looked up at Mazaryk and let out a bullish huff through his nose. Mazaryk stood silently for a moment in the middle of the dance floor amid the screaming and scrambling. He sucked air through his teeth as he thought how this changed things, and then he walked over to the splayed body of the Silver captain, Yves Noel, and spat upon it.

"You have no respect for this organization," said Mazaryk, speaking into Yves' dead ears. *"Do you see what happens when you treat this like a game?"*

Slowly Mazaryk stood and looked around him. People pressed themselves against the far walls like terrified caged animals. Nobody moved against him, and he could see why. He counted fifteen people motionless on the floor, not including the three Frenchmen and his own striker. He knew his team had hit nine; the other six had to have been hurt in the rush to get away from the fray. Those would be the worst injuries.

"You brought this upon yourselves! The blood of these innocents

rests upon you and your foolish brothers," Mazaryk hissed, bending low towards the still face of Yves once more. *"Remember that when you wake up. Remember that you deserved this."*

He stood and walked to where Ales was gently wiping the slack face of Goran Brander. He reached over and drew up one of Brander's eyelids. There was only white. Then he walked to the door and out into the darkness of the derelict buildings, Ales close in tow. They could hear the approaching helicopters and saw that several flashing cars were already on the horizon.

Team Silver was out.

CHAPTER NINETEEN

"TOTALLY WIPED OUT. In a bad way."

Johnnie Northern rested his chin in one hand and a cup of black coffee in the other. Team Blue was gathered together on the porch of a late-night coffee house ten minutes from the San Diego beach, just southwest of the UCSD campus. Nikkie Hix studied Northern. Max Haulden stirred his own coffee as he watched the leaves of a nearby wooded area rustle about under the street lights in the night wind.

"But they got Brander," Northern said. "No small feat."

"Really!" said Hix. "Brander hasn't been hit for quite a while. How did that happen?"

"They shot it out in a dance club in east Paris. It's a mess. Didn't take Black very long to move, did it?" Northern asked, looking at Max, who still looked elsewhere.

"So France is out," Max said, smiling cryptically as he swirled around the dregs of his coffee. "What an stupid plan, to hide in a dance club. They must have been drunk. A band of fools."

"Fifteen civilians injured. They opened up on the crowd. Indiscriminately. Destroyed the place. A million and a quarter in fines, according to Greer's report," said Northern.

"My God," whispered Nikkie. "What happened?"

"Mazaryk's insane, that's what happened. He's turning this organization into a gang war. Things are changing. Greer says we should stay heads up," said Northern.

"The Japs are coming?"

"From what I can tell Red ain't moving at all," Northern said, before yawning hugely. He tapped the table top rapidly and leaned back in his seat, hands behind his head. "Teams are moving all around us, yet we sit. And drink coffee," he added, tipping his cup and squinting into the grounds as if to read the future.

"John, we agreed. It would be stupid to move on them. If we don't move, we have to wait, it's the name of the game," Max said.

"Yes. The waiting game," Northern said, his voice only briefly betraying his annoyance before he smiled again. "I've never been much good at the waiting game."

Max furrowed his brow and was about to speak again when a woman who was passing by their table suddenly hitched up and leaned backwards to look at them. All three turned to her.

"John?" she asked.

"Sarah," said Northern, as he might speak the name of a song or a movie that he'd struggled to remember all day. He stood. Nikkie looked from him to this new girl, her face a careful mask. She thought the greeting awfully familiar. She was unnerved. It was the nature of their work that each should know of the other's contacts in the places in which they stayed. And she was beautiful. She immediately disliked the woman.

Max looked up at Sarah blankly, annoyed at the interruption but willing to wait. He briefly eyed two others, her friends no doubt, who stood a polite distance away. No danger there.

"I haven't seen you in a while," said Sarah, eyeing the other two at the table uneasily. Only Northern smiled, his teeth pointed and white in the gathering night.

"I thought you were gone for good," she said.

"Work has been busy, but I'm always around." His eyes were but blue glints in the dark, yet she found herself looking away and back again.

"Fair enough," she said, nodding and fussing with the zipper on her coat. It was unlike her to avert a gaze. She felt foreign to herself; laid bare. She looked at him again in self-defiance.

He smiled, drawing out the silence before speaking. "These are my associates, Max and Nicole."

Northern nodded at each in turn. Max offered a half smile so as not to look overly disinterested. To him this was an interference; they were essentially on the clock and this wasn't part of their job. But the competitive spirit within Nikkie was stirred. She stood up, flashed a southern smile, and stuck out her hand.

"Very nice to meet you. John has said good things about you," she said, shaking her hand with three brisk pumps.

Sarah looked from Hix to Northern and blinked. "Has he?"

"I did mention that I met you," he said softly, eyeing Hix, who still smiled at Sarah. Sarah was confused as to where she should look, so she settled upon Max, who was focusing on the tree again.

"Well, I'll have to keep an eye out for you then. If you're around, I mean," said Sarah.

"I have to leave for a few days, for work, but I'll be back," Northern said, dipping his gaze to beg her pardon. Max and Nikkie stared at him. He looked only at Sarah.

"Good luck," she said. "I should head out." She gestured back at her friends still waiting just beyond, smiled a farewell, and walked off.

His two teammates still watched him. He turned back to them.

"What's all this now?" Max asked flatly. "Are we going somewhere? Did you not just say *we wait*? What was all this talk about sticking out like a sore thumb over there, and making easy targets and whatnot?"

Nikkie, more concerned about Sarah than any newly formed travel plans, judged it best to wait to bring up the girl. She settled for cocking an eyebrow at her captain. Northern took in a breath and exhaled slowly.

"Waiting has its merits," began Northern.

Max rubbed his eyes, already weary with the travel he now knew was coming.

"…But it rarely gets anyone anywhere," Northern finished with flourish.

Max could only shake his head. His captain had made up his mind.

"Pack your bags," Northern said. "We're going to Japan."

CHAPTER TWENTY

I N THE BEGINNING, TAKURO Obata doubted his team. They didn't look anything like he expected. These men weren't muscular, nor did they look particularly menacing in the way certain stringy men can look. Amon Jinbo, his striker, looked like a prepubescent boy, dressed in clothes too large, with thick black plastic eyeglasses that seemed about to fall off of his face. Initially Obata thought something might be mentally wrong with the boy as well. He fidgeted too much, often scratching absently at his hands. When he stood, he draped one arm across his body and onto his opposite shoulder as if he was holding himself—a posture borne out of a lack of confidence. He looked weak. Obata recalled thinking that the boy was nearly cradling himself.

His sweeper was a different character altogether and no more promising at first glance. Tenri Fuse spoke like a pervert, drawing out certain odd words in his sentences and enunciating others with undue care while petting his thin strip of a goatee. He craved attention and was a strutting spectacle unto himself. Obata remembered thinking that if these men were expected to do what he thought they were supposed to do, and what the Tournament told him they were supposed to do, Japan was in a lot of trouble.

But what must he have looked like to them? He rarely spoke, and often caught himself staring blankly at nothing. His mind was always working, but how were they to know that? They probably thought him boring, or worse, stupid. When he did speak, his voice was low and soft. Perhaps they thought this betrayed weakness. He was no storybook general. He would never be the one to deliver a rallying speech as the three of them faced the breach. He'd been told he often scowled when he was lost in thought, so they may have thought him an angry, brooding man. Thankfully these first impressions, whatever they may have been, no longer mattered. Appearances were deceiving. They now knew exactly what each was capable of.

The tipping point, the point when Takuro Obata was fully able to say to himself that all three of them were an unbroken circle—a team that was three made one instead of one made of three—came when he took them into the mountains of Toyama prefecture, almost a year after they met:

The three trudged up the pathless wilderness in single-filed silence, soaked through to the bone as they parted the masses of greenery with their bare hands. Pollen and dirt dripped down their exposed faces, arms, and legs in rivulets of fine yellow and brown grit. It had beaded upon the dull metal of their newly acquired guns and, like paint, streaked the leather of their holsters. Every so often one of them spit to clear their mouth. Amon Jinbo had long since stopped trying to clean his glasses, and instead peered out through their grimy lenses half blind, trusting the direction of his captain in front of him. As Tenri Fuse, the last in line, passed though the greenery, it closed behind him like a theatre curtain, solid and undulating.

For two hours they trudged uphill in silence, through the roiling mist that fell down the mountain as the cool night air met the hot overgrowth all around them. As they climbed higher the vegetation thinned out by degrees, but so slowly that when the team first stopped both Fuse and Jinbo looked around themselves bewildered by the change. Thin-trunked bamboo trees stood in clumps, straining to find what sunshine the massive canopies of

Red Cedar leaves allowed them. Here and there animals of all kinds had torn the spongy undergrowth in swaths to reveal dark mulch beneath. All around them the cicadas were awakening in the dark, each of their saw-like calls melting into one another to form one long, continuous scream.

As the red rays of the setting sun sliced through the trees, elongating their shadows east and up the mountain, Obata found a carved rock. It was surrounded by four other rocks of similar size, all devoid of moss and dirt, and rounded to a smooth egg shape. On the rock were written the characters *Heiwana Tooge.* Restful Road. Obata seemed to have been looking for it, because after sighting it he turned around and gave a rare smile to his two teammates.

"*Just ahead,*" he said.

Five minutes later the three turned a sharp corner around a jutting boulder and came upon a simple gazebo that was invisible even ten paces back. Four worn oak poles held up a small pointed roof of thatched grass and mud. It sheltered a flat, square patch of land in which dwelt a simple and beautiful garden of sand and stone. In the middle of the garden a small monk was raking very slow and precise circles in the sand around a flat center stone of pure white. Fuse and Jinbo froze, as much out of surprise at finding such a secluded, secret place as out of respect. They feared that perhaps they would startle him and ruin the sanctity of everything in front of them. The monk continued his infinitely slow raking until he reached the precise area in which he had first set rake to sand. When he saw that the grooves in the sand fit perfectly together, he stood and turned without surprise to look at the three men. When he saw Obata he smiled so widely that the wrinkles of his face seemed to fall upon themselves and squeeze his bright eyes shut of their own accord.

"*We've come, grandfather,*" Obata said, gesturing openly at the men to either side of him.

"Yes, yes, yes," the old man said. He stepped deftly from rock to rock, his wooden sandals clacking once upon each, and alighted upon the forest ground. He wore a swath of burnt-orange cloth that wrapped around one shoulder and hung barely above the ground. His other shoulder was bare and brown. His *geta* sandals were worn clean of lacquering. His head was completely bald, devoid even of the beginnings of stubble. He took one look at each of the three men in turn, all of whom bowed deeply, before setting off to the right of the garden towards a small wooden building in the near distance. With one hand he held up the hem of his robe like a debutante might, and with the other he motioned for the three men to follow.

The wooden building was the monk's sleeping quarters, but also doubled as an outdoor noodle shop and bar. Whom it might serve in this wilderness, none could say. It was a simple structure of worn wood. The side facing the garden was opened and had a single, slightly uneven wooden bar-top that ran its length at about waist height. Two polished stumps acted as stools. The three men stood and waited while the monk went into his house by the back and came to the bar. But instead of serving them, he moved to the back corner of the shack's interior and dug in the soft earth there with his cupped hands. Minutes later he withdrew a small clay jug from the ground, blew on its label to clear it of dirt, and eyed it at arm's length. He nodded to himself and rose to his feet holding it out before him. He grabbed three small *sake* cups and turned to the men waiting outside.

"Bring a stump," he croaked, and gestured behind him to the forest beyond. *"Come, come, come,"* he chirped.

Obata nodded at Amon Jinbo, who picked up one of the stumps in front of him and held it ponderously to his chest, leaning back so as not to pitch himself over. He eyed Obata with one cocked eyebrow as his bulky glasses slid to the tip of his nose. Tenri Fuse was absorbed in the fairytale scene, his head swept slowly this way and that as if he expected a talking animal or other living mythology to materialize from the low-lying mists. Obata walked around the shack and his team followed, the old monk was already many steps ahead near the border of the mists and wasn't looking back.

They followed the monk to a flat section of the mountain that might at one time have been a place in which crops grew as part of a tiered block of farmland, but had long since been abandoned to the elements. The monk, or somebody, had carved steps out of the earth leading up to the flat slice of land; each step was paved with small white pebbles. At the top of the steps a section of the flat land was hacked clean of brush and vegetation and re-sown with a soft lichen of vibrant green. The monk removed his wooden sandals and stepped upon it and immediately began to examine its parameters for upkeep. The three men removed their shoes as well, and their socks, and walked upon the lichen with their bare feet. It was like walking on a heavy liquid; a thick cream of green. The monk motioned for Jinbo to place the stump he carried in the center of the lichen patch, and when he did, the monk placed the sake gourd and the three cups upon it. Obata thanked the monk and gave him a small brown parcel. The monk bowed and withdrew, stepped deftly into his sandals and then flitted off into the mist below.

Obata looked at the two men for a moment. They said nothing.

"*Sit,*" Obata said quietly, folding himself into a cross legged position on the ground.

Jinbo and Fuse sat so that all three of them surrounded the low stump and the sake. Obata poured his partner's cups full, replaced the sake, and then took out his gun and set it next to the cups. Jinbo eyed it warily, but Fuse picked up the sake again to fill his captain's cup. Once done, he set the gourd back down and he too removed his firearm, a long and thin-barreled Smith and Wesson 622 that resembled a target pistol. He placed it on the stump next to Obata's gun before grasping his cup.

Jinbo paused and pushed his glasses up and scratched at himself before he, too, took out his bulky chrome Colt Anaconda .45 revolver and set it on the stump where it overhung the edge a bit. He then took out a second gun, a standard issue Colt .45 automatic, and set it upon his first. He took up his cup and then he sat back and eyed both of his guns. They seemed particularly ugly in this place.

Then Obata spoke. *"I've seen you work and train this past year, and you've seen me,"* he began, speaking awkwardly into the glass held out in front of him. *"I know your strengths and your weaknesses and you know mine."* He paused. He seemed to ponder elaborating, but then decided against it. He was unaccustomed to speeches and a great believer in the economy of words. *"Let us first drink to that knowledge. That we have come to know each other and those weapons in front of us."*

He rose his cup a notch higher in silence, and then all three drank the sake down at once. Obata took the cups and the gourd of sake and set them aside on the ground.

"If I know anything about what lies before us, it is that gunfire is but a small part of the competition—a fraction! More, it is a pitting of wits. The battles are won or lost before the actual match begins."

Both men were watching him. That he should be this enigmatic when it was not normally his custom to speak at all concerned them. As Jinbo saw it, people started philosophizing only when they wanted to announce something serious in a roundabout way. Jinbo was beginning to believe all of this Tournament nonsense, to really and truly grasp that he would be devoting his life to this cause, but his grip was precarious. If it was all the same, he would just as soon have Obata return to his stoic, inwardly seething self.

"When we win, it will be because we are more prepared than our opponents in every way," Obata continued as he slowly reached for his gun. *"And if we ever lose, it is because our opponents are more prepared than us."*

He held his gun in his hand as he might present a sword, its flat edge balanced on his open palm. He contemplated it for several moments as shadow chased the sun down the mountain to the sound of wind rushing about the leaves of the trees.

He slowly grasped the gun around its handle and rested his finger lightly upon the trigger.

"In order to understand this business, we must feel the worst of it. On our terms. Only then can we know fully what we go into."

Obata turned to Fuse, who eased his gaze from the gun to his captain's face. He squared his shoulders and set his hands loosely in his lap.

"Fuse, do you trust me?" Obata asked, his voice just above a whisper.

Tenri Fuse bowed theatrically, sweeping the ground from his sitting position. *"I do,"* he said.

"Will you follow me? Even into darkness?"

Fuse bowed again.

In a single fluid motion, Obata leveled his 9mm at Fuse's left shoulder. Fuse had only enough time to slightly raise his thin eyebrows before Obata fired. The noise startled the mountain around them; birds nearby took flight in the sulfur aftermath, their shrill caws joining the clapping echo. Fuse lay prone. He was groaning, his long, manicured fingers draped over his right shoulder, tapping it gently as if probing for a puncture, although there was none.

"*Sit up,*" Obata said.

Slowly, Fuse sat up, grappling at the spongy moss like a climber seeking purchase. He had gone very pale and was whimpering. Every movement seemed to grind an invisible set of steel teeth further into his shoulders. He sat slumped, head down, as if he wanted to nuzzle up against his wound. Jinbo was torn between watching his colleague and grabbing his own guns.

"*We must feel the spreading effects of the diode first hand,*" Obata said, his voice flat as he watched his partner suffer.

"*The pain will spread, followed by a numbness that will eventually take you under. But fight against it as long as you can. Slow your breathing. Clear your mind.*"

He turned to Jinbo and saw that he was reaching for his weapons.

"*I won't shoot you, Jinbo,*" Obata said, setting his gun back on the stump and sighing. He had hoped by now to have Jinbo's full trust. The boy was eccentric, probably had been ridiculed in the past. Trust was a long time coming with one such as him.

"*If you allow him to, I want Fuse to do it,*" Obata said.

Jinbo looked at Fuse and pinched his lips. The sight of a well poised man brought so low was almost revolting for Jinbo, although it was Fuse himself that looked about to be ill.

"No one is forcing you to do anything. As you can see, he is in no shape to overpower you."

Jinbo shook his head, not in answer to Obata, but at the situation as a whole. Obata had given Jinbo a choice, but Jinbo knew a refusal irreparably harmed his standing in the group. He watched Fuse try to work moisture back into his mouth while taking deep, haggard breaths.

Obata looked at Jinbo for a moment more and then, turning to Fuse, gave a single sharp nod. Fuse reached for his gun on the stump, hissed as a violent cramp wracked his left shoulder and upper chest, then moved a good deal slower to finally grab it. He dragged it heavily off of the stump and dropped it to the ground before he could hoist it up again to a position leveled at Jinbo's left shoulder. Obata turned to Jinbo once more, awaiting answer. Jinbo leaned his head back and away, fluttering his eyelashes slightly in anticipation. He whined, but nodded.

Fuse took a deep breath, sighted, and fired.

Jinbo too was slammed back, but he caught himself with his left palm briefly before a shooting pain collapsed him in an awkward, turned about position. He held his forehead to the cool lichen floor and uttered a stream of epithets. Despite everything he heard about the tearing, raw, nerves-exposed pain of getting hit by a diode, he was in no way prepared for the actuality of it. His mouth watered heavily in anticipation of vomiting, and then just as suddenly went dry as he realized that already the locus of the pain was slowly expanding. His shoulder felt horribly warm as well, as if blood now saturated his shirt.

"Now," Obata said, "You will shoot me."

As his wits returned and he once again placed himself in the little clearing in the woods on the mountainside of Toyama,

Jinbo grabbed his own gun, unsure if he was going to shoot out of anger or obedience. For the first time in his life he seriously regretted choosing weapons of such weight and size. At first he thought he could use his dominant hand regardless of the wound, but the gun dropped to the floor like a rock. He switched to his right hand to bring it up and to sight it at his captain's shoulder.

The gun fired with such a loud cannonade that all was a muted ringing for several seconds afterwards. When it cleared Obata still sat upright, but his dark eyes were glossy.

"Now we wait," he said, his voice hoarse.

The three men said very little over the course of the next several hours as the pain spread across their bodies like a smoldering brush line. The rending burn was followed by a dead cold. Near the end, Fuse began to lilt his head forward against his will. Then he fell over. Minutes later Jinbo panicked under an onslaught of numbness-induced claustrophobia, then he crumpled like a hobbled deer. Last of all was Obata. He watched his colleagues lie motionless for almost fifteen minutes more before he too went under. His head tilted forward and his chin pressed against his chest.

When all three men were out, the monk came back up the trail, walking lightly and bobbing about like a man on a summer stroll. He seemed not at all surprised. He methodically picked each man up, one at a time, and effortlessly draped each over his shoulder like a bag of rice. He moved each back down the trail and placed them in front of the large out-jutting rock that hid his house and gardens from view. Once all three were lying against it, their heads flopped on their shoulders, their arms lying palm up on the ground like a strange assortment of rag-dolls, he stepped back and cocked his head as if admiring a painting. Then he hopped up the trail and back into his grounds beyond.

When the Tournament medevac helicopter chopped its way through the skies above twenty minutes later, the medics dropped into the foliage to find all three still sitting peacefully against the rock, faces blank. A small cleanup team circled the surrounding area but found nothing more than an immaculate sand-garden and what looked to be an old, abandoned sake bar.

So it was, five years ago, that Team Red initiated themselves into the organization that would become their life's blood.

CHAPTER TWENTY-ONE

THE MEXICANS WERE ON the run, and Alex Auldborne's patience was wearing thin. He knew it was the natural progression of things; They would have to blow through Team White before they could then meet up with Northern, provided Northern and his crew got past the Japanese. But he was already thinking beyond White. The ultimate victory would ring hollow if it didn't at some point involve walking over Northern's face.

The *Bludgeon Blackout* was a new term in Tournament vernacular, developed during the last cycle, and one that Auldborne and his team were intimately familiar with. In every previous Tournament cycle, every team member brought down was done for with a diode. And until Blue faced Grey in the last Tournament, everyone assumed that was how it would continue to be done. But on that day, the two teams had run out of ammunition. With every bullet spent and two members on each team still standing, something had to be done. Northern had thrown himself upon Auldborne like a whole pack of wolves, and Auldborne had learned, to his detriment, that a gun butt to the temple can count a player just as dead as a diode to the face.

Auldborne was never fooled twice. Not only did he intend to break Blue; he intended to do it with style and flair. Perhaps add a new term of his own to the annals of the Tournament. He was determined that the Yank's humiliation at his hands go down in history.

In the meantime, however, he had to catch these god-damn Mexicans. He had no idea that they could be so fast. He and Christina and Draden landed three days ago in Puebla, just about one hundred kilometers southeast of Mexico City, and had been chasing them north ever since. Auldborne hated Mexico. It was entirely too hot. Nobody from England ever went to Mexico. When the English vacationed they went to Brighton, where it was only marginally warmer than London on a good day. In November it would be a comfortable ten degrees Celsius there, perfect weather for a greatcoat and a strong gin. Here, however, over a thousand kilometers northwest in the city of Teocaltiche, a name that Auldborne refused even to try to pronounce, it had to be at least twenty-five degrees Celsius—in November! Ridiculous! But he was too hot even to work up any anger.

Auldborne wiped the moisture off his brow with a handkerchief and tucked it back into the breast pocket of his wilting button-down shirt. He'd decided to ditch his jacket, tailored linen though it was, three towns back. His shoulder holster was blatantly displayed now, but he no longer cared. He'd found that the ratty beggar children were less prone to approach him when they saw the gun.

Christina bitched constantly about the heat, ignored everyone who talked to her outside of the team, and refused to touch anything she didn't absolutely have to touch. She walked around with a look of perpetual disgust, as if there were was a rotting stench at every turn. Only Draden Tate seemed unaffected; he spent most of the time glowering at everything, especially the cheap map they'd purchased.

The drill went as follows: A member of Team Grey administration would phone them with coordinates of the area in which White had last been seen. Auldborne had no idea how they found these, nor did he care, as long as they continued to find them. Once they had the coordinates, Draden would place them on a map, convene with Auldborne and Stoke, and the three of them would calculate how best to get where they had to go in the shortest time possible.

They had already been through several odd towns, if they could indeed be called towns, and they had already experienced too much of the local flavor. One day of this traipsing about was all it took for Auldborne to become thoroughly convinced that Mexico was the armpit of its particular hemisphere. Thankfully the natives seemed not to understand the horror in which they lived and breathed. If they did, he'd no doubt there would be some sort of uprising.

They were forced to go inside a bar to ask for directions in a ramshackle little town called San Miguel El Alto. Apparently, the roads in Mexico were not always reliable—often they were not named, and in some cases they simply disappeared. They were looking for a specific passage out of the city that allowed for them to go through the foothills to the north instead of around them. The car that they rented (and that they intended to leave in a ditch at the earliest convenient opportunity) was overheating again, and they needed water anyway; might as well ask how the hell to get out of there at the same time.

Everything was going nicely in the bar: Auldborne was doing all the talking as per usual while Draden stood by the door, shimmering in the heat like a big block of black lacquered wood. Then one of the men touched Christina. Whether this was intentional or not didn't matter. Auldborne heard a sound like a piece of paper ripping and turned just in time to see a man scream and fall from his stool onto the dirty wooden floor.

"Oh my," Alex said with understated surprise. "What did he do to you?"

Christina screamed at the man lying on the floor bunched up in a ball.

"You *prick!* You absolute *sodding prick!* Don't *ever* touch me. *Ever!*"

She spat at him as he struggled to sit up, and spat at him again as he took his hand away from his face and Auldborne saw that Christina had split open the cornea of his right eye. The man looked as though he was weeping blood. Auldborne glanced at Tate.

"Everythin' okay?" Tate asked.

"Not for this gentleman," Auldborne smiled. "Seems to have had his eye on the wrong woman. Taking it rather hard though, isn't he?"

Auldborne looked down at the writhing man and cocked his head like a curious animal. Christina, sickened by the very air she breathed, hurried past Draden and outside. She paced the wood planked deck and seethed.

"There you are," Auldborne soothed the man. "See? It's nothing. Nothing a friendly patch can't fix. You'll look like a pirate! It might even serve you well here," he said, looking about the bar distastefully at the smattering of horrified patrons.

That was how they left the sleepy little town of San Miguel el Alto.

Even Draden Tate, a man who usually kept his anger at bay until a time of his own choosing, was feeling the monotony. In Tepic, three days into the chase, he lost his cool. He was standing on the dust sidewalk outside of the car and discussing further coordinates with their administration when two men walked out of a nearby building and one of them made a comment in his general direction. Tate had no idea what they were saying, or indeed if it even was in reference to him, but it was too late. A combination of things set him off, most notably that the car was overheating again, and that Diego Vega and his team seemed to be gaining ground ahead of them.

He paused his phone conversation and eyed the men as they walked past. Then he covered the receiver almost daintily, as if to spare Administration the indignity, and blew up at them.

"Whatchu lookin' at man? Keep fuckin' walkin' if you know what's good for ya." The two men couldn't have been more surprised if the car itself had just bellowed at them. After a moment, one of them chuckled nervously. Tate snuffed loudly and curled his lip, set the phone gingerly on the hood of the car, and took out his .45 just as Alex Auldborne exited the building in front of them.

"No shooting, Draden," Auldborne said as if idly commenting on the weather. He continued to the passenger's side of the vehicle, took the phone from the roof, and sat inside the car.

Draden spat hard, a habit recently acquired from Christina, who watched the incident unfold from the back seat with a smirking grin. The men were still rooted to the earth in shock when Draden flipped his gun around and slammed it onto the top of each of their heads once like it was a carnival game. As both collapsed, Draden returned to the car and sat in the driver's side.

"What was that all about?" Auldborne asked.

"Just practicin'," he said, looking directly ahead as he started the car and pulled it out into the street. Christina laughed from behind him.

"This isn't working," Auldborne said, scanning the twisted

brush and bits of trash on the shoulder of the road as if he might find Diego Vega hidden within them.

"Goddamn Mexicans! If we keep this up, we'll all be in Canada before long. Give me the map," he said, motioning for it with his hand. "And the phone. I need Admin to do some digging."

Alex smoothed the map out on his knees. "We won't catch them—that's clear. And since we can't catch them, we'll have to draw them back down to us. It's very simple, really. Turn around, Draden."

CHAPTER TWENTY-TWO

IT WAS FOUR DAYS before any of them could walk unassisted. Before that, the Noel triplets were, for all intents and purposes, dead to the world.

An adrenal concoction tapped into their veins took each out of the diode coma, but it didn't immediately revive them. Tournament Medical advised against forcing consciousness upon fallen players, reasoning that increased mobility risked damaging already bruised organs. Also, the players were spared the pain when asleep. Conversely, Medical refused to prolong the unconscious state once a player awoke naturally, although many begged for it.

Dominique Noel, the striker, was the first to regain movement, having sustained only two shots to his person, one to the stomach and one to the right front quadrant of the top of his head, both from Eddie Mazaryk's weapon. Although the stomach shot pained him the most with a continual nausea on par with the worst depths of the stomach flu, it was the headshot that most worried the doctors. The electrical stimulation inflicted by a diode occasionally interfered with the brain's natural electrical synapse. Thus far, only severe headaches and minor vision impairment had been noted as serious side effects of a direct head shot, but Tournament doctors worldwide were of the almost unanimous opinion that the true extent of the damage could be far worse.

Yves Noel, the captain, was the second to awaken, with pain a good deal more considerable than his youngest brother's. He had sustained a direct shot to the neck, and two shots to the small of his lower back, courtesy of Ales Radomir. The shot to his neck caused severe tracheal bruising. It would be almost a week before Yves could eat anything solid and a month before he wasn't reminded of his wound every time he swallowed. The shots to the lower back welted his skin to a crushed grape color and induced random and debilitating back spasms for weeks. The ripping pain could drive him to the floor, frozen stiff, as if tiny shards of metal were coursing through his spinal fluid. Sometimes they would last for the better part of an hour before vanishing as quickly as they hit.

But by far the worst off was Tristan, the sweeper. The shot to the shoulder had left a fist-sized green and brown bruise with an angry red eye in its middle, but what had finished him was when Eddie Mazaryk fired three point blank shots into a single spot on his head, right where the skull met the neck. When his two brothers were finally able to shuffle about under supervision, they would move to and from Tristan's bedside where he lay unconscious, attached to a ventilator. Its hissing, the methodical beeping of the monitor, and the bulbous and erratic movements of his lidded eyes were the only indications of life about him. He never twitched, and he looked pale to the point of translucence. The Pitié-Salpêtrière Hospital's Tournament neurosurgeon stated flatly, in the way that only surgeons can, that Tristan might never wake up, and warned that if he did there would most likely be some irreparable damage to his motor functions.

But he did wake up. Ten days after Yves, and a full two weeks after the battle at Frieze nightclub, he opened his eyes, shut them again, opened them once more, declared in a raspy voice that he was blind, and then threw up on his bedding.

Tristan's darkness was complete. He could not move. He could not talk with the speed he had once been able to. He slurred often, and occasionally he would mix up the word order of his sentences so that what came out sounded like a made up language from the triplets' childhood. When this happened he would stop himself, take a deep breath, and speak one word at a time slowly until the sentence was correct. This sometimes took several minutes. He was also plagued by terrible migraines, more intense even than those suffered by his youngest brother Dominique. He couldn't bear touch of any kind on his skin, and voices above a whisper set him moaning, moans he quickly clipped because they too induced pain. His brothers held on to the fact that he still possessed the capabilities of movement and speech, even if they caused him such pain that he said it felt like his brain was boiling.

For two weeks after waking up Tristan was inconsolable over his blindness. He locked himself away in a dark room in the basement of the hospital's secluded Tournament wing and didn't attempt to speak. He ate very little, drank sparingly, and didn't bathe, preferring to wallow in his own filth and misery. He played the scenario over and over again in his head. How Black had outgunned them and outmaneuvered them, even in the chaotic nightclub. Not even the fact that he had dropped the indomitable Goran Brander consoled him. Blindness was the price he'd paid. Mazaryk's vengeance was terrible. He was useless now as a striker, his life in the Tournament was over. His life as he knew it was over: a dreadful trade off.

With Tristan having sequestered himself from all contact, Dominique sat alone with Yves as he recovered. His brother's swallowing was prolonged and painful, his hitching Adam's apple looked like a rolling pin trying to smooth a stubborn piece of dough. He communicated only in grunts or single syllables and he often paused for long stretches. All the while he sat statue still so as not to inflame his lower back. With his jaw clenched against twinges of pain he looked like an actor playing a corpse on stage. Their conversations were rather one sided. For his part, Dominique would hold his aching head in his hands as he spoke to his brother, and wear his ever present aviators to protect himself from the light that often set off his hair-trigger migraines. Both wore medical gowns and ward slippers, although Dominique was the only brother who could shuffle about in them.

"It's because they have no women on their team. I could talk to the women, confuse them," Dominique said, to which Yves rolled his eyes.

Yves kept flashing back to Eddie Mazaryk and the furious look in his eye as he hovered over him, his small jaw clenched as he spoke through grated teeth, seconds before Ales had finished him: *You think this is a game?* he'd said. *The blood tonight is on your hands!* This after Mazaryk's team gunned down at least eight innocent bystanders without a word. Their pain wouldn't be on the level of the players, but they were no doubt hurting all the same. And Mazaryk had the gall to call his swath of destruction *their* fault?

"Insane..." Yves mumbled.

"Tristan? I don't think he's insane. He's too busy puking and moaning to be insane," Dominique asserted. *"He won't even take a drink. That's what worries me. Tristan Noel refusing to touch a stiff drink. This has to be the longest stretch of sobriety he's had since he was twelve."*

Yves would have shaken his head if he could. He wasn't talking about Tristan; he was talking about Eddie Mazaryk. The man was crazy. His mouth and his gun had two totally different agendas.

There had to be something he could take from this disaster. His team would persevere. They had to. He wouldn't allow himself to think in terms of total defeat. He would hunt down Mazaryk in time. He grew surer of this with every sucking breath and dribbled swallow.

So Mazaryk thought he didn't take the Tournament seriously. No surprise: that's what everyone thought. Not giving a fuck was something of a Silver trademark. How *could* he take it seriously? It was a big game. Yves had the vague notion that extraordinary things were wagered on every shootout, but the players were never told how much, or by whom. The Tournament was nothing more than the product of fabulously wealthy men and women who had been born in the wrong era and yearned for the days of the gladiator and the Coliseum. It didn't deserve to be taken seriously. He owed them nothing. At first he fought only to maintain the extravagant lifestyle being a member of Silver afforded him. Over the years, though, he had grown to hate those he fought, Mazaryk especially. And the goddamn English. Who didn't hate the goddamn English? But he still had no loyalty to the organization itself. He didn't represent France…he represented himself.

He had the feeling, however, that something about the Noel philosophy didn't sit well with Eddie Mazaryk and Black. It was hard to read Mazaryk, he was less like a man than he was like a dream of a man, here one minute and gone the next. His expression was transitory, as if changed by the very light surrounding him. That night at club Frieze Mazaryk had been genuinely angry. Three shots point blank to the gristle at the base of his brother's skull made sure that they all understood just how angry he was.

Yves also knew that unbridled anger was a weakness, a loss of control. Perhaps, just perhaps, it was a chink in his armor. Tristan had shot Brander, after all. Even the big man was only human.

He would think on it. Lord knew he had the time.

—

Two weeks later, Tristan saw a light.

It was blurry at first, like a candle viewed through eye-lashes, and it arrived by such slow degrees that he took notice of it only when it triggered a migraine, but sure enough, he was beginning to see the green electronic display of his monitoring system. It slowly gained in strength until Tristan was both ecstatic and crippled with nausea. Even what little light he could see was enough to make him vomit up everything he had within him. Doctors set him on an IV drip and left him alone, afraid to disrupt what they saw as nothing short of a modern miracle.

Tournament Medical determined that the concussive force of the shots, coupled with the trauma of his head striking the ground, had temporarily damaged the optic nerves behind both eyes. They had settled back into place in the ensuing week and were beginning to heal. The migraines, however, would remain intense for some time, and might resurface intermittently for the rest of his life. There was no record of any player taking three diode hits to the head from as closely as Tristan had. His case was the worst head trauma of the Tournament, and they would watch it carefully. Tristan imagined his migraines as a scaly monster lying in wait in the cold, dark depths of his brain, muddying its waters with oily effluence while waiting to surface.

Shortly after the incident itself, and well before Team Silver's convalescence, Team Black and their administration were fined 50,000 Euros for damages to the club, over one and a half million Euros for medical damages to individuals outside of the organization, and an even half of a million Euros for what the collective administration deemed "severe and endangering offensive tactics."

For administrative reasons, and for secrecy's sake, the fine needed to be hand-delivered. Allen Lockton was dispatched to courier.

CHAPTER TWENTY-THREE

SARAH BLAMED THE WEATHER. November is the beginning of the rainy season in San Diego, and were she to go out she would have to wear a coat, or at least a sweatshirt, and Sarah hated coats and sweatshirts because she thought they made her look frumpy. And what was the point of going out to the bars all covered up? Her friends bought the weather excuse for a little while, but it never rains forever, even in November on the west coast.

The truth was Sarah just didn't feel like doing anything. This was as much of a surprise to her as it was to her friends. When she did allow herself to be dragged to the bars at night, she wasn't her usual self either. Where once she would have moved about from table to table, chatting with people here and there and forgetting to sign out her various tabs, now she would sit quietly in a corner and check her phone or sip slowly on the tiny straw of her gin and tonic, waiting patiently for her friends to finish up whatever they were doing.

When Sarah became the one to remind others to close out their tabs, her roommates knew something was wrong.

"I can't believe you haven't told either of us," Annie said one night at a loud karaoke bar. Both Annie and Jessica had sequestered Sarah in a corner, refusing to let her up until she talked.

"Who is he, Sarah?" Jessica asked.

"Who is who?" replied Sarah, playing intently with her straw.

"We see how you look around each place just as you get in and then go sit in a corner and pout all night. Who is he?"

Jessica leaned in conspiratorially, "That bartender? The one with the sideburns? He only works on Tuesdays and Thursdays."

"No. Not him."

"Aha! But it is a boy!"

"No. I mean I'm not sure. I don't even know him. So it's weird that I think about him like this." Sarah bunched her sandy blond hair up into a controlled mess behind her head as she spoke. It didn't matter how it looked anymore. He wasn't here.

"Aww, it's love!" Annie squeaked, hands together and blinking up to the ceiling.

"No. I'd just like to see him again. It's been a while."

"How long? Did you sleep with him? What's his name?"

"Nothing like that. I've just seen him a few times, around campus."

"*His name! His name!*"

"John. John Northern."

"John Northern? Sounds like a porn star!"

Both roommates cackled, lit up by the idea of Sarah Walcott, the Grande Dame of their flat, smitten with serious feelings for anyone. Sarah rolled her eyes. Playing the sober one was new.

She didn't much like it. Usually she did the drunken cackling.

"What year is he?" asked Jessica, steadying herself.

"You do of course realize that it is our duty to help you in every way we can. It's a roommate code," said Annie.

"I don't think he goes to school," Sarah said.

This threw the girls, who arched their eyebrows and took a few sips in thought. It certainly wasn't uncommon to date outside of the school. San Diego was huge, after all, but neither of them had ever done it.

"Is he older? Like a rich older guy?"

"No. He looks mid-twenties," Sarah said, flashing back to when they had met off of Gillman that night in October, when he had seemed like he was expecting her.

I believe I was told to stay away from you, he'd said.

Did she like this guy? *Really* like him? It had been a long time since she'd had a crush on anyone, ever.

"And anyway, it's probably nothing. Like I said, I haven't seen him in weeks," she added.

"Sarah, you dress to kill then sit in a corner and put on a sweatshirt when you see he's not here. Look—somebody bought you a drink and you haven't even touched it. It's clearly not *nothing.*"

And they were right. Sarah knew it when she asked her father about him at their monthly meal. Her mom seemed surprised. Her dad had stopped eating altogether. Sarah had never voluntarily brought up a boy as the topic of conversation in the past. It led to uncomfortable questions.

Sarah loved her parents, but they were...her parents. It disconcerted her that they were getting older, her father in particular. He would go through periods in which he looked terrible. In the interims between dinners, time seemed to physically beat upon him. His normally combed and parted gray hair was sometimes frazzled, and his whole face would sag just a bit. He was beginning to hunch too, and at his age once you started to hunch you never went back to straight again. Both of her parents were becoming frail, just like her grandparents before them, and this terrified Sarah. She was increasingly aware that they were going to die one day. It could come at any time and she would be left alone.

And then she thought again of John Northern.

She wondered if he had aging parents or dying grandparents who kept trying to give him old lamps and strange china. She couldn't picture them. Here was a man that breathed life, a man who seemed to walk above it all. In her mind he owed nobody anything and was prone to nothing. He was everything that her family was not. At times her father seemed a flickering and guttering candle. John Northern was a bed of coal, ready to flare at the slightest breath of wind. That her father had told her to stay away from him only served to show how different the two of them were.

So she would keep looking for him. He'd said he had to go away for a time. In typically alluring fashion, he hadn't offered a hint of where he was going. But he had said he'd be back.

So Sarah sipped her gin and tonic and waited.

CHAPTER TWENTY-FOUR

L OST WITHIN THE CROWDED outskirts of Mexico City there was a dusty public park, still unnamed, that rested in the center of the Santa Anna housing development. It was a simple, square block of land, mostly dirt, but flecked here and there by scrub bushes and floundering young trees. It was newly renovated and still recovering from the crushing weight of bulldozers and backhoes. It lay in an area that a onetime mayor of the city had set aside as part of a "greening" campaign. The idea was to spare any new developments the same fate as many others in the inner city. There the housing was stacked and squeezed, additional units of stained concrete tacked on to already precariously overpopulated zones. The campaign was ill fated and underfunded, as were most developed by the local government, but in the Santa Anna development there was at least still some room to breathe.

The Vega family had always wanted to move from their cramped, inner city flat out to a place with more space, a place to accommodate a growing family. Miguel Vega, Diego's older brother and business partner in Vega lawn services, was particularly adamant about this. He was claustrophobic and not fond of the city in the first place. Their first child, a small and frail boy named after his father, was prone to lung infections, and Miguel blamed the city air. When his wife Maria became pregnant with their second child he insisted that they move out to where the air was clearer and the water better. It would be good for Miguel Jr., he said, and nothing would interfere with the health of his wife and the growth of his child still in the womb.

And so the Vega family moved. With the business as collateral, Miguel secured a modest home loan. This, paired with a small but healthy savings, was enough for a down payment on a small ranch style house of four rooms, with two bathrooms and a porch. For Miguel and Maria Vega it was a palace. They had a room of their own, one for Diego, and even a spare room that they agreed to rent to Luis, at a family discount of course. As soon as Diego saw the house he immediately went out and bought a rocking chair for the porch. He declared that he wouldn't even need the room, and if anyone wanted him they need look no further than his chair.

The Vega brothers and their family had lived in Santa Anna for almost two years now, in which Maria gave birth to a baby girl, now just over a year old. The constitution of Miguel Jr. was also improved, and although Miguel was convinced it was due to the new surroundings, Maria secretly thought that he had just grown out of whatever childhood malady was ailing him. He was now a rambunctious seven years old, and he knew the nooks and crannies of their neighborhood like the back of his often dirty and occasionally scraped hands. He had his uncle's coarse hair and ten-gallon smile, and his father's narrow face and sharp nose. He was also tall for his age, like his father. Miguel was fond of telling him how he would easily overlook his uncle Diego by the time he was a teenager.

On this day, Miguel Jr. was going out to the park of which his father was so proud, the park where several young children met almost every night to carouse, especially now that the temperature had moderated. He opened the whitewashed front door of the Vega household and was about to bound down the cinder block steps when he froze, his hand on the screen. There were two white people just down the street, standing together and looking about at the houses as if they were lost. One was on a phone, the type of phone his papa and uncle Diego had, that you could take anywhere. If they were lost, he could help. He knew everything about the park, even where his neighbor Martin had buried a shiny metal square that said *BOBCAT* on it and had a picture of a tiger. Martin had made him promise not to look while he buried it, but he had looked anyway.

Then, as Miguel Jr. watched, a big black man came out of a car nearby and stood next to the other two. The man was very black. Blacker than he was. Blacker than Uncle Diego even. He looked from the black man to the other two, torn as to what to do. The nice looking man on the phone was pointing at a house nearby and talking at the same time. The man shook his head and seemed sad, or mad. Maybe both. What if they were neighbors? They sure didn't look like neighbors, but mama had told him to always help neighbors. Maybe he could just go out and call at them. See if they were okay. Maybe it was their *BOBCAT* treasure Martin had found.

Then the man on the phone looked directly at Miguel Jr. and stopped talking. Maybe he smiled, but Miguel Jr. was suddenly shy and so he jumped back inside and slammed the door shut and called for his mama before he could see for sure.

"MAMA! There are people outside!"

Maria was in her bedroom wiping down the shutters, amazed by the dust's persistence as she moved about the fixtures, maneuvering her full figure in between the light stand and the window. The door to the master bedroom was never open, the windows were always closed, and still the dust came. But she'd take the dust of the Santa Anna developments over the grime of inner Mexico City any day.

"MAMA!" Miguel Jr. called again.

Maria shook her head and pushed back her long black hair, repositioning a clip here and there. What did that boy want now?

"I'm coming, I'm coming," she said. She gave the window bordering one last wipe and went to see her son.

"There," Miguel Jr. said, pointing out of one of the windows. Maria peered out. She saw two white people, a man and woman, casually walking up to the house. The man was dressed in clean slacks and slightly smudged collared shirt. The woman had a nice skirt and a top just a bit too revealing for Maria's tastes. Both wore exasperated smiles, as if they had been running around the whole city looking for something and finally found it. The man was even quite handsome, if you liked gringos. The woman could be pretty, but her smile harbored a smirk and she looked a tad constipated. They were probably just tourists, a young globetrotting couple, and they were most likely looking for a main road to town. Maria saw no wedding ring on the woman, but the man was walking with his hands clasped loosely behind his back, as if he was on a country stroll, so perhaps he had a ring. She watched as they came to the door. The man rapped lightly three times and then stepped back a few paces and waited, rocking back and forth on his heels.

Maria looked down at Miguel Jr., who shrugged and stepped behind her, grabbing on to her leg. Maria slid the door catch in place and opened the door just a crack.

"Yes?"

The man leaned to his left to see her through the crack and flashed a fetching smile. He cleared his throat and brought a hand from behind his back. He carried in it a small Spanish phrase booklet, in which he had written something down and translated it. He held it in front of him like a caroler and began to read, his accent broken and atrociously Anglo.

"Hello ma'am. My name is Alex. This next-to-me woman is Christina. We work with your brother from husband. His name is Diego."

At that point Auldborne stopped and looked up at her with eyebrows raised, as if to ask whether or not she could understand him. She nodded vigorously. *They're police,* she thought. *Oh God. Something's happened to him. They wouldn't send white people unless something has happened to Diego.*

Auldborne continued:

"There has been a problem," he said.

Maria sucked in a breath and put her hand to her mouth. She looked down at Miguel Jr. *"Go out back and get your father,"* she whispered. He ran out the back door calling for his dad, and Auldborne paused upon hearing him tramp away. Stoke glanced at him before turning back to watch Maria.

"Diego has been very hurt. He is in hospital," Auldborne said, still reading.

"Was he trying to fix the mower? I told him never fix the mower himself!" Maria said, her voice frantic. Auldborne cocked his head and frowned. He looked down to the sheet once more.

"May we come in?" he read, then promptly snapped the book closed and held it behind his back once more as he watched Maria.

Maria looked around herself and the house, then waited for Miguel to come in from the back. She heard him clomping through the kitchen in his garden work boots. He rounded the corner, his face paling.

"What is it?"

"They say something has happened to Diego! They're Americans, maybe. Maybe police or lawyers."

Miguel looked through the crack at the two people standing calmly on his porch. He sized them both up briefly and nodded. She undid the latch and slowly opened the door.

"Please, please, come in. Tell me what has happened."

Auldborne took three steps over the threshold before he drew his other hand from behind his back, and in it he carried a dull gray nine-millimeter handgun. With the same flat expression he wore in reading his Spanish he leveled the gun at Miguel, but he watched Maria, waiting for a reaction. Christina Stoke stepped in the house after him and swiftly turned and closed the door. She then took her own small snub-nosed revolver from a holster on her inner thigh.

Maria had her back turned to the intruders and was readying a place for her guests to sit in the living room, so it was Miguel who saw what was happening first. His eyes grew wide and his mouth worked about but no words came out.

"Eaaaasy Miguel," Auldborne said.

Maria turned around to speak to the two and, upon seeing the guns, immediately screamed bloody murder. She yelled for Miguel Jr., who then started screaming, which only fueled her hysterics so that she started throwing things in their direction thinking they were hurting her child. Auldborne deflected a knitted sham and two sofa pillows before Stoke stepped up and grabbed the boy and held a gun to his head.

"Hey!" she screamed. "Hey bitch! Stop it! Shut up or I'll shoot the boy!"

She jangled the revolver around by his temple to emphasize her point. Maria went from screams to sobs, which were notably quieter. She reached out for her son, but Miguel held her back and looked up at Auldborne, his eyes big pleading pools of water. Already the smallest child had betrayed herself in the back room.

"Please. Please. Please. No, no shoot," Miguel said, his already broken English faltering further in his dry mouth. "Take," he said, pointing around the small living room.

Auldborne sighed in annoyance, dropped his phrase book on the coffee table with a bang, and began picking stray bits of lint off of his front with his free hand. He pushed the doily patterned curtains back from the nearest window and looked out. The boy was whimpering and a baby in the back was screaming, but things sounded natural, at least. With any luck, nobody would think anything amiss.

After a moment Draden Tate entered through the back door, tracking bits of garden mud through the kitchen. He caught Auldborne's eye and shook his head. "Nobody comin'."

"Keep watch," Auldborne instructed. Tate nodded as he receded back out of the room. "And shut that baby up."

For a horrendous moment in which both parents could only watch, the hulking man made his way to the back room in which their daughter wailed. Maria began to scrabble forward out of her husband's grip again. Miguel started to move, but was stilled by a visible increase of pressure upon his son's temple.

Without pausing, Tate simply shoved the door to the

child's room shut and continued his way out the back. The wailing was still evident, but muted. Both parents sagged. Auldborne shrugged.

"Now then," Auldborne said, taking a deep, cleansing breath. "All of that nastiness is done with." He smiled at the family each in turn, but none would meet his eye.

"The idea is *not* to shoot any of you. That's the idea, anyway. Do help us out."

"They can't understand you, Alex," Christina said, the cold barrel of her gun pulsing along with the boy's left temple.

"I know that. But I feel I should say it anyway. Pretenses must be made."

"You see," he continued, turning back to the family, "I wasn't entirely lying back then. This *is* about Diego."

At the mention of his brother's name Miguel's eyes gave a flash of recognition.

"Nothing has happened to him *as of yet*," said Auldborne, enunciating with his hands, "But we're hoping to change all of that, naturally. So let's all just sit tight for a bit, shall we?"

—

As his house was being invaded and his family held at gunpoint, Diego Vega and his team were resting momentarily on the Mazatlan coastline, many miles away. They were road weary and, although she would never admit it, at least one of their numbers was ashamed of running.

"You of all people should understand the idea of misdirection," Diego had said. *"The power of the bait. They chase us, but we want it!*

We are in control."

Lilia Alvarez didn't buy it. What they were doing still felt cowardly. *"Well when does it stop being 'misdirection' and become 'running?"* she asked Diego.

"They must be tired," Felix said as he sat looking out upon the foamy crash of the waves on the trash strewn beach. This stretch of the coastline wasn't privately owned and tended to accumulate debris. He followed a faded detergent bottle with his quiet eyes as it tumbled about the concrete breakers, alternately sucked under and spit out.

"This is the best way to deal with hotheaded teams. Let them work themselves into a fit and then hit them when they're confused and clean up the mess," Felix said.

Lilia shook her head and stood up, her hands on her slender hips. She wore pants of a smooth, stretchy fabric that clenched around her thighs and fluttered in the wind at her ankles. Felix crossed his arms in a manner that made him look like an old man on a stoop, pondering. Even his speech was low and calm. But his iron gaze hinted at the true rapid fire synapse he possessed, that he could take in an entire scene at a glance and could place objects and people perfectly after a moment's look. His peripheral vision was as strong as his direct vision, a rare talent and an invaluable tool for a sweeper.

"Of course you would say that," Lilia said. *"That is what you do. You sweep. But me? I strike. I create the mess that you clean up."*

"And I lead," Diego said, quieting the other two just as Ortiz was about to speak. Lilia sat back down and slid over to Diego's side, where she put her arm around his shoulder.

"You do. And we follow. I just get worried. Grey makes me nervous. I'm not so sure Alex Auldborne is the type of person to 'beat

himself.' He likes to beat others. And he is very good at it. "

Just as these words fell from Lilia's lips, Diego's phone rang. White's administration rarely called their team, preferring instead to let them work as they would, so the ring had a distinct weight of foreboding once Diego saw who was calling.

"What news?" he asked.

"Something happened," said the other line, a woman, her Spanish laced with poorly veiled panic.

"Where are they?" he asked, straightening in his seat.

"They've left a very deliberate electronic signature in eight separate spots in Mexico City in the past forty-five minutes," said the woman.

Diego stood.

"They're all leading in one direction."

"No."

"Yes. Santa Anna. The last hit was just four miles southwest."

"Call Tournament Security, get someone to intervene," he instructed, his breathing short and rapid as he looked from Lilia to Ortiz. *"This is a blatant violation—"*

"We called! But our people in the Federales *are too far out! A day away, at least!"*

"I've got to get to Mexico City," he said, his voice suddenly cold and flat.

"I've got three seats on the next flight out from Buelna Airport. You've got forty-five minutes until takeoff."

He hung up and looked at his team, already gathering their things. His eyes were wide and his face long and down-turned. He looked a good ten years older than his age and his voice was distant as he spoke, his mind trying to wrap itself around the type of team that would openly involve a man's family in a private war.

"Change of plans," he said, sweeping up his bag and shouldering it in one move. *"We go to Mexico City."*

CHAPTER TWENTY-FIVE

THE IRISH HAD FILED a Tournament-wide flight plan and made it known to the Italian administration, effectively issuing a challenge to meet.

"Can you believe this? Those Irish bastards think they can tell us where *our fight is gonna be!"* spat Ignazio Andizi, his wristlets jangling as he paced back and forth, mildly outraged.

"Portugal," Tessa said calmly. She was used to Andizi's bravado.

"Portugal," echoed Andizi, *"They say it's half way. Who the hell do they think they are? Am I supposed to be impressed by their geography? That they can pick something halfway in between our two countries? They assume we'll just meet up like backyard bullies, like—"* Andizi momentarily lost his train of thought. *"I say we go right over to their drunken country and smash their pale asses right into the blarney stone—*

"—I'll decide what we do, Ignazio," Tessa said.

Andizzi paused, shrugged, and flopped on a nearby couch. He turned to look out of the apartment window at the evening rush of Rome, his legs up and crossed on a nearby chair. He never wore socks, the better to expose his right ankle, across which was inked the Team Gold insignia shared by all three members. It resembled a decorative shin guard, but sharper and more angular, running from the top of the right foot, where it spanned ankle to ankle, and shooting up to a point around mid-shin. It was made of curling and sweeping vine shapes like those found tooled on the barrel of an old western gun, and from a distance it looked like a Spartan's armored shin guard. Andizzi liked to show it off at every possible opportunity, but he didn't like people to know that he was showing it off, so he would often wear slacks and prop his right foot up exposing just a bit of it.

"I appreciate your confidence, Ignazio—" said Tessa.

"You say confident, I say loud…" said Lorenzo Aldobrandi, their hardened sweeper, smiling widely across his half-moon face as he lay prone upon the floor. He looked as if he might be sleeping in the late fall sun, his back propped up against the wall of his captain's apartment, his arm slung lazily over his eyes. His teammates knew better. Aldobrandi often rested, but rarely slept.

"I'm just glad I don't have to deal with him," he said.

Andizzi smiled and plucked at his cuff, admiring the insignia. To him it was a crown wrapped around his leg, a symbol of his mighty country's past, once the jewel of the world. He intended to restore that glory. In his mind the Italians were the best at everything: They wore the best clothes, drank the best wine, and ate the best food. They drove the best cars, and brewed the best coffee. Their language was the most beautiful, most expressive in the world. It was the well from which a myriad of other, inferior dialects had sprung. Why shouldn't they rule the world again? And why shouldn't Gold be the one to usher in that new era?

In truth, Gold was the youngest of the eight Tournament teams, and the other seven never let the Italians forget it. The irony of the newest Tournament team being representative of one of the oldest cultures on earth, headquartered in one of

the world's oldest cities, didn't escape them. Andizzi thought it
fitting. He loved it when others called them a group of rookies.
He almost flushed at the thought of the pleasure he would derive
in standing over one of the women of Ireland's team, his knee in
her chest, whispering *How do you like this rookie now?* into her ear
as he softly ran his gun up the small hairs of her stomach, stopped
at the belly button, and pulled the trigger. He'd never seen Team
Green in person, but he'd studied them. He wanted to do it to the
sweeper. The feisty one. Kayla MacQuillan.

But before that, there was the goddamn striker. Ian Finn.
His matchup. He would have to get rid of him first. And from
what Andizzi had heard, the man was nothing to spit at. Not
while he stood, anyway. When he was on the ground Andizzi
would do all the spitting he wanted.

Too wired to sit, Andizzi stood once more and moved
to the kitchen table where his guns lay. He was the only member
of the Tournament who fought with two guns at all times. He
knew the young nerd boy that fought for Japan had two guns on
him, but he fired one after the other. Ignazio Andizzi used both
together. He was aware that he sacrificed some accuracy in firing
one handed, but he also believed that with twice the bullets, accuracy didn't much matter. His two 9mm handguns gleamed in
the sun, both engraved with the same pattern found on all of their
right shins. One was made of gold chromed steel, the other of silver chromed steel. Both had mother of pearl inlays on the handles.
They were his children.

He picked up one and then the other, analyzing each
with a surgeon's eye and slowly dismantling each for inspection.
Before his team moved out, he would place them both in a modified holster at his lower-back, hammer to hammer, handles out so
that they formed a T.

Lorenzo watched the striker from under the crook of his

elbow. Andizzi took an enormous pleasure from this ritual cleaning. He wore a telltale, eager smirk. Lorenzo frowned. If Andizzi wasn't careful, he might just strut and preen himself straight into a coma.

"You need to be shooting before you even see Ian Finn. If we run into him without our guns out, it'll already be too late," Lorenzo said. *"He's far too fast."*

Andizzi nodded slowly as he popped a clip into his golden gun. He allowed few people to tell him what he *needed* to do, but his soft-spoken sweeper was one of them.

"We'll have to surprise him," Andizzi said.

Tessa ran sharp nails through her chestnut brown hair while she watched Andizzi clean.

"Surprise isn't necessary. We just have to ensure that he doesn't shoot until we're ready," she said. *"He shoots on our terms. When we want. We can't have him appearing out of nowhere with that left hand of his."*

"Pyper Hurley, the captain, she knows how to use him. She's very good at that. If we go to Portugal, they'll be on us as soon as we get off the plane," Lorenzo said.

"Then we'll have to catch them before that," Tessa said.

"Where? Ireland?"

"No. On the way," Tessa said.

Andizzi paused his cleaning and furrowed his dark brow.

"It's a direct flight, Tessa. No layovers," Lorenzo said.

"Then we catch them in transit," Tessa said simply.

"You mean…like in the air?" Andizzi asked.

"On the airplane," Tessa said, nodding. *"That miracle arm of his won't be of much use to him in the cabin of a jet, thousands of kilometers high, will it?"*

"But neither will ours, nobody'll shoot," Andizzi said.

"All I ask is for a level playing field. We'll de-plane ahead of them. Pick them off as they disembark. Every angle will be ours. If the madmen of Black can destroy a dance club with impunity, then we can certainly make a bit of a stir on a runway. We'll corner them is all. Push them back until we're clear of the airplane, then pick them off as they are forced to disembark."

She pursed her lips, and then blew a kiss out of the window.

"Then it's farewell to the fools of the emerald isle," she said, smiling.

CHAPTER TWENTY-SIX

S HINJUKU STATION PROVIDES ACCESS to all manner of rail
transportation, public and private, as well as a myriad of bus
lines. Seven island platforms serve fourteen JR line tracks. People
from all over the country converge through one of the stations
more than two hundred entrances, at least three million people on
any given day, making it the busiest train station on earth.

At noon, on the last day of November, it was where Team
Blue disembarked.

It was a drizzly day in Tokyo—not enough to stop people
from venturing about in the city, but enough to keep them to
the eves and awnings when possible. It was also the midday lunch
rush. The kiosk level of Shinjuku station, where the main exits are,
looked like an anthill in turmoil. People walked every which way,
dashing when they had to, taking advantage of open lanes. They
moved around the shops and stalls with a practiced efficiency,
brushing by people and goods with millimeters to spare. Japanese
businessmen dressed in ties of every color but suits of only two:
blue and black. The women wore skirts and blouses, business drab.
Students from Tokyo's many metropolitan high schools shuffled
about in groups dressed in variations of a single style of uniform:
pleated skirt and a button up shirt for girls, slack and ties for the
boys, and leather loafers for both. A handful of kids did what they
could to distinguish themselves, using temporary hair dyes of
every color of the rainbow often coupled with clip-on extensions

and odd piercings, but only during after-school hours. Otherwise they settled for a hip disheveled look by hiking up skirts and rolling up jacket sleeves.

Typically, these commuters wore a constant look of grim determination. It was a battle of sorts just to move about in Tokyo. Their fixed gazes were rarely diverted, their pace rarely shaken, but on that day a good many were distracted by the three Americans walking through their station.

In an area accustomed to tourists, these three stood out nonetheless. For one, they walked with a broad shouldered gate that was all the more confident for its slow pace. They formed a triangle wide enough to walk in between, yet nobody did. Their very presence was a moving wall through which none would enter. They wore a sort of uniform as well: weathered canvas jackets of deep blue, modified with extra zippers at the sleeves and shoulders.

In the lead point was Johnnie Northern; he carried a small duffel bag with his left hand and popped the knuckles of his right with his thumb. He was barely smiling and his blue eyes, a rarity in that area of the world, were shielded by yellow-lensed sunglasses. Behind and to his left walked Max Haulden, swinging his head from side to side as if mechanized. Occasionally, he would absently tap on the left side of his chest like he had an involuntary tic. Someone who didn't know him might say he looked nervous, his brow slightly ridged, or even sad on account of his soft brown eyes just shy of fully open. But that was how Max always looked, and it was best not to assume with a man like him.

To Northern's right walked Nikkie Hix. She was cute and blonde in all of the ways many of the Japanese girls wished that they were, but with a heavier presence. She seemed focused on something just beyond the view of everyone else; as a sweeper she had the habit of seeing two steps ahead. Anticipation was her game.

"Jesus, John. They could be any one of these people," said Max as he panned the suited, black-haired men and women. It was hard for him to pinpoint the age of many of them to within a decade. And everyone looked at them suspiciously. Any one of them could pull a gun at any second. Max tapped his own in his jacket again as a young Japanese man eyed him suspiciously before moving on.

"We'll know them when we see them," said Northern. "It's what we do."

"Let's just get to the hotel," said Hix, her voice the sort of calm one might use in the cave of a hibernating bear. "That's a good base of operations. I'll be able to stake out perimeters."

"They must know we're here," said Max.

"They do, no doubt," Northern said, "but they can't know where we are. This city is too big. Too saturated with people. We have some time."

As they exited the station they came upon a street crossing. There they waited alongside a thousand others for the light to change so they could move to the taxi rank on the west side. They split themselves apart, each moving to an area in which other foreigners, mostly tourists, also waited to cross. Max was suddenly reminded of how he used to tuck away in the cubbies of his high school library whenever classes of students ventured near. He would stay completely still, sometimes even shallow his breathing to hide in plain sight. No doubt they saw him, but he liked to think it helped make him invisible. He did that now, in Tokyo, surrounded by the masses, and he couldn't help thinking that they, too, were being seen by the very people they sought to avoid. He looked at Northern, carrying himself like a man born in the city, and couldn't help but wonder if his confidence wasn't part ignorance. The three of them were the up-thrust nails here, just waiting for the hammer.

When they finally reached their cab Northern flashed a small grin.

"See? Nothing to it," he said, ushering them both in and even gazing about one last time, as if to bait anyone who might be looking; to prove that they were, in fact, never in danger, not with him at the helm. He sat himself in the passenger's seat and gave the white gloved cabbie a slip of paper with directions to the Hotel New Otani. Max let out a heavy breath as the cabbie pulled a lever to close the door behind him and the trio set off down the streets of Tokyo.

Northern's oozing calm was grating upon Max by the time they pushed through the wide double doors of the New Otani into its lush, marble floored atrium. The lulling sound of a small waterfall came from the hotel's large interior gardens and mixed with the soft taps of patent leather shoes on stone as attendants bustled about. Two uniformed doormen in bucket hats bowed in welcome.

—

Their room was on the fourth floor, as low to the ground as they could manage and in the least crowded wing, as requested. Their room was number 426, an elaborately appointed suite with two king beds and one rollout, three rooms all told, not including the bathroom. But they never even went into it. Northern set the duffle bag down in front of 426 then moved over to 427 across the hall and knocked gently. After a moment he nodded at Max, who unzipped the bag and took out a small electronic device the size of a cellphone. He plugged one end of a single pronged cord into its top and the other into a small receiver at the base of the electronic lock on the door. He ran a scanning program and waited. The two men watched for any sign from Hix as she leaned casually against the wall back by the elevators on guard. After a moment the device beeped.

"The key card," he said. Northern took it out of its sleeve and handed it to his striker.

"It'll erase the original unlock code." He slipped the card into a thin opening on the side of the device.

"That's fine," said Northern.

The device whirred and snapped like a camera taking a picture, then spit the card back out. Max took it, examined it briefly, and slid it into the lock on the door. The LED light on the lockbox went green. He pushed open the door. Northern called softly for Hix and all three went in to the new room.

"I know we're exhausted but we have to post watch. We'll go two up, one down, to help each other combat the jetlag," Northern said, glancing about the room and pushing open the curtains at the far window.

"I'll stay up first," Hix said, plopping down in the desk chair by the far wall. "I slept most of the flight."

"Me too," Max said quickly. "I'll stay up."

Northern glanced up at his striker, vaguely surprised. "Well I didn't mean to make both of you stay up."

"I can't sleep right now anyway," Max said hastily, "I'm… unsettled. By the flight and all."

Northern shrugged. "Fine by me." He flopped out on

one of the two beds. "Wake me in two hours."

Northern was asleep almost instantly, his breath slowing to a soft, rhythmic pull and hiss. Max and Nikkie spoke in low tones about nothing in particular, remarking about the oddness of the culture in which they were steeped, exemplified by the intricate and toilet in the bathroom. They spoke of the qualms of air travel and trials of jetlag. It wasn't long until they returned, once again, to profiling the team they faced, continuing a conversation that had been on and off ever since they got their draw.

"His firing report proves it," Max said, speaking of Amon Jinbo, the Red striker. "He's trigger happy. Obsessed with firepower. He shoots that huge gun and it jars his arms, throws him off. Every time he hits too high. He's been this way for years, ever since we first met them. You just can't make yourself a moving target for him. That's when he gets you. He may be just a kid, but he's excellent at leading a target."

Hix had pulled her legs to her chest and was resting her chin on her knees. As she listened to Max she occasionally nodded off, succumbing to the sandbag weight of sleep deprivation. Although it was five in the afternoon in Tokyo, it was midnight in San Diego. At first Max would wake her as soon as she started to slip, prompting her with questions or tapping her shoulder. He didn't feel tired, but it was always best to have two people up on watch to look out for each other. After the third time that she lowered her head in small hitch steps against her will, he just watched her as she slept. He especially liked her neck, brushed lightly here and there by her sandy blonde hair. It was a golden-brown neck, and it looked soft, and dipped and cupped beautifully. He wondered what it might be like to touch it, perhaps drink water from it in the shower like a tiny teacup. Her ears were tiny too, and even they looked soft. Everything about her looked soft, but Max also knew just how hard she could be. He liked her even more for that side of her, the side only he saw. He and Northern.

He watched her for perhaps thirty seconds before he tapped her shoulder again.

"Nikkie," he said softly. She slowly opened her eyes again, and then sat up abruptly. She looked at Max and smiled, her face reddened.

"Sorry. I guess I'm more tired than I thought."

"That's all right. I'd let you sleep, but…"

"No no. You're right to wake me."

"Tell me about their sweeper," he said, although he already knew everything he could know. "That might help you stay awake."

"Tenri Fuse kind of creeps me out, actually. He moves strangely. Kind of prances, even when he shoots. I dunno, it's hard to explain."

"Keep going."

"When I survey the field, it's mechanical. I go into a zone and it becomes a chess game. But him…when I imagine him sweeping, I picture him creeping about the edges of the field, watching us like a voyeur. Does that make any sense?"

"You think he's a pervert."

Nikkie laughed then quickly shut up and glanced over at Northern, who stirred briefly but slept on.

"I guess, sort of. Who knows," she said, shrugging. In the silence that followed she looked over at Northern again and rubbed her eyes to stay awake.

"Do you think he's doing the right thing?" Max whispered, watching her as she looked at Northern.

"The right thing?"

"Do you think this is smart? Coming here like this?"

She looked hard at Max for a long moment in which Max dearly wished he had never asked. What if she thought him a coward? What if she thought him insubordinate when he was just looking at things realistically?

"I can't claim to know what he's thinking all the time," she said. "I really wish I could, but I can't. I do know this. Johnnie's very good at what he does, and I'm willing to follow him anywhere he leads."

"Of course. I only wonder sometimes—"

"And it's good to wonder. And it's good to challenge him even. He appreciates that. But we're already here, Max. It's already done."

After several minutes in which Max was quiet, Nikkie spoke up once more.

"He's one of the best out there, and he's only going to get better. But we're nothing without you. We're a team. Understand?"

Max smiled and gave a very small nod.

Moments later Max heard a rustling in the hallway. Nikkie jumped up and tapped Northern. His eyes opened instantly.

"What?" he asked hoarsely. She placed one finger over his mouth. Max was already by the door listening, his gun out. The rustling became louder and then passed, fading away into silence.

Max shook his head. Nikkie let out a breath.

"You sure you want us to wake you every time?"

"Every time. Their people will have found the booking by now. They could come at any minute."

Max slumped back down in his chair, facing the door. Nikkie sat on the bed to his left.

Twenty minutes later, just when Northern was drifting off, there was another shuffling. And again ten minutes later. And again thirty minutes after that.

"If we keep this up we're going to be worse off than when we got off the plane," said Max.

"You want to go after them," Northern said, more of a statement than a question.

"At this point it might be better."

"You know as well as I do that they are near. If we go out there we lose the advantage," he said, but his voice seemed distant, as if he was trying to focus on some insubstantial, floating thing. On the bed Hix propped herself more severely against the backboard, trying to will herself into wakefulness. Max was wide eyed, but only because he was past tired and into the zone where his body was overcompensating. It was a second wind that couldn't last long and the crash would be that much harder.

They heard another shuffling. Max wearily rose and positioned himself by the door again. This time the shuffling stopped before fading. Max tensed and Nikkie crept up beside him, her own gun out.

They heard an agitated rattling nearby. Northern took his

gun from the nightstand and flicked off the safety. Suddenly their door handle was rattling, Northern raised and aimed, but signaled for his team to hold. The rattling stopped and was followed by a slew of unintelligible cursing and a fit of hiccups. Then more shuffling, a pause, and another bit of rattling one door down. More drunken slurring and hiccupping.

Northern lowered his gun and rubbed his eyes. Max shook his head.

"Unpopulated my ass," he muttered, sitting down once more.

"Stay alert," said Northern. Nikkie crept up on the bed again and sagged against the headboard, her eyes cast down.

Team Blue waited.

CHAPTER TWENTY-SEVEN

ALLEN LOCKTON'S WORK NEVER stopped. His was a job not confined to pre-Tournament activity. Lock was a full time employee, beholden to no one team, only the overarching organization itself. He often tried to identify precisely which time was the busiest for him: before, during, or after a Tournament. Inevitably, he settled on the present.

While it might be hard to identify when he was busiest, it was very easy for him to identify who always seemed, in one way or another, to make him run the most:

Eddie Mazaryk.

No team contributed more to his workload than Black, and their captain specifically. He was the one client that infallibly proved to be a pain in the ass. Back when he was running documents across Chicago for the courier service, one law firm always hired him to run correspondence to their sister office just across the Chicago River, maybe one quarter mile away as the crow flies. The problem was Lock couldn't fly, and the closest bike-worthy crossing was at Ping Tom Memorial park, almost a mile away, after which a prolonged and convoluted route finally took you to the building twenty minutes later—at best. The run had a reputation amongst couriers, who had come to call it the 'legal lashing.' Nobody ever figured out a quicker route as long as he worked there. Lock delivered for that firm over twenty times, and on the outset of every one of them he would look across the highway at his destination and scowl.

That's how he felt now, in St. Petersburg once more, looking for Eddie Mazaryk again. No other Tournament courier could ever seem to find him with any regularity, and so the job was invariably his. Back as a bike-courier, Lock had to deal with only snooty lawyers or snappy executives when he finally reached his destinations. They could talk at him if he was late, but that was about it, and that was some measure of comfort. At the tail end of this trip was a gun-toting sociopath to whom he was supposed to hand-deliver a fine statement totaling well over a million Euros.

What a pain in the ass.

Mazaryk had been angry with fines in the past. Lock recalled having to serve Black a fine last cycle for what the organization had termed "reckless endangerment." Mazaryk had been furious. In his own seething, ice-water way, he stated that he took issue with the use of the term "reckless" and flatly refused to pay the fine until the wording was changed. Six days and another round trip ticket later, the newly phrased fine was delivered by Lock and he promptly agreed to pay in full.

This time the collective administration painstakingly phrased this newest infraction, charging Black with "severe and endangering offensive tactics." While this seemed indisputable to Lock, or anyone else that had seen the Club Frieze security tapes for that night, you just never knew with Eddie Mazaryk. The man was a loose cannon.

When tracking Black, Lock found it best to first go to where he'd last found them, in this case, the small ale house in the back alley of western St. Petersburg. Because of his knack for re-membering routes and places, Lock managed to trace his way past the crumbling courtyard and back down the alley strung above with washing. He found the sideway where the little boy in the rain slicker had directed him, but there was no boy this time. In all likelihood, there would be no Mazaryk either. That would be far, far too easy.

At least the pub was open. A single, guttering flame still flickered in an old lantern above the faded sign. He pushed open the door and stepped in to the very same smoky gloom he had visited mere weeks ago. If he wasn't mistaken the same two men were playing chess at the same table. The same bartender looked up with the same complacent expectancy, and took a slow, hissing drag off of a cigarette made from the same cloyingly sweet tobacco. The same man even read a paper by the back stairway. But the atmosphere wasn't as heavy, the silence not as intense, and Lock immediately knew that Team Black had gone. Nonetheless, it was worth a shot. Maybe they left something behind, some clue.

"I don't suppose any of you speak any English," Lock snipped, looking about the room. No one spoke. No one even moved. It was as if the very sound of his voice had hardened to stone and fallen flat to the floor.

"Naturally," he sighed, smoothing his track pants with his hands. Determined to try nonetheless he moved over to the bartender, who watched him blankly.

"I'm looking for Eddie Mazaryk. You know him? Pale guy? Long hair? Kind of looks like a girl?"

The bartender didn't even blink.

"He was here, in that room," Lock said, pointing upward.

The bartender pointed at one of two cask ale pull draughts at his side.

"No, I don't drink."

The bartender pointed again. Lock sighed.

"You people know who he is. I know you at least understand his name."

Nothing. The rustling of a newspaper and the slide-click of a chess piece on an old wooden table.

"Fine. Since you all seem to be so occupied, I'll just take a look around upstairs. Okay?"

Lock moved slowly to the rod-iron spiral staircase at the back of the bar. Nobody challenged him. He placed one foot on the first step and nobody spoke. The bartender watched him as he might watch a squirrel playing in the yard.

Lock went up the stairs.

The room above the bar in which he had last found Black was the same as before, albeit empty and cold, having no fire in the hearth. Lock could see his own breath. One of the small windows was open and two pigeons perched on the overhang just outside of it, sleeping with their heads tucked under their wings. An empty sunlight filtered into the room around their silhouettes.

"Damn," he muttered.

He walked slowly about the room. His steps kicked up flurries of dust motes from the dark red carpet undertow. He saw nothing. The room was not only empty; it seemed hollow. The soft cooing of the sleeping birds echoed about him as he sat heavily in the empty wingback chair and stared at the cold hearth. He swung his leg up to his knee, in a sad impression of Eddie Mazaryk as he had been when Lock first saw him there, and in doing so he kicked a small mesh trashcan under the nightstand to his left. It wobbled for a moment and then fell over, dislodging a single, crumpled piece of paper. Lock looked at it for a moment, and then reached over and picked it up.

It was a small, lined slip of notebook paper on which something had been written in Russian. Lock didn't understand a word of Russian, but he scanned the slip anyway and found one line that had been repeated several times in what looked to be English: *Vorkuta—Adrytski*

Still sitting, he powered up his mobile and opened a browser. He queried the first word and was rewarded with coordinates and an overhead satellite feed of an area in northern Siberia. Apparently, Vorkuta was a struggling coal town made infamous by a forced labor camp once stationed there as part of the Gulag system. Adrytski was an even smaller settlement just to the east of Vorkuta.

Charming, thought Lock.

They were due northeast of him. Instinctively he caught his bearings and found the north-easternmost facing side of the room. He looked up and saw that it was the one in which the window stood open and the pigeons slept. Naturally. It had been left open deliberately. The slip of paper had probably been strategically placed as well.

Lock folded the paper and stored it in his pack. He would try to get a full translation of the document but he sensed that it would prove to be useless beyond the one location. No matter. Lock could find them.

He stood and walked to the window, just above his eye level, taking care not to spook the birds. From where he stood he saw only gray skies. The red carpeting just under the window was darker than elsewhere, damp. He looked up and blinked as a smattering of wet snowflakes hit his eyes. In the time he had taken to figure this all out, it had begun to snow.

The town of Vorkuta was serviceable by a small airport just south
of the city. Lock took off that day from St. Petersburg in the
snow and landed half of a day later in even worse snow. Soon the
snow-covered roads of the town converged into a single choppy,
rutted track that went east towards the outlying Adrytski settlement. Harsh, unchecked winds and the inclement weather of the
Arctic Circle prevented anything more substantial than sickly
brush and small trees to live in the area. The ground was frozen
year round and covered with at least a foot of snow in the late
fall and winter months. Nonetheless it was dotted here and there
with small shacks, several miles apart. Some were abandoned huts,
others were government operated filling and service stations for
the army vehicles that crossed the tundra on their way east. Still
fewer of them were small houses and way-stations for those un-
lucky civilian travelers that came this way, one of whom was Allen
Lockton.

Lock had procured a stripped dune buggy for the trip
that he had located at a dealership not far from the airport that
sold equipment for trans-Siberian crossings. The buggy was drafty
and rusted, noisy as a freight-train, and sucked gas like a thirsty
camel drinks water, but it was durable and the best he could get
on short notice. He had been ripped off, having the discernible
disadvantage of not understanding anything anyone said, but as
usual time was short while money was plentiful. That was the
nature of the Tournament.

Trying to make up for lost time in getting to the fields,
and annoyed at being run about like a dog, Lock flew over the
narrow, snow packed roadway. He treated its two tire ruts as if
they were train tracks, trusting them to keep him on the right
line, and for the most part they did, although Lock's teeth popped

against each other continually as the larger bumps got through the buggy's enormous shocks and shot through his body. His neck grew tired from his constant effort to keep it stabilized and his eyes grew strained from the evening snow glare. He looked a tad suspicious, speeding down the treacherous road like a diesel fueled comet, kicking up a tail of snow for a good fifteen feet behind him.

As expected, Lock had gotten nothing more of use from the slip of paper and so he was going on instinct. After all, there was only one road to Adrytski.

As each successive outbuilding came into view on the horizon he would check to see if any recent tracks led up to it. Typically, there was nothing, but if there were recent tracks Lock went on gut feeling. Many of these huts were dark and derelict. Lock felt that Mazaryk wouldn't shore up in a ramshackle building; he would want someplace quiet and peaceful to plan for his next round, somewhere out of this roaring tundra wind. He passed outbuilding after outbuilding for almost thirty miles; none of them felt right. Two of them were government filling stations but Lock blew by them in a vortex of snow, barely catching the bewildered look on the officers' faces as he went. He hoped that they either thought him far too fast to be pursued, or that the weather was far too cold and they couldn't be bothered to leave their card games and vodka. Whatever it was, Lock went on unhindered.

As the dark grew the wind lessened and Lock could see thick flakes of snow passing through the high beams of the buggy. When Lock hit the 56th kilometer marker, just as he was pondering stopping to unhook one of several gas canisters from the back to refill the tank, a brightly lit shack jumped out of the snow. He braked heavily and the rear of the buggy fish-tailed through a long skid before stopping. Lock watched the lights of the shack for several minutes. Things seemed unnaturally quiet here, the snow thick and heavy. The shack had the look.

He was here.

Lock pulled off the road towards it. As he approached the hut he saw the hulking black outline of a large man leaning against a single fencepost by the door. Lock recognized him immediately.

Lock killed the engine just outside of the sphere of light cast by the house. He stepped out, popped the collar of his snow-jacket against the wet flakes and the fitful wind, and crunched his way up to the skeletal fence. Goran Brander nodded as he approached, unsurprised at his appearance, as usual, but he didn't look well. He leaned heavily against the post, using it not as an idle perch, but more as a cane. His long face seemed less powerfully aquiline, more droopy and haggard, and he had weighty, dark bags under his eyes. Lock could just see the top of a diode wound creeping above the scarf he wore; it was very black and toxic looking in the night snow.

"Hi Lock," he croaked with a visibly painful effort.

"Brander," Lock said in greeting. All vitriol he may have mustered towards Team Black because of the chase was lost at the sight of such a powerful man so painfully injured.

"Does your captain realize the insanity of posting a look-out man in this place? And one who can't properly sound warning?"

Brander dropped his gaze and gestured for Lock to go inside, and Lock realized that Brander was ashamed. Ashamed that he had been shot. Mazaryk obviously wasn't expecting trouble out here but had ordered the weakened man to stand lookout in the freezing snow regardless, as punishment. Brander might have been out here for hours. Lock shook his head as he stepped aside and towards the small wooden house just beyond. Behind him, Brander hitched himself up a bit against the pole and watched the deep dark encroach.

The building was small, one square room of perhaps two hundred square feet, but brightly lit, and warmed by two kerosene space heaters. Rolled up bedding was stacked in one corner, and in the center of the room, under a naked light bulb, stood a large table. There was no other furniture.

Eddie Mazaryk, clothed entirely in black save for slim white boots, stood next to the table. He motioned Lock inside while speaking in low tones to Ales Radomir. Radomir was dressed impeccably in dark slacks and a button up shirt fastened all of the way to the collar. He watched Lock with a silent, disconcerting attentiveness. Neither seemed at all surprised to see him in the middle of the frozen plains of the Siberian tundra.

Lock saw that the table was entirely covered in intricately colored maps of all scales, including several topographic sheets. A quick glance and Lock saw that every habitable continent on Earth was mapped in some form within the room. On the far wall, behind the two men, was nailed a larger world map surrounded by timesheets and stuck extensively with colored pins. Lock was unsettled to see a small circle of red affixed over the city of Tokyo, no doubt representative of the impending conflict between Red and Blue. Not even Lock himself was as sure of those coordinates as these men seemed to be.

From the corner of his eye he saw Ales Radomir watching him with a trace of a grin. He shivered the last of the cold away as Eddie Mazaryk finally addressed him.

"Allen," greeted Mazaryk, his English perfect. "You found

us. Impressive, as always."

"Natasha looked for you. You remember Natasha Saslow, don't you? Your *assigned courier?*"

"I know of her."

"She didn't find you."

"No she didn't."

"You do know," Lock began, struggling to keep cynicism out of his voice, keeping in mind that he was, after all, delivering a rather hefty bill. "You do know that my quadrant's teams, the teams I'm *supposed* to be running for, are either in transit right now, or minutes away from gunfire in their own matchups?"

"I do."

Lock sighed.

"Eddie, I can't run for you anymore. I'm stretched too thin. The Tournament has an entire host of couriers."

Mazaryk smiled. "Then it would appear as though I won't have to worry about being levied any further fines," he said, flicking a hand at Ales Radomir. Ales stepped forward and for a moment Lock thought he might be frisked, or worse, but Ales stopped short of him and held out a hand. He wanted the fine sheet. Lock fished around in the breast pocket of his coat for a moment and then handed Ales a sealed envelope. Ales brought it to Mazaryk who ripped it open with the nail on his small finger, withdrew the official fine, and read it carefully. Lock held his breath.

"This all looks in order," he said quietly.

"Pardon me?"

"This is fair."

Lock exhaled a tad louder than he wished. "Fine," he said, pulling his mobile from its front pocket on his single-strap bag. "Then let's get this over with. Thumbprint here to authorize receipt of the fine."

He held out the screen. Mazaryk thumbed it and watched Lock while he waited for the beep. He looked amused.

"You're aware, then, of what happened in France?" Mazaryk asked.

"Yes."

"And?"

"And what? I'm not authorized to weigh in."

"But you don't approve."

"I'm not authorized to weigh in, Eddie."

"Hmm," Mazaryk said, as if pondering an odd puzzle piece.

The screen beeped. Lock secured it once more in his pack.

"It's unfortunate," Mazaryk said, "that those idiot Frenchmen still think they are playing a children's game. It was a hard lesson for them. Dearly bought."

Lock zipped his pack up and shouldered it, turning to go. As he stepped forward, Mazaryk placed one hand lightly on his shoulder. It was the first time Lock had ever been touched by any member of Black. It stopped him cold.

"I want you to deliver a message for me."

"From you?"

"Yes. To Northern."

"Johnnie Northern? Eddie, I'm not going to play a part in any sort of strategy—"

"And I wouldn't ask you to. I'm afraid you can't read it, nor can anyone else other than him. I'll need to see your handheld again."

"This is ridiculous—"

"It's your job!" Mazaryk snapped, sudden fury washing like a quick gale across his face.

Lock froze mid-sentence. The snow whipped at the windows and the heaters hissed loudly.

"Forgive me," Mazaryk said, as he exhaled a singular breath. "You deliver correspondence, and this is important. The handheld, please."

Lock looked at Ales, who braced himself on the table with both hands as if it was the only thing keeping him from ripping Lock apart. Lock swallowed. He didn't want to be bleeding heavily this far from help. He flipped his pack around, unzipped it, and took out the handheld again. He looked at it for a moment before surrendering it to Mazaryk.

"Thank you," Mazaryk said, as he took a flash drive from his pocket and clicked it into a port on its side. After a moment he took it out again and handed the device back to Lock.

"The message is thumbprint activated and he's going to want it immediately. Hopefully it isn't already too late."

"I swear Eddie, if this is some tracer program, or key logger…"

"Don't patronize me, Allen," Mazaryk said, his small beaded eyes reflecting glints of terrible emotion, like sunlight off roiling water. This clearly meant more to Eddie Mazaryk than the fine did. No doubt it was the reason he wanted Lock in the first place. A personalized message between teams was unheard of. Teams never communicated. Lock felt as if his trusty handheld had suddenly turned into a time bomb.

He stood his ground for half a beat longer, then turned to go.

"Immediately," Mazaryk said once more, fitting his silk brown hair behind either ear and straightening himself.

Lock trudged back out into the silent night. Brander, dusted with white, was hunched over and seemed not even to notice his passing.

CHAPTER TWENTY-EIGHT

ALEX AULDBORNE HELPED HIMSELF to a bottled water from the small refrigerator in the Vega's kitchen while Christina Stoke huddled their three captives on the couch. Her gun remained trained on Miguel Jr., its hammer locked back. Maria petted her son's hair until he was calmed and now he sat on her lap, his tear streaked face watching Auldborne with a newfound curiosity. Auldborne held the cool bottle to his forehead for a moment before cracking it open and taking a long drink. Miguel Jr. watched him through bleary eyes, his little hands palm up in his lap. Auldborne sat heavily in a faded green chair and set his burnished handgun on his leg.

"Cuál es éste?" squeaked the boy. His mother hissed at him to be quiet. Auldborne looked at him.

"What?"

The boy stared at the gun but hunched down into his mother's arms.

"Ah. You want to know what this is," Auldborne said, picking up the gun and spinning it about. The boy's eyes danced with it.

"This," Auldborne said with authority, "is called a gun. Say it with me. *Gun.*"

The boy was preemptively hushed again by his mother, who was growing increasingly terrified with this newest interaction. Miguel Sr. muttered a prayer, his head between his hands.

"Watch," Auldborne instructed.

With a snap he released a round, popping it from the side of the gun and catching it in midair. The boy gave a small smile despite himself.

"But it's a special gun. See? Do you see this?" asked Auldborne, twirling the diode around his fingers like one might flip a pen. "This isn't a real bullet! It's much better because with this I can kill the same person again and again!" He held it out to Miguel Jr. who snatched it up like a small piece of candy. Caught up in Auldborne's jovial tone, the boy even giggled. Auldborne tussled his hair and winked at his horrified mother, who grabbed it from him and tossed it away.

Auldborne thoughtfully finished his bottle of water, capped it and set it gingerly upon the television.

"I've an idea," he told the boy. He called Draden Tate back inside.

"Draden, watch the man. If he moves, shoot him until he cannot. Christina, get me the boy."

As soon as Christina moved towards Miguel Jr., Maria started screaming again. Christina flipped her revolver around and slammed it once into her left temple and she went limp. Then the boy screamed. His father moved to get up. Draden Tate quickly planted his knee into the man's sternum and shoved a gun into his nostril. So pinned, the man resorted to a throaty bellowing.

"My God," Auldborne said wearily. "Such a production."

"He might rouse da neighbors," growled Tate. "Do I beat 'ihm down?"

"No. The neighbors are of no further consequence. Hearing his brother scream will no doubt prove a useful distraction when Diego comes. Give me the boy," Auldborne said again.

Christina whipped the boy up from his mother's lap and flung him towards Auldborne, who snatched him and pinned his arms at his sides. His crying hampered his breathing. Saliva dripped from his gaping mouth and snot ran down his face. The house had turned into a cacophony.

"Shh. Shhhh. Come now, we'll be gone soon," Auldborne assured the boy. "I just want to show you one more thing."

"Diego's goin' be furious, Alex," Tate warned, his knee pinning Miguel to the couch.

"I know," Auldborne said, still speaking soothingly at the boy. "But what's the first thing you do in a battle? Get the opponent out of their right mind. Right my boy?"

Auldborne tried to walk with the boy, but something his father was saying in rapid Spanish put some fight in him, so Auldborne was forced to drag him, flailing, into the back bedroom next to the wailing baby. Miguel Jr. landed several square kicks into Auldborne's ribs and even managed to tear his shirt, popping several buttons. Auldborne dropped him with force right in front of a full length mirror by the crib. The boy bounced up and tried to run around him and back out of the bedroom door, but Auldborne yoked him about the collar just in time. This time he put the boy in a chokehold, positioning the crook of his elbow tightly over his small windpipe.

For a moment man and child looked at each other in the

mirror, the boy gasping and coughing, Auldborne's normally pale complexion pinked with the struggle and the heat. Then the boy shied away from Auldborne's coal-gray gaze as if it could turn him to stone by reflection.

"Now then. Close your eyes," said Auldborne, closing them for the boy as a coroner might. The boy snapped them back open and struggled to look at the door.

"No. No, no. Close them," he said, brushing down his face again.

The boy snapped them open.

"Listen to me boy!" Auldborne hissed, his spittle flicking the boy's ear. "I'm trying to help you! My magic bullets don't like glass! Close your goddamn eyes!"

The boy kept them closed.

Very quickly, Auldborne ducked behind the boy, brought his gun up and rested it on the boy's shoulder, and fired one shot into the mirror in front of them both.

The noise of the gun was especially horrendous to Miguel Jr. His ears immediately set to the muted ringing of hearing loss. The mirror made the sound a revolving door might make if it exploded shortly after brushing closed. With a *whooshbang* it shattered into tiny pieces and blew outward, slicing the boy with hundreds of razor sharp shards.

Miguel Jr.'s choking cries of fear fast became shrill cries of pain. Every exposed surface of his body began to seep blood. He seemed to be sweating little beads of blood from his face; from his cheekbones, and from behind the folds of his eyelids. Auldborne stood up from behind him, untouched. Behind them both the baby's wailing was renewed.

From then on the boy had no fight. Auldborne led him back into the family room as if he was blind. His father had screamed himself hoarse, but upon seeing his son he bucked as hard as he could, to no avail. Draden Tate was simply too much weight for him.

Auldborne gently pressed his hand on the boy's bloody face, then he opened the door and planted his hand on its pristine white front, right in the center. When he took it away there was a perfect handprint of deep red, like a horrible mockup of a child's finger painting. Auldborne came back inside the house and closed the door with a soft click.

"Not long now." He smiled.

Miguel Jr. went back to his unconscious mother and, weeping, burrowed his bleeding face into her apron. From where he lay pinned on the couch, his father did the same.

CHAPTER TWENTY-NINE

THIRTY–FIVE THOUSAND FEET in the air, Ian Finn watched the digital map embedded in the seat in front of him. It showed a graphic of his airplane as it traversed from Ireland to its final destination in Portugal, where his battle awaited. He watched it crawl its way across the English Channel at an agonizingly slow pace. He'd worked out that the little airplane graphic moved a hairsbreadth every ten minutes. Far too slow. He sipped on another whisky straight from the miniature bottle. It was American whisky and it went down about as smooth as a pinecone, but it was all the airline had left.

Ian was uneasy.

His gun hadn't spooked security at all. None of theirs had. He'd been on a lot of flights with his gun and getting through security was always a pain in the ass. It usually involved back rooms and hushed phone calls and waiting before they were inevitably allowed to pass. This time it was as if the transport officers were prepared for them…as if they had been through the drill before, recently. But that was impossible.

The three of them had reserved seats in the back half of the airplane. Most seats were occupied by the time the three slowly shuffled their way down the aisle. All around them people were preoccupied, settling themselves and jockeying for what space remained in the overhead bins. Many buried themselves in books or newspapers as they awaited takeoff. Some already attempted sleep, covered in blankets with their heads propped uncomfortably against the headrests or windows.

Pyper refused to fly business or first class, preferring to keep as low of a profile as possible, but she did agree to purchase three seats in the exit row. As they took their seats, the attendants closed the hatch and locked it shut. Kayla let out a breath and grinned at Ian. They were safe.

But Ian couldn't return her half-smile. Flying was hell for him under the best of circumstances and at the moment he badly needed a cigarette, the whisky was giving him a headache even as he ordered another, and he was hot. Things just didn't feel right. To him, the hatch doors of the airplane had never looked more like prison doors, and as the hissing sound of stale air filled the cabin, Ian noted that the encircling walls of the airplane resembled those of a coffin.

He wondered, as he watched the map, what the other teams were doing. Perhaps some were fighting as he flew. He wondered what the Americans were doing. They had drawn Japan, a formidable team, but he also thought he knew Johnnie Northern fairly well. If he was a betting man he'd place his money on Northern's squad; on the solemn Max Haulden, and on the deceptively dangerous Nikkie Hix. All American killers, they were.

Although Ian would never admit it, he held a grudging affinity for Blue. Oddly enough, Finn met Northern before he fought him. Years ago they had drawn each other in the first round. He remembered their two teams meeting at a college campus in California, outside of a café late at night. Ian still remembered the palm trees, the fibrous strands of their fronds swaying in the hot breeze of the passing traffic. They met like medieval nobility might before a pitched battle. How strange it seemed now, tactics such as those. Neither team would dream of approaching a battle that way anymore, even with each other. They had been young, it was both teams' first fight, and in retrospect it seemed outrageously naïve.

But looking back, Finn wasn't convinced the approach was so bad after all. Hix had been the last woman standing, Green had lost, but it had been a good, clean fight; no team member was unduly injured, certainly no civilians had been hurt, or even inconvenienced, really. Neither team would have dreamed of shooting up a dance club, mowing down anyone just to get at each other. Things were still decent back then.

It was folly to think that anything resembling that first meeting would be feasible anymore. The Tournament was morphing: changing itself and also changing everyone involved. Ian saw that now, and it was disconcerting. What once was an experiment, a World Cup of team shooting, was turning into a war. The power each team had been given made their true colors rise to the top, and what had emerged wasn't always pretty, specifically when it was Grey or Black.

Ian hated Team Grey and he freely admitted it. He wondered how much of this came from his father, perhaps some latent gene that had been passed on, and how much of it was simply a loathing for what he had seen the English do over the years he had been a part of this organization. They used terror tactics. This hit dangerously close to home for him, and yet he often wondered how far he would go to bring them down. Would he cut down the innocent to cut down Auldborne?

Perhaps he and his father were more alike than he thought.

The thought chilled him and he took his last slug of whisky. He tucked the small bottle in the seat pocket in front of him with two others and was looking about for a stewardess when

Kayla tugged on his sleeve. She was sunk deep into her chair, and had turned so pale that the splash of freckles across the bridge of her nose stood out like cinnamon. She was just able to peer over the seat before her and was fixated upon a point down the aisle.

"Are you gonna be sick?" asked Ian. Pyper looked up from her reading.

"We have a very big problem," Kayla whispered.

"There's a bag here somewhere," Pyper said, shuffling through the pocket in front of her own seat.

"Get. Down." hissed Kayla. She fumbled inside her front jacket pocket.

"Kayla, what are you doing—"

"Row sixteen, aisle seat," she said, snapping the button off of the holster inside her jacket. Ian traced down the rows until he found the sixteenth. There sat a woman. Her back was to them, but she was dark skinned and had big, full hair. She turned to the side and revealed the profile of her face as she spoke to someone across the aisle. The woman did look remarkably similar to the most recent pictures of Tessa Crocifissa. Or it could just be another young Italian woman. They did have a distinctive look, after all.

"Kayla, wait a minute," said Pyper. "Let's not do anything foolish. If you pull that out, they'll turn this plane right around and throw us all in jail. Think about it—why on earth would they be on this airplane?"

Kayla turned to Ian, her eyes wide as dinner plates. There was not a doubt in her mind.

"To keep you from shooting," Kayla said slowly, as if it all had clicked in to place.

Ian looked at Pyper, and then at Kayla. Both seemed to be pleading with him, but for different reasons.

"I'mna go check," he said, unbuckling his belt.

"Ian—"

"It's all right, I'm just going to get a little closer."

He stood and pulled his jacket down over his own gun, steadying himself against the seats as the plane jittered a bit. He still couldn't tell that the woman wasn't Tessa. He crept closer, but she was facing forward again. He would have to get in front of her or wait for her to turn around. He inched forward once more, aisle by aisle, but still without a clear view.

And then he was stopped.

A man stood up right in front of him, blocking his way. It took Ian a few moments to recognize the sneer, but even then he couldn't quite believe it. He stood dumb. The leather bangles on the man's wrists, the silver rings on his fingers as they rested upon the tops of the chairs to either side, the hair, slicked back in stripes as black as night.

Ignazio Andizzi grinned into his face. "Tha's far eenough, Finn," he said, his voice dripping with smug satisfaction.

CHAPTER THIRTY

NORTHERN WAS UP, SPLASHING water from a pristine marble basin in the bathroom into his bleary eyes. Max refused to sleep and Northern could tell he was unhappy with the progression of things. Max was a powerful striker, fiercely loyal, but he had a way of making everyone uncomfortably aware of how he'd be running the show if he could. The last thing Northern needed right now was disruption from within.

"New plan," he said, walking back into the bedroom.

"There was a plan?" Max asked, his voice low. Northern stopped and stared at him, face dripping wet. Nikkie closed her eyes.

"Max, are you with me on this or not?"

"What's the new plan, John?" sighed Max.

"Nikkie and I are going across the hall, to our original room," Northern said, snapping back the action on his .40 caliber automatic. "We'll make a bit of noise, and with any luck, they'll think all three of us are in there and turn their backs to this room. That's when you jump out, pop everyone, and *bam*. Done and done, and I'm sleeping all the way home. First class. Quickly now, they've got to be close. They may be in the building."

"And what if they come in here?" Max asked.

"They'll buy the dummy room bit."

"But if they don't—"

"Then we'll pick them off as they go to you, Max!" Northern snapped. "But they'll buy the dummy room bit!"

Max shrugged, glanced at Nikkie, then fitted his earpiece around the back of his ear. "All right. I'll be right here," he said, shouldering up against the interior crook of the door.

Northern fitted his own earpiece, as did Nikkie, blinking herself truly awake. Northern eased his head out of the door, using angles to shield him as he surveyed the hallway, still empty. Only the brief crunching of a nearby ice machine could be heard. He nodded at Nikkie, who darted across the hallway, popped in her keycard to room 426, and snapped open the door. Once she was safely inside, Northern followed, both doors shut with the soft swoosh of wood on carpet, and all was again quiet.

Northern was right about one thing. They didn't have long to wait.

The Japanese quickly learned which room the Americans were in and split up in their approach; the striker and the sweeper as one group, and the captain alone. Tenri Fuse and Amon Jinbo took the elevator to the fourth floor, and Takuro Obata took the stairway. They wasted no time.

Each walked down opposite ends of the wing like a man on thin ice, slow and low and constantly moving. An older couple hurried past Fuse and Jinbo on their way to the elevator, oblivious. They saw no one else. Eventually they came to the 430 block and they stopped, waiting for the signal from their captain to move as one. With a flick of his hand Obata called Jinbo forward and told Fuse to hold and guard the hallway.

Jinbo seemed a different man as he approached room 426. Gone were the nervous tics and twitches, gone was the boyish awkwardness. He presented an odd sight for sure, a small man, eyeglasses smudged and pinched low on his nose as he peered down the barrel of a massive gun, half again as long as his hand, and yet this was clearly his element, his aggressive posture and the hunger with which his eyes snapped up the scene in front of him stood as testament. The two men, creeping down the hallway from opposite ends, registered each other without so much as a glance. Their eyes were focused on two separate doors.

One was notched open, resting on its popped deadbolt, most likely secured by a chain slip. This was 426, the room in question, clearly occupied. It was an inviting site. Too convenient. Obata glanced at Jinbo, who cocked an eyebrow. He braced against the wall, weapon in hand. He awaited his signal to kick in the door. He was ready.

But Obata was not. Obata was looking across the hall at rooms 427 and 429. It was one of these. They would come from one of these. But how best to lure them out? He soft-stepped over to Jinbo, who stood ready to unleash hell. With a series of punctuated gestures he mimed for his striker to watch the rooms across the hall, and those only. Jinbo furrowed his brow, but turned around to face rooms 427 and 429. Obata himself would take 426.

Inside 427, Max Haulden rubbed his eyes and replaced his glasses, clear lensed wraparounds in case of fragmented glass. He pressed his ear to the door, but heard nothing. The view from the peephole showed an empty hallway, but something was up. He was suddenly possessed of an almost overwhelming urge to pop his head out and check. He thought he heard whispering. Or was it the ice machine? He readjusted his grip on his gun and wiped his brow and wondered what Nikkie and John were talking about.

Outside in the hallway, Obata nodded to Jinbo, nodded to himself, took a breath, and slammed his heel into the door of room 426. It was a violent kick, heel first, a finishing move drilled into him back in his Judo days at University. The door snapped back and the chain popped with a crack of splitting wood, but Obata didn't move in. Instead, he stepped back out of the doorway and pressed himself against the hallway wall once more. He decided he would shoot whoever came out of any door within this vicinity no matter who they were.

But no one came out.

For a few moments, Obata thought he might have over-analyzed the whole situation. With almost comical slowness, the door to room 426 began to close again. Down the hallway Tenri Fuse poked his head out from behind the corner, questioning. Jinbo's guns aimed everywhere at once, but nothing moved.

The anti-climax of it all bothered Jinbo greatly. Where was the blazing retaliation? Could this be wrong room? Would Obata try to kick it open again? Two door kickings were foolish. That's not how these things went. There was one kick and then shooting.

With three inches to spare before the door closed totally, Jinbo stuck his toe in the gap.

—

Northern heard them all along. They were remarkably quiet, like rabbits moving on a crust of snow, but he knew how to listen. Then something had given one or more of them pause. For several seconds Northern thought they might have figured out the dummy door ploy, and he thought how Max would hold it over him, saying nothing but silently gloating. He thought all of this in the four seconds it took Obata to breathe deep and kick the door to the room wide open.

But then no one came in.

This disconcerted Northern just enough to stay him as the door slowly swung closed. Nikkie looked at him, surprised more by his lack of action than by the door. And where was Max? He had to have heard or seen something by now. Wasn't that the sign for him to start shooting?

Then someone stuck a toe in the gap, and Northern saw the thin, boyish form of Amon Jinbo, the striker, slip between door and jamb like a wraith. The metal barrel of an absurdly large revolver clicked gently against the doorframe as Jinbo brought it up to eye level. Milliseconds later it roared to life.

The wanton, destructive impartiality with which Jinbo raked the entirety of room 426 was ultimately what actually saved Northern and Hix. He shot at anything and everything, swinging in a slow, wide arc. The diodes tore through lampshades and exploded cut-glass table tops, ripped runs in the comforters, dislodged bits of plaster from the walls, and blew out both rear facing windows. The room was acrid with gun smoke and deafeningly loud.

Nikkie Hix recognized Jinbo immediately and recalled Max's advice of not providing him with a moving target. She simply dropped to the ground. Northern dove into the bathroom to his right. He was very nearly hit in the process, but the diode passed over his left shoulder and shattered the window behind him. He slid on the polished marble floor and smacked his head on the doors to the cabinet under the sink. His first instinct was to slam the bathroom door shut, but the sight of Nikkie Hix crawling to the far side of the bed stayed him.

Six, seven, eight, nine shots and still nothing from Max.

What the hell was he doing? Northern screamed at him through
his earpiece, but the gunfire was too loud. Ten, eleven, twelve
shots. Nikkie was moving very slowly. It occurred to Northern
that she might be hit. But no, she reached the far wall up by the
headboard, turned around, brought her gun up to her chest and
nodded at him. Her lips were pressed into thin white lines, her
blond hair hung over her face in wisps. She didn't look to be in
pain, but she did look angry and quite beautiful. *BLAM BLAM
BLAM.* Where was his goddamn striker?

And then everything fell into a ringing silence.

And the fire alarm rang.

Takuro Obata literally had to pull Amon Jinbo back from
the room out into the hall. He slammed the door shut behind
him.

"How many?"

"Two."

"Did you hit either of them?"

"No."

"Then what the hell was that all about?"

Jinbo, breathing hard, said nothing, and would not meet
his captain's glare.

"That means there is one other—"

And then the door to the room across the hall cracked
open and both men saw a sliver of a face: Maxwell Haulden. Max
tried to slam it shut, but Obata was too quick. He kicked out at
the door and it snapped back into Max's face. His teeth clacked
together and for a brief second everything in his vision wavered

in primary colors. Blood ran from his forehead down and into his eyes, stinging like warm soap. He screamed into the earpiece. Both men on the other side were kicking furiously at the door and it was crushing over his shoe where he held it precariously closed. His big toenail was slowly tearing from its bed as the door gained ground. The pain made him suck in a quick breath of blood through his nose. He coughed and sneezed a metallic spatter all over the wood of the door and still they slammed against his foot, taking quick turns at kicking. This was not how things were supposed to go. What a fabulous plan his captain had devised.

He couldn't stand the tearing pain. Without thinking he pulled his foot back and flattened himself against the wall of the room's entryway just as both men exploded through the door and right past him. Seeing the opportunity to escape, he took it. Dashing outside into the hall he slammed the door shut behind him and threw all his weight into pulling back on the handle to keep it closed. Immediately he felt a pulling from the other way. He braced his knee against the wall for leverage. How quickly things had flipped.

"John! They're inside the room! I've got them!" he screamed, before it occurred to him that nobody might answer, that both of his teammates might be lying dead to the world in the room across the hall. That Nikkie might be bleeding out onto the satin coverlet or the pristine white carpet.

And he realized that there were only two people inside of the room, not three. But before he could dwell upon this newest disturbing fact, Northern and Hix rushed out and to his side.

"What *happened*?" Northern yelled. "Where the fuck *were* you—Jesus! You're bleeding everywh—"

"The sweeper!" Max yelled. "Tenri Fuse! Where is their sweep—"

There was a single crack of gunfire, and Nikkie Hix fell to the ground.

What in reality probably took no more than five seconds seemed a hundred times that long for Max Haulden. He forgot himself entirely, his split forehead with its steady, thin faucet-stream of blood, his throbbing toe and stinging headache, all of that left him. He didn't remember ever having let go of the door; he knew only that he looked at Nikkie for what seemed an inordinately long time as she clutched her left shoulder, rolled herself over, and kicked her way against the wall. She made no sound, never cried out once, but her eyes were watering.

Suddenly he was firing down the hall. One shot was all Fuse got off before disappearing around the corner, bits of the plaster wall about him flecking off as Max unloaded half of his clip, but one was all he had needed to hit her. Max wanted to run towards the man, perhaps unload the other half right into his eye, but Northern was holding him back by the collar of his shirt and screaming something about retreat.

"We've gotta get her out of here! We've gotta get ourselves out of here!"

When the door to his left holding the other two at bay began to open, everything snapped back to real time. In a flash, Northern let go of his shirt and swept up Nikkie with his free hand. Hip to hip, they ran off down the hallway. Max spat out an accumulation of blood and kicked wildly at the opening door. It popped back in upon the two men with a meaty thunk and he heard two distinctive yelps. His empty grin was streaked with red as he ran down the corridor after his teammates, firing behind him all the way.

CHAPTER THIRTY-ONE

"WHAT IS THAT ON *the door?*" asked Diego, squinting into the distance at his own house.

Lilia looked through binoculars. *"Oh God,"* she muttered.

"'Oh God?' What's 'Oh God?'" Diego asked again, his inflection a breathy panic barely veiled. To him it looked like an angry red sore had sprung up on the clean white door to his home, but Lilia saw it loud and clear.

"Is it blood?" Felix asked, the low calm of his voice odd and unnatural. He stood behind Lilia, hands clasped in front of him as he, too, squinted into the distance, like a somber choir boy scanning the audience for his family.

Lilia brought the binoculars down to her waist, wiped her brow, and looked strangely at her own hand.

"Lilia, give me the binoculars," Diego said, his voice dead flat, his face sheet white.

But Lilia looked out at the house in the distance and then back at her own hand, fingers spread wide. She seemed not to hear her captain, lost instead somewhere between the lines and curves of her own hand and the dark ink eagle marking just above it on her right outer forearm. The eagle mark was good and pure and she tried to focus on it as she looked back out at the house.

In that very house Diego Vega had offered her succor and shelter when nobody else on earth did. That house was her only home. It was the polar opposite of the streets she'd prowled before. It was permanence and safety—until now. Now there was blood upon it. The red mark was blasphemous, a gross violation of the only place she had ever felt welcome. She could hardly control herself, and if it was this hard for her, it would be nearly impossible for Diego.

But he was already gazing through the binoculars.

"No." he said, *"No no no."*

"Diego…" Felix began, approaching him as he might an unstable animal.

"No!"

Diego removed his wide brimmed hat and raked a hand harshly down his face.

"He's doing this on purpose, Diego!" said Felix. *"He wants you to lose your composure! He wants you to make a stupid decision!"*

Diego began to walk towards the house but Felix grabbed him and spun him around. His look was wild and wide-eyed, his pulse hammering out of the side of his neck.

"Diego! Listen to me! Rush down there and you will play right into his hands! Don't you understand?"

"Diego, please," Lilia pleaded. *"Please let me look first. There is an open window around the side. I can sneak in. Let me get an idea of the situation. I'll come back and report. It might be that the English simply wish to bait us."*

"Not even Auldborne would dare—"

Diego waved his sweeper off with an angry flick of his

hat.

"Dare? Of course he would dare! That man is the worst thing that has ever happened to this organization. Can't you see! The writing is on that door!"

"Diego, please, let me look. Five minutes. I'll be back."

"Go!" Diego spat. "Go and see what there is to see. If he has hurt my family, I will kill him."

So Lilia went. She wriggled through almost fifty meters of dirt on her belly then crouched low just outside of the chain link fence surrounding the small backyard plot of the house garden. Her olive face and dark hair were streaked with dry grit. Dust hung about her as she flattened herself further on the floor, but she was almost positive she had made it without alerting anyone. Just inside the fence was a low lying window, cracked slightly at the base, where she might be able to get a better idea of what was happening. She might even be able to pop in the window, look around, and then get out again. She'd done it back in her thieving days.

Of course, the little produce stands and bread cart owners she'd snuck in on back then hadn't had guns. She could be fairly sure of that whenever she decided to steal. Still, there had been risk, and she had, on the whole, performed beautifully.

But back then, she risked only herself. She quite clearly heard the muted wailing of a child inside. Or maybe of a woman. She would have to get to the window to take a more educated guess.

So much of the art of silent movement was instinct. She couldn't see through the glare of the sun on the window, but she felt that nobody was watching. In one deft movement she flipped up onto the fence, and in another she dropped over to the other side, landing expertly with cat-like agility. The chain links tinked softly against each other once. She froze and listened. There was only the soft mewling, nothing more. Lilia always prided herself on being able to *feel* when someone became aware of her presence, of sensing the precise moment when their bubble of privacy popped. She had practiced by sneaking up on ratty street cats in her youth, the kind that were both abnormally patchy and abnormally large, and she got to the point where she could identify the precise moment when she knew that they knew she was there, even when they made no movement as such. She still felt the bubble emanating from the house, but it was fragile. She crept to a point directly beneath the window sill when she heard footsteps and froze, not daring to breathe. They were heavy and they were coming her way.

Back on the hill, away from the house, an agitated Diego Vega was watching his striker's painfully slow progress through the binoculars. Felix Ortiz was in turn watching Diego warily, half expecting him to take off down the hill towards the house at any moment. Suddenly, Diego paused his rapid scanning and hitched up, mid breath.

"What is it?"

"The big black man, Tate, he's walking towards her."

"Does he see her?" Ortiz asked, shading his gaze as he peered down the hill. With the other hand he unbuttoned his collar and fanned himself. Dark sweat stains streaked the back of his shirt.

"I don't know. No, not yet."

"He might just be checking the perimeter, making the rounds," Ortiz said, but he checked and rechecked that his gun was cham-

bered nonetheless. For a long moment, Diego simply watched.

"*No,*" said Diego, still gazing at the house. *"He's either heard something or he's waiting. Either way she's got seconds before he looks down and sees her. Not even Lilia can get that low."*

Diego started walking down the hill. Felix grabbed for him, but Diego snatched his arm and bored his gaze into the sweeper.

"I'm going, Felix. You will let go of me now. Cover me."

Ortiz gently let go, his arm dropped to his side.

Diego replaced his hat and walked on.

———

Miraculously, Tate hadn't seen her. She was staring right up his nose. She greatly regretted not having her weapon in hand, but if she moved to grab it she'd be dead in the dust, so she watched. *Jesus the man is big,* she thought. In profile as he was, all she could see were his bulging pecks and the superhero angles of his massive jaw, of a black as pure and dark as obsidian. His dreadlocks hung like frayed ropes down to the windowsill, some spilling over. *They must go down to his ass! Where do you even find a guy like this?*

And he *was* going to see her. She felt like she'd stumbled into the cage of some deadly animal that, by the grace of God, had been too preoccupied with current prey to notice her. Yet.

But then she heard a voice calling. This one came from outside of the house, around the front, and she realized with a sort of gleeful horror that it was Diego Vega. He had foregone his broken English in favor of a deep and robust Spanish, and he was screaming with authority.

"I always knew you were all petty criminals and cowards! Why don't you get up from behind the women and children and come outside?"

In a flash, Draden Tate was gone. It was now or never. Lilia slid up the wall, peered in, and saw an empty kitchen. She popped herself up onto the ledge and into the house.

———

Inside the living room it was getting hot. The air hung about Alex Auldborne like a fog. Michael Vega had simply shut down, but his wife kept muttering to herself like a bag lady and the boy would not stop wailing. It was enough to drive a normal man crazy, and was beginning to tax even his patience.

But then he heard the calling from out front, and he knew his wait was almost over. He peered around the side of the curtains and smiled to see Diego Vega walking towards the house and shouting.

"What the hell is that Mexican saying?" Auldborne asked.

"I've no fucking idea," said Christina. She still trained her gun on the three on the sofa, but the heat had forced her, very reluctantly and with visible distaste, to sit down upon the lounge chair across the table. Her legs were crossed.

"Just shoot him," she said, just as Draden Tate came in from the kitchen.

"What are you doing here?" Alex asked, his voice suddenly hard.

"I heard shouting."

"Yes. You did. It's their damn fool captain finally arrived, drawing you to the front of the house," Auldborne said quickly, snapping each word. Tate narrowed his eyes.

"Which means that someone is coming in the back, you idiot," he continued, physically turning the big man around and pushing him back towards the kitchen.

"These Mexicans are tricky!" he called after Tate. "They love to sneak about!"

Tate loped back into the kitchen and saw that the window was opened. Had it been opened before? Surely not that much.

"Someone is in!" he called back, his voice only slightly annoyed.

"Fine," Alex said from behind him. "It's most likely that lithe bitch Alvarez, and now she's trapped in this mess of a house. I trust you can take care of her."

Tate grunted in agreement and pulled his gun.

Outside, Diego was bellowing and gesturing wildly like a man on a pulpit.

"Listen to him! He's having a fit!" Alex said, grinning.

"He's going to bring the neighbors out. If you don't shut him up, I will," Christina asserted, rubbing her temple with her free hand. Auldborne shrugged. He stepped over to the door, turned the knob, and with one fluid motion he swung it open and stepped to the side, covering himself. The door swept silently outward, as if in anticipation of a grand exit. Diego paused in his diatribe. He could see inside the house. It looked dark and hazy.

Suddenly Alex Auldborne appeared in the silhouette, his thin figure set perfectly in the center of the door frame like a

Victorian painting of a man and his gun. Diego hit the ground seconds before a volley of shots exploded outward on to the common park. He scrambled on all fours into the shelter of the small playground to his left, where Miguel Jr. and his ragtag band of young friends would gather. He came to rest under a polished wooden slide. The firing stopped. He heard laughter.

But Auldborne's aristocratic guffawing was cut short by a second explosive volley of shots, these in response from up the hill: Felix Ortiz was answering. Auldborne wasn't prepared for this. He jumped about and dashed back inside, slamming the door shut. Although he was far too modest to gloat openly, Diego imagined his sweeper laughing a bit to himself, perched on high with the sun behind him. Unfortunately, Auldborne was way out of Felix's range. Diego doubted his shots had even hit the front of the house.

Inside, Auldborne cursed and spat on the carpet, mortified at his display of indignity. "One of the bloody Mexicans is up on the hill somewhere. I can't move on Vega unless he's out of the picture. You'll have to go after him." His grin was now a glare, his lips peeled away from the tips of his teeth. Christina nodded and slowly stood. She knew better than to try her captain when he was like this. There was a time for jibes and a time for action.

"I'll keep an eye on these three," Auldborne said, flicking a hand absently in the direction of the couch. The boy still sobbed mutely onto his woozy mother. Miguel Sr. had gone catatonic.

"Draden!" Auldborne screamed. "What the bloody hell are you doing in there? Why isn't she dead yet?"

"I dunno mon!" came the gruff reply. "I don' see 'er, and I don' wanna move about too much or she'll get me in da back."

"Get you in *da back*? Christ! Do you need me to come

hold your hand?"

"I'll take care of her," he said, his voice a growl.

—

From under the slide outside, Diego saw a small shape dart from his house out and into the neighborhood towards the hill from whence his team had come. He screamed a warning to Felix.

"Felix! Someone is coming your way! I think it's the girl!"

"Stoke?" came the muted reply from on high.

"Yes!"

"I hate that girl!"

"Then take care of her!"

"All right!"

That left two English in the house, plus his own striker. Diego wiped the dust from his gun with his left hand and spread it on the brim of his hat.

It was time to put an end to Alex Auldborne.

CHAPTER THIRTY-TWO

NIKKIE HIX DESPERATELY WANTED to stop in the stairwell, at least to try to catch her breath, but she knew that if you were shot in this game and could somehow still run, you ran. Once they were on ground level she insisted that she stand and run on her own while still able. She remembered now just how visceral the pain was, like her innards were jerked around with every hitched stride. At her side, Northern helped her steady herself and stood back to check her wound.

"If it's just above the bicep, it's probably a moderate diffusion. It's not a quick killer, but it's awfully close to the brachial artery. Once the spreading gets that far, you're done. If you stay passive, I'd give an hour before you're comatose."

"And what if I can't stay passive?" she replied, breathless. Max was already slamming down the stairs, nearly with them.

"With an elevated heart rate I'd give you thirty minutes. Maybe less."

Max caught up and immediately reached out to Nikkie before stopping himself.

"Max, run ahead and clear a way to the cab. We'll be right behind," said Northern.

Max slowed down momentarily next to her, his eyes

pleading with her, then he dashed off towards the doors and the awaiting line of pristine cabs.

Northern checked behind him as he trotted along with Hix, urging her as much as he dared. The lobby was in the process of a remarkably orderly evacuation. Several attendants were actually smiling as they directed bleary and sleepy guests towards one of the fire exits amidst a siren's droning blare. The crowd gawked at Max Haulden as he shoved his way through in a sprint for the doors, creating a small wake for his teammates. For a moment it looked like others might run in a contagious panic, but the soothing, repetitive monotone of the desk help prevailed and the slow shuffle outdoors continued on, the crowd seething back together behind the crazy Americans' exit.

Max had just grabbed the closest cab to hand, its doors already open, when they heard screaming from inside the hotel. Now people started to push their way out of the front doors. Something was coming up behind them. Hix grunted and ducked her way into the back seat where Max took hold of her for a moment and righted her, carefully steering clear of her wounded shoulder. There was a small tear in her shirt under which the skin was a mottled red. A thin line of dried blood tracked its way down to her elbow, and then stopped. The diode had broken the skin. He gingerly placed a hand on her knee and removed it just as quickly.

"I'll be all right," she said between gritted teeth. But like Northern, Max was just as familiar with the slow, numbing spread of a diode hit. She'd been shot too close to the heart. She didn't have long.

Northern ran around to the passenger's side and hopped in.

"Take us somewhere," he said. "Anywhere."

The cabbie looked at him, confused. Northern cursed under his breath and glanced at the crowded foyer. Someone was clearly shoving at the back of the mass exodus; people were bursting through the double doorway now, and not of their own accord. He snatched up a tourist map from a pocket in front of him. He pointed at random.

"Here! Take us here!"

"*Ah! Akihabara,*" the cabbie said, nodding. Moments later they were cruising towards the center of Tokyo.

—

His team could tell by his look that Obata was furious. Since he rarely spoke to begin with, Jinbo and Fuse could divine his mood only from his facial expressions. When he was angry his brow protruded and his round face tensed up, as if he was lifting a heavy weight.

He wasn't as considerate to the mass of evacuating people as the Americans had been. Once he saw that Blue was outside he started shoving, cleaving through them like a knife. But Obata wasn't a tall man, nor was his appearance all that imposing, and so people got angry. When a pair of young men shoved him back, Jinbo pulled out his massive revolver and then all hell broke loose. Obata hissed at him to holster it, but the damage was done: the herd had smelled the wolf. Those nearest him shoved violently away, eyes rolling like those of spooked horses. These people then ran into others, and so a wild ripple seemed to bounce against the doors and then return back on itself, creating a jam worse than before. By the time Obata fought his way outside there were already squads of police cars and fire trucks approaching, and a single cab speeding out of the parking lot, headed northeast into Tokyo proper.

"We should get out of here," Tenri Fuse whispered, uncomfortably close in the pressing crowd. Obata snapped around and glared at him.

"The police are many, and more come," murmured Jinbo, resetting his boxy glasses upon his nose and dabbing gingerly at a streak of blood with the sleeve of his jacket. He'd taken the brunt of the door's kickback. *"What do we do?"* he stammered.

Obata seethed, taking in deep breaths through his nose.

"If they take us to the police station, it will be a while before we're cleared…" Fuse said, nervously smoothing his thin goatee.

"You think I don't know that?" spat Obata as he grabbed both men and pulled them behind the topiary to the left of the door.

"Well if you talked to us—"

"Don't ever take that tone with me! How many shots, Jinbo? How many shots did you fire?"

Jinbo stared at the ground and said nothing. His glasses slowly slid down his nose.

"Answer me."

"I don't know. Eight, maybe nine…"

"Liar. You lie. You know exactly how many."

"Fourteen."

"Fourteen! And not one of them hit anybody," Obata said, shaking his head in disgust.

"And you," he said, turning to Fuse, who shrank under

his devastatingly even tone. *"You actually had a shot. A clear line. All three of them like gaping carp and you hit the girl. The girl. Once. In the arm. She's still walking, Fuse."*

Neither man spoke in their defense.

"We had them. You've both failed me."

The men bored holes in the ground with their gaze.

"But all is not lost," said Obata, looking into the distance in the direction the cabbie had taken. *"The woman is wounded and the other two are attached to her. They cannot go far."*

—

In Akihabara, the teeming electronics district of Tokyo, block after block of shops too numerous to count flashed, buzzed, blared, and honked their gadgets and gizmos to thousands of passersby. People with megaphones stood at corners chirping away in persistent Japanese. Rows of the newest televisions flashed patterns that rivaled anything found on the Vegas Strip. Odd and inane promotional booths dotted the major thoroughfares, complete with men and women in an embarrassing array of costumes hocking sleek new products and metallic odds and ends. It was all too much for Nikkie Hix, who was getting dizzy with pain as they dashed about this mayhem with no clear direction.

"John, my shoulder is numb," Hix said with a calm she didn't feel.

"I know, we're almost there."

"Almost where?" Max said. "We've been outside too long. They'll spot us a mile away."

Northern turned about. Everywhere he looked there was

a sea of black hair, broken only rarely by swells of tall white foreigners as evident as the frothy caps of waves. Max was right. They shouldn't be outside. He grasped at the first relatively secluded place he saw: what looked to be some sort of check-in desk for something in the back corner of a side street.

"There. We'll go in there," Northern said, looking at Nikkie as she leaned heavily against a wall of digital screens nearby. Sweat darkened her blonde hair where it clung to brow. She looked up at him and smiled weakly. Max simply shook his head and said nothing, his silence somehow heavier than the ringing around them as they dashed for cover.

CHAPTER THIRTY-THREE

NIKKIE SAT DOWN HARD in a small, private room of what turned out to be a karaoke joint. Northern had thrown money at the hapless young man at the front desk and this is where they ended up. They sat down opposite, watching her. To their left was a large flat-screen television, and under that sat a stack of blinking boxes. On the screen a computer- generated Japanese woman was bowing and chirping out a greeting none of them could understand. Her high pitched voice came out of several speakers situated in the corners. On a table in the center of the room an ornamental basket contained two individually wrapped microphones. All around them the collective off-key crooning and screeching of parties of Japanese filtered through the walls and blended into a continuous and indecipherable, dog-kennel of a buzz. Occasionally, the sound would get louder as doors to other rooms were opened and closed.

"You can't go back out there," Max said, drumming nervously on the low table in front of him. "You've got to slow your breathing, calm your heart."

Nikkie Hix laughed, and then sucked in a quick breath.

"I'll be lucky to get off of this couch again." She smiled weakly.

Max glared at Northern. "Now what? Looks like the

dummy room plan didn't quite work like we thought it would, did it John?"

Northern narrowed his eyes to blue slits, but said nothing.

"Where *were* you Max?" Nikkie asked, her voice almost sad. She leaned back in her seat and looking up at the ceiling. "What took you so long? Jinbo must have shot at us at least ten times."

Max went suddenly sallow at Hix's cut. He swallowed several times and searched for a reply in the back of his throat, but Northern cut in and saved him.

"Nothing went quite as we had planned, but it's in the past now. Time to move on," he said, his voice flat. "We're still three and three."

"But she's been *shot,* John—"

"And if you and I do our jobs quick enough she'll still have enough in her to do hers, and then maybe we can get her to the nearest Tournament equipped hospital. But every second we waste is a second closer to her going under."

In the ensuing silence Northern seemed to dare Max to speak. Max looked hard at the basket on the table before him.

"Nikkie, if you stay here you should be safe. We'll go out and move away. Create some ruckus to draw them off. We'll make them think Max and I split up. With a little luck, they'll try to team up on one of us and the other can catch them off guard. If we need you to sweep in, we'll call you."

Nikkie nodded, propping her legs up on the couch. Max hunched and glanced at her.

"Max," said Northern. "Are you with me?"

Max nodded, his eyes flicked to and from Hix. "Of course," he said, but his voice sounded vacant.

"We need to get far enough away from her before we make any noise. We passed a train station on the way in. That's where we're headed."

—

Red lingered outside of the hotel, lost for true direction as Obata stood away in silence, mulling his options. Fuse's gaze snaked back and forth over the shivering crowd. Jinbo nursed the trickle of blood from his nose.

Suddenly the radio inside of an idle cab nearby cut mid-song and warbled about a disturbance near Akihabara station. An explosion of some sort. Two large front windows blown totally out. Obata walked over to it.

"Take us there," Obata said.

The cabbie hesitated.

"Did you hear him?" hissed Fuse, leaning his face nearly to the driver's ear.

The cabbie nodded. They drove in silence. When Obata abruptly called a halt the cabbie braked immediately and propped open the rear doors, eager to get these three gone.

"There. Look. By the windows. That's Max Haulden. He's all alone," Obata said, pointing. *"So Northern is either an idiot, or this is a trap. And I don't think he's an idiot. One of us will approach. The other two will hold up here in case he tries some American underhanded trick."*

"I'll go in," Jinbo announced, eager to get back in to

his captain's good graces. *"Max Haulden is my match-up. Striker to striker."*

"Then go," Obata nodded, *"and go quickly. He's proficient. As soon as you get near him he'll see you."*

Jinbo bowed awkwardly from a sitting position, pushed his glasses up his nose and brushed flakes of dried blood from his upper lip. He gripped his gun inside his coat and took off at an awkward half-run towards the station.

Jinbo got no more than ten steps towards the entrance before he saw Max move inside and onto the first platform. Jinbo hesitated. He glanced back at the cab where his team waited. Obata nodded. Jinbo continued inside the station, moving at a slower clip, gripping his largest gun tight.

All of the JR platforms were jammed, but only the first had a departure scheduled within the next several minutes. Platform five serviced an inbound local line, one frequented by college students, businessmen, and tourists. During the week it was impossible to distinguish the rush hour from any other hour. Every train was standing-room only; white gloved attendants physically pushed more people into the bulging train than was entirely safe, and then apologized profusely for doing so. Amon Jinbo ran face-first into this wall of humanity and saw Max Haulden in the middle of it. By the looks of it, Max was going to get on the train, and by the looks of it, Jinbo was not. He hunched and popped up his collar, sniffing a trickle of blood back into his nose. He tried to pry his way in between flashes of holes in the crowd in front, anything to keep a closer tab on the man, but he was shouldered back. He cursed and was cursed at in return.

"Where do you think you're going boy? You wait like everyone else."

"There's an American," Jinbo stammered, scratching his neck with his free hand. *"A friend, he's up there somewhere. I have to see him."*

"You'll wait like everyone else!"

"But—"

"But nothing. You wait!" said a drab older businessman, who promptly turned away and puffed his shoulders up haughtily. Those around him nodded in approval and glared at Jinbo, muttering half-heard insults.

Flashes and dings signaled the train's impending arrival. People shuffled in anticipation. Max was well in front of where Jinbo stood, near the front ranks. Jinbo chanced a jump, trying to catch a glimpse. He couldn't risk losing his man and disgracing himself further. He had to get on the train.

The businessman turned again to Jinbo.

"Why are you jumping? It won't move us any faster."

Jinbo's face reddened. He scratched his neck again, and tightened his grip on the Colt .45 inside his jacket.

"It might not," Jinbo stammered, *"but this will."* He pulled out his gun and pointed it up and into the man's face. Out of the corner of his eye he saw the train pulling in and slowing. He had perhaps fifteen seconds to break through five hundred people. Those who saw the gun just looked at it, wide-eyed. Nobody could move. A panicked run was not physically possible. There were several gasps, but oddly enough no one screamed. Perhaps they didn't believe him.

Jinbo saw the train stop. The doors hissed open and people began squeezing their way out, single file, through tiny rivulets in the crowd.

"That's not real," the man said, narrowing his eyes.

"Get on the ground old man," Jinbo ordered, his voice now as steady as stone.

He pointed the gun into the sky, fired once—and hell broke loose. The man did as he was told as did a hundred or so people directly around him. Somewhere, finally, someone screamed. Hundreds followed suit. The train platform sounded like a maddened concert.

Jinbo started to walk, stepping over people like puddles. Ahead of him, the white-gloved pushers were, incredibly, still at work, either oblivious to the gunshot amidst the normal platform racket, or extremely devoted to duty.

And then Jinbo saw him.

Max was already on the train, in a far corner by the window. He was speaking into an earpiece. Now Jinbo *really* had to get on the train.

He fired again, once, into the air. Another hundred hit the deck. More muffled screaming but mostly just confusion. He stepped forward. He was close. He fired once more, and as the attendant turned toward the noise he shoved his way forward and onto the train, two cars behind Max. He jammed his gun back in his jacket, to the mute horror of a few observant passengers nearby, just as the doors hissed closed behind him.

—

Back in the karaoke room Nikkie Hix was getting worse. There was a nauseating, hollow feeling in the pit of her stomach and her arm was a painful, swollen numbness. She had horrible thoughts of going comatose here, in a claustrophobic little room, surrounded by Japanese screeching songs by *Wham!*. She told herself that she would not allow it. By God, if the train station was where her team was, the train station was where she was going to go.

Saying and doing were different things, however, and Nikkie feared she was going to puke everywhere. The telltale signs were there: gathering spit in her mouth, involuntary deep breaths soft on the exhale; both bad omens. She allowed herself a few more deep breaths, rocked to gather some momentum, and then grunted into a standing position.

The act was ludicrously draining. She'd seen flashes of purple after standing up too quickly before, but they had never lasted this long. She felt she might fall right down again, perhaps on to the table in front of her. She even rotated to protect her left arm in anticipation, but when she found herself still standing a full minute later, she knew that she could do it. She told herself that getting up was the worst part, and was halfway convinced. One thing was for sure: now or never.

She shambled outside and down the hall to the exit, ignoring the stringent calls of the Japanese man at the desk who wanted something that he wasn't going to get from her. She pushed her damp hair behind her left ear and walked out into the late afternoon sun. It, too, seemed abnormally intense. She felt exposed, like an unearthed tree root flayed and damaged. With her good hand she flagged a cab and sat down hard in the back seat, her heart hammering like she'd just sprinted up a flight of stairs with a hangover. After several moments in which the driver glanced suspiciously back at her while she gathered her breath, she told him to take her to Akihabara station. By the grace of God he seemed to understand, or at least he started moving. She quietly reached for her gun inside of her jacket. Her curtain call was coming. It was time to flare out big.

—

Jinbo thought he knew exactly where Max Haulden was: two
train cars in front of him, in the back left corner. But by the time
he snaked his way through his own car and the one in front of
him, Max was gone. Jinbo scratched at his arm and tried to calm
himself. Max couldn't have gone far. He had to be on the train. A
quick perusal told him that there was clearly no white boy here,
so he must have moved towards the front. A small shuddering motion also told him that the train was already slowing. Approaching
a stop.

This presented another problem. What if Max got off?
Then all was lost. He would miss his mark again *and* end up out
of all of the action entirely. He couldn't possibly monitor everyone as they got off of the train, but since Max had to be in one of
the two cars ahead, he could perhaps hang just outside the door
and watch for a brown mop of hair a good head above everyone
else. He might even get a shot off and end this foolish chase. He
would spare no expense this time. He grabbed the hilts of both
of his guns, crossing his arms over his chest. He sniffed up the
last of the blood that dripped from his swollen nose as he heard
the harsh squealing of the brakes. As the train lurched to a stop
he shuffled to a position just outside of the door, one foot on the
train and one foot on the platform. He ignored the grumbling as
passengers pushed their way behind him and outside, and focused
on scanning the heads of the people exiting in the two cars in
front. Max wasn't hard to spot. He was in line to exit, and he
seemed none the wiser. Jinbo could hardly believe his luck. He
gingerly loosed both guns from their respective shoulder holsters.
He would wait until the last minute to align his shot with the
side of the train; he wanted to get Max just as his head appeared
outside, but before anyone noticed his weapons.

"Jinbo."

He didn't hear his name—or he refused to hear it. Concentrated as he was, he didn't even register the strange rising hum of noise coming from behind him.

"Jinbo!"

It was loud this time, shouted. Confused, he turned his head. Standing there like some horrific reckoning out of the romantic old west of Jinbo's dreams was Johnnie Northern, his blue eyes glinting in the afternoon light. The gaping barrel of Northern's gun yawned toward Jinbo's forehead.

Jinbo didn't have time to even blink. The shot was loud, its effect immediate. He dropped right where he stood, half in and half out of the train, as screams erupted from every direction. The closing doors bumped softly upon his body and then opened again. Bumped then opened. Northern watched him for a moment as Max shoved his way through the retreating crowd and to his captain.

"Just one of them," said Max.

"Better than none," said Northern, and the two of them dashed off down the platform.

—

As her cab approached, Nikkie Hix could see Obata and Fuse from a distance. Both still stood in front of the station, waiting for a team member who would never come. Northern had called her, his voice constrained, no hint of celebration as he told her Jinbo was out. Sit tight, he'd said. We'll finish them and get you out of here. No problem.

From the looks of it, Obata and Fuse were just coming to the conclusion themselves. She could see Obata shake his head and snap his phone shut with one hand, his other forming a tight

fist. Fuse leaned away from his captain, as if anticipating an explosion of anger. She smiled in spite of her pain. They had no idea
she was near.

"Stop here," she told the cabbie. He pulled to the side
perhaps one hundred feet from the two members of Red. They
didn't give it a glance. Cabs pulled up and departed from around
the station regularly. Two others were pulling up at that moment
and another was leaving with a fresh fare.

The cabbie pressed a switch to open the door. Nikkie
calmly paid the man. Then she took out her gun and propped
herself up behind the door, her pistol leveled at the two.

She opened fire.

She got two good shots off before the cab abruptly pulled
away, leaving her out in the open. Both shots slammed into Fuse
as he turned to locate the noise. She grinned as he staggered
backwards into Obata like a man whose chair has been whisked
out from under him. He hit the pavement and writhed there,
leaving the captain wide open.

But Obata was quick. As she squeezed off a third and
fourth shot, he turned sideways and stepped back, forcing her to
reposition her already wobbly stance and sight one handed. Her
own body seemed to rebel; her arm was infuriatingly slow. She
fired off one more haphazard shot, missing Obata entirely, before
she felt the first diode punch into her gut. She managed to fall
onto the sidewalk rather than the street behind her, but she could
no longer raise her hand to shoot.

She vomited in earnest as a second diode hit her back. It
felt worse than the gut punch, like a hammer slammed down on
her spine. She vaguely heard the screams of several people around
her mush together with her own cries. She tilted her neck and

saw that her gun was away from her. She had dropped it. She dared not move; the pain was too intense. Everything about and around her screamed.

She heard Obata walk up behind her but couldn't turn to see him. His steps were sure and quick. She hadn't even come close to hitting him. He halted. All around him was blaring, siren filled mayhem. She closed her eyes and tried to slow her breathing but she felt like she was choking on air.

"Look at me," he said, his English accent strained and juvenile sounding.

"Fuck you," she croaked.

The diode crashed into her skull, knocking her into a full coma before she could even hear the report of Obata's handgun.

CHAPTER THIRTY-FOUR

I GNAZIO ANDIZZI GOT THE drop on him.

The first thing that went through Ian Finn's head as he stood face to face with his cocksure Italian counterpart was *we're all dead.*

The second thought was *why hasn't he shot me yet?* And as the hammering of his heart and the whistle of blood rushing through his ears was slowly displaced once more by the muted whine of turbine engines and the hiss of re-circulated air, Finn remembered that he was on an airplane. You don't shoot on an airplane. It's just not done. Andizzi smirked because he had surprised Finn, but also because he knew Finn wouldn't shoot. He saw Finn's hand go to the holster under his jacket and grinned even further. It was as if both men were trapped in a room full of explosive gas. Ian was able to fully take in the presence of a rival team member without shooting, and the effect was unsettling, like coming face to face with a snake.

Finn chanced a glance down the aisle; Kayla was right. Tessa Crocifissa, captain of Gold, was turned around and watching them intensely. Her eyes were wide and her nostrils flared with anticipation. Finn was sure that their sweeper, Lorenzo Aldobrandi, was also nearby, no doubt also conveniently placed between all three of his own team and the exit.

They had planned this from the beginning. Green was

trapped.

Ian badly wanted to see what his own team was doing behind him, but he dared not turn his back on Andizzi. The man smelled strongly of hair gel and cologne. He practically oozed.

Andizzi spoke in overly enunciated English, his Italian accent slamming home the first syllable of each word.

"Drink cart," he said.

Ian furrowed his brow.

"The drink cart, Finn. For the drink. It is behind you."

A stewardess tapped his shoulder and indicated that she wanted to pass with the metal bulk of the drink cart. Her smile was practiced. Ian shifted his gaze from her to Andizzi, his head throbbing.

"Sorry sir. May I get by?"

Ian stepped inside the nearest row, annoying a large bald man seated there who ruffled his newspaper loudly.

"Sorry," Ian mumbled, his eyes fixed once again on Andizzi.

"Would you like a drink?" the stewardess asked.

"I'll take a whisky. Neat," Ian said, staring straight ahead at his smirking opponent.

She rummaged about the cart and handed him a small bottle. Ian took it without looking. The woman looked back and forth between the two men in their odd, silent standoff, shrugged, and moved the cart forward. Ian watched Andizzi take a small cup of orange juice and sip on it thoughtfully, his metal bangles sliding up his tan arm as he drank. Ian realized that his team would never leave this plane. The Italians were blocking the exits. They would pop out as soon as the hatches opened and just wait. They would watch every exit from the outside. He and Pyper and Kayla would have to leave sometime and then they'd walk right into the bullets, like weevils popping up for the hammer. Ian had never been so resentful of first class in his life. Why hadn't they just sat first class? They'd wanted to see everything that happened in the airplane, but they had never thought what to do if something *did* happen.

Andizzi toasted to him with his orange juice as he backed his way down the aisle and to his captain.

Kayla crept up behind Ian.

"I think the sweeper is in the front right. See him? All three of them are here."

Ian saw. "What is Pyper saying we should do?"

"Wait. They're obviously not going to shoot us in the air. There is a lot of time left in the flight. She says the situation might change," Kayla said flatly. She clearly gave little credence to this theory.

"How might it change?"

"I don't know. I think we should just shoot them."

"We're ten-thousand meters in the air Kayla."

"These windows are plastic, not glass. The diodes won't rip through the hull."

"You don't have a gunfight in an airplane. There are hundreds of people here crammed right next to each other."

"You're worried about the people?"

"Of course I am."

There was a silence in which both teammates watched Andizzi yawn luxuriously.

"He sees us talking. Slimy fucking little prick that he is," Kayla said.

"I know."

"Think he can understand us?"

"Maybe."

"Well shit."

"Shit."

"Just look at him," Kayla said, disgusted at everything. "Look how pleased he is with himself. He's already gloating."

Andizzi was tapping the butts of his two pistols, covered loosely by a thin linen jacket, but their outline evident nonetheless to anyone who was looking for them.

Ian shook his head. Was this how their short run would end? Never even seeing the English? Gunned down by Gold as they left the airplane? The ringing in Ian Finn's ears increased as he thought of how Alex Auldborne would take the news. He'd probably give a little guffaw, maybe a single, derisive snort, as if he knew all along that Green wouldn't pass the first round. Or worse, he wouldn't even care enough to guffaw. Ian grinded his teeth, and seeing his expression, Andizzi laughed. Ian wondered how hard it would be to rip a man's tongue out.

But there were too many people. It was too dangerous.

He couldn't allow himself to potentially risk the lives of three hundred people just for a chance of dropping three. This was their own fight in their own world. No need to involve others.

But would he for the chance to drop six? The three Italians and then the three they would get next round? What if those three were the English? What then?

The buzzing in his ears turned to ringing.

To drop nine? To become champions?

Would he do it to wipe Alex Auldborne out?

The ringing turned to roaring.

He shook his head violently to clear it. No. It was foolish to risk innocent people to further his own agenda. There were children on this plane for God's sake. It was selfish. But still his heart raced. He couldn't swallow. He gripped the chair in front of him and tried to will his left hand away from the barely covered holster above his hip. Half of his brain pleaded with him to sit down. To acknowledge that the Italians had gotten the upper hand and chance what would almost surely be a disastrous exiting of the airplane. A walk right into the fire.

But the other half, the half of him that was his father, demanded that he remain standing.

Down the aisle, Ignazio Andizzi saw Ian Finn struggle with his helpless situation, he saw him trying to work saliva down his throat and he saw him dig his nails into the headrest in front of him, and he guffawed. He let out a single, derisive snort. Something Auldborne would do.

Ian snapped.

Andizzi didn't even have time to change the expression on his face. One second, Ian Finn stood squeezing the chair, and the next second there were shots flying down the plane. Andizzi was still mid-guffaw, it happened so fast. Then everything went to hell.

—

The airplane's captain and first officer were locked in the cockpit, as per FAA rules. Both were senior officers with many thousands of hours of flying under their belts. The captain was a slightly gaunt, gray haired man, who, as a result of his occupation, had a slightly discombobulated look, as if always confused about the time of day. He was pleasant in an older uncle sort of way, although he had been sometimes a little forward with the female attendants on transatlantic flights.

The first officer was a paunchy, ambitious fellow who wanted nothing more than to be the gray haired, slightly gaunt man sitting to his left. He immediately recognized the popping sounds emitting from the cabin for what they were. It took the ensuing screams to convince the captain, who radioed in a dazed distress call and asked his first officer to ensure that the door to the cockpit was, in fact, locked tight.

The first officer jumped up and double checked the lock, full of a fierce sense of duty and an even fiercer sense of terror.

"We should land the plane no matter what, captain. No matter what those terrorists threaten us with."

The captain, who had worked too damn hard for this over the years, began to tear up at the thought of dying in this cockpit. In this seat. He took several controlled breaths to stave off weeping. His first mate, jittering about like a caged rabbit, was none the wiser.

"Sit down," ordered the captain. "You're making me nervous."

Finally, the control tower at Dublin International responded. In an infuriatingly calm and controlled voice, they were told turn the plane around and make an emergency landing at London Heathrow.

"I'm not sure you understand the situation—"

"We do understand the situation," said Tower.

"We have what are most likely several Arabs with machine guns—"

"Three Irish nationals and three Italian nationals," corrected the Tower.

Both officers paused.

"How the hell do you know? Is this some sort of mob fight?"

"No. You'll be landing on runway 12."

"Listen to me," insisted the captain, pressing his com to his face. "They are shooting right now. Do you hear that? My cabin crew hasn't checked in yet. For all anybody knows—"

"We've been told the bullets won't pierce the cabin walls or windows," said Tower.

"—What's that supposed to mean? By who?"

"Divert the plane to Heathrow, runway 12. You'll be debriefed. We'll keep this channel clear."

And that was that.

As another volley of shots popped off behind them, the two officers looked at each other in muted disbelief. They banked the plane hard to the left and back towards England.

———

Ian was fast as lightening, but he wasn't always accurate. Two of his first three shots hit the carpeted cockpit wall behind Ignazio Andizzi. The third hit him in the collarbone. When Andizzi slumped backwards onto the knees of those sitting in the row to his left, Ian thought he'd gotten him for good. When Ian saw him kick his way further into the aisle atop the screaming passengers, like some trust fall gone horribly awry, he cursed under his breath and dove for the ground himself.

Ian didn't want to face his captain. He knew Pyper would be seething; he'd disobeyed a direct order. He couldn't quite believe what he'd done himself, something about a ringing in his ears and Andizzi snorting and then he thought of his father and then he'd unloaded three shots. This was all his doing. With any luck they wouldn't plummet from the sky and Ian could spend the rest of his life in jail right next to his dad.

Somewhere to his right, Kayla was being her usual brash self. Whatever Pyper might be thinking of what Ian had done, Kayla was supportive.

"I shoulda figured you greasy fucks would pull something like this!" she screamed from somewhere under the seats. "In a goddamn plane! Unbelievable!"

Tessa gave an Amazonian scream of rage, and fired seven distinct shots at absolutely nobody from way down the aisle. Ian flattened himself lower onto the floor, flinching at each pop of her gun. Each report was painfully loud and rang in his ears long after the diode hit. They sounded like a car backfiring in a parking garage.

"Typical micks!" Tessa screamed in remarkably clear English. "Always shooting, never thinking, probably drunk!"

Ian remembered that he'd had several whiskies what seemed a thousand years ago, but if she thought he was drunk she was dead wrong. He'd rarely felt so alert.

"In case you didn't notice, you crazy bitch, it wasn't looking good for us from back here," Kayla said. "We decided to change things up!"

Figuring he should at least look confident, Ian tried to power his voice over the screams and the clawing sounds: "How's that shoulder, Andizzi? Or did I get your neck? Must not feel too good."

Andizzi let off a gurgling stream of Italian vulgarity. Ian noted with some chagrin that he didn't seem to be on his deathbed, just winged. Suddenly he was thrust to the right. The plane was banking. They were turning back. The other passengers felt the change in direction as well and a swell of pitiful cries arose once more.

"People! People!" Kayla shouted from the floor, "Calm down, now! Calm down! We're not trying to blow up the fuckin' plane or anythin'! We only want to shoot the wogs!"

Rather than mollify the crowd, this increased the shrieking. Ian tried to gauge the reactions of those nearest to him. None would meet his gaze or even look up from between their knees. They reminded him of ostriches trembling in the sand. One, a teenage boy, had replaced his headphones and was humming softly, eyes squeezed tight against tears rolling down his face. Another woman seemed to be hyperventilating. Ian thought about speaking to her but was afraid of inducing some sort of fit.

The panic level in the cabin was palpable, as if the air itself had thinned and couldn't be consumed fast enough. If even one person snapped, they would undoubtedly have a small scale stampede on their hands—an ugly event inside a Boeing 777. Ian took all of this in with an unsettling detachment. Part of him felt sick. Part of him knew he'd made a terrible mistake, but a larger part was eager to keep moving in order to stave off reflection, for he knew that if he stopped to think, the crushing weight of what he'd done to endanger these people would smother him. There was no denying that he'd fired the first shot. He tried to console himself with the fact that if they did indeed drop out of the sky, he wouldn't have to feel guilty for long.

Suddenly, Pyper Hurley was heard over the com system. She had somehow gotten hold of the aft cabin phone. Calm and resolute, its pacifying effect was instantaneous, like a cold cloth on the brow.

"Unfortunately, you've all been caught up in a conflict that isn't yours," she observed sadly, as if reading aloud a poignant passage in a children's book. "And while we won't hurt you, you can hurt yourself. I beg you to please stay seated, and for the love of God keep your heads down."

She clicked off.

Ian could breathe clearly again.

"You hear that, you whore?" Kayla screamed. "That means you can't unload entire clips at nothing! How 'bout you shoot at us instead of the wall!"

"You have a foul mouth you little pixie bitch," Tessa snapped back, her voice hoarse. She popped out into the aisle with remarkable agility and fired two shots at Kayla before any member of Green could think to respond. Both were angled too high; one slammed into the headrest in front of Kayla, ripping the fabric slightly. The other slammed into the console above with a loud rap, like a knuckle on wood.

"Kayla," Ian hissed, loud enough for her to hear across the middle isle. "Hold tight. Stupid shooting gets us nowhere."

Ian had to get back to Pyper. She could see everything from the rear galley. She could stand behind cover when everyone else was plastered to the floor. He marveled at the clear, quick thinking of his captain—the opposite of his own. He slid over to the aisle and chanced a glance backwards. Pyper was right there looking at him, barely visible behind the wall of the galley, as if she had been anticipating him. At first he tried to explain himself, make amends for losing his cool.

"Pyper, I—"

"Let's just win it and get back on the ground, Ian," she said coolly. She was truly a Mother Superior.

"You and Kayla need to move up the two aisles in shifts. One dashes while the other fires. Quickly, before they realize what's happening."

Ian slid back to the ground in front of his seat.

"Kayla," he hissed again, just above the whining of the engines and the moaning of the people. "To the other aisle! Then forward in shifts! Five up, five down! Wait for my fire!"

He started counting down. Five, four, three, two...

He was firing before he was up on his knees, alternating from where he knew Tessa to be, over to where he thought Lorenzo Aldobrandi might be, and back to Tessa. He fired five shots, one for each count. He didn't get a chance to see if it was working or not. He could only duck and shove himself into position to dash forward again, like a sprinter on a platform. Sure enough, seconds later Kayla was firing from her new position over on the other aisle, several rows up. Ian scrambled forward like the floor was hot pavement, covering his head and pawing his way onward. He counted down five seconds then slammed himself sideways into the nearest row of seats and people, knocking knees together like swinging pendulums. He shoved his gun into all three of the unfortunate passengers' faces, taking the offensive in case anybody tried to be a hero.

"Don'tmoveI'llbegoneinasecond!"

They begged for their lives but Ian had no time to listen. It was his turn to give cover fire. He popped up and pulled the trigger five more times, once a second. He saw Kayla briefly as she threw herself forward down the opposite aisle. He then ducked down and placed himself on the mark once more. Kayla stopped firing and Ian was about to dash, but he heard someone else dashing instead. He chanced a look out in time to see the wounded Ignazio Andizzi retreating backwards at a severe angle, literally falling his way to the front rows and managing to force his way into the same aisle his captain had holed herself up in.

Ian dashed into an empty seat, immediately threatening all nearby. Someone retched on the floor near him and he was hit by a sprinkle of bile. He was close: ten rows from Tessa and the wounded Andizzi. Up until this point, the Italians had been strangely silent, especially the sweeper, somewhere over on Kayla's side of the plane. This worried Ian. He was more cautious with his cover fire when his turn came; he popped out from the side of the seat in front of him, and then the top, then the side again. He still couldn't pinpoint Lorenzo's exact location. What was he doing? Why hadn't he made himself known? Kayla had to be close to him, probably fewer than ten rows away.

—

Javier Renaldo was on his third flight in two days. He was coming back from a disastrous sales pitch in Dublin that he was sure would net him nothing, and was contemplating how to break the news to his regional manager. He was under his parts quota for the month, hadn't slept more than six of the last forty-eight hours, and had terrible cuts on the inside of his nose from the cabin's dry air. Even worse, he was positive that the seat in front of him was broken; it seemed to recline a good five inches farther back than anyone else's. When he heard the first pop, he was sure the airplane was exploding. It fit perfectly with the current trend of things.

Several loud pops later, it was clear he was in the middle of a hostile takeover. Then some woman had gotten on the loudspeaker and actually told them all to calm down. *Calm down!* As if he could just shut out the gunfire! Javier wasn't calm, yet strangely enough, Javier wasn't that scared.

Javier was pissed off.

And now he was forced to sit, like a constipated child, with his head between his bony knees and watch through his legs as one of the crazy gunmen—actually a woman— dashed up the aisle towards him.

He thought about the loans he was still paying off. If these crazy assholes slammed the plane into a building he would die in debt. And that was what they were going to do, he was positive; he'd seen the footage of 9/11. He'd watched the made for T.V. movies. They were heading for the fiftieth storey of some building, and when they slammed into it, he'd die without a nickel to his name.

And the whole time he could only watch as his death approached, a few rows at a time. She looked about 18 years old.

Javier blinked.

She was just a girl. She was actually kind of cute. Was she really the one making all this noise? He watched as she popped up like a groundhog, fired five swift shots, and then ducked down again. He shivered over his knees as the woman to his right screamed again and then cut herself off just as quickly. Yes, she was making the noise. This girl was a cold blooded killer. A vixen. She was going to get to the cockpit, shoot the door open, and fly them all straight to hell.

Unless he could stop her. He wasn't screaming or crying or pissing himself like the rest of them. He had his wits. She was just a girl. He could be a hero. They'd give him the key to some city. He'd be on cereal boxes and cable news channels. He might even get a book deal. Goodbye debt!

She wasn't that far back now. She'd be next to him in half a minute. Through his legs he assessed her stature. She looked maybe a hundred pounds. He wasn't a big guy, but he could handle a hundred pound girl. He'd knock her out and take her gun. No problem. Surely by then people would see his heroism and be inspired to follow.

Very slowly, Javier unfastened his safety belt.

Lorenzo Aldobrandi also saw Kayla MacQuillan approaching his row one dash at a time. Twice he moved to shoot her when she popped out to run, and twice Ian Finn's cover fire kept him pinned in his seat as surely as if he'd forgotten to unbuckle. Finn didn't know exactly where he was, but his shots were close enough. They moved quickly as a team, sweeping the plane from aft to fore. Every time he thought he saw one of them, the other started shooting and forced him to hunch over in his seat again. If you didn't notice the gun he was holding right at the pit of his stomach, you might mistake him for another hapless bystander, just like the terrified couple to his right, heads bowed low and stuck together, hands intertwined. Aldobrandi wasn't sure, since they were speaking in English, but he thought they might be praying.

And all the while, Kayla was making moves, row by row. She was more cautious now. She knew that he was nearby. He knew that if he made any move, he'd be seen. If he even repositioned his gun to where he might have a shot, much less stood up, he'd be blown away, if not by her, then by Ian Finn from the wide angle. But he was getting desperate. In moments he might have to risk it all. Maybe he could get a shot off before he went under.

He was steadying himself for his suicidal stand, taking a few deep breaths hunched over in his seat, when he looked to his left and saw a man just two rows back slowly unbuckling his seatbelt. The conspiratorial manner in which he lifted the clasp and gently pulled apart the two ends meant he wasn't doing this for comfort. He looked bedraggled. His suit was crumpled and his hair was sticking up oddly. He looked like a man at the end of his rope.

Now this was interesting…he was making a fist, flexing his knuckles.

Lorenzo relaxed. He was just going to wait. If things panned out how he thought they were about to, this poor fellow might just turn the tables for his entire team.

—

Kayla was going to allow herself two more rows. Two more rows and then she would make her stand. She would be at a good angle to pin down both Tessa and the wounded Andizzi on the other side of the plane, and she was sure that Lorenzo was just four rows up, somewhere on the right side, hunched over like a sissy. She kept her eye on that row, watching for the slightest movement. She waited for Ian to start his five seconds of cover fire, and she ran.

She had gone two steps when someone tripped her. Some idiot snapped his leg out into the aisle and tripped her up. Before she could look up at him he'd lashed out a hand, more of a whip than a punch, and caught her right in the eye. There was an explosion of color behind her retina, and then everything started to water.

"What the—"

She snapped her gun around and saw a shabby, terrified businessman in a bad suit. She paused, one hand over her weepy eye. There was a break in the cover fire as Ian Finn crouched and prepared to move up again in pattern, totally unaware.

Lorenzo merely had to reach over with his gun. He fired from one foot away. The diode slammed into the base of her skull, and she collapsed into the businessman's arms. Her head was thrown onto his lap where she lay limp, like a child asleep.

CHAPTER THIRTY-FIVE

GREER NICHOLS WAS FINDING it a very inconvenient time to be the Master of Ceremonies. Not only was he in charge of maintaining his *own* team, Team Blue, but for this series of rounds he was also in charge of mediating larger disputes and is-sues. He had problems hand over fist: there was an unprecedented increase in the number of civilians who found themselves on the wrong side of a gun, he was still trying to explain away a major firefight in the middle of a hotel in Tokyo, and now there were reports of an airplane incident—and all this before the second round! Greer took a deep breath, ran his hand over his gleaming, bald dome, and squared himself once more in front of his guests. There was no time for self-pity. He was paid to facilitate and to mediate. He planned on doing just that.

"I know time is precious for all of us, so I'll be brief," said Greer. "You men will no doubt remember each other," he gestured first to his left. "Tom Pierson, head of this hemisphere's intellectual property and contracts division. Tom, the man next to you is Baron Miller, our criminal law specialist. You both are very expensive, and you both round up by the hour. So let's get down to it."

Miller and Pierson nodded respectfully at each other. Both were venerable looking men. Miller was balding slightly, and Pierson was graying slightly more, but doing it well.

"First things first." Greer flipped open a dossier marked *Youngsmith*. He cleared his throat and his voice dropped to its natural baritone octave. "Almost a month ago this guy showed up on our radar. His name is Frank Youngsmith, and he was digging around for his work as a claims adjuster. Now, ordinarily this is no big deal. Occasionally people cross paths with us, but generally this type of stuff is restricted to rumor mills and conspiracy websites. The press often writes us off as gang activity or something of the like, and people go on their way. But our techs flagged him nonetheless and we put a watch out for him.

"For several weeks, there was no further activity from Frank, and it was assumed he had lost interest. But then, unexpectedly, he came back online. He was much more direct this time. He was looking for BlueHorse Limited. BlueHorse, as you'll know, is Team Blue's financial holdings firm, and the focal point of investment and betting in the Americas. It's a legitimate company, but very closed doors, and not one Frank Youngsmith should bother himself with in any case.

"Because he was already on watch status, Frank was fully reported this time. We shut his office IP down, but nothing stopped this guy. Somehow he caught Lock's trail as he was delivering correspondence at the UCSD Hospital. Lock managed to lose him, but not before something happened."

"What was that?" Baron Miller asked, writing with a brilliant silver pen on a yellow pad in his lap. Tom Pierson had crossed his arms over his chest and was leaning back in his chair, pondering.

"We're fairly sure he talked to a doctor out there. Dr. Baxter Walcott, one of our top medical men. Walcott has a history of…disagreeing with what the Tournament does. He says it flies in the face of the Hippocratic Oath."

"Did you bring Walcott in?"

"Walcott has a certain amount of leverage with us. He's very important. One of the best. Diode hits, they're pretty brutal. And the learning curve as a physician for treating diode injuries is severe. Many years of training. Bottom line is we need Walcott and he knows it. Especially now."

"And this Youngsmith," Pierson prodded. "Where is he?"

"I think we spooked him. Either that, or some combination of work stress and what he was learning about us finally caused him to snap. By the time we could send men to his Colorado Springs home, he was already gone."

Tom sucked in air through his teeth. "That's unfortunate."

Miller shrugged. "So he's gone. No harm, no foul."

Greer held up a finger. "Here's where it gets tricky."

He reached under his desk and pulled up a leather portfolio. After a moment's deliberation, he popped open the brass clasps and withdrew two stapled packets. He passed these out to Pierson and Miller.

The cover page read THE TOURNAMENT, and then, under that, BY FRANK YOUNGSMITH.

"Oh shit," said Tom Pierson, his voice flat.

Baron Miller briefly flipped through about half of the report before he had to close it up again, take off his square framed spectacles, and rub his eyes. He let out a tired sigh.

"I know," said Greer, tapping the cover. "He even got the name right."

"Well, in all fairness, it's not a very original name, now, is it?" noted Miller.

"You think this is funny, Baron?" Greer asked. "If we can't contain this, it's a shit storm for you, too. People love a good gunfight. They'll come out to watch."

"Jesus," Tom said, leafing through the packet. "He's taken it upon himself to document this entire organization."

"Something Walcott must have said to him at UCSD sure lit a fire under his ass. He started digging. He got a basic idea of the diode, probably from Walcott, and he went from there. Ostensibly this is a file documenting his company's investigation of Bill Beauchamp's death, from the insurance perspective. But it's thorough—which is not good for us. He also sent copies to his work," Greer said.

"It's hardly complete" said Bowen. "He only has a basic grasp."

"True. He's missing quite a bit, and quite a bit more is clearly conjecture, but it doesn't matter. This document is public now."

"How many copies are out there?"

"We can't know. It's online through Barringer Insurance. God knows who else Frank has told, or mailed, to try and save his own ass."

Greer tossed his own copy across his desk in disgust.

"What can we do here?" Greer asked. "Can we censor this stuff? Sue?"

"If an individual or an entity came forward and claimed

to own the patent for the diode, we might be able to prosecute Frank Youngsmith for divulgence of trade secrets," suggested Tom.

"That would never happen. I don't even know who would come forward."

"Of course it wouldn't. Admitting to the diode would mean admitting to the whole thing," Tom said, holding up his packet.

"We don't prosecute in this organization, Greer," said Baron. "It's far too messy. We use our extensive knowledge of the criminal and civil legal systems to pay people off at exorbitant rates. We find what people want and trade it to them in exchange for silence or cooperation. Find out what this Youngsmith character wants."

"By the looks of it, he wants to be left alone," said Greer.

"We can't do that," said Tom. "He knows too much, and he's telling people. If he catches the right ear…We have a hard enough time keeping this organization under wraps as it is."

The men were silent for a moment in which only the muted, white noise of the office computers could be heard.

"Maybe we should go on the offensive," Greer said.

"Damage control?" asked Baron.

"Are you talking about going public?" asked Tom, incredulous. "That's ridiculous, Greer. This thing is *illegal.*"

"*Very* illegal," said Baron. "For one, it's a massive off the books gambling operation, and that's not even factoring in what these teams do. The public is not ready for this. Do you know who gambles on these teams?"

"No," Greer said, eyeing the dull glass eyes of the camera lenses above him.

"Neither do I. Nobody does. But I can guess, and so can you. Your team is brokering a troop movement based on the outcome of what's happening in Tokyo right now. The type of people who can do that have a lot of power and they like their privacy."

Greer said nothing. He rubbed his head.

"Greer," said Tom, warily. "Greer, I don't like that look. That staring look you get. Promise me you'll tell me if you're thinking of doing something stupid like go public. Give me enough time to move my assets overseas. And my family."

"I think we're losing control here," admitted Greer. "We've never seen this level of violence, in all of our years here. We're already sliding down the slope. If we sit around and wait for this story to break, we lose. If we react, maybe we can shape what the world will think of us."

Baron rubbed the bridge of his nose. Tom flipped his pad shut and stood up.

"All right Greer, you're clearly under a lot of stress. It's been a bloody round, and as the chips fell you're forced to moderate for the collective administrations. It's a lot to ask. You're not in your right mind, so I'm going to come back when you are."

"If you ask me, we were lucky to get what years of secrecy out of it we did," said Greer. "And now we're losing control. Time for a new approach."

"We're not losing control! It's just a particularly heavy round!" Baron stated, standing up.

"I don't think either of you really believe that. We aren't

even through round one and we've got one destroyed nightclub, a gunfight in the middle of Tokyo, and reports of some fresh hell on an airplane above the English Channel. You think we're not losing control? Well here's what I say. I say we never had it in the first place. Only now are we realizing what we've truly done out there, and it's far too late for us to stop it. Either start packing or stand tall, but either way I think you boys need to get ready for a new dawn. Consider yourselves warned."

CHAPTER THIRTY-SIX

THEY SHUT DOWN THE trains.

Amidst the gunshots, someone pulled the full stop emergency alarm on the station platform and the outgoing and incoming trains went dead on their tracks. The people were another matter. Even as Northern and Max ran out of the platform to the streets, the panicked wave followed. People had heard by now of the shootings. Japan didn't have many shootings. In fact, it hardly ever had shootings. And this one was big. Live news feeds reported that three foreigners were creating mayhem, and both men were easily spotted.

And now Nikkie Hix was gone, and Northern was screaming into his cell phone as he tore around corners and across streets, getting briefed on the situation by his administration as he tried to shake the panic that was tailing him. He pocketed his phone and looked about, blue eyes wild.

"Where is her body?" asked Max, breathless.

"Medical already picked her up," said Northern. "This way, quickly."

All around them people were pointing and crying, or on their phones taking pictures. Pictures that would be everywhere in a matter of seconds.

"She got Tenri Fuse though, right in the gut," Northern said, ducking down the nearest and darkest alley, pulling Max along.

"So he's gone?"

"Gone. It's just Takuro Obata now."

"Well done, Nikkie, well done," Max said, but his sidelong glance at Northern was grim, almost affronted. Even wounded, Hix was worth five of that sniveling Tenri Fuse. They shouldn't have left her. *He* shouldn't have left her.

"The Tournament can only confuse the police for so long," Northern said, oblivious. "If we go back into the center of the ward we're going to get shot by the cops. Greer said they're swarming Akihabara station, right alongside our cleanup crews."

"Where is Obata?" asked Max, lips barely moving

Northern glanced around him. Everywhere people stared and pointed. When his gaze fell upon them they scattered, but only enough to lose his attention. People peered out of windows and from around buildings.

"He's going to find us before we find him, if we stay outside like this."

"The police," Max said, dazed. He was pointing back the way they'd come, where two starch-hatted Japanese men in pristine blue suits with white gloves had just pushed their way out of a door. An elastic loop ran like a wallet chain from the butts of their guns to the hips of their belts. Their guns were in their hands.

The Americans ran, turning corners wildly, bowling over the old and young to escape the pervasive eyes, but with every step they made themselves more conspicuous. Stares stuck to them like gossamer webs. Whenever they stopped to breathe, someone pointed. There was no escaping Japan. It was everywhere.

Northern slammed open the sliding wooden door of a small noodle shop close to hand and threw Max and himself inside. He closed the door and rested his head against the wood for a moment. Then he turned around. A small, elderly Japanese woman studied him from behind a smoke yellowed countertop. No other people were inside. Her face was lined and compressed like a cabbage. It was impossible to read her impression of them, each with a hand under their jacket.

"This place is as good as any," Northern said.

Max watched the woman and nodded slowly. She said something unintelligible in scratchy, toothless Japanese and hobbled through a sooty curtain into the back of the shop. Max walked over to the curtain and pulled it aside.

"She's going outside. She's leaving."

"Fine. Let her go."

Both men heard the faint thumping of distant helicopter blades.

"Jesus," whispered Max. "What the hell is going on out there?"

"They're probably telling people to get off the streets. Maybe it's a Tournament chopper. Waiting to see how things turn out. Waiting to clean up."

The late afternoon sun was throwing long shadows across the muddled glass paneling of the door, creating illusions.

"There are people out there," Max said, pulling his gun out from his jacket, "They're pointing at the building."

"What the hell is wrong with these people? Do they want to get shot?"

"Well if they don't already know who are, they're about to," Northern said.

"What?"

"The Tournament. This is going to be a hard one to cover up."

"John, if we get out of this one alive—"

But Max never got the chance to finish. The glass door Northern was leaning upon exploded.

—

It hadn't been hard for Takuro Obata to find the small ramen shop where the Americans were hiding.

After he shot Nikkie Hix in the head he caught a cab to Kanda station, one up the line, where Max and Northern had shot his striker. When he got out of the cab in the neighborhood district, people were pointing and calling on their phones and floating about in contagious excitement.

"What happened here?" he asked the nearest group.

"Two foreigners were shooting. They ran that way."

All Obata had to do was follow.

The path to the shop was erratic, the two men had panicked, but their trail was as clear as day. Obata simply followed the twittering of the people like a bloodhound on a scent. Whenever he didn't know which way to turn, inevitably someone would be standing on a corner, talking in hushed tones and eyeing in a certain direction. His countrymen were helping him without knowing so. It was an odd sensation. He'd always assumed he would fight on their behalf, but he had never imagined that they might work for *him*.

An eclectic crowd had already gathered outside of the shop; schoolchildren in uniform mixed with elderly neighbors and passing businessmen who had stopped to see what the fuss was about. Very small children ran about his legs giggling. The atmosphere reminded him of the neighborhood festivals of his youth, but all the more alluring for the sense of danger in the air. These people knew that there was some sort of monster holed up inside the shop. Something legendary and mythic that they could tell their children about.

Then he noticed that many of the people were watching him.

And then he realized that he was holding his gun, but the people weren't afraid. They nodded at him and gave small whispers of encouragement.

"Good luck, sir," they said, using the most honorific Japanese.

"Keep struggling," they whispered.

They parted for him. He saw a glass paneled door, its panes muddled and impossible to see through clearly. But he saw a shape. Someone inside was leaning on it.

A very old woman with a pinched face pushed through to him and patted him gingerly on his hip. She whispered something he couldn't understand and pointed at the door.

Obata knew that this was two on one. If he started a shooting match he would get killed right in the midst of this crowd, but if he turned away he would dishonor himself in front of his people. The thought made him sick. No. He would have to fly like the wind. One shot to take out the glass panel; his body would follow his diode and he would throw himself forward upon them, meet his fate head on. That was his only chance. It was a fitting attack.

He took a breath and squared himself into a shooting stance. The people quieted.

He fired once and then dashed.

Obata buried his face inside his coat as he ran. As the diode hit the glass it exploded out towards him in a shower of dime sized fragments, like a hose set on wide spray, and he tore through them like they were water. He dropped his shoulder and blew through the wooden frame.

Northern was blindsided. He became a ragdoll folded over Obata's shoulder as Obata drove him into the overhang of the countertop. Northern's gun popped out of his grasp as if spring loaded. The vertebrate of his spine popped like the knuckles of a fist, and air exploded out of his lungs with such force that he felt as flat as paper. He tried to breathe and sucked only the hollow of his empty chest. Struggling for air, he focused only on keeping Obata's gun away from his body. He tore at it like an animal and caught the Japanese captain unawares, Obata's gun skittered out of his hand and puffed through the back curtain of the shop, missing Max by inches.

Max turned to fire but had no target, only a twisting, flailing mass of humanity. There was no clear distinction between where Northern stopped and Obata began. They flipped around each other like spinning tops, but Obata was clearly in his element. He deliberately positioned Northern between Max and himself. He knew exactly where Max was, and knew what would happen if he exposed his back to the striker.

Obata fought with trained efficiency, staying low, grappling Northern about the knees and keeping a wide stance. Northern was still sucking wind and trying his best to defend himself. Obata caught him in the temple with the point of his elbow and Northern's vision blurred. He dipped slightly, stunned, and Obata took advantage. Grabbing Northern by the lapels of his jacket, Obata pulled him back and around the bar and threw him into Max. Northern's head popped back into Max's already bruised nose, squelching a teaspoon's worth of thick blood from both nostrils. Max choked out a sloppy groan and staggered back.

Obata stepped forward and repositioned himself, then slashed out with an axe kick that struck Max's gun hand. It drove his gun straight into the floor where it bounced nearly to Obata's waist. Obata tried to grab it, but his hand snatched only air. It landed on the grimy linoleum floor, partially propped up against the wall fifteen feet away. He turned to chase it but Northern grabbed him and spun him right back around and into his fist.

Obata managed to tense his neck muscles and bob his head in time to deflect much of the punch down his jaw. With both hands, he shoved Northern back into Max again, turned, and dashed for Max's gun. Northern pushed off of Max and dove after him, slamming Obata forward into the wall above the gun as he made a grab for it himself. Obata wrenched around and slammed the heel of his palm into Northern's mouth. His skin split on Northern's wolfish I-teeth and Northern choked and sputtered before he could bite down. Obata grunted and reached down for the gun. Northern kneed him in the balls. Both men collapsed. Northern spat blood.

"Max! Get my gun! Behind the count—"

Obata chopped Northern's windpipe and again grabbed for Max's gun. Gurgling out a cry, Northern reached for it as well. Obata clasped it first, but Northern gripped over Obata's hand and immediately yanked down on his trigger finger. The men fought for control of the gun as it fired in every direction. Max dove for the floor.

"Max!" Northern pleaded, coughing hoarsely. "Max! Please!"

Obata was slowly curling the gun inwards and down at Northern. It fired again and again, closer by the shot. Northern could feel the heat of the barrel on his face. He heard only explosions and ringing. Muzzle flash singed the fine blonde hairs on his forehead. Obata was turning the gun on him now point blank. He could see down the oily chamber. Obata pulled the trigger.

The gun clicked.

The gun clicked again.

Obata hissed in anger and slammed his fist into Northern's kidney. Northern lashed his legs out, sweeping Obata to the ground. He fell hard on his hip, hitched up, and tried to rise but fell again.

"Max, for Christ's sake! Get a fucking gun!" Northern croaked, struggling to sit up under the overhang of the counter. Obata pushed back to the wall and began to rise; his nostrils flared and his rounded brow creased as he looked about for a weapon. Both guns were somewhere behind the counter, with Max.

Northern was still on the floor, clutching his side. Obata slowly stood. He pushed himself off of the wall just as Max appeared from behind the curtain, his nose crunched up to stem the blood flow.

He leveled his gun at Obata as the captain charged forward with a bellow. Max fired three times in quick succession. All three shots jack hammered into Obata's sternum and he was driven right back into the wall as if he had been tethered there. He sucked in one heavy breath, dropped to a sitting position, and closed his eyes. His head drooped to his shoulder. His breathing became very shallow and small, but consistent. He was out.

"I can't believe he just charged in here like that!" Max cried, shaking his head. Drops of blood spattered all over the counter.

Northern grunted as he massaged his jawbone. He spat out the last of Obata's blood and some of his own.

"You all right, John?"

"Help me up."

Max grabbed a bar towel and pressed it to his nose as he walked around the counter. He pulled Northern up. Once standing, Northern saw that his striker was nursing an already purpling right wrist.

"It's not a break. I've broken bones before. Just a sprain," Max said, taking down the reddened towel.

Max looked even worse for the wear than Northern did himself. His lower face was splotchy and streaked from the blood he'd wiped off using both sleeves. His teeth were a reddish brown. His nose looked squished, as if he was leaning face first on a pane of glass.

"The nose I'm not so sure about."

"Jesus, Max."

"I'll be fine."

Approaching sirens now mixed in with the methodical whumping of helicopters.

"We've got to go," Max drily observed.

"So we live to fight another day," said Northern, hobbling gingerly towards the window to peer outside. "Barely."

Max said nothing. He moved behind the counter and held the curtain aside for his limping captain.

CHAPTER THIRTY-SEVEN

Draden Tate found her.

She went straight to check on the whimpering family. Lilia Alvarez had somehow slithered her way in the back window, around him in the kitchen, and now leaned against a wall, casting furtive glances towards the living room and the couch where the Vega family sat in all their misery.

Tate shook his head in disbelief. What did she think she was going to do? Even with Christina off after Felix Ortiz, was she really stupid enough to think she could single-handedly take down both Alex Auldborne and himself at once? It was suicide. Perhaps she thought she could just get a nice look at everyone and then sneak out of the window again unharmed. Draden almost laughed to himself. What a stupid little girl.

Her back was facing him. She wore a dusty black tank top that exposed her dark brown shoulders, and her slender arms braced against the wall. She carried a gun, but she didn't aim at anything. She just held it loosely in her hand. From time to time she glanced behind herself towards the kitchen, looking for him. She never saw him, of course. He was hidden himself, kitty corner to where she stood in the same room, between the wall and a freestanding cabinet full of dishes. He watched her reflection on the glass front of that cabinet and could see her every move clearly. Every time she looked behind her, her gaze swept the room briefly, and always missed him. She thought he was in front of her, not behind.

He marveled at her confidence. She was like a rabbit, thinking that by flattening herself she would escape notice. She had the gall to throw herself into the lion's den and now she believed she was going to escape again.

Not today.

Grey had a new policy when handed situations such as this. When an opponent had their back to them like she did, none the wiser, they were to go for the *Bludgeon Blackout*. Auldborne had decreed that anytime any of them was offered the chance to bludgeon, they were to take it. They were to practice in the hopes that they would match up with Blue again. Draden had the feeling that when Auldborne eventually got a hold of Johnnie Northern he wouldn't stop at a gun butt to the head. And Draden, for one, didn't blame him.

So it was time to practice.

He breathed very slowly and watched her look for him. She was so small. Slamming his gun into her face might break her, or kill her. He didn't want to kill her, really, just hurt her. Maybe he'd use his fists—not that they were much better. But what could he do? Blue had forced them into this. Lilia had only the Americans to blame for the fate of her face.

She would see him coming at the last minute. He would make sure of that. What fun was a kill if the poor sap never even saw who brought down the wrath? It was like pulling off a robbery and never being able to take credit. Draden never understood criminals who wore masks. There was no glory in that.

And so he lumbered out of the dark corner like a bear,

and she did see him, and it was too late for her.

He went for her gun arm first. He brought his fist down on her shoulder like a mallet. He could actually feel the bone underneath slip its muscle holding, like shifting a marble around in a sack. She barked out a brief scream and swung her other hand around right into Tate's face. She wanted to tear his eyes out, but he closed them and she could only rake him, shaving small slivers of skin. She grabbed at his mouth and managed to tear his lip before collapsing into the wall. He roared and reared his head back. She fought against the numb, wrong feeling in her shoulder and used the time to try to switch her gun to her good arm. Then he kicked her knee in.

She was just able to shift and move with the momentum of his boot enough to prevent total cartilage rip, but something tore. She felt fluid rushing into her knee seconds before she lost all purchase on the ground and collapsed in a heap at Tate's feet. But he was still feeling about his face. She had but a moment. She grabbed her gun and fired.

The diode hammered into his forearm. He let out a low "Oh," and slapped the gun away with his other hand, swinging it like the pendulum of a grandfather clock. It flew across the room. Her knee was puffing with pain. Even the barest touch of the wall grated against her shoulder. She looked at her knee; she looked at her shoulder. Then she looked up at Tate in silence and in pain and shook her head as if sorry for the man.

"Don' be blamin' me for this, yeah?" he said.

He popped up the middle knuckle on his right fist and batted it into Lilia's temple. She collapsed.

After ten or fifteen seconds of silence, Alex Auldborne chimed in from the front room.

"Are you quite done in there?"

"Bitch tore up my face."

"But is she out?"

"Bludgeon. Special present for you."

"Wonderful! Let's report it to our heroic captain Diego Vega just outside, shall we? See how he reacts?"

Draden cast one last look over Lilia's prone, barely breathing body before walking into the front room, his hand over his left eye. He tongued his flap of lip.

"Look here man. Look what she did."

Auldborne glanced at him, angled his gaze, and sniffed. "You'll live. Do you think Christina is anywhere near that sweeper on the hill?"

"How long she been out there?"

"Five minutes."

"Maybe."

"Thanks. Wonderful help."

"So sorry. I been actually doin' things. Not just lookin' and runnin' aroun'. Maybe you should call her," Draden said, voice flat.

Auldborne looked back at him once more and cocked an eyebrow. He smiled. "See now? You're just fine."

Draden grunted.

"No, I won't call her. I'm sure she's where she needs to

be." As if that had decided everything, he opened the door again.

———

Diego Vega heard the shot from inside the house as he sat under cover in the dusty park's playground. He prayed it was Lilia and that she had hit someone. Preferably Auldborne.

Seconds later, the door to his house opened. No one stepped into the slanted square of light cast inside the house, but Diego heard the nasally, drawn out voice of Auldborne. He sighed. He didn't have to understand English to pick up on the triumphant tone.

"She put up a fight, Diego! She really did! Or so I hear. I was too busy keeping an eye on your shifty family and I thought it lasted all of about five seconds, but my striker tells me she scratched at him like a little Mexican cat!" Auldborne laughed. "But she's gone now!"

Diego's phone started buzzing: Ortiz was calling from the hill. He dismissed the call as he continued to stare into the sunlit patch of the inside of his house and the darkness beyond. His family was in that darkness, and now Lilia was too, lying unconscious, or worse. The doorway called to him. Auldborne's voice called to him. He felt sick. He felt cramped from his crouching there, under the slide, hiding like a boy.

Diego stood. He chambered a diode.

Up on the hill, Felix Ortiz pocketed his phone and swore softly. He peered up from around the mound of earth he had positioned himself behind and tried to get a bead on his captain. He could see the playground; it was about 20 meters below and off to the left. The house was another 30 meters beyond that. He'd be lucky to hit the house itself at 50 meters, much less anybody in it or near it. There was nothing for it; he'd have to move in with Diego. The man was walking to his death if he went alone. This business with his family had thrown his brain off. He wasn't being rational. Ortiz shook his head and cocked his gun. He'd have to swing wide and come in from the side of the house.

He scampered around the mound of earth and walked right into Christina Stoke. She stuck the snub nosed end of her revolver into his gut and fired three times before he could even think to say or do anything. She blew him a kiss as he staggered back and fell onto the dirt, out in a matter of seconds.

She wiped dust from her hands off on his shirt and saw Diego running for the house. She was amused. He must have mistaken her shooting for Felix Ortiz trying to cover his run. She might as well give him a few more. She lazily raised her revolver and laughed as she fired haphazardly. He was running to his doom. The idiocy of it struck her as particularly funny, how by plucking one string a man could become so unhinged. He'd been debased. Auldborne had been right. Everyone had a string like that; the key was to find it and to pluck it. The Mexicans had made a mistake when they hired a family man for this job. This was no job for a family man.

Diego Vega ran for the door like a man afire, leaning forward, tearing with his hands at the air in front of him as if he could grab hold of it and use it to propel himself. His face was contorted in an emasculated rage that was more sorrow than anger, and as he ran forward Alex Auldborne sauntered out of the door frame. Diego tried to hitch up and take a stance to fire, but he couldn't stop himself in time.

Auldborne fired at the shoulder of Diego's gun arm. The diode went exactly where he wanted it to, slamming into Diego's arm and flinging his body around. For a moment, he was a puppet jerked hard by one string. Then he tripped over his own feet and crashed face first in the dirt not ten feet from the porch of his house.

Auldborne watched Diego as he spat out grit and moaned in the dirt, trying first to will his gun arm to work, and when that proved too much, to switch hands. It was like watching a fish out of water.

Diego looked behind him for Felix to back him up but he saw only the girl, Christina Stoke, strolling towards him with exaggerated slowness.

"Felix is gone, Diego," Auldborne said.

Diego flopped himself around and grabbed his gun. He squinted up at Auldborne through a yellow haze of dust.

Auldborne shrugged. "Go on then. Raise your arm and take aim. I've been told I'm the best shot in this humble outfit, but I enjoy proving it to myself. Let's all see who gets shot first then, shall we?"

Diego raised his arm. Auldborne allowed him to get very close to a full-on sight before shooting his gun directly from his hand, as sure as if he was right next to him and had plucked it from his grasp. Diego's fingers went numb as his gun skittered in the dust behind him. He didn't follow it with his eyes. He dropped his head onto the dirt. It felt very cool on his forehead.

"You don't even want to look at me, Diego?"

Diego shifted the coolness of the dirt to his cheek. He said nothing. He didn't understand Alex Auldborne, and he figured that even if he could, the man was saying nothing that he wanted to hear. Let him have his fun.

"Look at me, Diego."

Diego's breathing burrowed a tiny divot in the soft dirt next to his nose. Auldborne walked to where he lay, kicked Diego's hat away, and pulled his head up by the hair.

"Look at me!"

But Diego looked past Auldborne to the marred white front door of his house. He saw the blood handprint, lurid and obscene, like a jagged scar cut through the canvas of a piece of art. Kicking with his legs, he struggled to crawl forward. Auldborne let go and stepped back, smiling.

"Look at you then! Bravo! Crawl my friend!"

Diego focused on the door. His face burned.

Auldborne got down next to him on one knee. "How about this? If you can crawl your way up to the door, I'll let you see your family before I shoot you. How does that sound?"

Diego was able to worm his way forward for almost thirty seconds before he was too exhausted to continue. Only then did he look up at Auldborne, directly into his slate gray eyes. They were a void, like glass globes of swirling fog, punctured black in the middle. Diego worked moisture into his mouth and ran his tongue over his teeth to gather the grit, then he spat directly into Alex Auldborne's face.

Auldborne recoiled and stood, wiping his face repeatedly on his sleeve long after all of the saliva was gone, and then switching to the other arm to wipe more. He turned away from Diego while he did this. Then he placed his hands on his hips and shook his head at the horizon. After a moment, he turned back around. Diego said nothing, neither smiled nor frowned. He set his cheek back down on the cool dirt.

"Pitiful, really, your efforts here. You call yourself a family man?"

Diego lay still.

"Disgusting." Auldborne pulled the hammer back with his thumb, paused for a moment, and when he saw that Diego wasn't going to move, he fired directly down on the top of his head. Diego's body hitched a fraction of an inch in the dirt and then lay as before, eyes closed.

Auldborne glanced at Christina and blew out a long breath.

Team White was out.

CHAPTER THIRTY-EIGHT

IAN WAITED FOR FIVE seconds and prepped to run, but he didn't hear Kayla start to shoot. He waited for ten. Then fifteen. Nothing. And then he knew that she was gone, and that he was now all alone in the fore of the airplane not even ten rows from two members of Gold. Worse, if he moved even two meters forward he would be at the perfect angle for the third member to stand up from across the airplane and drop him as he stood. He was trapped.

He pushed himself farther back into the row of terrified passengers, thanking God that they were old and cowered instead of fought. He wiped his brow and looked backward for his captain. The old woman whose legs he was crammed up against began to sob.

"I'm not gonna hurt you," he hissed. The last thing he needed was to realize how guilty he felt about this disaster he had created. A bawling grandmother would do just that. Then he heard movement up ahead. He froze. He popped his head out and looked back towards the front of the cabin and saw the metal drink cart slowly rolling back down the aisle towards him. He brought himself back around and looked again for Pyper. She was out of sight in the galley. He had to get back there. He needed direction. Pyper always knew what to do.

He chanced another look around the seat and saw that

the drink cart had rolled to a stop perhaps ten rows up, near where Andizzi scrambled to safety after he'd shot him. In fact, exactly where Andizzi had scrambled.

Ian went cold.

The drink cart wasn't rolling of its own accord. Someone was behind it, and that someone was Tessa Crocifissa. She'd stopped at Andizzi's row to gather her wounded. He could hear them now. Andizzi was groaning, cursing in a spit heavy, guttural Italian. It struck Ian as odd that there were others witnessing this small war. Andizzi hadn't actually fired his gun yet; those seated nearby probably mistook him for some poor passenger that the rowdy Irishman had shot for no good reason. The lack of blood likely confounded them, but they only had to look at Andizzi to see that the pain was real. They probably thought that *he*, Ian Finn, was the bad guy. And were they so wrong? He'd started all of this.

Ian's head hurt. The whisky was wearing off. He badly needed a cigarette.

Suddenly the cart started moving again. Ian furrowed his brow.

A small voice inside of his head said, *They're coming for you. What are you going to do now? Are you going to start this thing only to lose it and get shot to pieces high in the sky?*

Ian shook his head. He had to get back to see Pyper.

He crouched and moved to the aisle and was immediately fired upon from across the airplane, a heavy cracking sound eerily devoid of echo that set the whole plane screaming again. Ian shoved himself back in the row and let out a gasping breath. He patted his back and his arms. Nothing. No numbness. He wasn't hit. Thank the Good Lord. He struggled to slow his breathing. He closed his mouth and tried to breathe through his nose but the air wasn't coming fast enough. He opened his mouth again, panting like a dog.

He should have figured that Lorenzo would pin him back from across the airplane. He'd shot Kayla, and was going to shoot him if he moved out into the isle. He was keeping him there, allowing his teammates to creep their way up and shoot him from behind the cart like a fish in a barrel.

He knew Pyper wasn't a big shooter, more of a field commander, but he could sure use some fire right now. He knew she was watching, waiting for the right time to act. Lorenzo was standing now, so he was vulnerable. He was probably switching his sight back and forth from Ian to the galley at the back of the plane where he knew Pyper was. He couldn't focus on one or the other for too long.

"Pyper!" he screamed. "Pyper! They're behind the cart!"

And then he saw her. She appeared on his side of the airplane, still in the galley and well out of sight of Lorenzo's cross fire, and she shushed him.

"Pyper!"

She shushed him again. He chanced a glance back at the cart. It was less than a meter away from him. He looked for any angle at all to shoot behind it. Nothing. It was flush to the seats. He turned back to Pyper again, eyes wide.

"Stick out your foot, Ian," she said with extraordinary calm.

Of course. What an idiot he'd been! If the cart was coming, stop the cart. You don't run away from a drink cart. You stop a drink cart. The stupid things were always slamming into his elbows and knees anyway. Why not just stick a leg out?

He flattened himself against the seat in front of him and slowly extended his leg into the aisle.

Ian closed his eyes and waited. He heard the cart squeak its way forward. He heard heavy breathing behind it and the metallic rustle of a gun. He didn't dare breathe.

He felt a little bump, like a polite tap on the side of his leg. The cart stopped. It tapped again and stopped once more. It was right next to him; he saw scuffs and dents on its dull gray side. Whispering rose from behind it. The voices sounded confused. Could it be that they thought he was farther back and that the cart had jammed itself on a seat?

There was another tap, more forceful. His leg held. Then came a prolonged push in which Ian had to use all of the muscles in his groin to keep his knee upright and holding. He gritted his teeth. There was a scraping sound of shoes on carpet and then a sharp, whispered string of Italian. Someone, probably Andizzi, began breathing very hard and groaning. He was hurt badly, and exerting himself was making it worse. Suddenly the groaning stopped— then the whispering.

Ian braced himself for a sudden slamming of force. He told himself he'd pop a hernia before he allowed that cart to roll forward another inch, but he knew that if Tessa slammed against it she'd make it move. He looked back at Pyper, who had taken out her gun and was now sighting it at the cart. She seemed nonplussed. Ian gestured wildly at his groin and at his knee and shook his head violently. She shushed him gently and nodded encouragement. Ian furrowed his brow and tried awkwardly to use his hand to brace his knee while positioning his gun to shoot through the small gap under the cart. Even if he managed to fire his gun sideways, the kickback might fling it out of reach, but he was desperate.

There was no big push. Instead he felt a mild pressure and heard a sliding sound: someone bracing against the cart and slowly rising.

Then Pyper fired three times in quick succession and the cart went slack on his leg. He heard a body crash on the far side.

"Ian! To me!" she yelled.

He ran low and with his hands over his head, like a soldier through a trench, expecting at any moment to feel the punching force of a shot from Lorenzo's gun, but it never came. Pyper picked Ian up off of his knees and brushed him off. She patted him on his shoulder. She told him to be quiet.

On the other side of the airplane, he heard Lorenzo calling for his captain, the normal calm in his voice strained, barely holding.

"Tessa?" he asked.

"Tessa? Ignazio? Hey, Ignazio! Ignazio?"

There was no answer.

"Ignazio!"

Pyper grabbed the intercom phone.

"Ignazio Andizzi is out. So is your captain. Disarm your gun, Lorenzo, and we can work this out on the ground. None of these people have to get hurt for this."

Lorenzo immediately sighted the galley, looking for any sign of the two of them. He tried to glimpse over the aisle at where his two teammates lay prone, but he couldn't see, and wouldn't allow himself to shift his focus completely. He curled his lip in grand disdain. His prominent chin raised high.

"Disarm my gun?" he asked, in thick English. "There is no disarm here. Once it start, it must finish!" he bellowed.

"Put your gun down, Lorenzo!" Ian screamed.

"Why don't you come take it, quick guy? Hey captain, why you no send your quick shot back here to take? Or you come?" Lorenzo sounded haughty, but his eyes were wide in his half-moon face, and he kept shifting his sight from one end of the galley to the other, waiting for the Irish to pop out from behind the wall.

"Ian, you agree I am a more accurate shot then you," Pyper whispered, a definite statement and not a question.

Ian paused. He looked over his shoulder and back down the aisle with the drink cart. Two passengers were cautiously peering down at the jumble of bodies behind it. They looked perplexed.

"Ian…"

"Yes. I suppose. If I had a gun to my head."

"Then I need you to run down the aisle towards him," she said.

"What? I just got here! You want me to run back down?"

"Get on his side of the galley. Wait for my signal."

"Wait just a minute here—"

"Get ready to run." She inched herself down the wall, millimeters from the open aisle.

"Pyper—"

"Go!"

Ian stepped out, propelled as much by Pyper's voice as by duty. It was the least he could do. He saw Lorenzo seeing him. He saw the proud rage in Lorenzo's face as he swung his aim towards him. Ian closed his eyes as he barreled down upon the man. He dropped his shoulder, ready to ram. He heard a single crack.

Ian tripped up and fell to the floor on all fours, scrambling for purchase. Already in a falling tumble, he met Lorenzo at the knees.

Pyper had stepped out immediately after Ian, sighted, and fired once across the airplane right into Lorenzo's sternum while he was adjusting his aim to Ian. He let out a tremendous *huff* sound, bounced his back off of the seat behind him, and then fell forward over Ian. There was a wave of screaming from front to back, like the cabin was on a rollercoaster. The passengers near him scrambled and pushed to avoid touching him as he lay draped over Ian.

Ian was still frozen, not breathing, not blinking. His heart hammered. Lorenzo's weight had him pinned to the floor. For the second time in as many minutes he waited for the pain to hit, for the terrible numbness to spread. But it never came.

Pyper dropped her gun to her side and took a measured breath. She walked around the galley and down to Ian and helped him to his feet. Lorenzo settled on his stomach, breathing softly in measured time.

"This wasn't good, Ian," Pyper said quietly, looking around the cabin. Not one head could be seen over any headrest. If it weren't for the crying, the occasional stifled screams, and the sickly sweet stench of vomit, one could almost believe the airplane was empty.

"I know. I know," Ian said, wiping his face and body, as if surprised to find it in one piece.

"But what's done is done, and Green still stands."

But not all of them. Kayla MacQuillan was still slumped into the aisle where she had been shot.

"Let's get Kayla, and get off this damn airplane," Pyper said.

CHAPTER THIRTY-NINE

ROUND TWO

G REER FACED THE CAMERAS with more apprehension than he had fourteen days ago. Then, he had simply announced the round one draw and the beginning of the Tournament. Now, everything was imploding.

He whisked his large hand over his gleaming head and brushed off the front of his suit coat. He unbuttoned one button further down on his deep blue shirt, decided against it, and re-buttoned. Just like he did two weeks ago, he would be speaking from his office. There was no in-house audience, only a battery of cold camera lenses. He watched as Bernard fiddled about with last minute alignment issues, assuring that each camera had a live feed and was focused on the desk. He went over his talking points in his mind once again.

White was out, Silver was out, Gold was out, Red was out.

Teams Green, Grey, Black, and Blue all managed to battle through to the second round—at extraordinary expense. Greer licked his teeth. This would not be easy. He had to speak to the extreme nature of this past round. He had to say *something.* In every case victory came at the cost of the unknowing public. By train and by plane, in homes and in clubs, no holds had been barred. But did he have any right to be surprised at this violent turn? This was a violent business, and if he looked back honestly

at the progression of things, the trend would have been obvious.
Hell, his own team stepped up the physicality of the rounds themselves when Johnnie Northern brained Alex Auldborne in the
last Tournament. What did he expect? Did he think the English
would take that one on the chin?

And the wagers were changing. Just as the players seemed
increasingly willing to go to extreme measures to win, so did the
anonymous bettors seem increasingly willing to wager the outrageous. As the most recent contract between Blue and Red had
proven, things were getting political. Blue won that fight, and so
the Americans would be staying at their bases in Yokohama and
Okinawa. Greer felt a great deal of pride in this: the first wager of
its kind, and his team won. But redress was inevitable—if not now,
then in the near future.

And then, of course, was the matter of discussing the
second round match ups. Any combination of the four remaining teams seemed explosive, but Greer had to admit that certain
combinations were more explosive than others.

Bernard signaled for Greer. He nodded, cleared his throat,
and settled himself below the big board. He set his hands on his
desk to keep them from fidgeting. Bernard began a soft countdown that went silent at *three, two, one…*

He was on.

He paused to allow for any delay, and then spoke.

"Ladies and gentlemen, welcome to round two of the
Tournament. I am Greer Nichols.

"Before the board matches the remaining teams, I should
voice some collective concerns with regards to the…inordinate
collateral damage accrued this round as compared to…really to

any other round in our history."

He paused and looked down briefly at his hands. The silence of the gleaming lenses of the cameras was deafening.

"The complete freedom of every team member has always been a top priority in this organization. The dream was to create a competition that had at its core total and absolute freedom. All we asked was that teams make a real effort to minimize civilian contact. We assumed that teams would abide by this, out of respect for human dignity. If we can take one thing away from this round, it is that we should no longer assume anything in this organization, ever.

"And now we have a problem. Victory at what expense? Is *any* price too high? We can levy fines against teams that lose control, but we're kidding ourselves if we think money, any amount of money, will be an effective deterrent for much longer. We need something else, something more, to make teams accountable.

"It's time to look at the teams you are supporting. They have evolved into something different. Something other than the men and women that they were when you contracted them or first followed their progress. Some for better, others, perhaps, for worse. I can't tell you what they fight for, what drives them and what controls them. Only you can."

Greer took a slow breath.

"The high visibility of these past four engagements is a turning point. We'd be fools not to acknowledge this, and we are not fools. The Tournament is changing. By now, many of you may be aware of a man named Frank Youngsmith, and of a report he has circulated on the nature of this business, for reasons of his own. His is the greatest single example, but for some time now awareness has grown on all fronts. Gunfights on airplanes, inside crowded nightclubs, and across busy city blocks do nothing to help this, and yet to tell our teams to stand down would fly in the face of our defining manifesto: Competition without limits. We're getting a taste of that in the truest form, and it would appear that we might not be ready for it.

"You need to look no further than the very nature of the wagers we are making to see firsthand how far this organization has come. When we started, betting billions was unthinkable. Now it is routine. Using engagements to settle long-standing business debts, determine contract awards, or to settle personal vendettas was unheard of. Now it happens regularly. And most recently, we have government contracts wagered on teams' performances. More will come.

"So how do we approach this new era? Should we play catch up? Work our people to the bone to stem what little they can of the flow of information to the world? Deny everything? Lay low for a period of time and hope that when we resurface all will be forgotten?"

Greer shook his head.

"Or," he said, gazing directly into the camera in front of him, "should we redirect this growing global interest, and go out and meet the world?"

He imagined the scoffs at this, in the various private estates, offices, and boardrooms worldwide. He hoped only that enough of those watching would pause and reflect. He was confident that those who did would see that obscurity was no longer a long term option. Meeting this head-on was the only way they would survive. Thankfully, all was quiet in the broadcast room. Cameras couldn't rabble or scoff.

"It is the belief of the Team Blue Administration, myself included, that we can no longer conceal the nature of the Tournament. Not anymore. However, we believe that we *can* control how people become aware of it. As you know, control of information is the key to winning, both on and off the field. Our players have their great battles, and now we have our own."

Greer stood to his full height and stepped aside. He popped his shoulders back slightly and brought his attention to the board above him.

"And now," he said, "it is time to announce the second draw."

The board clattered and the letters fell into place. Greer blinked several times. He cleared his throat.

"The Russians of Team Black will fight the Irish of Team Green. The Americans of Team Blue will fight the English of Team Grey. As this conference comes to a close, betting will officially open. I ask all of you to carefully consider what I've said and determine where your own administration stands. The longer we wait to make a collective decision, the worse our position becomes.

"Best of luck to all the remaining teams," concluded Greer, and as he nodded one last time the live feed shut off with a barely audible click, and all of the lenses once more went dead.

CHAPTER FORTY

THE TWO HIX BROTHERS were well known about Shelby County, in Memphis, Tennessee. Tall blond boys, each attractive in his own way, they shaped trends at Shelby's East High. They walked with a rare confidence that refused to even brook the notion of the insecurities that plagued almost everyone else in high school. They had broad shoulders, smooth skin, and seemed to come into puberty with a proportioned, pre-developed physique that most men approach in their twenties. People watched what they wore, how they acted, and where they stood, and then, when people weren't around, they would wear, act, and stand in the same manner and think hard about how they could adopt these traits without looking too derivative.

The boys were polite, and never went out of their way to abuse their social status, nor did they speak of their popularity, although they tacitly acknowledged it. If anything, they could be accused of being slightly aloof, but only because far more people knew of them than they actually knew themselves. There simply wasn't enough of them to go around.

Very few people knew they had a younger sister, and fewer still could name her. Nikkie Hix was a quiet girl, a late-blooming fifteen in a garden dominated by the brilliance of her seventeen and eighteen year old brothers. They had smiles that created a presence. Nikkie Hix was in her second year of braces, and her smile was metallic and awkward. Her brothers were tall and shaped like v-cut wedges of wood. Nikkie was short and shaped like a rectangle.

Sometimes Nikkie thought that the world didn't know what to do with a *girl* Hix. She swore she saw surprise whenever she introduced herself, like on the first day of class, for instance, as if there had been a mistake somewhere along the line in the Hix family tree. She sensed that even her parents seemed at an occasional loss with what to do with her. They'd had two boys in a row. They had the growing boy blueprint blazed in their minds. But a young girl? She'd followed her brothers in almost everything: sports, clothes, even their manner of speaking and walking, but she wasn't one of them, and sometimes she felt it terribly. The formula didn't work with her. Popular boys and popular girls weren't cut from the same tree, even if they were of the same genes. Nikkie wasn't exactly unpopular, but she seemed diminished in comparison, like a flashlight in broad daylight.

The oddness of her braces hit her at the beginning of her sophomore year, when she looked around herself that first week in August and saw that almost everyone else had gotten theirs taken off, including her closest friend Brianne, who, one way or another, never seemed to let her forget it. The first thing Brianne did when she got her braces off was ask Nikkie to come over.

"Look!" she said, licking her teeth. "Gone!"

Nikkie never had reason to cover her mouth next to her best friend until then. And soon enough Brianne was getting boys to lick her teeth for her, very publicly, and very near wherever Nikkie was, it seemed. In the arms of a boy, she saw her childhood friend differently. In the way Brianne's flowing black hair cascaded and bumped softly over the boy's arm, she saw her own small, blonde ponytail, limp and boring. In the way his hands rested on Brianne's curving hips, Nikkie saw how blocky her own still were. In the way each boy subtly pressed against Brianne's perky chest,

Nikkie saw her own smaller chest, and crossed her arms over herself. She became withdrawn, tired of waiting for beauty that was promised her, and angry that she wanted it. So she focused on tennis.

She proved herself on the court where she couldn't in the social scene. She was fast, and honed exceptional reflexes. On the weekends, while Brianne was out getting drunk growing a paunch, Nikkie was getting lean and strong. She enjoyed losing herself on the court and reveled in the confidence she had inside the paint. She liked the woman she became when she played tennis. If only the rest of the world played by the same rules.

When she finally did get her braces off she was almost eighteen. They had been the scapegoat of all her social ills for so long that she had convinced herself that once they were removed, she would become a true Hix. She would become like her brothers. She would make a place for herself in school, no matter what. The eldest Hix brother had just graduated, and there was a spot to be filled. And yet, as she studied her smooth smile in the mirror, unhindered and bright, she couldn't help but admit to herself that she felt no different.

She missed both her junior prom and her senior prom. No one pushed her to go, and so she didn't. Often she wished that even one of her brothers would come in and drag her out of her room, or off of the tennis court, and throw her into a situation she couldn't walk out of without getting a date. She knew they could—they could do anything. But they never did, and she cried for it, but only when she was alone in her room or out on the tennis court and her tears could be disguised as sweat.

She was still a virgin in all senses when she went to college, and while she never let on, it tore at her deeply. She was honest about it with her small circle of friends, but their quips made in jest jarred her. Just as she was angry at herself for wanting the type of oozing beauty her old friend Brianne had once possessed, she was now angry for wanting to lose her virginity. What was worse, with every quip and every sexual discussion, of which there were many, her inexperience was boosted that much higher on its pedestal. What was once a mere monkey on her back quickly became an elephant in the room of her mind; it stomped and blew and huffed over everything she did. Even tennis wasn't the opiate it once was, despite its increased NCAA competitiveness.

Her first true romance bloomed in the only place it could: on the court, where she couldn't run from it. Occasionally the men's team scrimmaged with the women's team, and one boy in particular took a liking to her. He saw in her what she admired in herself: her core strength and her fierce competitiveness. He also saw what she couldn't see in herself: her trim figure, her tan legs, her flat stomach. He lavished attention upon her, calling out to her by name across all of the courts in practice to compliment a shot, and often waiting after practice to walk with her the fifty feet back to the gymnasium and their locker rooms. During one such time, he asked her out.

As she said yes, she knew she didn't much like him. She liked that he liked her, but she felt no affection for him. She was ashamed that she saw him as nothing more than an opportunity to break the cycle she had foisted upon herself. She guessed he must find her attractive, or he wouldn't have asked her out. She resolved to wait until the third date. They split a bottle of wine in his dorm room and ordered Chinese food and talked tennis. She stayed late, and in a lull in the conversation she moved over to him. He leaned in to kiss her, hitched up, and leaned in again. They wet each other's lips and he moved his hands over her.

She shivered involuntarily, stopping him.

"Are you all right?"

"Yes," she said, a little too quickly.

Propped over her, he asked her again if she was ready, and again she said yes, and as he pushed his way inside of her she imagined herself standing before the mirror at her old room back home, smiling a smooth, white smile for the first time, but smiling only because it showed her teeth.

It didn't hurt as much as she'd been led to believe. She felt no real pleasure, only the strangeness of having something inside of you that wasn't yours. As he moved himself she whispered and made soft moans because she'd heard that would help him. She was very aware of the time. She focused on trying to feel the exact moment when a change would come over her, when she would explode into sexual experience. She tried to separate each part of her into its own center of nerves, wanting to catch and freeze that moment forever. But the moment never came. After several minutes the boy exhausted himself in a series of pulses.

He rolled off of her and the damp on her hips began to cool. He looked at her and smiled but his eyes betrayed vulnerability. Nikkie recognized that moment as one in which she controlled him; One cruel word, one flippant comment, would destroy the boy. She could lay him low or build him high. She watched him for a moment in the low light and saw his smile fade, but then she smiled and stroked his hair and he closed his eyes and grinned like a dog. She couldn't bear to break him, but inside she was disappointed. All human sexuality seemed a fragile façade.

She couldn't in good conscience continue to see him after that, although it hurt her a bit when he didn't seem to mind. She always thought that after she'd slept with a man for the first time, she could consider herself truly equal with everyone else, that she'd attain a new status, but again she was disappointed. Instead of bringing her up, sex brought everyone else down; They never were any different from her to begin with. They were all just people, wasting energy worrying about stupid things together.

During coed scrimmage, the lower ranked men would play the higher ranked women, for fun and for practice, but also for bragging rights. The highest ranked men didn't bother with the girls; they played only each other. It bothered Nikkie that regardless of how well she played, she would never be in the same court as the top men. It also seemed unfair that their matches drew all of the spectators, while her sidelines remained empty. So she was surprised when, on one such scrimmage day at the end of her sophomore year, as she wiped her dripping brow on her shoulder, she caught the forms of two men out of the corner of her eye.

Every now and then one or two boys would watch her, not because they cared much—more because they liked to watch a woman bent over playing tennis, and sometimes one or another of her teammates would stop by to cheer her on or critique her form, but these two were different. One was a tall black man with a bald head that gleamed in the sun. He was dressed like a broker out to lunch, in a dark, well cut jacket and a dark blue shirt with a sharp collar, no tie. She didn't recognize him, but perhaps he was one of the new younger professors, or maybe he worked for the sports department.

The second man was a blonde fellow, younger than the black man, perhaps even around Nikkie's age, maybe a student, but she hadn't seen him before. She would have remembered him. She caught all of this in a glance, before turning back to play out another point, which she lost.

She turned around again. They were still there, standing calmly behind the chain link fence. The black man leaned in a fraction and said a word to the blonde, who nodded. Nikkie turned back around. She racked her brain as she played, trying to place the two of them, and she lost her concentration. She gave up another point. She was ad-out now. She wiped her brow again. The last thing she needed to do in front of these two was lose. For all she knew they could be scouts for an invitational. She licked her dry teeth and squared her jaw and set herself for the serve. She popped the ball up and snapped her body forward, all of it a motion so ingrained that she hardly needed to think. She felt a solid connect, a thrum of the strings as she slammed the ball directly at the feet of her opponent. He backed out of the way and deflected it high and off the court and let out a shout. Her point. She glanced back at the two men. Neither moved.

The next serve her partner returned with force, but she volleyed, approaching to attack. She would never last in a baseline battle against him; his shots were too strong, but she could beat him at the net. He let loose a cannon forearm shot at her face, perhaps in retaliation for the serve the point before. She snapped her racket up and caught it, shot it down onto his side of the court, where it bounced once at the edge of the line and went out. He couldn't catch it. The game was hers. She allowed herself one fist pump and glanced behind once more to see how her company reacted. They didn't. Or maybe the blonde was smiling ever so slightly. She could see the blue of his eyes even from where she stood. They were very blue, almost tropical, and they drew her gaze like the glint of water in the distance. It took a surprising amount of control to turn around again. She resolved to finish the match without another look.

She went on to lose the match. She simply couldn't return the man's serve. Point after point she proved faster than him, but she couldn't match his arm. That his raw power could ultimately beat her finesse disappointed her, and, after shaking his hand over the net, she turned around again and saw that her visitors had left. She wasn't surprised. She couldn't pull out a win, after all. She was even a little relieved. The blonde in particular made her feel strangely, gave her a barely noticeable unsettling in her stomach and a bump in her heart rate. It wasn't unpleasant, though—just strange that the mere sight of a person could do that to her.

She gathered her equipment, finished off her water, and zipped up bag. She contemplated watching the men's number one and two singles match. It looked to be quite a game and had drawn a bit of a crowd. No doubt that was where the two had moved off to. But she decided against it and instead exited the courts towards the locker rooms.

As she closed the gate behind her, she turned around and saw him. He had been waiting. For a split second she felt a bizarre desire to run away, but she quickly gained control. That was ridiculous. It was broad daylight and there were people all around her. And what was it about this man that made her think he was going to hurt her, anyway? He was a clean cut blonde guy in a collared t-shirt, jeans, and flip-flops. His blue eyes were reduced to slits in the late afternoon sun, but the color still peeked through. He even seemed to be smiling, albeit in a small, private joke kind of way. He had a bit of blonde stubble glinting off his angled chin that made him seem both clean and dirty, but that was no reason to run. Out of habit she ran her tongue over her teeth, as she often did while playing. She caught herself mid-motion when it occurred to her how strange it must look.

"I saw you doing that," he said.

"I only do it when…" When what? When she was nervous? Afraid? She didn't finish her sentence.

He waited calmly.

"…I'm sorry. Do I know you?"

He broke into a real smile at this, showing a magnificent

set of teeth, incisors that were nearly vampiric. "Not yet."

CHAPTER FORTY-ONE

NORTHERN AND MAX STOOD over Nikkie's bed and looked down in silence. Northern moved over to examine her chart hanging from a metal hook at the foot of the bed while Max continued to watch her sleep. Both men were swollen and discolored about the face in patches of purple and red, like pools of wine beneath the skin. They both looked far worse than Hix, lying peacefully asleep. Her breathing was soft, but no longer the barely perceptible shallow indicative of a diode coma. The doctors had brought her back with adrenal before the two men had arrived. Now she was just sleeping.

Northern flipped through page after page in the low light of the room. He reached a diagram indicating where she had been shot, and paused. She'd been hit four times. The first had been on the arm. She'd taken that in the hotel. Then she'd been hit once in the stomach and once in the back, but the finishing blow had been a diode to the top of her head. Head shots were the worst, worse even than gut shots. No wonder the lights were so low. Anything more would have been unbearable to her.

Northern turned to look at her and saw Max reaching for her. Max saw Northern watching him and slowed. Northern said nothing, but Max gently clasped Nikkie's hand when it looked like he might have been reaching for her cheek. She stirred slightly and opened her eyes a fraction, seeing everything through a partial blind of her eyelashes. She saw Max and managed a feeble smile. He still held her hand. She shifted a bit and saw Northern.

"My boys," she mumbled.

Northern moved to the other side of her bed.

"John, I'm sorry, I couldn't get both of them…"

"Shhh," Northern whispered as he brushed her cheek. Max watched him and moved his own fingers on her hand.

"You did it," Northern said. "We just finished them off. We got them all. We won."

As he talked, he gently and mechanically checked where the diodes had hit her. First, the top of her head. He parted her blonde hair with such a light touch he might have brushed a sleeping tiger to no effect. He slipped strands behind her ear as he leaned over her. There was no blood, but he saw clearly what looked like a big purple birthmark where the diode had hit. The crown of her head was swollen and upraised. Hix closed her eyes again. She didn't seem to mind his probing. Max now watched Northern very closely.

"I had to go in," said Nikkie, her eyes still closed.

"I know," Northern said.

"I was going to pass out," she mumbled.

"Try to sleep, Nikkie."

He checked her right arm, just above her bicep, where the first diode had struck. He turned down the blue hospital gown only slightly and saw that the wound still looked painful. Her smooth, golden skin was disrupted by violent shades of red and white, feathering out from a pale blue epicenter. It looked like a terrible spider bite, or blood poisoning. Northern gently ran a finger over the wound and felt small abrasions, as if her skin was piled upon itself at the edges, but stretched too thin on the interior. He took a slow, deep breath and rolled the gown back up over it. The aftereffects shocked him every time. He knew that they would fade, but a wound like that—that caused a reaction like that—had to be more than skin deep. The wound feathered out with the veins for a reason. Something traveled in the blood-stream every time a diode hit skin, and bruised as it went. Northern wondered, not for the first time, if the internal mottling ever faded. Or if he himself still looked like that, only on the inside. He spared himself the stomach shot. It no doubt looked the same.

"What happened Max?" she asked, eyes still closed.

Max snapped up at the mention of his name.

"I…I'm sorry. I couldn't get out of the hotel room. They were right there," he said, looking away again. "I would have if I had any way—"

"No, your face. You look terrible," she said, her lips barely moving.

Max paused.

"Well, first there was the door…and then a head-butt—"

"They got very physical," Northern said.

"I believe we started it," Nikkie said, still with a trace of her soft southern drawl.

"No, they attacked us with the hand to hand stuff," Northern said.

"That's not what I meant."

"Oh. In general. With the bludgeoning and the English and all. Yes, I suppose we are partly to blame for that," Northern said. "Or I am," he added. He didn't seem sorry for it.

"Is England still in?" Hix asked. The men looked at each other, unsure how to speak.

"Yes…" Northern said.

"And? All of the teams were in action when I went under. It's been a while. The second round draw must be out." Hix took in a slow breath. Prolonged speaking pained her.

"Nikkie, you should really rest."

"Spare me, John. It's us and them, isn't it?"

"Yes. It's us and them."

"Guess I'd better heal up quick then, huh?" she said, cracking a smile through chapped lips.

"Two weeks," Max said, cocking his head as he watched her speak.

"Two weeks." She nodded slightly.

"Once you can move, we'll get you back to Dr. Walcott in San Diego. You can recoup there, close to home" Northern said. "Don't worry about Grey right now."

"Who said I was worried? One step at a time."

"One step at a time," Northern echoed.

—

"We almost lost everything in Japan," said Christina Stoke, safely away from the dried blood and dust of Mexico City, sipping a gin and tonic in the forward cabin of an airplane cruising at altitude to the Northeast and home. The seats were big bucket recliners, one to a row. She spoke to Auldborne, on her left across the aisle. Draden Tate was to her right, gazing out of the window. His bulging right forearm was wrapped in gauze. If it caused him any pain at all, he gave no indication.

"Yes," Auldborne said, reclining further and resting his own drink on his stomach. "The Japanese do fight on. And on. And on. Crazy bastards. They very nearly did it themselves."

"Hix took four shots? Haulden and Northern almost beaten down? The stupid asses almost lost. Then what? Our glory robbed. End of story."

"But they didn't lose, did they? They couldn't beat Northern in the end, could they? No," Auldborne said, emphasizing his point with a sip of scotch, like amber medicine in its plastic cup. "No, that's for *me* to do."

"Pretty close though," Draden said, still looking out the window.

Stoke slammed down the rest of her drink and began rattling the ice loudly, glass upheld.

The stewardess made her way to where she sat. "Another?"

"Yes another," Stoke snapped, as if the question was the most ridiculous imaginable.

She took the glass and hustled off, eager to be away.

"I predict Northern will make a stand in California," Auldborne said. "His sweeper is too injured to travel far."

"Goin' on offense nearly ruined him in Japan. He be thinkin' twice now 'bout leavin' his home."

"He's afraid," Stoke smiled.

"Perhaps," Auldborne said. "Or maybe Hix is hurt worse than we think. Either way, after the two week moratorium, the move is ours to make."

"So we go to them. Beat them into their own dirt," said Stoke, snatching her drink from the proffered tray without a word to the stewardess.

"I say why not? It'll be a massacre," said Auldborne. He sipped and hissed in a slow breath. "It'll be *our* massacre. They'll name it for us. It'll be historic.

"California it is then," Stoke said.

Auldborne looked at Draden Tate, who nodded as he stared out of the window, slowly balling his left hand into a fist and relaxing it again. Squeezing and releasing, squeezing and releasing, as the ground below flew by.

Chapter Forty-Two

W HEN THE PLANE FINALLY landed, the entire runway had already been taped off. Ian saw flashes of cameras and the twirling of red and blue lights in the distance, but only several large, black SUV's and a single row of idling ambulances were allowed past the lines. Pyper and Ian were told to exit first, while everyone else was held back for a debriefing by the Tournament legal wing. The inert bodies of the four players shot down were hustled away and placed into the awaiting ambulances.

Ian and Pyper were ushered into a black car with tinted windows and driven through a cordon of flashing bulbs. They were admitted to the Royal Hospital Chelsea through a basement entrance monitored by two armed guards. Once there, they waited for Kayla to slowly come back to them.

Just over 24 hours later, when she could finally move of her own accord, Kayla insisted that they leave England immediately and would brook no argument otherwise. She became so agitated that Pyper finally agreed, and so they subtly exited the hospital and flew directly to Dublin. Thinking Kayla would benefit best from a few home amenities, Pyper suggested they all eat and regroup at her father's house on the city's outskirts.

Daniel Hurley kept a modest, three bedroom ranch house. On

this day, Daniel was off on a quick trip to the supermarket around the corner, and Bailey answered the door to the members of Green. She squealed when she saw her older sister, and squealed louder when she saw Ian Finn. Kayla MacQuillan she abided because whenever she came around, Ian was usually there too. Pyper picked up the girl, still a waif, but with hair that was already nearly as long and as striking as her older sister's. She had none of Pyper's quiet, regal carrying, however, and screamed her hellos to the three of them, saving Ian for last.

"Where's dad?" Pyper asked.

"At the store," she said, hugging her sister's leg and peering up at Ian.

"Why did you answer the door then, Bailey? Never answer the door when you're alone."

"But I saw Ian!"

"And I saw you! How are you?" Ian knelt down and put his hands on his knees, which Bailey mistook for an open invitation and squealed as she threw herself into his arms. She hugged him for barely a moment before she dashed out of his reach again and around the table.

"Wish I had half of her energy," Kayla said, leaning hard against the doorframe and breathing heavily.

"Let's get you something to eat. Sugar always helps for me," Pyper said.

The three of them sat down at the dining room table, but Kayla pushed the soda and bit of chocolate away. She was piqued and pale. The smattering of freckles across the bridge of her nose stood out starkly on her gray pallor. Her normally mischievous, dark eyes were puffy and shot through with red. Her spiked auburn hair was plastered to her head. Ian Finn watched her with concern.

"You have to eat, Kayla," Pyper said.

"I'm fine," she snipped. She looked at Pyper and then away again. "Sorry. It's just that I'm not hungry."

"Kayla—"

"If I look off, it's because it makes me sick that we can't fight those bastard English in the second round. Instead we get the lunatics from Russia."

Pyper glanced at her little sister drawing on the coffee table in the next room. Bailey doodled while shooting furtive glances at them.

"Keep your voice down," said Pyper.

"Sorry," Kayla said again as she deflated once more. The burst of righteous anger had spent what little wind was in her sails. She wouldn't even meet Ian's eye. Ian knew she was embarrassed, as if by getting shot she had failed them in some way and every pain reminded her again and again of this failure. Her shame hurt her as much as the diode hit. Ian didn't know how to comfort her without seeming patronizing, so he said nothing.

They sat in silence until Daniel came through the door, laden with plastic bags. He stopped dead in the hallway and broke into a wide, whiskered smile.

"Pyper! You're back! And with Ian and Kayla as well!"

Pyper hugged her father before he was able even to set down his groceries.

"We have a few days in Dublin," she said. "The company

put us up in the city, but I thought I'd pop in for supper when I can."

"You should be staying with us! All of you!"

"We wouldn't want to be a bother, Mr. Hurley, and the hotel is almost as comfortable," Ian said.

"Well, at least I get you for meals. Here, you kids help me put this away," he enthused, handing off the bags. Kayla tried to rise from the table, but was forced into her seat again by Pyper's subtle pressing as she passed. Daniel paused in his unloading.

"Kayla is feeling a bit under the weather," Pyper said, watching her sweeper carefully. Kayla swallowed and mumbled something about food poisoning and how she might lie down for just a bit. She forced a feeble smile as she glanced up at Daniel, concern evident in his furrowed, freckled brow.

"Of course, of course, why don't you rest in the bedroom?" he suggested, moving over to her as he spoke and gingerly raising her up. He walked her down the hall and into the spare bedroom, muttering warnings about raw meat before they were lost to sight. Ian looked squarely at Pyper and shook his head.

"It's normal," Pyper consoled. "She took a point blank head shot. The light bothers her. We've all been there."

"Is it just me, or is it getting worse?" Ian asked in a whisper.

"It'll get worse before it gets better, but it'll get better."

"No, each time. Each time we're hit it seems worse."

"It's just because you forget how bad it really is."

Ian resolutely shook his head. "No, I—"

But Daniel was coming back down the hallway. The conversation stopped. To cut into the sudden silence, Pyper spoke up. "Dad, you didn't cash my check."

"Oh, Love, save your money," Daniel said, brushing away the notion with a sweep of his calloused hands.

"Dad, I can help you out. They pay me quite well. Trust me," Pyper said, her voice taking on that softly insistent tone that held such sway over her team. Her father, however, seemed immune. He rolled the slight stoop out of his shoulders and shook his head proudly as he walked into the kitchen to busy himself with pots and pans. Pyper continued nonetheless, raising her voice.

"I was hoping you'd relax a bit more. You don't have to work so late. Spend more time with Bailey."

"She's only alone for an hour between school and when I come home," Daniel said, pouring water and setting it to boil. "And she's the better part of ten. Your mother and I were letting you babysit other kids when you were ten."

"She's seven."

"Almost ten. She sees plenty of her old man, Love. Trust me. And I like to work. It keeps me busy. We're doing just fine."

Pyper watched the little girl as she ran into the kitchen and presented Ian with a crayon picture. She didn't wait for his response, only giggled and dashed out into the living room again. Ian held it up for all to see. It depicted a little stick figure of a girl with Bailey's long brown hair holding the hand of a larger stick figure with Ian's floppy curls. The two of them were surrounded by orange colored trees and several smiling, stick-legged dogs. The scene was enclosed in a large, lopsided heart. Her signature was prominent in the bottom right hand corner.

"She wants a dog," Daniel said, bringing plates to the table before returning to the kitchen.

"She's getting quite good at me," said Ian as he carefully folded the picture and placed it in his front pocket, like he always did.

The two of them alone at the table once more, Ian again spoke of Kayla. "She'll take the full two weeks. That's for sure. And she won't be one-hundred percent. Not by a long shot."

"Neither will they," Pyper said, laying a calming hand on her striker's shoulder. Ian continued to look in the direction of the silent room down the hall. Daniel had closed the door to give Kayla quiet, and also to keep Bailey from exploring.

"Eddie Mazaryk isn't like Alex Auldborne," Ian said. "Black isn't like any other team."

Pyper watched her little sister roll to the floor to start another drawing and said nothing. She wouldn't argue with that.

"Some say they're worse," Ian added.

"Goran Brander was gunned down as well. Remember that. We're both working with one wounded."

Ian moved close to his captain and lowered his voice further.

"Goran Brander is almost 200 centimeters tall. He's a brick wall. And he's had much longer to recover. Kayla is shorter than me, weighs as much as a pinecone, and has two weeks."

"What are you saying, Ian?" Pyper asked, looking directly at him.

"I'm saying I think we should assume Mazaryk is going to use her against us, and she's already badly hurt."

Pyper narrowed her eyes. "She's our sweeper. She comes with us. In everything."

Ian looked away. Daniel came back with more place settings. Ian offered to help but was hushed and told he was a guest. When Daniel had gone out again, Ian turned back to his captain. Pyper was still watching him.

"I didn't mean—" he began.

"Yes you did," Pyper said, her voice deadly calm. "You want Kayla out of this round. Out of harm's way. It would destroy her to hear you talk like this."

Ian knew it was true. He searched for the right words: "I'm just not sure…"

"About what?"

"Everything. It's changing. I don't think anyone is really aware of what those three Russians are capable of."

"Says the man who started a gun fight in an airplane."

"You know what I mean."

"Yes. I do. But only because I know you. To everyone else, what you just did up there looks twice as reckless as anything Grey or Black ever did."

"You disapprove."

For the first time in what seemed to Ian like many minutes, Pyper pulled her gaze away from him and back to her little sister.

"I can't answer that," she said, "because I'm not sure myself. What I can tell you is that I disapprove of losing, especially now. Because you're dead on about one thing—this organization is changing. The stakes are too high. And as long as England is represented, Ireland must be too. This is my country. And your country. If they escalate and we back down, we'll lose everything, and I cannot let that happen."

Ian found himself smiling for the first time since the hospital. He was suddenly steeled by his captain's simple words and the light touch of her hand on his shoulder. He knew that the Tournament had made a terrible mistake in allowing someone to arm the English criminals—and the Russians they would fight in less than two weeks. They might even have made a mistake when they allowed Father Darby to choose him, rehabilitate his arm, give him a gun, and tell him that the country he loved was now his to serve.

But one thing was for sure. They clearly had done the right thing by commissioning his captain.

CHAPTER FORTY-THREE

SARAH WALCOTT ALMOST DIDN'T recognize him. He was sitting at the same café where she'd last spoken to him, gazing out at a park across the street through the palm trees and sipping a Coke.

She was strolling with her two roommates and stopped in her tracks right next to him. The full power of his pool-blue gaze was set on the park, or perhaps beyond. He looked pensive, even troubled. His eyebrows drooped as if he was trying to recall a distant thought or feeling and it was eluding him. Her friends continued apace before stopping, and when they looked back at her, so did he. Whatever might have been troubling him disappeared under a wolfish grin while Sarah's mind ran circles around itself trying to think of something to say. She'd forgotten what great teeth he had.

"Sarah," he said. It was almost a sigh, like an exhalation of smoke. His focus was exclusively upon her now, as if nothing else existed.

She wanted to back away and run towards him at the same time. She made a conscious effort to root herself, and said the first coherent thought that came to her mind.

"So you did come back."

"Of course I did. This is my home."

She noticed a portion of what looked to be a masterwork of a tattoo peeking below the short sleeve of his right arm. It was vivid and dark in color, but abstract in design. It seemed to flow over the contours of his upper arm. She hadn't noticed it before. Forgetting herself, she bent closer to look at it and saw that it consisted of many smaller designs and only appeared filled-in from a distance. She extended her forefinger.

He didn't move.

She touched it, half expecting her finger to come away wet. "Is this new?" she asked, enthralled.

"No."

"What does it mean?"

"A lot of things. Kind of a family crest."

"It looks like water," she said, pulling her finger away.

"And it looks like fire up here," he said, tapping his shoulder twice as he watched her.

She stepped back and looked at him. They were silent for a moment. Her friends began to walk back her way, seeking an introduction. When Northern spoke again, they stopped.

"If I take you out to dinner," he said, "will your father ever find out?"

"M—my father?" she stammered. She couldn't help it; the question was so matter of fact.

"I really can't have him angry at me."

"Oh, he'll live," she said.

"He cannot know. This is very important."

"Then he won't know."

Northern smiled again. "Good. Sooner rather than later is best for me."

"How about this weekend?" She cocked an eyebrow. Having regained some of her composure she was eager to take him off his guard, to push back a little.

"Friday night. We'll meet here." He gestured with a brief opening of his hands. "It's my favorite café."

"I'd guessed."

Northern glanced at her friends. Their eyes were wide. Then he was looking over Sarah's shoulder at a man approaching in the distance. His glance away from all of them was brief but noticeable. Sarah almost looked behind her, but caught herself; it amazed her how much she wanted to follow the man, even when he didn't speak.

"Until then?" Northern asked. A polite dismissal.

"Until then." She stood straight once more, nodded one final time, hitched up her purse, and turned to catch up with her friends.

"Bye Sarah."

She looked over her shoulder. "Bye, John," she smiled.

As soon as she no longer watched him, he transferred his gaze back to the approaching man. He walked with a prim sort of energy, very nearly on the balls of his feet. His brown hair was neatly parted in a tight wave. He wore an immaculate track suit of shiny polyester, zipped open just above the ankles. His shoes were the only part of him that looked worn: scuffed, dark blue trainers with a gray sole that was peeling away at the walking creases. He carried a single-strapped messenger's bag slung tightly over his right shoulder.

"Hello, Lock," Northern said, still sitting.

"John," Lock said in reply. "What was that all about?" He looked down the sidewalk at Sarah and her friends. "Official business?"

"In this business, everything is business," Northern said, sipping his Coke.

"I'm sure," Lock muttered, unconvinced. "Well, it's not like you're in the middle of a war or anything. Moratorium ends Saturday. Let me guess. Date Friday night?"

Northern nodded, watching Sarah fade in the distance. "She's a nice girl."

"She looks a lot like someone else I know…"

Northern turned his gaze to Lock and froze his words in his mouth.

"Fine," Lock said, after a minute. "It'll go unsaid." He loosened his strap and flipped his bag frontward. "As much as this might surprise you, I'm not here just to chat." Lock dug around inside a pocket. "Eddie Mazaryk is pulling his eccentric nonsense again and refuses to let his assigned courier carry for him."

"Aw. He likes you," Northern said, his eyes glittering.

Lock withdrew his handheld and tapped his way through

various screens.

"Yes. Well. I caught him recently and he asked me to hand deliver this to you, and only to you."

Lock flipped the screen around to face Northern. "Press your thumb to the pad."

"A message?" Northern narrowed his eyes. He leaned away from the screen.

"God only knows."

"For me only?"

"For you only. He was adamant."

Northern slowly took the device. Lock seemed reluctant to give it up completely, but eventually let go. Northern looked from the screen to Lock. After a moment, Lock sighed and turned around to give him privacy.

Northern pressed his thumb to the pad.

For what seemed like a full minute, Lock heard nothing from behind him, not even a shuffle or a breath. After two minutes, Lock turned his head slightly. Northern was completely still, his face a mask.

"John?"

Northern said nothing. Lock turned full around again, but stayed back. Northern paid him no mind. His eyes were unfocused and distant. He was looking at the screen, but didn't seem to be seeing it.

"John?" Lock tried again, and this time he was rewarded with a dazed look. He resisted the unprofessional temptation of asking what the message was about. It was clearly of a personal nature. His job was not to ask why; his was just to carry and fly. Still, this change in character alarmed him.

"If you need me to carry for you, I can do it. I can be anywhere in the world in one day. Anywhere."

"Is this set to delete itself?" Northern asked, his voice slightly hoarse, as if he had just awakened.

"Yes. Close the file and you can watch it go."

Northern closed the file.

"Do you need me to run for you John?"

"No," Northern said, with something of his old confidence back. "That won't be necessary. Thank you, Lock. It's fine. Everything is fine."

Lock shrugged. "If you say so." After a moment, Lock spoke again. "If that's all you need then, I should be going."

Northern nodded. "Safe travels, Lock."

"Call me if you need me," Lock said, replacing the console and zipping his bag once more. He flipped it behind him. "I'm off." Lock turned around and walked back the way he came, receding to the distance until Northern was left alone once again.

CHAPTER FORTY-FOUR

COMMUNION SEEMED PARTICULARLY HEAVY at Mass that Sunday.

Kayla and Ian went alongside Pyper Hurley and her family to the service. The moratorium was in effect for another three hours, enough to accommodate the service, but in all likelihood they would have attended regardless. Ian stood last in line and he watched his captain approach the priest. She looked remarkably calm, stepping forward a little at a time, waiting patiently with her hands on the shoulders of her little sister in front of her. She seemed a portrait unto herself, her face smooth and flat, her eyes straightforward. Even Bailey, who would receive only a blessing, seemed calmed under her touch. He envied Pyper's poise. If he didn't know her so well, he might think she had no idea what approached. The thought of the fight that awaited them unsettled his empty stomach. It took effort just to keep it together in front of Pyper's family.

Bailey looked up to receive her blessing and Pyper knelt to receive Communion before they returned to their seats. Ian stepped forward. Just ahead of him stood Kayla. Whatever was in store, Ian was afraid Kayla was not going to fare well. She was only now regaining a semblance of her freckled coloring. Only recently was she able to go the whole day without significant rest. Basic activities tired her and she was often left winded just walking apace with him. She described her pain as a lingering hangover that she couldn't sleep away. She closed her eyes to receive Communion and her eyelashes twitched. Ian could read upon her face her frustration at her condition. His stomach twinged again. He would have to watch out for her, and that was a burden he didn't need.

He stepped up last of all and knelt. The paper thin wafer caught in his throat and he swallowed the juice awkwardly—it hitched going down. He coughed gruffly and moved on.

—

Kayla checked her watch on the quiet ride home. Rain clouds gathered and made it seem darker than it was, but the short fall day was already drawing to a close. Not long now until round two officially opened. They would take no chances of endangering their own people. Once home, they would gather their things and leave Daniel and Bailey, move away from them and the city out to the country where they would await Black. She slowed her breathing by taking three deep breaths. On the long road to recovery she'd found this technique effective at stifling the pangs of nausea that occasionally still crept up from her gut. Each time, Ian glanced at her and then away. She knew he was concerned, and she loved him all the more for how much he tried and failed to hide it, but she was hiding things of her own.

For starters, she wasn't nearly as weak as she let on. She was in pain, surely, but it was nothing she couldn't cram down inside herself for a few hours when she had to, when the time came.

Also, she was going to bring down Eddie Mazaryk all by herself.

Ian thought she didn't understand the full threat of Black when in fact she felt she was the only one who did. She understood Black well enough to know that Eddie Mazaryk *always knows*. If you want to get the drop on any of them, you must never utter a syllable of your plan. You must not say anything about it to anyone, not even your own team.

      She *wanted* Pyper to tell her to hold back. She *wanted* Ian to worry enough to convince Pyper to keep her in the rear out of harm's way, and it looked as if it was going to work. Then, when everyone thought she was far and away, including Black, she would hunt down the man himself. She would take him out. She harbored no delusions of grandeur, she would most likely end up in a second coma, but it would be an even trade this time. Her for him. With him gone, Pyper and Ian would have a chance of taking out Brander and Ales Radomir. It was the only way.

———

As Pyper watched the gathering dark and the fluorescent streetlights of Dublin float by her window, she prepared. The trick was to take it one step at a time. The first step was getting out of Dublin and assuring the safety of her family. The task was simple enough and her only focus at the moment. Conjecture and hypothesis beyond that was pointless, especially against Black. *What-if* thinking could drive a woman crazy. Once they were away, she would tackle the next issue as it presented itself; she always had, and she always would. Ian and Kayla had their own thoughts, she knew, but she also knew that in the end they would look to her, just like her sister did, and just like her father did. The pressure calmed her. She constantly reminded herself that the manner in which she gave the orders, when the time came, was as important as the orders themselves in the eyes of her team. Her calm was integral and contagious and they needed it. She knew Kayla was hurt, and she knew Ian could very well get himself shot taking care of her, so she would order Kayla to stay back. No questions. It was as simple as that. As for whatever was next, she would take it as it came, head on.

The rain was coming down consistently now, and the horizon was black. Water formed in rivulets that streamed across the windows, blurring the steady progression of muted brick buildings and the looming fall foliage of the trees in the dusk as they passed by. They spoke very little, instead taking the time to reflect. Even Bailey sensed the need for quiet, and busied herself with breathing softly on her window and slowly brushing her finger through the brief fog that appeared there.

Once back at the Hurley house, Daniel made a cup of tea and sat watching Bailey scamper about with her crayons while the three members of Green gathered their belongings. It didn't take Ian long; anymore nowadays he packed light, a few t-shirts and some tried and true pairs of jeans, perhaps a week's worth of undergarments. Enough to look presentable. He could throw everything into his small duffle bag in under a minute. The girls always took longer—Kayla especially, now that she was injured. Every move seemed to take her twice as long. So it was that he found himself sharing a cup of tea with Daniel at their small dinner table while they both waited. Ian flipped a cigarette end over end, itching to smoke as soon as they left.

"So you're off again, eh?" Daniel said.

Ian nodded and sipped at his tea.

"Any idea when you'll be back?" he asked, with a hint of eagerness that seemed sad to Ian.

"I wish I could tell you. Trust me when I say I would much rather be here, sipping tea with you, than off working at the moment."

"The road can get long, I know."

"Yes it can."

"You take care of my daughter, hey?" he said, half smiling.

"Pyper's quite good at taking care of herself, but I always watch out for her."

Daniel nodded and sat back, hands clasped over his mug. Ian was pondering a second cup as Pyper and Kayla came in, their packs over their shoulders.

"That's that then?" asked Daniel.

"Time to go," Pyper said, "but we'll be back, da. We always are."

"I know," Daniel said, clasping his daughter into a deep hug. "Be good."

Kayla and Ian said their goodbyes, and just as they turned to go Bailey tore out of her bedroom and, beaming a smile, stopped Ian and held out another of her drawings.

"Is this for me?" Ian asked.

Bailey nodded vigorously. "I wish" she began, struggled with the precise words for a moment before exhausting herself with an explosive: "You'll come back!"

"Of course I will," he said, as he unfolded it for his customary perusal before packing it away in his breast pocket.

It took until Pyper and Kayla were almost out of the door before they realized he hadn't moved. Pyper peeked back around the doorframe and smiled.

"Are you coming with us, Mr. Finn, or has she smitten you?"

But Ian wasn't smiling.

"Ian?" she asked, her smile fading.

"Where did you see this, Bailey?" Ian asked, his voice hollow.

"Yesterday," Bailey said, confused at Ian's change. "They waved at me. When I walked home. Do you like it?" she added after a moment.

Pyper quickly moved over to Ian and looked at the picture. It was of three men, crudely outlined, but clearly dressed in black. They wore small black ties that Bailey noted with single lines down the middle of their bodies. One man was very tall and another had large, round spectacles. The man in the middle had a scribbling of black hair that went to his squared shoulders. He was smiling a small black smile.

"Oh God," Pyper whispered.

"Did they do anything to you?" Ian asked, words spilling out of his mouth.

"No!" Bailey said. Her eyes widened. "They just waved at me, and told me to tell you hello." She began to cry.

CHAPTER FORTY-FIVE

WHILE GREEN RECEIVED COMMUNION, with the moratorium in its final hours, Johnnie Northern sat at his favorite café just off of Gilman Street in the waning light of a November evening. A cool fall California breeze fussed with the loose collar of his dark shirt as he sat, one arm upon the back of his neighboring chair, gazing mutely at the shaded, tree ringed park across the street where it was dead quiet and peaceful. He swirled the remnants of a cup of coffee in his left hand. He was waiting for Sarah Walcott to appear, but he didn't look as though he was.

As the last of the fall sunlight streaked down the street, Sarah came walking. He turned to watch her and smiled. She wore low cut jeans, painted around her hips. Her top was an auburn silk and lace number that might, under other circumstances, have doubled as a classy piece of lingerie. Her sandy blonde hair was straightened and smoothly parted and wisps fell down the right side of her face. She saw Northern and waved. He raised a hand.

"I was afraid you might not be here," she said, as she approached and he stood. "Sometimes you disappear."

"Not this time. I thought this time I'd stick around." He motioned for a waiting cab to approach the curb. He popped open the back door and ushered her in. "Shall we?"

"We shall."

As they spoke in the cab, touching on this and that, she asked him how long he'd lived in the area and what he'd been doing with his time. She kept her tone light, trying not to betray her intense curiosity. His responses were perfectly non-committal; he seemed to have been most everywhere and done most everything. He was full of entertaining digressions.

His focused interest in everything around him, including her, was just shy of alarming. As he spoke she sensed that his eyes took in not only her, and not only their surroundings, but both at the same time and with more intensity than the average man could devote to any single one. When they glinted in the passing lights, she imagined seeing flashes of thought in him, although she couldn't guess at their form. She shifted closer to him nonetheless.

The restaurant was a small, intimate affair he'd chosen, and Sarah was surprised not to have heard of it. The walls were a dark red and each table was lit softly by milky globes suspended above. At the far end was a large bay window, and Sarah thought she saw him glance furtively at it a handful of times, but she couldn't be sure. He leaned forward to listen and slightly back to speak, and his eyes rarely left her otherwise.

His very presence intrigued her, from his wry wolfish smile to the small white scars on his left hand, thin and long, like gossamer threads running under his cuff. He had a deep, clean smell, like cold water, and Sarah found herself leaning in and breathing softly to catch it. But perhaps most mysterious of all was the tattoo. He wore his shirt two-buttons down from the collar, and she could see a bit of a softly sloping line of dark ink appear when he leaned in to listen. She wanted very badly to see its entirety. It seemed somehow integral to his being. He'd said it was like a family crest, and she imagined it as a map that held a key to understanding him.

Given courage by the wine, she chanced to speak about what she'd seen as he got out of the cab: A slight bulge on his lower back, resting just above his tailbone. A flash of cold metal.

"I know you carry a gun, John. But you don't look like a policeman. Are you a policeman? Please don't be a policeman…" she said, trailing off and watching his reaction carefully. At first he leaned back and crossed his arms over his chest, and she was afraid she'd overstepped. He seemed to appraise her intensely for a moment. Then he leaned in very close. She could smell his hair and his skin.

"I'm no policeman, Sarah," he said, smiling. "Don't worry."

She wondered how eyes could possibly be that deep of a blue in real life.

"Then what, exactly, do you do?" she asked, popping one eyebrow.

"I work for a group of people that represent this country. In a way," he said, pausing to pick the right words.

She furrowed her brow. "Do you kill people?"

He looked down, thinking.

"You don't have to answer that," she said quickly. "Sorry."

"Then I won't," he said, but he was smiling again.

"And my father…"

"You're father works for the same group, although on the medical end."

"And what 'end' are you on?"

"You could call it the business end."

On the way back from the restaurant, the cab slowed outside of the dark café. Northern shifted to pull his wallet out of his pocket when Sarah, buzzed by the wine and company, tapped the driver on the back and signaled him to continue forward. Northern watched her in silence for a moment but she only turned to look out of the window, smiling.

Her apartment consisted of one main room with an apportioned kitchen, two bedrooms, and a sunroom converted to a third bedroom. Pictures of her roommates were peppered about the walls and on the coffee table, but they themselves were conspicuously absent. The floors were wooden and the walls were painted a pleasing array of light reds. There was a well worn, plush couch in the center of the main room, situated opposite a television, and a small bar of mostly sweet liqueurs and one large bottle of rum. The doors to her roommates' bedrooms were closed and covered in cutouts and clippings and labeled *Annie* and *JESS!* in clever magazine montages. Sarah's bedroom door was adorned similarly, although it was wide open.

Sarah gave him an abbreviated tour, to which Northern smiled and nodded and occasionally commented, his eyes always watching, taking in everything. She poured them both a drink from the bar that neither of them finished before taking him into her bedroom.

She sat him down on her puffy queen bed, not bothering to remove any of the decorative pillows, and all the while he wore an amused look, but he seemed more than willing to be moved. She stopped speaking and moved between his knees and unbuttoned his shirt from the bottom up, surely and quickly. When she finally pushed it off of him, she sucked in a breath and pushed herself back to take in the full measure of the art on his right shoulder.

"My God. That is unreal," she said.

Northern said nothing. He didn't have to. She gently pushed him back and padded her way on to him and leaned her face towards the inking. Very slowly she began to kiss it, running her lips across it with the barest hint of pressure, leaving here and there markings of her lip gloss. He inclined his head to watch her as she took in every dark curve and arc of it before moving across his chest. She didn't even stop when he raised his hips into hers and reached under himself to pull his gun from its place on his lower back. She pressed back. With one hand he set the gun onto her nightstand. The other hand he ran over her back and the sides of her stomach, his touch sliding with the silk of her shirt like soap.

CHAPTER FORTY-SIX

"ONE HOUR UNTIL THEY can shoot, and they're here somewhere," Ian said, peering under the shuttered blinds of Pyper Hurley's front window. They had ushered Daniel and Bailey into the small storage basement of the house, dropped all blinds, and shut off every light. Although Bailey was skittish with a fear she couldn't quite understand, she went easily enough when Pyper and Daniel held her hands. Daniel, however, came right back into the front room, determined to understand what was happening in his home. He was about to speak when he saw the faint, dull gleam of a gun in the dark, resting gently in Ian's left hand. He gawked for a moment, and moved to speak again just as his eldest daughter pulled a small revolver from a holster under her light jacket. His eyes bulged.

There was a prolonged silence. Suddenly Kayla spoke, returning to something of her old self in the adrenaline of the situation as she came in from checking the rear of the house.

"I don't see them," she said, picking up Bailey's ominous drawing from the dinner table, "but it's pitch black and pouring rain out and I can't see anything. They could be out there."

"They're out there," Ian said again, pulling an unlit cigarette from his lips and tucking it back in his pack. He'd have to wait for that smoke.

"I agree," said Pyper, her voice quiet but clear in the dark. "I can feel it."

"Is this what you do for work?" Daniel asked, his voice an angry whisper. "Guns, Pyper? Guns?" He took in the full measure of his daughter as if seeing her for the first time. The disappointment Pyper could hear in her father's harsh whisper hurt her to the quick, but she had no time for it right now. Now, she would focus only on the task at hand. No more.

"Yes da," she said, her voice as flat and honest as her gaze. "But we do it for Ireland," she added, as if that explained it all, and perhaps it did, because Daniel said nothing more, although he worked his jaw about as if he wanted to speak and stared down at his shaking hands.

"They can't touch us for the next fifty-five minutes," Ian said, breaking the silence. "If we're gonna move, we'd best move."

"You don't know that," Kayla said quickly. "We don't have any idea what Mazaryk will do."

"Eddie Mazaryk and his company are ruthless," Pyper said calmly. "But they've always had the greatest respect for a level playing field. He won't break the moratorium. That is one rule he will not break."

"Dad," she said, turning to Daniel, who looked up and then away from her. "Dad," she said again, softer this time, "the three of us have to get away. It's us these men want, not you or Bailey, but they'll likely walk over you to get to us if they have to."

Daniel sputtered an attempt to speak, but Pyper simply kissed him on his forehead.

"I'm sorry da, I'll explain everything in time. Bailey is scared. She needs you."

Daniel gave one last look at them all, and even though it was dark Ian could see the hurt on his face. He tried to think of something to say, but everything rang hollow. He thought about apologizing to Daniel, but he would not apologize for what he was, only perhaps for keeping it from this increasingly vulnerable man, this man who had become a surrogate father to Ian over the years. But before he could speak, Daniel hurried from the room back to the basement and his youngest daughter. Ian was left to wonder at how yet another of his countrymen had come to think of him as a monster.

"We need to get out of this house. Now." Pyper said, clearing the air.

"Bastard's probably been here for days," Kayla muttered, shaking her head and squinting at the crayon picture in the slatted moonlight.

Outside there was a crack of thunder and the rain worsened, its timbre near howling. It fell in sheets, as though someone was running a hose across the windows and back again.

"What's our move?" Ian asked.

"Someplace deserted."

"We'll have to get out of the city. Phoenix Park will be deserted in this weather. We'll go there," said Pyper.

"Damn rain," said Kayla, shaking her head. "The guns don't like the rain."

"Rain is what we're given, so in rain we'll work. Watch your first shots for flaring and be sure to factor in water-numbing in your positioning. Put on your glasses."

The three of them each took a pair of yellow tinted sunglasses from their jacket pockets and put them on. The lenses had been treated and were water repellent.

"Right then, time to move. We'll take my car."

Ian moved to the door and popped it open, propping it with his shoe as he aimed into the gloom beyond. The tint of his lenses picked up any faint nearby light. He saw a thin sheet of water pouring from the awning onto the sidewalk in front of him like a yellow beaded curtain. Beyond that all was awash in shapeless mist.

He walked out under the awning, gun up in both hands, his body close to the rain-dark bricks of the wall. He was immediately damp about the shoulders and on the top of his head. He checked his angles of visibility as best he could before motioning for Pyper to come out, and then Kayla. He soaked in the rain as they darted past him and into the car. His eyes played tricks on him, forming shapes in the erratic blowing droplets. He wiped his forehead with his sleeve but succeeded only in plastering his hair down. They could be anywhere out there just beyond his vision, and he was fairly sure that they were. As if they'd planned the rain.

Finally, with both in the car, Ian moved. He walked quickly to the driver's side, opened the door, and closed it behind him with much the same feeling he used to get as a small boy running up the stairs from the darkened basement.

As Ian pulled on to the street, a car three lengths behind them flipped on their lights and began slowly, almost leisurely, to follow them.

"Jesus. Fuckers don't waste time, do they?" Kayla quipped, squinting over her shoulder.

"That can't possibly be them," Ian said, his eyes flicking

from the mirror to his front view and back again. 'Right outside of the house? We passed right by them!"

"Of course it's them," Kayla said, chambering the first bullet of her clip.

"How much time until the moratorium expires?" Pyper asked, leaning down and across the back seat, away from the rear window.

"Twenty minutes. My guess is they start shooting in twenty minutes."

"Then so do we," Pyper said.

CHAPTER FORTY-SEVEN

FRANK YOUNGSMITH WAS TIRED. He hadn't shaved, returned to work, or been to his apartment in nearly a month. His beard had grown in patchy and unevenly, and the tight curls of hair that ringed his head frizzed wildly out in all directions. Although both of his eyes sported impressive bags, his right looked more tired than his left, and he walked about with an off-kilter half-squint, suggesting a drunken pirate. He had a few buck-shot sized holes in the crotch of his trusty Dockers, and both buttons on the seat of his pants had come off some time ago, their threads left to dangle like tassels.

He was literally falling apart.

When he'd slept, he slept poorly, and since he was paid only through this weekend at the Lucky U motel off I-70, just west of Topeka, Kansas, he had resigned himself to many more nights of little to no sleep. It wasn't his fault. They were after him. They were after him, and the more he learned about these people, the more he felt the need to run.

He couldn't trust anyone. Literally nobody. He was convinced now that no one on earth was out of their reach. The police? Please. The police were in their pocket. Their people were peppered about the municipal, state, and federal government at every level. He was convinced that half the time he picked up the phone they were listening on the other end. The internet was an open book to them; they flipped through the whole damn thing at their leisure, ripping pages from it like paper when the content didn't suit them. More and more he was catching looks out of the corner of his eye. He could feel people watching him with undue curiosity. Truck drivers and hotel lobby workers, convenience store clerks and bums on the streets. Even a father of three on a road trip in his minivan seemed to watch him unnaturally as he passed by Frank's battered coupe. The Tournament was everywhere once you knew how to look, and it was Frank's singular misfortune to know how to look. He knew he was most likely on the cusp of insanity. He walked a strand of hair in his mind. It was only a matter of time until it snapped.

Thank God the report was done, or as done as it was gonna get, anyway. He was sure he was fired by now, naturally, but the report was submitted. He wasn't sure why he'd kept at it except to say that the doctor's words placed enough of a burden of guilt on him to look a bit deeper into the organization that was the Tournament—and from there he'd fallen of the cliff. They learned who he was, ransacked his apartment and probably harassed his hapless neighbor. He smiled to himself as he sat against the thin headboard of a twin bed in his ratty hotel room. Then he frowned. That was no reason to smile. For all he knew, Andy could be dead.

Presidents, heads of state, rulers and kings were involved. Frank knew he was less than nothing to them. Hell, he was less than nothing to most people he knew, much less to *them*. If they found him, they'd kill him. Few people were more easily disposed of than himself. At this point really a loud *Boo!* ought to do it.

On the other hand, there was still so much more to discover. It was *worldwide,* for God's sake. He'd done a whole report on it and was sure he'd barely scratched the surface. Right? There had to be more, right? But he needed money. He needed money, and he needed to shave and to brush his teeth. In fact, he'd worry about the money later. First, the teeth and the shaving. The money would come. Hopefully. An evening shave would do him good, both a literal and a symbolic cleansing.

He flopped out of bed and padded over to the yellowish bathroom and grabbed his stained daub kit. He lathered himself up and fussed around to find his old razor. Then he heard a knock on the door.

He froze. A glop of shaving cream plopped from his chin into the basin. He suddenly had to urinate. There was absolutely no one else it could be. He contemplated forcing his ample gut through the small bathroom window, but he was too tired and too asthmatic to run, he'd only embarrass himself. He looked about for a weapon: he saw the rough towel, he saw a spare roll of toilet paper, he saw his frayed toothbrush.

Then the door opened. Frank turned, white faced and dumbfounded, to face two men standing in his room. They were dressed entirely too professionally to be frequenting the Lucky U. Their expressions were indecipherable, the masks of the professionally anonymous.

"How did you get in here?" Frank moaned, spraying flecks of shaving cream out upon the floor.

"You didn't lock the door Frank," one said, shrugging.

"Please," Frank said, holding his hands up as if to ward them off. "Please, I have…" What? A wife? Nope. Kids? Nope. He didn't even have a dog.

"…I have a, a neighbor," he stuttered, "and he worries." Frank backed up onto the toilet and sat down hard upon its seat. The men continued towards him. He looked from one to the other, breathing heavy, panicked-animal breaths. He slowly brought his fat legs up and hugged them, his paunchy belly pressed against his knees. The shaving cream was beginning to sting his upper lip.

"Relax, Frank," one of them said. "You of all people should know by now that we aren't in the business of killing people forever in this organization. We also bring people back from the dead."

The other chuckled as he looked about the hotel room.

Frank blinked several times. Was that a joke? The man didn't look like the joking type. He closed his eyes and rested his head back on the scummy linoleum tiling of the wall and waited for the cold press of a gun to his temple. Instead, he got the sharp hammering of a fist, and everything went dark.

CHAPTER FORTY-EIGHT

THERE WERE FIVE MINUTES left in the moratorium. Five slippery minutes was all that stood between them and the hell that tailed them. The Irish knew that when the time was up, Black would erupt with the ferocity of the storm now battering every side of their car.

Green hadn't gotten very far. The downpour slowed traffic out of Dublin to a crawl, and up ahead the runoff had pooled deeply in a depressed section of the road. The few cars that chanced it had stalled out, their hazard lights blinking worthlessly into the roaring rain. They'd gone a measly two kilometers on the westbound N3, and the dark car close behind them had followed every step.

Ian Finn was watching the clock and driving, the knuckles on his right hand white on the steering wheel while he cooled his left palm in front of an air vent. Kayla was chancing frequent glances behind her and holding loosely to her gun. In the back Pyper lounged across the seats as if asleep.

Four minutes. The traffic slowed further, then limped, then stopped. The freeway had turned into a parking lot.

"Park the car," Pyper said, her eyes still closed.

Glad to finally be doing something, Ian threw the car

into park and pulled his gun from his holster, where it had been digging into his lower ribs as he hunched over to see through the sheets of water pouring down the windshield.

"When the time comes, we need to get out of this car and fan out into a line. Use other cars as cover, duck and run. Keep the line. I'll be in the middle. Ian you get to my left, and Kayla you stay to my right. We'll slowly sweep down the highway towards them."

The rain drummed loudly on the windshield. The wipers couldn't keep up.

"Is that clear?" Pyper asked.

Ian and Kayla nodded.

"Good. Ear pieces in."

All three of them popped small, blinking com devices into their ears and secured them with a plastic wraparound strip.

Less than one minute. The car close behind them idled innocently, its passengers impossible to discern. No matter. There was no doubt in anyone's mind who sat within. With seconds left, Pyper grabbed a door handle. Ian felt his blood tearing about his veins. Everything seemed very damp and close and there was suddenly little air in the car. A strange, roaring stillness descended; all the cars seemed frozen, as if the water were molasses. Kayla also positioned herself to run, her face suddenly pale once more. Then, with no flair whatsoever, the clock flipped.

The moratorium was over.

At once all three of them popped open their doors and dashed out into the downpour, Kayla and Pyper on one side and Ian on the other. If they'd thought to catch Black unawares, they failed. Three men popped out of the car behind them. As soon as Ian saw the black door of their old Cadillac glint with rainy movement, he fired as fast and as true as he was able while scrambling for his life behind the front bumper of the nearest car.

The electrical charge of his diodes snapped and popped as they slammed into the water pouring down Mazaryk's car door. One hit the driver's side window and the entire pane flashed a brilliant electric-blue before exploding outward, a thousand tiny fragments vanishing into the rainfall. Water and glass: two things the guns didn't work well with.

The car he ran to for cover was closer than he thought, and he hadn't been watching for it as he shot. He hit it awkwardly and bucked himself over the front hood like a deer. He heard the loud honk of the surprised driver and sucked in a gulp of rainy air as he landed hard on his hip. He brought his gun around and froze for half a beat, trying to make out any sound at all, but the rain was deafening, like God was pouring out sacks of marbles from on high. The car honked again, right into his face, and he scrambled back and away.

Two shots narrowly missed his head and crackled into the rear bumper of a car directly behind him. He'd stumbled back into their line of fire. He vaguely registered the wet heat of an exhaust pipe bursting smoke as a nearby car shot forward and directly into the car ahead of it. He heard a muted crash in the distance, but he was already running again. Up and over cars. Sliding and slipping on hoods. He sliced his shin on the sharp edge of a protruding license plate and backed up into another car's side-view mirror, snapping it clean off. Then he was on the wet concrete again, water already pooling about his hands and body, and someone else was honking at him. He pointed his gun at their windshield without thinking. The rain was loud and the honking was loud and he could barely see despite the eye protection. His shin was warm with blood.

"Shut up!" he screamed, and then he ducked down again. His ears were ringing with the racket and the adrenaline as he tried to position himself. He'd done his best to fan out in a straight line like Pyper said, but he'd been in a partial panic. He couldn't be sure he'd gone where he wanted. Nobody was shooting at him any longer, which was a good thing—and a bad thing. He depressed a small button on his earpiece and spoke directly to anyone on the team that could hear him.

"Did we get away? Where is everyone?"

Pyper's voice chimed in. "Ian, you're not far from us. See the speed limit sign? Work your way back down the side of the highway to that point. They're still in the middle…" Her voice crackled out for a moment. "—get to either side of them."

Ian pushed his dripping hair back from his forehead and popped up into a crouch. He dashed past the passenger side of the car that was providing him cover and stopped just back of the brake lights of another car. He chanced a glance out and down the center of the highway. He couldn't see anyone; the rain blurred even the cars very near to him. He looked warily at their darkened passengers. Any one of them could fly at him in a panic, thinking he was going to hurt them. Staying in one place here was dangerous in more ways than one.

He bolted away, always low, towards the concrete barrier marking the left most edge of the highway. Thankfully, this far from their initial exit the motorists couldn't possibly have seen the fight, and no sound, even gunfire, could penetrate the loud rain. Hopefully they just assumed he was some sap running from his swamped car.

He ran up and kept left, popping and ducking like a

groundhog until he reached the concrete barrier and there he
crouched. He was instantly awash up to his lower calf with runoff
sweeping down the street. Perhaps four cars ahead of him stood
the speed limit sign Pyper spoke of, waddling in place with the
force of the rainfall. He peered past it and to the center of the
highway but all the cars blended into one ill-defined mass. There
were people in those cars. So many people. He'd pointed his gun
at one of them without even thinking. He wondered if Eddie
Mazaryk thought of all these people as anything more than ob-
stacles. It suddenly became very clear to him that he would never
survive this night if he paid these bystanders any more accord than
Eddie Mazaryk did.

Wide eyed, a small child looked at him from a rear window as he passed, her breath fogging the glass. He turned away. It
was no good looking at them. He had a job to do.

He tried to make out any shape that moved, but could
see nothing. He pressed the com button on his earpiece with one
dripping finger and held his gun loosely with the other. Water
poured down his sleeve and off the barrel like it was a squirt gun.
He blew the rain out of his nose. He badly wanted a cigarette, but
his jacket was soaking and his softpack was a mush of tobacco and
paper. These cravings hit him at the worst possible times.

"I'm on the far left side, maybe four cars back from the
sign," he said.

He heard several sharp bursts of white noise before he
was able to make out the words "move forward." He frowned.
Either the storm was disrupting the com signal, or the earpieces
weren't waterproof. But if the order was to sweep forward, he
would sweep forward. Keeping tight to the barrier, he moved.

He'd gone fully three steps before the windshield of the
car directly to his right exploded with a bright flash and a reso-

nant thud, like a deep sea mine. He ducked with his hands over his head as another shot rang off the metal siding of the car inches from his. The diode popped and crackled and the left side of his face went numb. Just before he fell back he caught the hulking shadow of what could only be Goran Brander crouched ineffectually behind another car in the distance. There was screaming and the slamming of car doors as a group of people hit the concrete and ran hysterically down the highway with the runoff.

Ian sat stunned with his back to the car and his gun up and out, daring anyone to appear. With the other hand he patted at the left side of his face. It felt swollen. He forced his breathing to slow. He hadn't been hit. This was just the spray-numbing Pyper had warned them about. It had happened to him once before, albeit on a much smaller scale, and on top of his forearm. When the diode cracked against the metal siding of the car the liquid inside misted out and onto his face. It was worse in rain, when the liquid could spread out with the splash of contact. That a tiny drop could numb him as surely as a shot of Novocain was shocking, but nothing had entered his blood. The feeling would fade, but probably not until whatever happened tonight was over.

He heard the scratchy, distant voice of Kayla MacQuillan through his earpiece, shouting his name.

"I saw the flashes! Are you—ight?"

He pressed the com button.

"It's okay, just numb about the face. It was Brander. Do you see him?"

"—left side...think I see somebody—not sure." She crackled out.

"Hello?" Ian pressed and repressed his com button. Nothing but static.

Before she cut off Kayla had spotted somebody, but whom? Where the hell was Eddie Mazaryk and why wasn't he shooting? He whipped around and pointed his gun behind him where he saw several figures scampering to the edge of the freeway. Nothing but stranded motorists. Damn this rain. It was deafening. He couldn't hear himself think. He yelled into his com once more.

"Kayla! Pyper!"

But there wasn't even static. The com was dead.

—

Pyper saw the flashes to her left where Ian was, two of them, like supercharged fireflies, but she knew Ian wasn't hit because she caught the tail end of chatter between him and Kayla just before her com died. She removed hers and tossed it to the swamped ground where it was swiftly picked up and washed away.

In the absence of the com she heard much more. She heard the full force of the pounding rain on nearby hoods. She heard distant snatches of screaming—not, she thought, from anyone she knew. She even thought she could hear, somewhere below the rainfall's drone, the flat thumping of a hovering tournament helicopter, waiting to rush in and clean up when everything was over. From her position, crouched low behind a car in the very center lane of the highway, the heat of its exhaust wafting over her at intervals with the shifting winds, she took stock of what she knew, and of what she could do.

She knew that Eddie Mazaryk had not yet fired a shot. She knew that Ales Radomir had not yet fired a shot. Nor had she, or Kayla, who crouched just barely visible to her right. Ian

and Goran Brander were tied up to her far left. Ales was somewhere in front of Kayla. That left Mazaryk and herself.

She also felt very strongly that Mazaryk had somehow
gotten behind them, maybe thirty meters or more. Somehow
he had deduced their plan to sweep up in a line, and had left his
striker and sweeper while he ran down the street and to their
other side. She hadn't seen him go back, but he was there; she
could feel it. What was disconcerting to her was that he hadn't
fired at anybody.

It was her job to find out precisely where he was and
what he was doing, and to take him down. With this clear in her
mind, she could act. She looked to Kayla to indicate that she was
going to drop back and find Eddie Mazaryk, but when she turned
to her right Kayla was already gone.

—

They thought she was sick. They thought she was weak. Of all
of the people to go after Eddie Mazaryk, Kayla was sure nobody
thought it would be her, least of all the man himself. This was her
advantage. She'd seen him. She'd seen him move past them to get
behind their position. He was up and out of the car even before
they were. He was so fast that she hadn't the time to pull her gun
around before he'd disappeared into the rain. Now they were
boxed in: Ales and Brander in front, and Eddie Mazaryk somewhere behind.

It was time: enough of this sneaking about like flushed
out rats. She would hit hard and fast, the exact opposite of what
everyone expected from her. The com was dead, but it made no
difference. She would act alone. She didn't hesitate; she didn't
even steady herself. She just popped up and sprinted through the
sheets of water towards a reckoning with the dread captain of
Black. Pyper didn't even see her go.

—

Ian almost shot her. He whipped around the back of the car he was using for cover and glimpsed Kayla tearing off through the rain to his right, back the way he'd come. Only a flash of her spikey hair glimpsed through the rain stayed his hand. He was sure Brander had seen her, probably Ales too, but they held their fire. They were letting her run towards what he could only assume was Mazaryk himself. They were toying with her. For another half of a minute Ian waited, dripping, for the looming hulk of Goran Brander to materialize out of the rain like some huge swamp monster, gunning for him. But Brander never came. Ian's mind raced. Ales Radomir had disappeared somewhere up to his right, near where Pyper was, and now Brander had disappeared to his left, probably moving back towards Pyper.

They were both going for Pyper Hurley.

Ian popped up from hiding, aiming wildly at nothing. He had to draw them off.

"Brander!" he screamed. No answer. The sound of his voice died feet from his mouth, battered like a bug to the ground.

"Brander, I'm over here!"

Still no answer. He screamed again but this time for Pyper, his voice cracked. Nothing. He ran towards the center of the highway where he'd last seen her.

—

Pyper saw Goran Brander coming for her, his long arms sweeping the rain in front of him. He was surprisingly fast for such a large man, shifting in and out of view like a ghoul with the passing sheets of rain. Just when she had a bead on him, he would disappear. Patiently, she waited. Ales Radomir was somewhere nearby, up where Kayla MacQuillan had been before she'd disappeared. If she fired, Ales would know and pinpoint her. She had but one shot at the hulking Brander and then she would have to run to try and escape Radomir. She followed him with her sight then jumped to where she thought he'd be, but never was. She took a deep breath and wiped the rain off her lips. It was as if he knew the limits of her sight exactly, as if he was staying just outside her range, distracting her.

And then she knew.

She spun around one second too late: Ales Radomir was already on top of her. He stopped her arm with one hand as she fired and her shot went wide. She'd startled him; she could see it in his eyes behind their round, gold rimmed spectacles. She took advantage and shoved him back as she sprang up. He made no sound as he fell, but he did shoot. The diode slammed into Pyper's knee just as she put pressure on it. She toppled to the side and her head bounced off of the grimy bumper of a nearby car. She lost focus.

Ales Radomir was not used to being on the ground. His eyes flashed and his mouth formed a white line on his face. He brought his gun up. Pyper fired into his gut just as he fired into her face.

Ian saw two flashes in the center lane, ten meters away from him. His heart was in his throat and his eyes went everywhere at once. For fear of hitting his own captain, he didn't dare risk firing into the tangle that grew visible before him. He screamed her name again and again but then heard a muffled crack, and then another, and he knew she was gone. He wheeled up just short of them, but was forced to take cover behind a nearby lorry as gunfire raked down its side. In the distance he heard the booming laugh of Goran Brander.

On the ground, Ales Radomir shifted and blinked several times as he watched the still body of Pyper Hurley. His wound was severe and he hadn't much time left, but if it pained him at all, he didn't let it show. Instead, he fumed. His nostrils flared and his mouth opened in a silent snarl. He pounded his fist into the water on the street. He spat on her. Then he shook his head and lay back so that his body cut the runoff around either side of him. He tucked his glasses into his pocket, and he closed his eyes.

"Two on two!" Brander boomed through the rain. His voice was a full octave lower than the average man's and the rain played a ventriloquist's tricks with it, making it seem to come from everywhere. "It looks like you and me, Mr. Finn! And I wouldn't hold out much hope for that little sweeper of yours," Brander added sadly. That he sounded genuinely sorry chilled Ian more than the pouring rain.

Ian threw himself onto the car immediately in front of him, up and over, praying that the lorry would still provide him with cover. The hood popped under his weight and he heard a muted scream from within, but no shots came after him. Safely in a new position, he ducked low and took stock. Whoever was in the car tried to open the passenger door, but Ian slammed it shut and heard a startled yelp. They didn't try to open it again.

His captain was gone. He felt her absence like a gash in the fabric of his team, deflating him. He shook his dripping head and brushed back his soaking hair. For all he knew, he was all that remained. He was angry at Kayla for running to face Mazaryk alone, yet he also admired her. It seemed to Ian like he'd spent the entire firefight scampering for his life, fighting from a defensive position, ducking and dodging like a terrified child. At least Kayla had taken matters into her own hands. He had to find her. He had to help her if she was still standing. But first he would have to take out Brander.

—

Donovan Debenham was a long haul trucker for Refrigerated Transport of Greater Britain and he was on the tail end of a drive from Cardiff when the storm hit just outside of Dublin. He'd been through heavy rain before, but rarely this severe, and he knew when the sluggish traffic halted that the rain must have washed away a barrier or formed a pool too deep to risk cross-ing—he would be there for a while. He threw his rig into park and his cab shuddered into place and began to idle with a soft rattle. He took out his cigarettes and swore under his breath as he lit one up. He was so close. He couldn't be more than twenty ki-lometers from his drop point. And a pub. A pub most importantly.

He inhaled deeply, cracked his window to let out the smoke, and then quickly rolled it back up as water poured in.

"Jesus," he muttered. If that was how it was, he'd just smoke out the cab.

His shortwave radio chirped with occasional bursts of chatter, people reporting the dead stop to their dispatchers and warning others away from the storm. He learned that barriers had been set up several kilometers back and that all traffic was being rerouted from this area. That was peculiar, blocking off the whole expressway like that. He reached over and flicked off the radio. He was tired, and it was beginning to give him a headache. He pre-ferred to listen to the steady thrum of the rain and gaze out of the windshield at the motion of the washers: clear, blurry, clear, blurry. Hypnotic. He let his seat back a tad and watched the fury of the storm rage around him from on high.

So it was that he saw the man approach from rather far back, materializing out of the distance as he made his way down the expressway. He walked quickly, but didn't seem rushed. He was well dressed, in a black suit and a thin black tie. He wore a knee length, dark gray raincoat. He kept his head down against the wind and the rain, and he had long, dark hair, pulled back and held together with a small band. His hands were in the pockets of his coat as he walked. He was surely soaked to the bone, but didn't act as though the rain bothered him.

About ten feet from the truck, the man stopped and looked directly at Donovan. Donovan froze mid-drag. The look wasn't threatening, not exactly, but it was deeply probing, as if he were taking in the entirety of Donovan: his job, his life, his truck, his whole being all at once. Then the man smiled and approached the passenger's side. With a strange thrill Donovan realized that he wanted to talk to him. He slid over and rolled the window down about halfway, letting rain pool on the floor of the cab. The man stood a respectable distance back, his hands still in his pockets.

"Hello," he said in flat English. His accent was almost American. Almost, but not quite. He was clearly not Irish. His face was delicate, almost feminine. He had a button nose and small pink lips and his skin was very pale.

"Are you all right?" Donovan asked.

"My car is stalled in a pool of water just up ahead. Could I perhaps wait out the storm in your cab?"

Donovan thought for a moment. The guy didn't look dangerous. He was slight, almost thin, like a bird. Donovan probably had three stone on him. He was most likely just some foreign businessman, stuck here on his way home.

Donovan shrugged and popped open the door. "Sure. Come on in. My name is Donovan."

The man smiled that strange smile again as he stepped up and into the cab. "Hello Donovan. My name is Eddie."

—

Kayla continued down the highway, running in bursts as her body would allow, until she saw the flares. At first they were nothing more than an odd brightening in the distance, a strange red coloring of the pouring rain. She paused, suddenly cautious. This was the type of place where that bastard Mazaryk would wait, she thought. He would exploit something like this, a disconcerting scene, an odd coloring, anything to disturb the system. Then he would pounce.

She ducked between the cars, skating the dotted lines as she edged closer to the phosphorescence. When she could smell the acrid tang of sulfur, burning so hot it was immune to the downpour, she stopped. He was somewhere close. A man popped out of the passenger's side door of a nearby car and she leveled her gun at him without a second thought. But he was fat; she could tell even in the rain, and when he saw her he immediately got back in the car. She swore under her breath. Things like that could give away her position.

The rain was dripping into her eyes. She wiped it away, cleared her nose, and spat. Her eyeglasses were basically useless. It was like standing under a shower. She was very conscious of at least two pairs of eyes watching her from either side as she edged her way forward, but neither of these strangers would meddle with her. It was a touchy science, determining who would act and who would not. She had been burned badly in the last round and the humiliation still stung her. And in front of Ian, too. She would not let that happen again. She wondered how they were faring behind her…not that she could do anything about it now. This was her battle. She had chosen it. She would make them proud by gunning down the legend.

She could see that the flares were ringing what looked to be a giant puddle. Perhaps you could even call it a small pond.

At the far end, directly across from Kayla, an abandoned car sat swamped, half in and half out of the bubbling water like the carcass of a dead animal stuck in tar. The water level was up above the bottom of the doors. She needed to avoid that at all costs. The wrong shot at the wrong time and she could slip under that mess and drown. No adrenal shot on earth would help her then. She turned away, panning the rain. He was out there somewhere, and his time was up.

—

"Look at this one," Donovan remarked, exhaling a jet of smoke through his nostrils and nodding out toward the rain. "You think she's okay?"

While Donovan had just noticed her, Eddie Mazaryk had been watching her since she had appeared in the distance— watching *for* her, in fact. He watched as she ran up the middle of two lanes. He watched her pull up ten or so feet back from where some poor municipal worker had set out a series of flares marking a large pool of runoff. He watched her push her hair out of her eyes and he smiled when she spat rainwater out of her mouth.

Donovan looked at him as he watched Kayla.

"Do you know her or something? There's room here. She can wait it out here too," he said, moving to roll his window down.

Eddie Mazaryk held his hand up and Donovan stopped mid-motion. "No," Mazaryk said softly. "I'll get her."

—

Crouched by the pool, Kayla was looking in all of the wrong places. She snapped her gaze from aisle to aisle in between the cars. She peered into the swampy distance. She even got low and looked for shoes. All the while, Mazaryk eased down his window and popped his shoulder out. Donovan watched with horror as Mazaryk withdrew a gun from his overcoat pocket. He brought it outside, sighted briefly, and fired three times in quick succession. Donovan couldn't scream; he couldn't say anything. The words caught with the smoke in his throat. He could only cough and scrape wildly for the handle of his door and shove himself as far away from Mazaryk as possible. Once the firing was done, Eddie Mazaryk turned slowly to look at Donovan.

"Goodbye," he said, as he opened the door and stepped carefully down and out of view. He closed the door softly behind him.

Once outside, he saw that she had fallen with her face half inside the ever growing pool. With his gun leveled at her, he pulled her back until she was clear of the water. He saw that there were two red welts on her face, one just below her right cheekbone, the other on her chin. A third spidery welt wrapped around the right side of her neck; he'd hit with all three shots. Still holding the scruff of her shirt, he bent down so that his cheek was beside her slackened mouth. He felt the barest cold brush of air. She was still breathing. She hadn't sucked in water. He gently propped her against the nearby concrete barrier. He even brushed her hair back from her forehead. Then he turned his attention back down the highway.

—

Goran Brander came around the far side of the lorry with his .50 caliber blazing. He fired at anything and everything near Ian. When Ian ducked behind a car, Brander shot through it. He pelted it like hail, exploding every window. The screams of the passengers didn't slow Brander in the slightest, but they rang like foghorns in Ian's ears. To spare them Ian would run, but no sooner did he stop to get his bearings when Brander would tear through his cover and new screams erupted. Ian got a shot off in his direction only when Brander paused to reload, and when he did this he was quick. When Ian was finally able to sight him through a windshield or passenger's window, his outline vague and watery behind wide eyed stares and screams, he couldn't bring himself to fire through them as Brander did. Ian screamed in fury at Brander, but also at himself.

He realized Brander was herding him like a stray sheep. He cut a startling figure, tall and thin, his arms flipped about him in the rain like a flag in the wind. His gun was everywhere at once. He seemed to part the rain around him, whereas it fell fully upon Ian as he scrambled about. And what was worse, Brander was smiling. Enjoying himself.

When Brander fired a cluster of shots to Ian's left, Ian ran right, and then he saw Eddie Mazaryk walking towards him. The captain of Black walked behind his gun, his head bowed, his left eye just visible over the hammer. He reached out to Ian like a pale wraith. Everything seemed to slow, and Ian could see fat drops of rain explode off of the epaulets on the shoulders of his raincoat. He knew it was over.

Mazaryk fired three shots and Ian saw them jump up his front, exploding in pops of blue like electric coat buttons. He jerked back and collapsed onto the hood of a car behind him, his slack face open to the rain. Mazaryk lowered his gun and paused, waiting for any movement at all from Ian. He cast a sideward glance at Brander, who was already holstering his gun.

Mazaryk walked over to Ian and gently closed his gaping mouth. He turned Ian to his side as one might a sleeping child, to the screams of the family in the car under him. Then he turned and walked towards Brander. Now that the action was over, the helicopters that had been at bay moved directly over the bodies and dropped lines down which medics scampered with harnesses.

Men and women in dark jumpsuits emblazoned with the white letter T ran from behind the barriers where they had been waiting and down the alleys of the gridlocked lanes into the combat zones. Brander watched all of this with mild interest as Mazaryk approached.

"Take care of Ales and meet me in St. Petersburg. I have an errand to run," he said in soft Russian, barely audible over the storm. Brander nodded.

The two men parted ways: Brander off to St. Vincent's Hospital and the secluded Tournament wing where Ales would awaken, and Eddie Mazaryk to the airport, where he would catch a plane.

They left Team Green to soak on the swamped streets of the N3.

CHAPTER FORTY-NINE

JOHNNIE NORTHERN WAS STILL asleep in Sarah Walcott's bed, one arm resting lightly over her curled body, when Greer Nichols called. The phone rattled lightly against the butt of his semi-automatic on her nightstand.

"Green is out," Greer said. "Three to one."

"Who did they get?" Northern asked quietly, looking over at the gentle slope of Sarah's back.

"Pyper Hurley got Ales Radomir. Brander and Mazaryk were unscathed."

"Pyper's a dangerous one. She's quiet, but she's dangerous."

"Not dangerous enough, apparently."

"No."

Sarah stirred and arched her back, stretching like a cat.

"I think we should assume that the English are in the air, coming for you," Greer said.

Northern sat up.

"Our people picked up increased activity surrounding

a flight that departed from Heathrow a half of an hour ago. Last minute reservations and all that. The typical indicators. Probably them."

Northern rubbed his face and his eyes. "All right. I figured as much."

"That gives you about eight hours until they find you."

Northern watched the sheets slip around Sarah's hips as she turned around to face him.

"What time is it?" she asked, her voice scratchy.

"Early," said Northern.

"Also," Greer continued, "one other thing…"

Northern slid out of bed and moved over to his clothes. He placed the phone in the crook of his neck as he stepped into his jeans.

"We're not quite sure what to make of this—"

"Just tell me."

"Eddie Mazaryk is coming."

Northern froze in the middle of buttoning his fly.

"*What*?"

"He registered his flight plan with the Tournament. Under his own name."

"He's coming to California?"

"Which means that he doesn't care who knows about it."

"Mazaryk is coming *here*? To *California?*"

"Yes, John. And he's coming alone."

"How do you know?"

"Ales Radomir is still under monitoring at St. Vincent's in Dublin, and Goran Brander is registered as a visitor there."

"*What* in the *world*—"

"We're working on it, we're working on it, but one lunatic at a time. I'd focus on the one you're actually slated to fight."

"You'd better stay on top of this. If that man gets anywhere *near* us—"

"—I'll tell you. Meantime, eight hours at the most. They're coming."

Northern hung up and stood with his hands on his hips, gazing out at the first light of dawn as it streaked across the sky.

"Is everything okay?" asked Sarah.

He turned to look at her, but his gaze was distant again and his eyes unfocused, the way she'd seen him at the café off of Gilman. She knew that the man she'd met last night was gone, at least for now.

"I'm on the clock." He buttoned up his shirt, then grabbed his automatic and slid it barrel first down the back of his jeans. He patted his pockets to make sure he had his keys and wallet.

"Will I see you again?"

"Yes." He smiled down at her briefly. He looked momentarily about the room as if seeing it for the first time. He picked up his drink, still full from last night, looked at it, and set it down again. For the first time since Sarah had met him he seemed unsure of himself. Then he turned and walked out of the door, leaving her in bed, half covered by the sheets.

Northern caught the first cab he saw and went directly to the Westgate hotel, where they moved Nikkie after Dr. Walcott had reluctantly allowed her discharge from UCSD Medical. As the cab moved up the roundabout outside of the front doors, Northern saw Max Haulden. He was waiting just outside, hands crossed in front of him to ward off the early morning chill. He watched Northern in silence as he arrived, paid the driver, and exited the cab.

"Rested?" he smirked.

"How is she?"

"Sleeping. She's still not ready," said Max. "She looks very tired," he added haltingly.

"They're coming."

"Greer told me."

Northern nodded for a moment before he moved through the doors. Max followed silently.

Up in the hotel room, Northern took a seat next to her. Max stood and leaned against the doorway. They both watched Nikkie in silence. She looked pale and fragile in the blue light of dawn, her skin like paper. She was a long way from healthy, but her face was set in defiance, even in sleep.

She opened her eyes, and Northern was relieved to see them clear and green. But when she turned to look at him, he saw sadness lurking there.

"You're back," she whispered, and then she looked away and up at the ceiling. Northern glanced at Max, who looked only at Nikkie. The silence took on weight.

"Is it time to go?" Nikkie asked, her eyes closed once again.

"No, not yet. Sleep, Nikkie. Max, you should sleep too."

Max nodded but didn't move.

Nikkie took a deep breath and turned to her side, facing away from Northern. He could see the gentle curve of her back through the old Memphis shirt she wore as her pajamas. Max slid down the wall and sat on the floor, leaning his head back and exhaling. Northern pulled his gun from his back and held it loosely in one hand, his elbows on his knees. He dropped his head and gazed at the floor.

They sat like this for five more hours, allowing Nikkie as much time as Northern thought safe to recover what little more she could before the approaching melee. At half past ten in the morning he stood and tapped her lightly on the shoulder. Max awoke with his movement and rolled his neck about.

"Time to go," Northern said.

———

To the south of San Diego proper stands the city of Chula Vista, just north of the Mexican border. Chula Vista is home to a deteriorating dock district known as the Lower Chula Vista Port. It's not one port so much as a long string of barely connected individual docks, constructed when the shipping business in San Diego was booming such that anyone with the startup capital could invest there, where the water depth dropped precipitously, and could make a fortune offloading rig equipment for the southern California oil fields. In the early eighties, when the oil industry went belly up and millions of dollars disappeared overnight, a good half of these docks were suddenly deserted as their owners found themselves without even the money to sell them or scrap them for materials.

The view from these blighted buildings was not pretty, and the water about them was strewn with trash and murky with waste runoff. Every waterside warehouse was anchored with at least twenty feet of solid concrete and constructed from thigh-thick steel bars and rivets as big as a man's fist. They were built to last, and so they did. Over the years they accumulated debris, gang tagging, and rust.

It was into these steel skeletons that Blue forayed that evening as they awaited the arrival of Alex Auldborne, Christina Stoke, and Draden Tate. Blue had been here before, had planned to use this area as a potential battleground should the fight ever be brought to their home. The three of them were confident and comfortable surrounded by the horror-show of rusted loading machines, scurrying animals, and the thick-cabled remains of crane-works. The idea was that whomever they fought wouldn't be.

Max Haulden walked carefully around one spattered metal chute, blood red in the waning sunlight, and took in his surroundings once again. Greer had called them thirty minutes prior and told them that the airplane in question had arrived and all passengers had disembarked.

"You're sure they'll follow us here?" asked Max.

Northern nodded. "Greer made it obvious to Grey Admin where we'd be. We humiliated Auldborne last time. I humiliated him. He's been obsessing over this for over a year now. They'll be here."

"And Eddie Mazaryk?" Nikkie asked, leaning a bit too heavily against a steel roof support that was twice her width. Her voice rang hollowly about the cavernous loading dock. Her very being was diminished, more than could be attributed to the aftereffects of the diode shots. The diodes could paralyze the body, but as Northern watched her in the shadows her very spirit was flickering.

"I don't know what Eddie Mazaryk is doing, but that's secondary now," said Northern. Nikkie continued to gaze at the ground in front of her. Max furrowed his brow.

"Max!" snapped Northern, his voice suddenly angry, "get just inside the entrance and watch the bottleneck there. They have to come in that way. Nikkie, up that flight of stairs and sit. You have the best angle. I'll be back and behind these metal crates. Just like we planned way back when. This is our ground. Cheer up everyone, for Christ's sake!"

Nikkie looked up, surprised by this change in tone. Max turned to the entry way: a small double door that opened into a bottleneck of concrete walling that ran ten feet to the interior. He hopped up the wall and began to move towards it.

"Look," Northern said suddenly, his hands out as if trying to tamp down his temper. He struggled for the correct words.

"Look," he said again, his voice kinder this time. "We know these three. They yell and stomp and talk a big game, but then they screw up, and we're there to catch them. Their pride ruined them last time, and it's gotten even worse. Use it against them, and we cannot lose."

Max nodded and continued to walk along the top of the concrete barrier towards the front door. Nikkie paused and looked at Northern, who glanced at her out of the side of his eye. She expected him to say something more, and when he didn't, she slowly brought herself over to the small flight of stairs behind them. She began to climb, her hand grasped tightly around the flaking banister.

Both of them gone, Northern took a deep breath and shook all thoughts from his head. He clicked his earpiece on and tested it, depressing a small button when he spoke.

"Is everyone in position?"

"Yes."

"Ready."

Northern walked back to the stack of metal crates behind him, pacing off in his head. He stopped. He turned around and saw clearly the swath of evening sun that cut through the massive glass skylight above. It fell upon the cluttered concrete floor in a long, sharp rectangle. To the left of the front door crouched Max, the cold glint of his gun reflecting the last of the light. Above him, through the grating of the suspended walkway, he saw the white rubber of Nikkie's sneakers and heard the rustle of her clothing as she settled into position.

Then all that could be heard was the distant lapping of the dirty water.

CHAPTER FIFTY

"NUMBERS ARE IN," said Bernard, after knocking gently on the open door to Greer Nichols' office. "Odds are all over the place, but the consensus is at two-to-one in favor of Blue. And the wagers, my God. We've never seen this much, or this variety."

"And the political wager?" Greer asked, not looking up from his monitor. "Have they agreed?"

"They have…" Bernard said. "Although Grey Admin would like it noted that Eddie Mazaryk is en route."

"What is that supposed to mean?" Greer was leaning back in his chair and watching a detailed map of south San Diego County and the city of Chula Vista on his screen.

"Grey's administration want it marked in the record as an *extenuating circumstance.*"

"How English of them. There is no such thing as an *extenuating circumstance* in this business."

"Just telling you what they said."

"Sounds to me like they want an excuse to bitch when they lose."

Bernard nodded, tucked his clipboard under his arm, and made a move for the door when Greer spoke again, halting him. "Any minute now."

Bernard glanced at Greer, confused as to whether he was being given a directive or not, or indeed if he was even being spoken to. Greer hadn't taken his eyes off of his screen, but Bernard lingered under the open doorframe just to be safe. Greer had been known to look one way and think another before.

"I saw it coming to this," Greer said, speaking softly, as if to himself.

"Sir?"

"But I couldn't believe it, back then."

"Saw what coming? Blue versus Grey?"

"I thought the people wouldn't understand," said Greer, oblivious. "I still don't know…" he snapped his gaze to Bernard, who blinked.

"If we win, England will commit to the Middle East. Militarily and diplomatically."

"That is the agreement," said Bernard. "Grey Admin insists that they have this capability within their power."

"And if we lose, they will draw down their current troop presence. And we will support that withdrawal publicly."

"Yes. We have told them that this is within our power."

Greer shook his head in wonder.

"A decades-long diplomatic issue resolved in a flash. People will never understand," said Greer, refocusing on his screen and narrowing his eyes, "but there's nothing we can do. The damage is already done. Frank Youngsmith, he was just one. The people know, and they'll know more."

"The people?"

"There was a time," said Greer, "long ago, when whole nations, entire races of people, pinned their hopes and futures on individual warriors. Whole wars were won and lost on the outcome of a single battle between heroes. Entire countries were moved. Empires rose and fell."

Bernard was silent. Greer did not look up.

"Not long now," Greer said, leaning back in his chair once more and running one damp hand over his head.

Chapter Fifty-One

FOR TWENTY MINUTES THE three members of Blue entrenched themselves within the silence of the dilapidated shipping building. Only the metallic scurrying sounds of rodents and the distant wash of water against the concrete broke the dead still. Twenty minutes in which Northern looked only up, trying to catch any sign that Nikkie Hix might be looking back down at him, and twenty minutes in which she never did. All the while Max Haulden stared at them both from across the concrete expanse of the floor, illuminated like a stage in the center where the skylight above was letting in the first of the moonlight. Then Grey came.

Alex Auldborne signaled a halt in Grey's approach by holding up his hand and closing his fist. He pointed for Christina Stoke, her white skin porcelain in the night, to take a walk around the left side of the building to the external stairway that jutted there like a broken bone. He signaled Draden Tate around the right of the building. He would linger at the front, and when the time was right, he would attack. His team made to move, but he held up his hand once more and stopped them both.

"Leave Northern to me," he muttered. "Now go."

—

Max strained every muscle to catch the slightest sound of movement outside of the doors, but he still heard no sign of them. He passed his gun from hand to hand and wiped his palms on his pants. His thoughts continually wandered back to Hix and Northern. He tried to blink his mind clean but thoughts weren't so easily dismissed. *She was distraught. He hurt her.* It was far too easy to continue down that line, about how exactly he had hurt her. Why she felt betrayed. What it meant. He placed his ear against the flaking metal of the wall and listened. Nothing.

Max was no idiot. He knew where Northern had been last night. He knew who he had been with. Northern hadn't attempted to hide anything. Hours before the moratorium was to end, he'd gone off with some college whore and this had cut Nikkie deeply. Northern's little tryst seemed to wound her far worse than Takuro Obata's diodes. Her whole light was dimmed. Didn't he realize that they were a team? That what he did had consequences?

A rustling sound from beyond the doors snapped him back to the present. There would be time to discuss this with Northern later. He waited.

Nothing.

A rustling again, more distant this time, as of footsteps walking away.

Suddenly Max knew that nobody would come through the front. With the door open anybody could see that the concrete walls would funnel them like cattle to the slaughterhouse. This bottleneck was too obvious. He was guarding a doorway nobody would walk through. Once again, Northern couldn't see what was right in front of his face. He hadn't even asked Max his opinion about the positioning.

Max stood, and as he did so he caught the barest glimpse

through the doorway of a figure moving around the left side of the building outside. A small figure. A woman. Christina Stoke.

He couldn't shoot through the opening; the angle was too thin. He snuffed a breath, annoyed at his impotence. He depressed the com button on his earpiece and whispered into it.

"Stoke is circling around the left of the building."

There was no access indoors anywhere but through the bottleneck. There was a crusty old external staircase on the left of the building. Daring to ascend it would take her to the top floor, but the door there was bolted shut—they'd made sure of it.

"Did anyone hear me? I see Christina Stoke, she's walking around the side of the building," he whispered again.

"Hold your position Max."

"I'm going to lose her."

"She's got no way in."

Max shook his head. Stoke was the sweeper. She would hole up somewhere until it was time for her to clean up, and she was particularly slippery. If they lost her now, they would regret it later. Once you lose sight of the wasp in the room…

"I'm going after her."

"Max. Hold. Your. Position." Northern insisted. Max could hear his gritted teeth even through the com.

Max weighed his options. There was a good chance at least one of the other two English was outside watching the door, but if he was quick he might be able to flit out and into cover outside; change up the stalemate that was sure to ensue otherwise. He backed up, gun out, and crouched to see what he could see through the doorway. There was a stack of large concrete piping not too far from the entrance that would cover him as he rounded the corner. He shot a glance back into the dark recesses of the building where Northern was watching. Then he slipped down the concrete bank and to the floor, pressing his back hard against the wall as he crept towards the opening.

"Max, what are you doing? Do not move!"

"John, you're going to have to trust me on this one."

Max peered sideways out of the door. Nobody. He shot to the other side of the bottleneck and flattened himself there and peered out the other way. Nobody.

Northern hissed his name again, but in the blink of an eye his striker had already ducked out of the door and disappeared.

Alex Auldborne saw Max leave, but Max was quick, and his instincts told him to hold his fire. Max shot around the corner and behind a set of huge concrete pipes like a mouse caught by a flashlight.

He guessed that Max was most likely the one guarding the entrance. Now that he was gone nobody was there. He stepped away from the shadows and walked directly to the open doorway. He paused and readjusted the grip on his gun while looking through into the darkness. Before Max could turn around again he'd walked inside.

Backlit by moonlight, Northern could see only the black shape of a man in the doorway. For several moments he assumed that Max had come to his senses and returned. It was Nikkie Hix who first understood who she was looking at: something in the hard squaring of the man's shoulders, the way he took in the interior of the building with a haughty sweep of his head. Max

Haulden would not do that.

"It's him!" she screamed, and she fired. Light burst from her gun in the dark, and the shots reverberated off the steel surrounding them, but he was too fast. He threw himself against the concrete wall of the bottleneck, and then hopped up and over it into the shadows of the interior.

Outside, the tinny popping sounds of gunfire stopped Christina Stoke in her tracks. She turned around just as Max Haulden rounded the corner, his gun up.

"Shit," she said, as if she'd done nothing more than step in something unpleasant. She tried to level her pug-nosed revolver and fire, but Max was already there. He fired three quick shots in a single cluster in the middle of her chest and dropped her to the floor like a ragdoll.

Max sniffed. *Just like that. How many times? How many times must I carry this team?*

He turned about and peered behind him. The firing from inside the building had stopped. He walked back the way he came, staying close to the wall. He pressed the com button in his ear. "Is everyone all right?" he asked.

No answer.

Max heard another quick succession of shots smack into the inside front wall with a dull ringing sound: they were coming from the far side, from Nikkie's position. Someone had snuck in the door when he'd gone out. Northern wasn't going to be happy about that. Never mind that Max had already taken care of one of them; never mind that now he was free to come up behind whoever was inside and trap them in the middle. Never mind that it was a *good* thing. Northern would see only that he had disobeyed a direct order.

Max sighed. He'd take care of this, too. He crouched low and pressed his com button again. "I'm going to get behind him and pin him—"

And in an instant Draden Tate came up behind Max. He moved like a shadow, unnaturally fluid for a man of his bulk. Max only heard him at the very last minute, when the butt of Tate's gun was smashing down upon him. Max couldn't bring his arm up; he couldn't even yelp in surprise. All he had time to do was move his head a fraction of an inch to the left so that instead of braining him, Tate's improvised bludgeon glanced off of his ear and slammed into the shoulder of his gun arm, separating it instantly.

Tate was ruthless. He hissed is unintelligible English as he beat Max about the head. Max brought his working arm up to protect his face even as he fell to the ground, grunting with every crushing impact. Tate hammered into Max's exposed forearm and split a toothy grin when he was rewarded with a muffled snap.

It was the pain that made Max squeeze the trigger of his gun. He still held it loosely, flopped flat on the ground like a dead fish. The pain of the break contracted his muscles and he squeezed the trigger. By pure dumb luck, his shot hit Draden Tate in the shin.

Tate sprang away as if he'd stepped on a wasp, bellowing and hopping. For a moment he seemed to forget about Max, and if he wasn't slowly slipping into unconsciousness Max might have found his bumbling amusing. As it was, Max's thoughts had become sluggish and his vision blurry. His comprehension of his pain and his surroundings became distant, as if everything was slipping down a tunnel.

When the immediate stinging subsided Draden whipped his head back around to Max, his dreadlocks sweeping a moment later. He limped over to him, grabbed him by his hair, and slammed his head back into the steel wall of the building one time. Max crumpled instantly. Then he spat on him as an afterthought. For Christina.

—

Northern swore under his breath. He heard the distant yelping from outside. He heard the single shot, and then, briefly, a dull smacking. None of it sounded good. He'd wanted to remain silent, what with Auldborne inside somewhere, but he had to know. He pressed his earpiece.

"Max," he whispered.

Nothing.

"Goddammit Max, answer if you're there."

Nothing.

He glanced up at Nikkie, who glanced back down at him for the first time since everything had started. Her face was dark and he couldn't see her expression. Both Americans looked back out into the expanse of the concrete warehouse. Auldborne was hidden in the shadows somewhere by the far wall. They could feel his gaze, even sense his snarl, but he did nothing to give away his position. Nikkie chanced another three shots into the dark, strafing against the back wall, probing for Auldborne. All three rang uselessly against the metal siding, same as before.

"Nikkie, hold up," Northern said, whispering through his earpiece. "We're wasting ammunition."

Nikkie didn't reply, but she did stop firing and sniff quietly. It occurred to Northern that she might be crying. He was about to ask her as much when the squatty bulk that could only be Draden Tate appeared briefly in silhouette at the door frame and just as quickly he, too, was lost in the shadows inside.

Northern cursed under his breath. Now there were two monsters in the closet.

He hadn't expected the darkness to be so complete inside of the building. Rather than help the situation, the skylight allowed in such a swath of brilliant moonlight that the farther reaches of the building were hidden in deep black contrast.

"I'm almost out," Nikkie whispered hoarsely.

"Then we need to get out of here," Northern replied. "Max has a nearly full clip in his gun and another in his jacket. If we can get to him—"

"We have no idea where Tate and Auldborne are," she whispered. "No way we're getting across to that doorway alive," mumbled Nikkie.

Northern knew this was true. He looked around himself for anything that might help them out, but their shelter was now their prison. He saw rotting wood, jagged metal, and shadows, nothing more. He rested his head back upon the cold wall and looked skyward. And then it came to him. Their ticket out was looming over them the entire time.

"Nikkie, I need you to come to me. We can get out of here together."

"The staircase is too open."

"Then you'll have to drop off the back of the catwalk. It's not that high. I'll catch you. I promise."

Nikkie was silent.

"There's no other way. Any minute they're going to move on us from God knows where."

Still she said nothing.

"Nikkie," Northern said again, pleading.

"Fine."

"Good. Quickly now, I'm moving back."

Still under cover of the crates, he backed up until he could see her back. She was facing forward, waiting for any sound or indication that the English were moving, but the silence around was so complete it was almost worse than if they had been shooting at her.

She shuffled back until her leg was extended over the catwalk. Then her knee. Northern shifted his eyes from her back to the warehouse in front of him. He knew how vulnerable they were. He could only pray that Auldborne didn't.

With painstaking slowness, Nikkie swung both legs down into the air so that she was laying on her stomach on the catwalk with her feet out, perhaps five feet above Northern.

"On three. One. Two…"

Nikkie shifted her weight.

"Three."

Wordlessly she dropped. Northern caught her true, right around her waist, and slid her safely down to the ground. When he was sure she had her footing, he snapped his gun up once more. Both of them froze, not even daring to breathe. In the silence, with his face close to hers, he saw that she had indeed been crying. She looked unabashedly up at him, her eyes swimming and her cheeks wet.

"Nikkie…"

She shook her head vigorously. "When this is over."

Northern looked away into the darkness. Somewhere out there, two men crept towards them.

"Cover your head," he said. "I'm hoping for a big glass reaction. Keep your eye on the door. When I shoot, run, no matter what. I'll be right next to you."

Nikkie nodded. She pulled off her jacket and covered her head with it.

Northern stepped away from the cover of the crates and aimed at the skylight. Then, taking no chances, he fired three quick shots at the swollen moon through the glass.

Nikkie had gone two steps when the entirety of the building flashed like lightning, There was a single crack, as if an enormous tree was split down the middle. In that moment she saw Auldborne, alone, halfway up the side wall, pressed flat perhaps fifty yards away. She had no doubt that Draden Tate would be halfway up along the opposite wall. Then the light was gone, replaced by an angry retina burn, and she was running blindly through a shower of glass shards, pouring down upon her like a razor waterfall.

When she faltered, shocked by the sheer weight of the glass raining upon her, Northern was there behind her pushing her forward, his arm around her waist. Then they were outside, and all they could hear was the tinkling of rebounding glass and a roar of anger behind them. Northern pulled her towards the stacked concrete tubing off to their right. Once there he swung Nikkie deeper under the cover and leveled his gun at the door.

Blood was seeping to the surface of his hands and dripping down in small rivulets. His grip twitched. He was dismayed to see his clip was spent.

Nikkie whispered his name and pointed down the concrete sidewalk that ran along the outside of the warehouse. There, in a heap, lay Max's body.

"Get his ammunition. Quickly. I'll watch the door," Northern said, and she hopped out into the open, her gun always facing the door, until it was out of sight and she was to the side of the building. She ran up to Max.

"God in heaven," she whispered, leaning down to feel for a pulse. She turned back to Northern and nodded that he was alive. She shook her jacket free of glass and balled it up to place behind his head, then she tore open Max's jacket and fished around inside of it for a clip, which she pocketed. She took Max's gun from where it lay in his limp hand, popped the clip, and loaded into her own gun.

Then she heard shuffling from the front of the building, just around the corner. She pressed herself flat against the wall and looked back for any sign from Northern, but Northern was gone.

The shuffling stopped. Nikkie could hear heavy breathing coming from just around the corner. She held her breath and angled her gun up.

Seconds later, a dreadlock appeared from around the wall, and then another. Like the waning of some dread moon, first the tip of Tate's nose, then his nostril, and then his upper lip appeared from around the corner, a mere foot from Nikkie's gun. His right eye appeared just in time to look down her barrel, and then Nikkie fired directly up and into his face.

Tate's neck popped back like a hanged man's and his body

staggered beyond the corner and onto the ground where he lay splayed like a marionette, motionless. Nikkie wasn't looking at him, though. Northern suddenly stepped back into view, beaming at her and nodding. He motioned vehemently for a clip. She tossed one his way.

From his spot just inside, Alex Auldborne had seen his striker stumble back and topple to the ground. His last comrade down, he took off into the dark as if pursued by demons. And perhaps he was, because Northern didn't even think—in a split second he had shoved himself off the wall after him. Nikkie yelled for him, but if her captain even heard her over the wind roaring past him as he shot along the wooden dock, he didn't respond.

Auldborne ran for hundreds of yards, his feet pounding on the warped wood with a sound like the rapid hammering of nails. The moon cast a flat light on the rotted slats that disguised how deteriorated they were. Northern knew about this and Auldborne did not. Northern ran off of the wood, in the dark dirt to the right, while Auldborne ran right next to the water.

Several times Northern saw Auldborne stumble ahead of him as he stepped badly, kicking up dust and flecks of wood as the slat strained to bear his weight. But Auldborne was fast and had the jump on Northern, so he stayed ahead until, at last, one plank gave completely.

The empty space caught his foot for a half second and threw the rest of his body forward just enough to tip him off balance. He stuck his hands out in front of him as he fell and lost his grip on his gun. He watched as his weapon jumped from his hand and bounced about in front of him. It skittered to the edge, half hanging off of the wood over the water.

Northern skidded to a stop and for a moment both men froze, waiting to see what gravity would dictate, but the gun held fast to the rotting wood and did not drop. Auldborne turned around and very casually took in Johnnie Northern and the gun Northern was pointing at him.

Nikkie Hix appeared from out of the dark behind him, slowing as she came upon the scene, wheezing hard, but Auldborne never stopped watching Northern. The moonlight seemed to reflect from Auldborne's eyes as if repelled by the very nature hidden behind them. He was winded, but he breathed only through his nose. His mouth was fixed in a disdaining curl.

"It's over, Alex," Northern said.

"What a ridiculous way to win. Dumb luck," Auldborne spat, repulsed. "But typical, coming from you."

"Call it in. Call in a surrender and I won't shoot you."

"*Call it in*? Who do you take me for?"

Nikkie moved directly behind Northern and watched Auldborne warily. "Shoot him," she whispered.

"What your thug Draden Tate did to my striker...that's not what I did to you last time around. I never went at you with the intention of humiliating you. It just happened that way. You didn't deserve to win then, and you don't now, so call it in and we're more than even. This bloodlust of yours needs to stop. You're beaten, Alex. I'm better than you."

"John, just shoot him. Please—"

"—Are you really?" Auldborne snapped. "That's easy to say behind a gun."

"Shut up, Alex!" Nikkie screamed as she raised her own gun to take aim at him, but Northern pushed it down and Auldborne laughed.

Northern then handed his own gun over to her. "Hold this," he said, his voice dead flat and as cold as steel.

"This is what he wants! This is exactly what he wants!" Nikkie said, pleading with him, tears running again.

"Shut up, you stupid bitch," Auldborne said smiling, dismissing her with a flick of his hand.

Northern launched himself at him.

Auldborne was still smiling as Northern hit him and they rolled back onto the old wood. Northern came up on top of Auldborne and went immediately for his face, holding the man's head in place with his left hand while he slammed at him with his right, the wet smacks mingling with the slap of the waves on the concrete below. But Auldborne managed to turn his head and bit hard into the pad of Northern's left hand, just below his thumb. He tore a chunk of it out and spit it as Northern grunted and reeled back a fraction. Auldborne writhed his way around, bucking the lower half of his body to throw Northern off balance. He swung at Northern's neck and landed a blow to his already bruised windpipe that sent him sprawling closer to the edge of the dock. Northern threw himself aside just as Auldborne launched at him in follow up, and he'd have thrown himself into the water had Northern not grabbed him by the buttons of his shirt just as he was about to fall in. With both hands full of fabric, he pulled as hard as he could and whipped Auldborne back around, releasing him like a discus in the opposite direction. Auldborne landed hard on his shoulder and Northern was there. In one swift motion he yanked him up by his hair and slammed his face down into the dusty concrete just off of the dock. He slammed again, and then Auldborne lay still.

Wheezing, Northern kicked himself away from where Auldborne lay. He put his bleeding hand to his mottled neck and struggled to push himself standing. When he faltered, Nikkie was there. She pulled him up and to her, and Northern realized that she was sobbing but making no sound. She shook with the effort.

"Nikkie," he whispered. "I'm so sorry. For everything."

She grabbed the back of his head and leaned up and kissed him, and as they kissed everything seemed to go out of the both of them and into the night. Their bodies sagged into one another and each stood only because of the other. The pain they both felt, their mingled blood and sweat, all was blown away. Forgotten.

Then the crack of a single shot echoed out across the ocean. Northern opened his eyes in time to see hers become unfocused. With an unasked question on her lips, Nikkie went limp and slid down him onto the splintered wood at their feet.

Northern turned and saw just as a second shot rang out and a diode slammed into his face. He crumpled where he stood and his body came to rest at Nikkie's feet.

For several seconds they lay unmolested as their shooter watched silently, but even now the thumping helicopters could be heard in the distance. And so the shooter approached.

Very slowly, methodically, they rolled Northern back-over-chest to the edge of the dock. The shooter paused for a moment, and then pushed Northern off into the ocean.

Then they turned to Hix and rolled her to the edge of the dock. They seemed to ponder something, or perhaps studied Northern as he floated face down in the water, slowly sucking the filthy ocean into his lungs, dying by degrees.

Then they pushed Hix over and into the water as well, turned around, and walked off into the darkness.

—

Johnnie Northern and Nikkie Hix were found by a Tournament medical crew five minutes later, floating face down against the concrete dock, bobbing along with the trash. Both were pulled from the water and administered CPR to no effect. They were pronounced dead at the scene.

Max Haulden was lifted via a back brace from where he lay by the external stairway of the abandoned shipping building. He was revived in the ambulance, en route to UCSD Medical

Christina Stoke and Draden Tate, still in diode comas, were transported to the tournament wing at UCSD Medical and revived under armed guard.

Although cleanup teams scanned the entire area, Alex Auldborne was nowhere to be found.

CHAPTER FIFTY-TWO

WHEN DR. BAXTER WALCOTT saw a sheet pulled over Nikkie Hix's head as he was attending, he thought a mistake had been made. When he pulled back the sheet to reveal the woman that so resembled his daughter, but blue and bloated, he had to support himself on the sidewalls of her gurney.

"Are you happy now?" he wailed. "You bastards finally killed her!"

He brushed several damp strands of sandy blonde hair off of her face and rested his hand on her forehead. There was no warmth to her, but neither was she cold. There was only a slick and clammy lack of warmth. She was long gone, only a shell now.

He stepped away and threaded his fingers behind his own head to support it. Then he saw the second body sheeted from head to toe, and went cold.

"And that one?"

"John Northern," said the medic, flipping back the sheet to expose his head.

"No," he said in flat disbelief.

Dr. Walcott closed his eyes and excused himself. In the hall he turned a full circle, unsure of what to do or where to look.

His hands seemed fat and clumsy as he pressed hard at his eyes. He straightened himself and stared at nothing while he forced himself to breathe normally again, like the professional he was supposed to be. He glanced back in the room at the medic as he charted, at the chrome plated gurneys and the lumps laying upon them. He cleared his throat. Then he took out his phone and called Greer Nichols.

As Walcott stepped away, a battered Max Haulden limped in and stopped dead. He had been told, but when he finally saw it, he refused to accept that this thing that lay motionless and bloated was his captain. It couldn't be. His blue eyes were dull and filmy. His burnished tan was a pale blue. His lips were swollen and stretched to an unnatural shine, his teeth dull and brittle in the coroner's light. The Northern Max knew had a subtle, natural scent, like a wide open field. This thing smelled of sewage water and formaldehyde. He'd been drowned like a kitten in a sack. It was no way for a man like him to die. It was not right.

For the first time since the terrible night had finally broken, Max Haulden grasped what he had become: a man without a family. A ronin.

Tournament teams were cohesive units, streamlined machines forged as one from three. It was with a sickening, sinking feeling that Max realized he had as much of a chance of continuing on now as did the rotting sack of flesh in front of him. It was over for him, as surely as it was over for Northern and for Nikkie Hix.

As for her, Max Haulden refused to even look at her and he wouldn't go near her body. He blanched and came close to running when she was pointed out to him. The walls seemed to rush in on him and he pushed his way back out of the doors in a panic, only wanting to get away from that place. He wept as he hitched his way down the halls, through the doors. Although he wasn't splayed out on a slab of cold steel, death had taken him too. The sight of Northern cut him deeply, but the mere thought of Nikkie had broken him apart.

Max Haulden was alone.

CHAPTER FIFTY-THREE

ALLEN LOCKTON PAUSED OUTSIDE of Greer's office door, a rare halt in momentum. He bobbed on the balls of his feet and flicked nervously at a speck of lint on his pressed tracksuit pants. He'd heard the rumblings. He feared the worst. Something had gone terribly wrong in California. He rubbed at his smooth jaw and gripped the doorknob. No sense in delaying the inevitable.

Inside it was very dark. Greer, sitting in his large chair behind the curve of his dark wooden desk, appeared to be asleep. Lock knew better.

"So it's true then. They're both dead," said Lock.

"It's true," Greer replied softly. There was no sadness on Greer's face, no tears. Only pure and total defeat. He sagged in his seat as if it was the only thing keeping him from lying prone on the floor.

"So what are you going to do?"

"I called you here for a reason," Greer said as he fumbled at the call button on his desk. After a few moments of silence there was a knocking at the door. Greer gestured for Lock to open it, and as he did, he was shouldered back into the room by a large man in a trim black suit. He half pushed and half dragged another man, who whimpered softly from inside a burlap sack slung over his head. Lock jumped back as the suited man shoved his captive into the room and then abruptly departed. The unfortunate fellow stumbled forward and bumped awkwardly into Greer's desk before stopping. His breathing was hard and panicked.

"Take that ridiculous bag off of his head," said Greer.

"Is he…dangerous?"

"Only to himself."

Lock stepped forward tentatively, then reached over and plucked it off. There, bewildered and terrified, stood Frank Youngsmith.

"You!"

Frank looked wildly about himself before settling on Lock.

"The mailman?" he asked, incredulous. He turned to Greer, who watched them both wearily.

"Are you going to kill me?" whimpered Frank.

Greer sighed. "Lock, you remember Frank. Frank, this is Allen Lockton. He's a courier for the Tournament."

"What the hell is going on here?" Frank whispered. Lock stared at him with outright distaste.

"We don't have time to explain, not now," Greer said. "Suffice to say, Frank, that you somehow managed to find and make public more about our work than anyone in the history of our organization. Looking at you you'd think you couldn't lick a stamp without fucking up, but there you go."

"I swear to God in heaven that I will never utter a word—"

"A little late for that," Greer said, before turning to Lock. "You two have more in common than you think, Lock."

"*What?* With him? Let's not get ahead of ourselves!"

"We have a serious problem," Greer continued, undeterred. "Two of my people, two good people, two friends, are dead. And the man who killed them is running free out there somewhere."

"This is what Walcott wanted to stop," Frank said.

"No, not this. This was awful. This was different."

"Who did it?"

"Most signs point to one man. Alex Auldborne. But I say *most* signs because there is another possibility."

"Mazaryk," Lock said. "The message. The message he gave Northern, the one that I delivered. It was a threat."

"Perhaps. And we know he was there that night. He could have been on that dock. He flew there under his own name and our people followed him from the airport to just outside of the lower dock area before he ducked us. So we've got a situation here where both men were there that night and both men have since disappeared."

"And you want me to find them," Lock said.

"No. You can't possibly take on both. I'll worry about Auldborne. I want the both of you to find Eddie Mazaryk."

"The *both* of us? I don't need Frank!"

"Wait, wait, back up a second. This guy maybe killed two people and you want us to go out *looking for him?*" Frank asked.

"This is different, Lock. You found Mazaryk in the past because he let you. Judging by the way he got the hell out of town, I don't think he wants to be found now. Frank can help you. He's quite…tenacious."

"This is outrageous," said Lock.

"This is *insane!*" said Frank.

Greer turned to look squarely at the disheveled man, still wide-eyed. His wiry and thinning hair jutted out in every direction and there was flaky scuzz trapped in the week old growth on his face.

"This is your chance, Frank. Even if you could go back to that shithole job you had in Colorado Springs, would you? You want a change? You want to live? Look at you, man. This is *it* for you. You've got nothing left. You can join us now, or you can turn away and live and die in that little duplex without anybody giving a good goddamn. That's how I see it."

Frank swallowed and worked his mouth about, but no sound came out. Lock shook his head and stared at the floor.

"You don't have a choice, Allen. You work for the Tournament. You deliver things. It's your job. Well now I want you and Frank to find Eddie Mazaryk. Find him quickly, and deliver him to me."

Epilogue

IAN FINN'S CHEST STILL pained him terribly. He felt as though he had a constant case of heartburn, or that he'd inhaled countless tiny shards of metal that tore at his lungs with every breath. It made smoking almost unbearable. Almost, but not quite. He took drags in small little puffs, like a jittery teenager. It was enough to drive a man to drink, and since Ian already drank, it drove him to drink more.

He'd been recovering with his team in Dublin for the past week. Kayla MacQuillan was the worst of them, having compounded her second round injuries on top of her first, from which she'd not fully recovered. But every time Ian thought of this, he thanked almighty God that at least she was alive.

In light of recent events, the bar had suddenly been set very low.

He couldn't quite believe what had happened in California. Johnnie Northern seemed the type of man to live forever, and Nikkie Hix was too perceptive, too sweet in one sense and too brutal in another to be murdered in that way. Their loss affected him deeply, but whether it was sadness or a sudden realization of his own vulnerability that was making him feel so, he couldn't quite tell. Probably both.

It also didn't hurt that Grey hated Blue, and Ian hated

Grey. Mutual enmity went a long way towards friendship, about as long as the circumstances could possibly allow. Now they were dead, and although details were hazy, he had no doubt that Alex Auldborne had done it and then disappeared, as cowards will do.

Ian spent a lot of time in the pub over the past few days, partly to ponder how in one night the entire Tournament had transformed, and partly to replace the stinging in his chest with a much preferable fiery warmth. His insides didn't feel quite right. He'd begun to shake. The movement was slight, just the barest tremor in his usually steady gun hand, but it was there. The liquor helped. A bit.

On one such foray, while he was sitting alone at the bar, contemplating stepping outside for his fifth cigarette while sipping away at his third double whisky, someone recognized the tattoo on his left forearm.

The man, a regular he'd seen several times in the past week, wore the monkey-suit uniform of a shipping factory stationed on the nearby Rhine. He was in his forties, thick and whiskered, with a bit of a belly. Ian had caught him glancing several times already, and when he leaned towards him Ian though it was going to end up in a fight, something he was in no way prepared for. The man spoke low, and looked cautiously about him.

"What you did on the plane, mate. Well done. Well done."

Ian's unlit cigarette dropped from his mouth onto the sticky bar. He snatched it up quickly and sputtered an awkward response:

"I'm sorry? Do I know you?"

"No," the man said, clearly pleased at Ian's flustered reply. He nodded blatantly at Ian's tattoo, which Ian immediately covered by wrapping his arm around his waist.

"Who do you think I am?" Ian asked.

"Only who you are, mate. Only who you are."

Ian sat back and looked at the man, who gleefully rocked on his stool and smiled forward. He popped the broken cigarette behind his ear and motioned for the bartender.

"I need to settle up," Ian said.

"No charge."

"I've had at least five drinks."

"No charge for you, brother."

Then it dawned on Ian that the entire pub had gone quiet. He stood up and turned about. Every eye was on him. A few people had their phones out and were snapping pictures, others were murmuring softly to each other as they watched him. Ian looked down at himself, then back at the bartender, who watched him placidly. He muttered thanks and pushed himself away from the bar. The eyes followed him. He saw that many were looking at his forearm and he pressed it harder against his body. He shuffled like this to the door then stopped. He turned back around, to prove to himself that he hadn't imagined what was happening.

They were still watching. The man who'd spoken to him took a big swig of his pint and toasted in his direction.

Ian turned back around. Someone, a small woman, pushed open the door for him. Bewildered, he walked out into the night.

About the Author

B. B. Griffith was born and raised in Denver, Colorado. After graduating from Washington University in St. Louis with a degree in English and American Literature, he wandered the world a bit before returning to Denver to set up shop with his wife. At times he's been a student, teacher, publisher, and editor, but he is and always was a writer. This is his first novel.

CPSIA information can be obtained at www.ICGtesting.com
Printed in the USA
BVOW041924260412

288814BV00001B/1/P